Melissa Good

Presents

Dar Roberts

and

Kerry Stuart

Hurricane Watch

In this sequel to Tropical Storm, Dar and Kerry are redefining themselves and their priorities to build a life and a family together. But with scheming colleagues and old flames trying to drive them apart and bring them down, the two women must overcome fear, prejudice, and their own pasts to protect the company and each other. Does their relationship have enough trust to survive the storm? (Book Two)

Tropical Storm

A corporate takeover pits mercenary IT executive Dar Roberts against soft-hearted manager Kerry Stuart. When Kerry comes up with a plan to save her employees' jobs and help Dar's company turn a profit, Dar discovers a new way to do business—and her heart. But when Kerry's father, a powerful Senator, gets wind, all hell breaks loose on the coast of Florida. (Book One)

Hurricane Watch

by

Melissa Good

Justice House Publishing, Inc.

Tacoma, Washington, USA

www.justicehouse.com

DEDICATION

Hurricane Watch is dedicated to all of us nerds who live inside the mass of wires, ports and protocols that make up the IT industry, and to those folks who believe love goes beyond labels.

ACKNOWLEDGMENTS

I'd like to thank my employers, Electronic Data Systems, for continuing to provide the inspiration for the technology in these novels; South Florida for providing the background and giving me an environment of unique color and composition to relate; my mother, for putting up with the keyboard rattling that goes on night and day here; and my Labrador Retriever, Gabrielle, for allowing me to include her in the story as Chino.

Chapter 1

 The boat bobbed lightly up and down in the gentle surf, the brass riggings clanking softly in the easterly wind. The sky was mostly cloudless with just a few puffy white intruders drifting across it, sending elongated shadows across the blue-green water as the sun tilted down towards the west.

To the east, a city skyline lifted, sturdy concrete nestled in clusters of green, as street lamps alternated with palm trees in a landscape overflowing with tropical foliage and lacking in any elevation which marked it definitely as that of Miami, Florida.

The deck of the boat was draped in various types of scuba gear, two regulators hung neatly to dry out, along with webbed belts, buoyancy vests, net bags, and wide, duck webbed fins nestled in the well in the center. On the front of the boat, two women were sprawled, soaking up the late afternoon sun dressed in sleek, one-piece bathing suits.

One was tall with long limbs, a swimmer's build, and dark hair. The other was shorter with much paler coloring and a more compact frame.

"Dar?" Kerry kept her eyes closed as she yawned a little.

"Mm?" her taller companion grunted in answer.

"You know, there's something really off kilter about spending the day before Christmas in my bathing suit, getting a suntan on the Atlantic Ocean."

"Yeah?" Dar lifted one eyelid, exposing a crystal clear blue eye.

"Yeah. Christmas is supposed to be about sleighs, and ice skating on the lake, and Jack Frost nipping at your nose, sweaters, static electricity, you know?" Kerry sighed. "I don't think I can do Christmas at 85 degrees."

"Ah. Not cold enough, huh?" Dar replied, opening her other eye and sparing her a wry glance. "I think you Northerners are nuts, out there singing in below zero weather, slipping on ice, crashing on the highway, having to have your driveways plowed, suffering with dry heat…" She spread her arms out across the soft deck pad they were sprawled on.

"No, no, you're missing the point," Kerry objected. "Christmas has to have cold weather, snow draped on the roof like in the movies, your nose has to tingle; it's part of the season."

"Okay, no problem. Here you go." A huge handful of shaved ice landed on Kerry's midsection. "How's that?"

"Yeeeeooowww!" The blond flipped over, brushing her stomach off and reaching for a towel. "Dar!" she yelped indignantly. "That was cold!"

"Wasn't that the point?" the dark-haired woman asked reasonably. "You were just complaining it was too hot, weren't you?" She bit off a grin as eyes the color of the surrounding ocean suddenly narrowed calculatingly. "Uh oh."

"Uh oh is right, you—" Kerry scrambled for the ice chest and grabbed a double handful, managing to get a good sized portion down Dar's back as she attempted to roll out of the way. "Aha! Gotcha."

Dar chuckled as she stood up and shook herself off, then stretched lazily. "Well, it's time to go in anyway; sun's going down, and I have three status reports to review." She extended a hand down to her friend. "I've been putting that off long enough. C'mon, it's getting a little breezy out here."

"Oh yeah." Kerry accepted the hand up. "It might go down to 80 degrees if we're not careful; that'd be dangerous." She slid up next to Dar and ran a hand over the taller woman's body, encased in white fabric. "I like this one," she complimented her companion. "Is it new?"

Dar padded over and stowed the cooler. "No, actually, it's an old one I came across when I was emptying out that chest of drawers the other day. Found some other stuff I'd forgotten I even had."

"Mm. Well, it's nice, and I like it." Kerry stepped carefully around the end of the bow and made her way down to where the steps lead to the cabin. "I'm going to put some dry clothes on. I think I have seaweed in places seaweed really has no business being."

The dark-haired woman chuckled. "Make sure you didn't collect any cuttlefish in there again; you scared me half to death when you screamed last week." She let her eyes wander over her lover's slim form in its rich burgundy suit. "You look pretty nice yourself, by the way."

Kerry paused on her way down the stairs and threw a glance over her shoulder. "Thanks, but if you're trying to butter me up so I won't pull any surprises on you tomorrow, forget it." Her eyes twinkled mischievously. "Birthday girl."

One dark brow rocketed skyward. "Oh brother," Dar muttered. "I'm in deep trouble. How did I let myself get talked into this, anyway?"

"What—the party, having a birthday, or putting up with me?" Kerry asked innocently, then came back up the stairs and relented. "I won't do anything horrible, I promise."

Dar took her hand off the throttle control as she listened for the anchor to finish retracting and gently cupped Kerry's chin, lifting it and kissing her with sincere passion. "Do your worst," she murmured, gazing into the sea green eyes. "But remember—paybacks are a bitch."

"Ooo, what are you gonna do to me?" Kerry growled teasingly.

"Mmm…cross-dressing full body stripper in the office?" Dar offered, with a full smile.

A momentary pause while Kerry blinked. "Uh, you wouldn't…do that…would you?"

Dazzling grin.

"Yikes!" Kerry laughed, then leaned forward and kissed her back. "Don't worry, I've got nothing planned that will rate me **that,**" she reassured her companion. "I was thinking more along the lines of making your favorite dessert for the party."

"Ah." Dar forgot about the controls and found more interesting things to explore. "I don't know that I have a favorite…" She nuzzled Kerry's ear and heard the soft sound of approval that trickled from the blond woman's throat. "Well, not that you could serve at a party, anyway."

"You saying…" Kerry paused a moment to let her breathing catch up with her. "…I'm better than Death by Chocolate?"

A low, seductive chuckle answered her as Dar slowly eased her left strap down her arm and ran a delicate finger across her sun-warmed skin. Kerry smiled at her answer as she nibbled her way up Dar's neck, taking a slow backward step towards the tiny bedroom and drawing the taller woman along with her.

Dar went willingly, already working her other strap down, her hands warm against Kerry's damp skin. She returned the attention, easing the thin fabric over Dar's broad shoulders and tugging it down her body, running her hands over the taller woman's powerful back.

The quilt's warmth surprised her as Dar caught her around the waist and boosted her up, joining her on the soft surface in one smooth motion, never letting up her nibbling. The windows in the cabin were open, and a rich, warm breeze came in, carrying in the salt smell of the ocean and brushing lightly over her bare shoulders as a lone gull called overhead.

"Still think we need snow?" Dar's voice purred into her ear, as the strong hands slid over her hip and down her thigh.

"No way." Kerry pushed her companion gently over on to her back and started a slow exploration downwards, starting at her collarbone, tasting the sea's richness on her body.

The sunlight bathed them in a golden glow in the fading sun of a tropical winter's day.

🐾 🐾 🐾

"Well." Kerry leaned against the console, now dressed in a pair of sweatpants and an overly large polo shirt. "I always wanted to see the skyline at night from this angle."

Dar sucked at a steaming cup of coffee, courtesy of the boat's small galley. "Lucky I have a position locator on this thing; we drifted a lot further than I thought we would." She aimed the boat northwest, roaring through the utter darkness of an Atlantic night. "Teach me to pull the damn anchor up and get distracted." She was wearing a sweatshirt over cutoff denim shorts and a baseball cap to tame her windblown hair. "My daddy would have tossed me overboard if he'd ever caught me doing that."

Kerry muffled a laugh, giving her friend a curious look. Dar seldom spoke of her father, a career Navy man who had been killed in the Persian Gulf. "I've never heard that many curse words strung together at one time, let me tell you," she admitted, peering ahead into the darkness, spotting a colorful string of lights. "Is that downtown?"

Dar shaded her eyes. "Yeah; that's the damn Centrust tower." She identified the tall structure, kitted out in blue lights with white bulbs interspersed to imitate ornaments. "And I can see the Metrogonowhere from here." The people mover, which traversed a downtown that nobody actually lived in, was lined with rainbow neon. The rest of the skyline came into view, tall buildings brilliant with lights.

"Is it still the Centrust tower?" Kerry inquired, enjoying the sight. "I think they went bankrupt, didn't they?"

"Yeah, yeah." Dar watched for the southern buoy. "I forget what it is now; it's changed three times since then, but I still remember it as the Centrust tower."

"Oh, there's Bayside. Wow, it's really lit up." Kerry pointed. "Is that a tree on top of the Hard Rock?"

"It's something," Dar replied with a chuckle. "Hang on. I'm going to make the turn up Government Cut."

Kerry obligingly slipped her arms around the taller woman, hugging her close. "Okay, I'm ready," she announced, feeling the chuckle go through Dar's body and the warmth as she circled Kerry's shoulder with one long, sweatshirt-covered arm. "It's nice to have a couple of days off, huh?" She poked her boss in the ribs with a finger. "Glad you let me talk you into it?"

It certainly was, Dar reflected, steering the boat into the channel and heading for the island her apartment was on. *First time for everything, I guess,* she mused. Previous years had seen her in the office even on Christmas, toasting the holiday with the grumpy cleaning staff who were forced to work. She'd brought eggnog last year, and it had actually turned out to be a little bit of fun, coaxing smiles from the maintenance workers who hadn't expected to see any of the office staff in.

Not this year. They'd left work at five yesterday and didn't have to be back until eight Monday morning, and she'd found herself looking forward to it, even with it being her birthday and having a party thrown for her. "Yeah, I'm having a pretty good time, you?" Dar answered with a grin.

Kerry nodded, stifling a yawn. "Very much so, even if I have to

settle for palm trees with strings of pink flamingo lights on them."
Dar's Michigan-born assistant had lived in Miami for several years, but
had not yet quite acclimated to the tropical urban culture so vastly
different from her northern birthplace.

Dar cut speed as she entered the marina and steered between the
concrete docks with casual skill. "Hey, palm trees are naturals for lights."
She pointed at the long row of the bushy topped trees that lined the
drive coming into the marina. Someone had painstakingly woven tiny
white lights between all the fronds on all the leaves. "See?"

Kerry peered. "Hey, that's not bad-looking, really," she conceded.
"But I like our tree better."

A real one. Dar had insisted that if she was being coerced into
getting a tree, it was at least going to smell like a pine tree and not like
extruded plastic. So they'd gone out and found one of the seven zillion
tents scattered around selling the darn things trucked from North Carolina packed in snow, and they'd picked out a Douglas Fir a little taller
than Dar herself was.

She docked the boat and they made their way up the winding path
towards the condo, waving to various neighbors that Dar hadn't even
known she had before the outgoing and friendly Kerry had started
spending most of her time with her. A soft strain of Christmas carols
was playing over the island-wide loudspeaker system, gentle hymns
that chased them from tree to tree along the path, and Dar found herself humming.

"Sorry, I didn't catch that." Kerry bent her head closer. "Did you
say something?"

"Um, no...I was just..." Dar flicked a hand at the speakers. "Humming along. I like that one." She put a hand on Kerry's back as they
walked up the path to her door. "I think there'll be roaming carolers
around tonight...you interested in listening?"

The blond woman gazed up at her. "Roaming carolers? I had no
idea they knew what that was down here. Sure, I love Christmas carols.
I can't sing worth a poop, but listening is great."

Dar opened the door and stood back to let her enter. Kerry lived in
an apartment in Kendall, but spent quite a few nights a week here since
Dar's place was undeniably larger, having a total of five bedrooms,
three upstairs and two downstairs, and three bathrooms, plus the huge
kitchen and living areas. And the stone patio had a hot tub in which
they both loved to soak under the stars, looking out over the ocean.

The effect was much more picturesque than at Kerry's yuppie-congested, though comfortable, apartment down south.

It was a tentative arrangement they'd developed as they cautiously felt out their fragile, little more than two month-old relationship, still a little unsure, still a little wary of accepting a growing dependence on each other. This was Kerry's first intimate relationship, and Dar had grown up an only child – it was an adjustment for both of them.

They maintained a polite separation during the week that allowed them both space to adjust, especially since they worked closely together at the large information services firm where Dar was the Operations Vice President, and Kerry her assistant.

At work, of course, they were strictly business, conscious of the avidly interested scrutiny of the several hundred staff members in their Miami office complex. Despite their efforts, the staff persisted in making them the occasional topic of coffee room gossip, something they'd both started becoming more aware of lately, snippy comments in the coffee room, meant for Kerry to overhear, and pointed remarks made to Dar in executive level meetings that Dar usually brushed off without answering.

They were both taking a big chance. Exposure meant a transfer or worse for Kerry, and potential legal difficulties for Dar, but they'd made the mutual decision to try and balance their personal lives with their demanding professional ones, and so far, things had worked out all right.

So far. Kerry glanced around at the now familiar condo with its marble tile floor and dark leather furniture, which had been transformed for the holiday season, mostly under her influence. The fluffy tree sat in one corner with strings of white lights nestled in its branches and colorful glass ornaments alternating with tiny carved ones Kerry had brought over from Kendall. Underneath the tree was a scattering…

No, Kerry corrected herself, piles of boxes. Gifts they'd gotten for each other and wrapped in a secretive frenzy. She'd never quite had a Christmas like this before, where most of her time and energy were focused on one person, and just looking at those piles, and knowing at least half were hers – that felt very weird.

They'd put green and red pillar candles around too, and a prettily woven wreath graced the front door, no doubt surprising Dar's neighbors, who had probably not even known anyone lived in the condo before Kerry started sharing space there. She liked Christmas, with all its traditions, and so far her new friend had been amiably cooperative in participating. Now, however, she was about to ask Dar to do something a little more formal, and she wasn't sure if her suggestion was going to go over well.

"Something wrong with the tree?" Dar came up behind her, and circled her with both arms, peering at what she thought Kerry was staring at. "And can I interest you in some eggnog?"

"Um, sure." Kerry took a breath, suddenly a little nervous about the request she was making. "Listen, Dar, I know you're not a religious person...but would you like to go to a church service with me tonight?"

The dark-haired woman paused, and studied her. "I thought you said there wasn't any of your brand around here?" she remarked curiously. "Or did you find one?"

Kerry tried to judge her companion's comfort level with the request. Dar was hard to read sometimes. She'd spent so many years hiding behind her frosty executive façade that her reactions occasionally weren't honest, but geared to what she thought her listener expected instead. Kerry didn't want her friend to be forced into an uncomfortable situation just because of her. "There aren't, really, but my old pastor at home gave me the names of a few he thought I'd be comfortable with; one's over here on South Beach." She paused. "It's...not very formal." Dar was, she knew, distinctly unreligious, and had shown little or no interest in theological topics Kerry had occasionally brought up.

Dar cocked her head, and considered that. "You mean it's no big deal if we go and hold hands?" she asked with typical bluntness, holding back a grin at the blush which colored Kerry's neck and face. "That kind of informal?"

"Something like that, yeah," the blond woman muttered. "Um...never mind. It's kind of a dumb idea." She hitched her gear back to her shoulder. "I'm going to put up a wash of this stuff; want me to get yours, too?" It had been a stupid thing to ask, after all. There were some interests, she'd discovered, that she and Dar simply did not share.

"Hey." Dar caught her arm, and swung her around so they were facing each other. "I know this stuff's important to you."

"It's okay." Kerry gave her a gentle push. "It's not your style...don't worry about it."

Dar hesitated, then glanced over her shoulder. "Listen, I dragged you down to watch those alligator wrestlers; fair's fair. I can survive a church service." She tugged on Kerry's shirt collar. "You have to poke me when I'm supposed to stand up or whatever though. I don't know much about any of it."

"Really?" Kerry peeked up at her. "Tell you what—I'll treat you to ice cream afterwards, how's that?"

A grin escaped Dar's usually serious face. "Ah. So you think I'll do anything for a hot fudge sundae, is that it?" She traced a fingertip over Kerry's visible blush. "Well, you're right. I'll take you up on your offer."

Kerry gave her a crooked grin. "I think I can do that. It's not that hard, this kind, not like we were going to Catholic Mass or something." She added offhandedly.

"I watched that on TV last year," Dar nodded. "The Pope one. It confused the hell out of me."

Kerry laughed, more at ease. "Yeah, I watched that too, the repeat after we got home from the late service…it's quite a circus." She considered her plans. "Okay, well, it's not until eleven, so…you up for dinner?"

"After eight hours diving?" Dar snorted. "I could eat the couch for dinner if you put a little A1 on it." She glanced outside. "It's beautiful tonight. Could I coax you into joining me at a little outside table up at the, um, nice restaurant?" She lifted a brow hopefully.

"Ooo…starlight, candelight, and you…I think I can twist my arm," Kerry agreed, relieved. "On the single condition that you let me pay." She raised a finger at Dar's protest. "Ah ah…remember our deal."

A sigh. "Okay," Dar grumbled. "But the champagne's on me."

"Deal," the blond woman relented cheerfully. "C'mon. I don't think sweats and polos are the dress code up there for Christmas Eve."

"Certainly not if you're wearing my polo shirt," Dar laughed. "But if you just add a belt to it, you could call it a dress, and that'd pass." The shirt hung almost to the blond's knees.

Kerry stuck her tongue out. "I like when they fit like this, and none of mine do."

"Well…." Dar drawled. "Now I know to buy your shirts two sizes too big and you'll be happy."

"Not the same," Kerry replied, a little shyly.

"No?" the dark-haired woman inquired.

"They don't smell like you," Kerry admitted, looking up at her through fair eyelashes as she delicately sniffed at her sleeve. "That's the part I like."

"Oh." Dar felt the blood heating her face. She cleared her throat. "I see… guess I'll just give you free reign of my closet, then."

Kerry sighed contentedly, determined to enjoy the evening now that she'd gotten Dar to join her. Even if the church was weird, and not what she was used to, it soothed her heart to know she'd be there at midnight, doing her part in the celebration of the Lord's birth.

If He chose not to listen…well, that was another thing all together. She impulsively turned, and hugged Dar, squeezing her tightly. "Thanks."

Dar patted her back, puzzled but pleased. "Anytime."

🐾   🐾   🐾

"Are you sure this is appropriate dress and all?" Dar deftly directed the Lexus off the ferry and through the terminal parking lot. "I'd always thought of church as being a lot more formal; you know, hats, floral arrangements, that kind of thing."

Kerry brushed a pine needle off her crisply pressed shirt, which was tucked neatly into a pair of dark chinos and surmounted by a festive, embroidered vest featuring running reindeer and holly wreathes. "Well, I called the pastor there, and he tried to get away with the 'whatever you feel comfortable in' line. I told him if I showed up in a bathing suit with a Santa hat on, and everyone laughed, I wasn't going to be very happy."

Dar laughed. "Oh my god, I'd have paid to see that."

"Dar." Kerry gave her a look. "Anyway, he said most people wore jeans or chinos and something other than t-shirts, one or two people wore dresses or suits, and there's one guy who comes in a reindeer outfit."

"With antlers or without?" the executive asked seriously.

"Dar!" The blond woman laughed.

"Sorry. Must have been those five glasses of champagne," Dar apologized. "Not to mention that Grand Marnier cake…wow." She exhaled a little. "I feel like I'm going to explode."

"Mm, tell me about it." Kerry rolled her head to one side, and regarded the dark water stretching away from the causeway they were on. "Should I be driving?" She gave her companion a concerned look. "You seemed okay."

"No, it's all right." Dar shook her head. "I don't feel it. I just tend to run off at the mouth when I've had a few glasses of anything." She gave her friend a light shrug. "Sorry."

Kerry patted her arm. "It's okay. I think it's really cute," she confided. "Turn left up there, and it's three blocks down on the right hand side."

"I know," Dar muttered, as she navigated through the very busy traffic. "Jesus, it's a mess down here."

Kerry regarded her lover out of the corner of her eye, approving the deep green sweater she'd put on over a collared shirt, which was tucked into her black silk slacks. The sweater was plain, but had pretty embroidery around the neck and cuffs, stylized birds chasing each other around and around in bold, clear colors. "I really like that sweater," she commented, reaching over to trace the embroidery. "It looks really good on you."

"Thanks…you look pretty hot yourself," Dar commented casually. "Here we go." She pulled into a small parking lot adjacent to an old fashioned, two story concrete building. The back half of the structure seemed to have been converted into a church, based on the stained glass windows, and that part faced the sea. "Must look nice inside during sunrise."

"Mm," Kerry agreed, feeling a little nervous now that they were here. Was this such a good idea? She really had no idea how to act, given the open nature of the church, or what kind of beliefs or services they'd have. The pastor had mentioned music, and when she'd told him her own denomination, he'd said she'd feel comfortable, but…

"You okay?" Dar studied her.

"Yeah…" Kerry folded her arms across her chest. "I've just never…um…this is really stupid, but I've never been in a place where mostly everyone was gay before."

"Oh." Dar chuckled. "Relax, just act normally. They don't stamp your forehead when you go in." She got out of the car and twitched her sweater straight, then she waited for Kerry to join her. "You're going to think everyone's looking at you, so just relax, because they are."

"Comforting. Thank you," Kerry muttered.

"Just think of what it was like for you the first couple days at work," her companion reassured her.

"Yippee." Being hired in as Dar's assistant over lots of other people had certainly turned a few heads, all right. "You've been down here before, to South Beach, I take it?" Kerry inquired as they started to walk across the lot, joining a small stream of others.

"Yes," Dar answered readily. "I used to cruise some of the bars down here in my younger years." She returned the appraising glances they were getting from some of the other attendees.

"Did you take your high school ring off then, Grandma?" Kerry poked her gently. "Listen to you—'in my younger years...yeah, when we had to walk to school uphill, both ways....'"

"Kerry..." Dar put an arm around her and leaned closer. "Being a Miami native means you never, ever have to walk to school uphill," she reminded her. "Unless you live under the highway overpass."

Laughing, they entered the building, nodding at the tall young man who was courteously holding the door open for them.

🐾 🐾 🐾

It was weird. Kerry found her eyes flicking here and there, her eyes absorbing the collection of assorted couples and singles assembled in the chapel. That, at least, was familiar, being roughly square with a raised platform at one end, and rows of pews stretching across the floor. The pews were donated from various building projects from other churches, she noticed, and in one case, a temple. They were a mixture of woods and sizes, but no one seemed to mind. Missing were the typical Bibles, but there were hymnbooks, and she took one, thumbing through its well-worn pages to see old favorites and some she didn't know.

She and Dar were sitting about midway on the left hand side, and as the room filled, she watched her lover's alert and interested eyes watching everything.

Of course, half the room, the female half, was also watching her. Kerry felt a mixture of pride and consternation at the veiled, and in some cases, not so veiled, looks of lust directed at her companion, but Dar seemed oblivious.

Or maybe not. She felt a warm arm slide around her shoulders as Dar leaned closer on the pretext of studying her hymnbook. "So. What's that?"

The pastor's arrival interrupted her somewhat meandering description of basic holiday services, and they both turned their attention to the man. He was of medium height with sandy brown hair and pale eyes, about their age. He gave everyone a friendly smile before launching into a short sermon.

It was...interesting. Kerry got the gist of it being a plea for more tolerance in the world, and she felt it probably was better off directed outside this room, since everyone in here seemed pretty darned tolerant to her. But she appreciated the sentiment, and he made several good points about how people who are persecuted tend to turn their anger outwards, and practice the same kinds of discrimination they themselves suffer.

Then three people got up, two men and one woman, to read some original poems they'd written. Kerry liked them a lot, as well as the fact that they were contributing something of themselves to the ceremony. That seemed to her to be a good idea, and something other churches would be better off adopting. Sometimes the overuse of the old traditions without infusing new blood made a church stagnate. She remembered being somewhat bored as a teenager in her own church, feeling that the people in charge really didn't have a handle on what was going on in her world.

These people had a handle. Their works spoke of the lonely feeling of standing out in a crowd, of having family turn away from you, and the last, spoken by a short, owlish man with horn-rimmed glasses and a buzz cut, was about what it felt like to be told that God hated you.

Kerry felt that one, but in a way it helped to hear it, because she understood she wasn't alone. She wondered briefly if someday maybe she'd have the guts to stand up there and mumble a piece of her own poetry, then decided it would be a cold day in Hell first.

Dar leaned over after the man finished. "That wasn't bad."

"Mm," Kerry agreed softly.

"Stuff you write is better, though," the dark-haired woman confided casually.

Kerry felt like an icicle had suddenly grown in the pit of her stomach. "What?" She put a hand on Dar's arm, and gripped it. A suspicion formed and she felt her heart lurch. "How did you know?" The thought of Dar taking advantage of their closeness to read her private files was chilling and sickening.

"Uh…" The blue eyes opened wider in consternation. "You…you left a couple pages on the printer, I didn't, um…" The crowd was rustling as the choir arranged themselves up front, and she glanced around. "I'm sorry, I didn't realize you…uh…" It was obvious that Kerry was very, very upset. "Kerry, I'm sorry." She hadn't meant to read the pages, exactly; it was just that she'd picked them up, and the first lines caught her eye, and she somehow managed to find her way at the bottom of the verse, unable to stop reading.

The printer. Right…of course, it hadn't been Dar's indiscretion, it had been her own, forgetting to pick up her stupid print job on their shared device. She slowly released the death grip on Dar's arm. "No, no, it's my stupid fault I left them on the printer," she got out. "That stuff is so personal, I just…" Then she stopped talking, and her brow creased as she replayed the words in her head. "Wait a minute—you liked it?"

Dar let out a very relieved breath. "Yeah…that one about the wind was great," she agreed enthusiastically. "And there was kind of a long one…um…" The taller woman fell silent, reaching up and tugging an ear in obvious discomfort. "It was kind of…ah…"

Oh, god, not that one. Kerry ducked her head. "Yeah, that one was about you." she murmured, hearing her heartbeat skip several paces. She peeked at her lover, who was definitely blushing.

Dar hesitantly pointed at her own chest "M…me?"

Kerry looked away, with a sick feeling. "You hated it, right?"

Dar folded her arms, and glanced around, the flush still very evident across her tanned skin. "It was beautiful," she muttered, "but it never occurred to me that you were writing it abou—" She stopped and took a breath. "I loved it."

Kerry nibbled her lip. "Wow. Cool." She tried to suppress a tiny smirk but failed. "Not the way I ever imagined showing them to you, but I guess that works."

Dar nodded, then straightened as the pastor reclaimed his podium. "I guess we've got something to talk about when we get home, eh?"

"Yeah," Kerry smiled, "I guess we do." She felt a quiet happiness lighten her mood considerably, and she turned the hymnbook over to the page he indicated. "Okay, this is simple. They sing, you sing," she instructed Dar, holding the book up. "I like this one. Have you ever…"

"Mm…yes, I've seen that one before," Dar replied blandly. "I think I can follow along."

They stood up and waited for the choir to finish the first section, then joined in when the pastor indicated. Kerry started to sing, then stopped as a crystal clear voice soared up from right next to her. She felt her jaw drop, and she turned to look at Dar, who was trying very hard not to laugh.

The chorus ended, and the choir started up again. "Something wrong?" Dar inquired, a definite smirk on her angular face.

"You can sing!" Kerry whispered incredulously. "I mean, not just sing, but like…that sounded incredible."

A light shrug. "Not something I use very often," Dar commented loftily, as she put her hands behind her back and gazed around the room. Some of their neighbors were giving her interested, sideways looks, and she lifted an eyebrow at them.

"You never told me you could sing!" Kerry warbled softly.

"I don't recall you mentioning poetry," her companion answered, in a low voice.

They exchanged shy glances and Kerry reached over and took Dar's hand, twining their fingers together as the rest of the congregation starting singing again.

The rest of the hymns went by in a blur, and before she knew it, Kerry found herself in a logjam of people all trying to get out of the small building and into the cool night air. Hands stopped them, though, and she found herself being introduced to a rapid succession of faces, most of whom seemed friendly, and they received quite a few invitations to coffee, conversation, and in one case, a psychic reading on the beach.

Everyone seemed fascinated by Dar, who assumed her business mien, all cool attention and brisk politeness, until the pastor caught up to them and offered a hand.

"You're new," he stated frankly. "Or is this just a convenient place to catch a service?"

"Um…actually, I called here earlier asking about the church," Kerry answered, a little hesitantly.

"Ah, bathing suit and Santa hat. I recognize your voice." The man smiled and gave her a wink. "Honey, you could have showed up like that, and I guarantee nobody would have minded a bit." He shook her hand. "I'm David Argnot, pastor, plumber, and all around handyman of the church."

That forced a chuckle from the mildly embarrassed Kerry. "Nice to meet you. My name is Kerry, and um…" She nodded her head towards Dar, who was fending off the choir mistress, a striking redhead almost the same height as the executive. "This is my friend Dar."

Hearing her name Dar turned, and regarded him, her pale blue eyes standing out with startling clarity against her tan. "Nice to meet you." She held a hand out.

He blinked. "Anyone ever tell you you've got fantastic eyes?" He took her hand and shook it gingerly. "Not to mention a killer voice."

Dar gave him a brief smile. "Thanks. That was a nice speech you made."

"Ah, it was nothing." He grinned. "You should hear me when I don't have a major worldwide holiday to deal with. Speaking of which, services are on Sundays in the late afternoons, in case I hadn't mentioned it."

"Late afternoons?" Kerry had to laugh, used to crack of dawn ceremonies at home.

"We're unabashed hedonists, and don't pretend otherwise," he told her solemnly. "I have a standing reservation with a beach, a blanket, and a picnic basket on Sunday mornings." He rocked back and forth. "So, how about it? You guys be back?"

Dar gave him a crooked grin. "Depends; do you serve refreshments?" Her eyes twinkled with amusement.

His brows waggled. "What, do we look like Catholics to you? All that wine and cheese... whoops, wafers..." He took some joshing from the nearby listeners. "Nah, just kidding. We usually get together after the service for some coffee over at the café across the street. They're used to us invading, and they make a killer seven layer dip."

"You should drop on by," the choir mistress urged. "There's lots of good talk, and stuff... we have a great time." She turned as a short, chestnut-haired woman came up and rested her chin on the redhead's shoulder. "Right, Anne?"

"Sure," the woman agreed. "As long as it involves orange juice and spanking." She gave Dar and Kerry a wicked grin. "Whoops, I'm in church...sorry about that."

Kerry had no idea if Dar liked, disliked or was thoroughly freaked out by the group. She had that politely intellectual look on her face that Kerry had last seen when Lou "Duks" Draefus, the company Finance VP, started explaining compound interest to her. "Sure. Sounds like fun," Kerry finally said, figuring she could drop by on her own, at any rate. It was strange, and not at all like what she was used to, but the people seemed pretty nice, and she liked the pastor, who definitely had a good sense of humor.

"Great, we'll see you guys next week, then." Pastor David smiled at them and loosened his collar. "Hey, surf's up...who's up for some midnight swimming?"

They edged their way out to the emptying parking lot under the twinkling stars of a clear tropical night. Kerry waited until they were in the car before she cleared her throat. "Um…that wasn't meant to agree on your behalf, by the way. I mean, it's kind of a weird place. Don't feel like you're obligated in any way to go back," she explained. "I can just go back by myself, maybe talk to some of those people. Two of the women are from the same denomination I am, so…"

Dar blew her wind disordered bangs out of her eyes and backed the Lexus out of its spot, then reached over and ruffled Kerry's hair. "Kerry, you know I love you, right?"

"Um, well, yes," the blond woman agreed shyly. "I'd sort of gotten that impression somehow, yeah."

"Have you ever seen what piranha can do to a cow in under a minute?" the taller woman inquired, turning onto the main street.

Kerry's brows knit. "What in the world does that have to do with anything?" she asked. "And yes, I saw that special, thanks." She made a face. "They almost ate Crocodile Man's parts." She referred to a favorite program on the cable channel.

Dar stopped at a red light, and turned to her. "Good, because that's what that crowd would do to you if you went back there alone." She grinned and chucked Kerry's chin. "They know an innocent when they see one."

"I am not an innocent," the blond woman protested, then paused. "Am I? I thought they were nice; they seemed okay."

"They were very nice, and I'm sure we'll find some great friends there," Dar reassured her. "But you gotta know the ground rules first, understand?"

Kerry thought about that for a minute. "Oh." She chewed her lip. "You mean the social side of things…yeah, they've got that in our church too, but it's different," she reflected. "They tend more to quilting circles."

Dar muffled a chuckle. "Well, I'm sure some of what this group does involves a quilt at some point," she muttered. "But it was a nice service, and I'm glad we went. Did it make you feel better?"

Kerry leaned back. "Yeah, it did. Maybe it's just the going through the motions thing, I don't know. But the poetry was good, and I liked his sermon, and that choir is not bad." She reflected. "It was really different, but I enjoyed it."

"Good." Dar gazed out the window at the now thinned out traffic.

"And I got to hear you sing!" Kerry remembered suddenly. "That was worth the whole trip." She poked Dar in the ribs. "You've been holding out on me, huh?"

The dark-haired woman chuckled faintly. "Not...." Dar hesitated. "Not on purpose, or anything. It's just not something I think about a lot." She changed lanes and leaned back.

They drove in silence for a bit, then Kerry glanced at her watch. "Hey, it's after midnight."

"Yep, it's Christmas," Dar commented. "Ho ho ho."

"It's your birthday," Kerry gently corrected her. "Pull over into that IHOP, Santa. I promised you a sundae."

The staff was busy serving a number of like-minded folks, but they were seated immediately. Dar leaned on her elbows and played with the edge of the menu. "Yeah, it is my birthday, isn't it?" She glanced up at Kerry with a wry look. "I can't believe I'm thirty years old." Her brows contracted together pensively.

"Given what you've accomplished, I can't believe it either," Kerry admitted. "I feel so inadequate."

Dar blinked at her. "Huh?"

"Well, Jesus, Dar, you're only two...okay, three years older than I am, and look what you've done already. I mean, you're a vice president, you've got a great career, this fantastic lifestyle...you're gorgeous...you're successful..." She threw up her hands. "It's incredible."

Her friend regarded her seriously. "I never considered it like that."

Kerry half smiled. "I know." She turned and ordered for both of them, having ordered ice cream enough for Dar to be confident in that, at least.

Dar's cell phone rang and she sighed. "Yeah?"

"Good morning, Dar." Mark's voice sounded annoyingly cheerful. "Merry Christmas." Mark Polenti was Dar's MIS Chief, and a good friend.

"Yeah, yeah, what's wrong?" Dar growled.

"Nothing," the MIS Chief drawled. "I was just calling to wish my favorite boss a happy birthday."

Dar drummed her fingers on the table, and gave her blond companion a suspicious look. "And just how did you find out it was my birthday, Mark?"

Kerry peered innocently out the window. "Gee, look at that moon, will you?"

"A bird told me," Mark replied, the grin very evident in his voice.

"Uh huh. Is this bird about five foot six, with blond hair and green eyes?" Dar inquired wryly.

"Sorry, Dar, that's secured info," the MIS chief clucked at her. "Anyway, you have a good birthday, okay? I'll see you tomorrow, at your, uh, Christmas party."

Uh huh. "Thanks, Mark; I'll remember this," Dar threatened, getting a wicked chuckle in response before Mark hung up.

Kerry was still peering out the window, apparently fascinated by the fake snow.

Dar reached over and tickled her ribs, making her jump and squeal. "Little bird, huh?"

The cell phone rang again, and Kerry muffled a laugh as Dar sighed, then answered it. "Yeah?" A pause. "Oh, hi Duks…yeah, thanks…I appreciate that…un huh…nope…what? Oh, sure…hi Mariana…thank you…no, well, if I have to tell you, okay, it's thirty." A longer pause. "Stop whining, it's not my fault…okay, yeah, I'll see you guys tomorrow." She turned off the phone as the ferry docked on the island. "What did you do, send out a message to MIAHQUSERS ALL?" she demanded.

Kerry whistled softly under her breath. The cell phone rang again. Dar glared at it, then turned her head as footsteps approached, seeing a huge bowl of ice cream approaching with a candle on top. She breathed in, then out, then looked at Kerry. "You are in such trouble."

Well, Kerry told herself, watching the bowl arrive, *I could always hide under my desk come October.*

Chapter 2

Soft strains of Christmas music intruded into Dar's dozing mind, and she sleepily identified "O Tannenbaum" as she nudged herself a little closer to consciousness. The other thing poking her was the smell of pancakes and biscuits.

"Mm." Her eyes opened, noting Kerry's conspicuous absence, which pretty much coincided with the delicious scents that now had her stomach growling. She rolled over and stretched, extending her arms out and yawning, as the morning light snuck through her blinds, and laid stripes across her bare body. She spared a glance down her length, tracing her recently reemerging abdominal muscles with an idle finger.

She'd kind of let that slip for a while, she admitted to herself, allowing the long work hours to nudge aside the frequent, long bouts of exercise that had been her habit. Then she'd met Kerry, and found herself dumped into an almost nonstop whirlwind of diving, climbing, running… and into a newly rediscovered involvement in the martial arts she'd only dabbled with for stress relief the past few years.

Which was a damn good thing, in retrospect, for both her and her newfound companion, because they both ate like starving wolves and if it hadn't been for their shared love of physical activity, they'd both be in some serious trouble.

Kerry was an excellent cook, though, and had found ways to introduce vegetables and other healthy things into their daily diet, and despite the late night raids on the ice cream container, Dar found herself in better shape than she had been for some time. She felt a lot more relaxed, in fact, and the bouts of dark depression she'd been experiencing had vanished, replaced with a sense of fragile happiness.

Which was also a little frightening. She was afraid of getting too used to this. After all, it could vanish just as quickly as it appeared, now couldn't it?

Damn, it hurt to think of that. Dar studied the ceiling. Every time she thought that maybe, just maybe this time she'd found the real thing, ugly memories of the times before taunted her, mocking her with warnings to be cautious, untrusting, remembering the pain of rejection all too clearly.

Knock it off, Dar. She took a deep breath, detecting the scent of the fir tree in the living room. *It's Christmas, and your birthday, so pull your head out of your ass and go have fun for a change.* She thought about the tree, and remembered the piles of neatly wrapped presents tucked under it. God, she'd had fun wrapping up Kerry's. She hadn't played with tinsel and ribbons in years, and she'd gone a little overboard making little colorful curls and bows. With a grin, she hoisted herself out of the waterbed and padded to the dresser, donning a t-shirt and her flannel boxers. After a trip to the bathroom to brush her teeth and splash a little water on her face, she poked her head into the living room, hearing a soft humming coming from nearby.

Dar followed the sound, ending up in the kitchen next to a busily flap-jacking Kerry, who was dressed in her favorite Tweety bird night-shirt with her hair twisted back off her face. "Good morning," Dar greeted her, with a smile, finding it hard to remember what it was like only two months before, when all she'd have walked out to was the utter quiet and sterility of loneliness.

No tree. No music. Just another day. Dar swallowed and took a shaky breath, then dismissed the thought, sliding both arms around Kerry's middle and squeezing her.

Kerry leaned back against her, and tilted her head back, returning her smile. "Happy birthday." She kissed Dar gently. "Merry Christmas."

Dar glanced over her shoulder at the griddle. "Is that my present? I'll have birthdays every week, in that case."

"Chocolate chip pancakes, eggs Benedict, biscuits, and that godawaful library paste you insist on eating," Kerry agreed. "It's almost done; go on out to the porch and let me bring it out." She'd been argued out of insisting on serving Dar breakfast in bed, curtailed only by the taller woman's demonstration of just how impossible it was to eat in a waterbed.

Food, anyway.

"Grits," Dar replied, nibbling her ear. "Not library paste. You just have to add enough stuff to it so it so they taste like something," she explained. "It's kind of like potatoes: a delivery mechanism for butter, salt, and maple syrup."

"Right." Kerry gave her a push. "Go on…here, take some coffee with you. I just put it in the carafe."

Dar took the pot and two cups and ambled out onto the porch, which was drenched in sunlight and washed with a freshening, cool breeze from the northeast. It was cool enough for the sun to feel good as it warmed her skin, and Dar took a seat, propping her bare feet up on the stone railing and regarding the blue waters that extended to the horizon before her. Above the beach, a gull soared, banking on long narrow wings in search of a tasty meal. The breeze ruffled Dar's hair, and she smiled in pure, animal satisfaction at the beauty of the day. The sliding door opened, and Kerry maneuvered her way out with a large tray, setting it on the table and looking out at the water with a smile. "Wow…nice day."

"Yeah," her dark-haired companion readily agreed. "You sure about this snow thing?"

Kerry pushed a lock of hair back behind an ear, and poured two glasses of very orange juice. "Well…" She handed one to her lover. "I'm starting to consider alternatives."

They shared breakfast, except that Kerry refused to touch the grits, even at Dar's insistent coaxing. "Sorry, sorry, I just can't. They look too gross, Dar," she laughingly refused, taking seconds of eggs instead. "Leave me in peace with my hollandaise sauce, please."

"You could put that on the grits," Dar replied, undaunted.

"No." Kerry waved her off with a fork.

"What about if I put chocolate on them?"

"NO. Ugh. Look, I don't force you to eat broccoli, do I?" Kerry complained.

"Yes, you do," Dar replied. "In fact, you sneaked it into the soup the other week and thought I wouldn't notice."

The blond grinned. "Whoops. Busted." She opened her mouth. "Okay, one tiny taste."

Dar scooped up a forkful of the southern staple and placed it on her companion's tongue with a chuckle at the trepidation on her face. "C'mon, it won't kill ya."

Kerry mouthed the substance, then paused thoughtfully. "Dar, all I taste is butter, salt, and maple syrup."

"Yes, thank you." Dar smiled. "Now, what's wrong with any of those?"

"Nothing." Kerry leaned over and took another forkful. "Share."

They wandered inside after breakfast and settled in the living room, where the tree nestled quietly in one corner, its twinkling white lights and bright ornaments livening up the room considerably. Kerry stretched herself out on the couch and pillowed her head in Dar's lap as the taller woman started up a new CD of Christmas music.

"This is very different," the blond woman commented, rubbing a thumb against Dar's skin idly. "At my parents' house, the first thing done on Christmas morning is everyone sits in the living room and my father presides over the gift allocation."

Dar patted her arm gently but didn't say anything. Kerry had spoken to her family only once since Thanksgiving, a several minute long, anger-filled, bitter confrontation that had left the blond woman shaken. She'd thought a little time would allow her parents to accept her relationship with Dar, but instead of understanding, she'd found only hatred instead. There would be no going back there, and she knew it. Kerry sadly accepted the estrangement, but Dar understood that it was still hard for her, even after what had happened, so deep was her innate love for her family.

"We never really had a tradition," Dar quietly said. "It was just whatever was going on at the time where we were. Dad would always have a present for me, but we didn't do a lot in the way of decorating, or trees…" She glanced at the colorful tree, which she found appealing in an odd way. "Too bad; they're kinda nice."

"Yeah." Kerry smiled a little. "So…you want to open stuff now, or later?"

Dar grinned like a little kid.

"I guess that answers that," the blond woman laughed, folding her arms over her stomach and gazing up. "Besides, we have to clear some space. I've got a feeling a few more things might end up under there during the party." Her eyes twinkled.

"Urgh." Dar winced. "Well, if I have to…" She tickled Kerry's ribs through the soft cotton of her shirt. "C'mon, let's go."

They settled at the foot of the tree among little stacks of wrapped packages. "I think we went a little overboard," Dar remarked dryly, observing the piles, "considering that there's only two of us here."

Kerry rubbed her nose. "Well, maybe, yeah, but…" She paused and took a breath. "I didn't have too many people to shop for this year, so…I guess I kinda made up for that with you."

Dar glanced down and fiddled with the edge of her shirt. "So what's my excuse?" she replied quietly. "My usual Christmas morning up till now has been a chocolate croissant, watching videos on VH1, and a run on the beach."

"I don't know." Kerry pushed her hair back. "Maybe we can make some new traditions. I always looked on Christmas shopping as kind of a chore, especially for my parents, but it didn't seem that way for you."

"Yeah." The dark-haired woman smiled a little, regarding the tile floor she was seated on. "I walked out of the mall the other week and couldn't believe all the stuff I had." She looked up. "Does that make you feel uncomfortable?" She knew Kerry felt very strongly about her own independence, and insisted on sharing all their expenses, regardless of the fact that Dar kept telling her she had more money than she knew what to do with.

"Well…" Kerry peered around at the veritable mountain of packages. "I'd probably freak out if you bought me a pony or something, but I guess I'll survive." She grinned engagingly at her companion. "Besides, I think I kept pace with you, but I think you know that if you'd gotten me a box of Kleenex for Christmas, I'd have been happy." She leaned over and curled her fingers around Dar's. "You're the only gift that really matters to me."

Dar smiled indulgently. "Likewise." She glanced around. "But we'd better get this stuff opened." She squeezed Kerry's hand. "Hey, the Disney parade is on at ten; let me put it on."

Kerry laughed and had started sorting the packages when her cell phone rang. "Oh hell." She glanced around. "Can you hand me that?" She'd arranged to have her apartment phone number forwarded to the mobile unit. "Hello?"

"Merry Christmas, chica," Colleen's laughing voice boomed. "I knew I wasn't gonna see you around here before the party, so I thought I'd call." Colleen was a good friend of Kerry's who lived in her apartment complex.

Kerry smiled. "Thanks. Merry Christmas to you, too, Col. How did it go at your mom's last night?" Colleen's family opened their presents on Christmas Eve, before they all trooped solemnly off to midnight Mass, being Irish Catholic and very traditional.

"O My God…" Colleen moaned. "I need a U-haul to get all the stuff back here. My mother, bless her little Irish heart, went berserk this year, and got me everything from new towels to underwear."

"Aw, that's so sweet," the blond woman laughed. "Did all your brothers and sisters show up?"

"Oh yeah. It was a real circus, let me tell ya. The blarney was flying like nothing doing. We had a great time, except my brothers got into the usual fistfight and we ended up dragging Mike to the emergency room after Mass to have a stitch put in his lip."

"Ow." Kerry made a face.

"How was your night?" Colleen asked.

"Well, we spent the day diving yesterday, then we had dinner overlooking the ocean, and we went to a service down at the beach…it was really nice." Kerry told her, watching Dar pluck at a corner of wrapping as she waited. "We just had breakfast, and we're about to get into some serious unwrapping."

"Trade ya," Colleen sighed. "I had to spend the night listening to my aunts and uncles tell me how it was in the good old days, and ask me when I was getting hitched, and tell me how chubby I am."

Interesting perspective, Kerry thought. "Funny, that's exactly what I'd have been doing," she commented. "No trade." She saw a slow, almost shy smile appear on Dar's face as she pieced together the conversation. "So, when you coming over here?"

"Weeeell…you said the party started at seven, but I figure if I show up a little bit early, you'll give me a tour, huh?" Colleen teased. "I want to see this famous fantasy island of yours."

"You got it," Kerry laughed. "See you then." She hung up and folded the phone, chuckling a little, then glanced up at her companion. "She's a lot of fun."

Dar smiled. "Yeah, she seems very nice, though I'm pretty sure she still has her doubts about me." She handed Kerry a package.

Kerry took it. "Is this invasion going to drive you crazy?" She carefully separated the bow from the ribbon and set it aside, then started working on the tape that held one end closed. "And Colleen does like you, by the way; it just took her a while to get past your reputation."

"You can just tear that," Dar observed. "And no, I can deal with the party. I'm a big girl."

Kerry patiently unfolded the wrapping, and set it to one side, revealing a large, golden foil box. "I never tear the wrapping," she informed her companion firmly. "Now go on and open one of yours so I don't feel so self-conscious." She looked at Dar until the dark-haired woman rolled her eyes and picked up a box, then she eased the top off her own and peeked inside. "Ooo." A beautifully embroidered shirt peeked back at her. She had a feeling this was going to be a very interesting morning.

They'd gotten about halfway through, exposing a trade of clothing and various computer trinkets, when her cell phone rang again. She picked it up as she opened a box of wonderfully scented bath beads and oils. "Hello?"

"Kerry?" The voice sounded strained.

"Angela?" She put down the box and listened. "Is that you?"

"Yeah," her sister sighed. "Michael's here too; we've kind of got a situation."

Kerry glanced at Dar, who had cocked her head upon hearing her sister's name. "What's wrong?"

"Well…" Angela cleared her throat. "It's been…kind of bad at home this past month… I'm sure you can imagine."

She could imagine. Kerry's father was Senator Roger Stuart, a conservative Republican recently embroiled in scandal and subsequently indicted by Congress. That, coupled with her own revelation of being gay had made it a somber and stressful holiday season for them.

"Sorry," Kerry answered quietly, and meaning it. The damning information about her father had fallen into her hands, and, in her anger at him after he'd thrown her out of the family, she'd released it anonymously to the press. Her siblings knew that. Her parents did not.

"No, don't be. I mean…." Her sister hesitated. "You did what you had to do, you know? But anyway, all we've been hearing for the last two days is how our lives are all ruined, and Michael and I kind of got sick of it this morning."

Kerry felt a pair of warm arms circle her, and she leaned back against Dar's comforting presence. "Angela, I'm sorry…I know I screwed things up for both of you… I…"

"No…hold on." Angela's voice muffled a bit, then came back. "Michael says don't you dare blame this on yourself. You didn't do any of that stuff, he did, and it's his fault, not yours." She cleared her throat again. "Anyway, we sort of went off this morning about that, and how if it was anyone's fault, it was his, and he lost it."

Kerry took a breath. "Lost it?"

"Yeah; he threw us out of the house," Angela laughed weakly. "Richard's on a business trip, Sally's with his mother because I didn't want her around all the poison for Christmas; she's too young, and she wouldn't understand."

"Wow." Kerry felt the hold tighten, and she pursed her lips. "Well, you can go by there, anyway…right?"

"Uh, actually…" Now Angela's voice got muffled again, and Kerry was aware of an echoing sound in the background. "Actually, Michael had this crazy idea, and before I could stop him, he kinda acted on it, so we're, um…" A slight laugh. "We're about to get on a flight down to Miami to spend a little time with our favorite sister instead."

She couldn't speak for a moment. "Angela, that's insane," Kerry finally breathed.

"Eyah…I know, but we're boarding…hope you don't mind," her sister laughed. "Honestly, we really want to see you. We've got tickets back for tomorrow. It was easier than I thought, because practically no one's flying today."

"No, I don't mind," Kerry reassured her. "We're having a big party here; it'll be great to have both of you. I'll come pick you up, we can spend some time before that…" She glanced at Dar helplessly.

The dark-haired woman just grinned. "I love spontaneity," she drawled, privately very glad Kerry would get to see at least a part of her family. "The more the merrier." And, of course, it would get some attention off Dar herself, which pleased her no end.

"Great! Gotta go." Angela sounded much more cheerful. "See you in a few hours." She hung up, leaving Kerry to exhale weightily.

"Well, that was a surprise."

Dar chuckled softly. "C'mon, we'd better get finished opening stuff." She turned toward the tree, scowling as her own cell phone rang. "Hello?"

"Merry Christmas, Dar!" Gerald Easton's voice boomed over the line. "I hope you got that little package I sent." The general was an old family friend of hers, and had known Dar's father well before his death.

Dar held the phone a little away from her ear. "Yep, and I hope mine got there all right."

"Sitting out under the tree even as we speak, my friend…we're about to start opening, and I thought I'd call to wish you a merry merry— oh, wait…here…all right, don't rip the damn thing out of my hands, you…"

"Hey Dar!"

"Merry Christmas, Jack," Dar smiled. "Got that shore leave, I see." Her childhood friend had really come through for her when she'd had to get to Michigan and Kerry in a hurry.

"One frigging day, yeah," the pilot snorted. "How're you doing? How's Kerry?"

"Fine and fine, thanks," the dark-haired woman assured him. "And you?"

"Busy, hectic, the usual," Jack answered. "Hey, Alabaster says hello, and wants to know if she can send you a present too?"

Kerry peered at her over one shoulder. "Alabaster?"

"Gerry's Labrador," Dar mouthed. "She has puppies."

"Oooooooo…." Kerry squealed. "Oh, Dar, those are such cute puppies…did you get to see them?" Her eyes lit up.

Dar regarded her with a solemn twinkle. "Had nine of them crawling all over me, in fact," she informed her lover. "Yeah," she finally replied into the phone. "Sorry, what was that, Jack?" His voice was muffled.

"Oh, nothing," Jack replied innocently. "So how's the weather?"

"Fine…why?" Dar asked suspiciously.

"Just wondering. I have to fly through Homestead on my way out tonight, thought maybe I'd stop by and say hello," Jack replied brightly.

This party was rapidly getting to be about the size of an inaugural ball, Dar mused. "Sure, why not. We're having a get together over here; I'll put your name on the list."

"Great, see you later!" Jack replied, a grin very evident in his voice as he handed the phone back.

"Well, that's lovely," Gerald stated, sounding pleased. "You two get along so nicely."

Dar sighed inwardly. "Yeah, we sure do…listen, tell Mom I said Merry Christmas, and I hope you like the gifts."

"Don't worry, rugrat…anything you send is always good stuff," Gerald chuckled. "Talk at you later." He hung up, and Dar let the phone drop to her knee.

"'Rugrat'?" Kerry grinned evilly.

"Don't start," Dar warned jokingly. "He's been calling me that since I was twelve."

"Rugrat; that's so cute." She leaned her head against Dar's arm. "He's nice."

"He is…he tries to be family to me," Dar replied quietly. "He was a good friend of Dad's. Jack and I grew practically in each other's houses." She reflected a moment. "I think both sets of parents thought we were going to…um…"

"Get married?"

A shrug. "Something like that. I do like Jack, a lot. If I had to marry a guy, he'd be the one," Dar admitted. "We have a lot in common."

"Yeah, I know what you mean," Kerry agreed quietly. "That's sort of how I feel about Brian." Her former fiancé was living back in Michigan and occasionally called her to see how she was doing. "Fortunately, I don't have to marry a guy, though."

"Mm…me either." Dar folded a piece of wrapping idly. "His wife's very sweet, and a great cook…which reminds me." A dark brow edged up. "I hear I have a spy in my camp."

Green eyes twinkled. "Whoops. Hey, you better be thanking me, because otherwise you'd have been munching on brussels sprouts for Thanksgiving because she called Maria first."

Dar leaned over and kissed her. "Thank you," she murmured sincerely. "For coming into my life and changing it for the better."

Kerry hadn't expected that, and she had to swallow and take a minute to get her breath back before she could answer. "I did that?" she uttered. "Funny…here I was thinking about how you'd done that for me."

They kissed again, then Dar gently nudged aside the wrapping they were nestled in and moved closer, pulling Kerry half into her lap so she could concentrate better. "Damn." She glanced up. "I forgot to hang mistletoe."

Kerry explored her lips. "That would be overkill, I think," she admitted softly, laying a hand along Dar's side and slipping it under the soft fabric of her shirt to the warm skin underneath. Her fingers traced familiar curves and tickled Dar's navel, which caused the taller woman to muffle a laugh.

Warm lips brushed hers, and Kerry let her body relax into the touch, tasting a faint hint of chocolate chips as Dar's palm slid under her nightshirt and up along her side, cupping her breast gently. A faint murmur escaped her, and she traced a line down Dar's middle, circling her navel, then moving lower.

They moved a little apart, and gazed into each other's eyes. Dar nibbled Kerry's nose just for fun, then kissed her again. "Thanks for the birthday," she whispered into one of Kerry's sensitive ears.

"We haven't had the party yet," Kerry answered, nipping her lightly through the fabric of her shirt, and feeling Dar's body jerk in reaction.

Dar cradled her head, as they shared breath. "It's already the best one in a long, long time," she admitted. "Thank you." Their lips found each other again, and a soft groan escaped Kerry's throat as Dar rolled them both over and onto the plush throw rug, its luxurious fur tickling skin grown sensitive and warm, a splash of light from the glass doors dazzling their eyes.

"Can we make this a tradition?" Kerry growled softly in Dar's ear, as she unbuttoned the taller woman's worn jersey. "Every year?"

Dar's eyes found the eggshell white ceiling for just an instant. "For as long as you want," she answered, sliding her hands under Kerry's t-shirt and lifting it up, as Kerry lowered her body and let their bare skin brush lightly together.

Kerry smiled. "You got it."

Dar gazed out over the water, leaning her body against the cool glass as she listened to the cheerful strains of "Jingle Bells" behind her. She heard soft footsteps approaching, her face tensed into a smile in unconscious reaction. Her body turned without prompting as her lover neared, and she found an answering smile spreading over Kerry's face as their glances touched.

"What do you think?" Kerry held up a pair of tiny, stuffed moose head earrings.

"I think you should hang those on the tree," Dar replied, plucking one out of her fingertips and doing just that. "There."

Kerry hung the other one on Dar's pocket. "I like them; I think they're cute." They were both dressed and showered now, the wrappings cleaned up and the condo prepared for the party.

Dar nodded, straightening little bits of the tree in an almost nervous fashion. "So." She turned, and folded her arms over her chest. "It's been quite a month, huh?"

"Mm," Kerry agreed, as she sat on the edge of the couch and folded her hands between her knees. "It sure has…a lot of changes to get used to."

"Yeah." Dar swallowed. "Hasn't been too bad, though, huh?" She furtively watched Kerry's face, trying to gauge her reaction.

Blond brows drew together in puzzlement. "It hasn't been bad at all… I mean, besides getting used to the traveling back and forth stuff, and trying to remember where I left what when, the apartment or here… it's been all right."

"I haven't scared you off then yet, I guess." She felt her voice come close to breaking, and she swallowed a few times, forcing down the nervous dread.

Kerry blinked a few times. "Scar…" Her eyes suddenly registered the tension in Dar's body and she got up and walked over to her. "You haven't scared me at all." She tangled her fingers in Dar's belt loops. "Have I driven you crazy yet?"

"No." The dark-haired woman visibly relaxed a little.

"Not even with force feeding you vegetables?"

A smile. "No, you put so much stuff on them, I hardly realize they're there," Dar reassured her.

"I don't make too much noise? Or bother your stuff? Get in your space?" Kerry persisted.

"No."

"Good." Kerry leaned against her and exhaled. "Because I really like being around you, and I'd hate to think it made you uncomfortable, or that you were regretting asking me to spend time here." They were, she'd thought, surprisingly compatible. More than Kerry had really hoped for, considering the vast differences in their natures and backgrounds.

They both enjoyed activities outdoors and in the water. They liked similar music, television programs, and movies. They both enjoyed pretty much the same types of food, give or take a vegetable here and there, and a grit or two.

Of course, Dar was moodier than she was, prone to moments of dark introspection that Kerry had learned to recognize. Sometimes she simply left her friend alone, but more often, she'd felt herself prompted to find a way to draw Dar out of her funk, treasuring the wry, twitching grin that always appeared when she was successful.

It wasn't always easy. They were two very different people, and it was more difficult in Kendall due to the apartment's small spaces. Here, at least, there was plenty of room, both inside the condo and on the island itself, which had a range of things to do within walking distance. "It's been a really happy month for me," Kerry added quietly.

"That's good to hear," Dar murmured, her face creasing into an unexpected smile. "It has been for me too." She reached over and plucked something from the tree. "I... thought maybe you could use one of these. I know the guards know you already but..." She offered Kerry a bit of plastic.

"What's that?" Kerry took it, peering at the colorful item.

"It's a...er...resident's decal." Dar coughed a bit. "For your car, you know..."

"Oh...oh! Right!" Kerry wondered if didn't go just a little deeper than that. "Thank you. Now I don't have to worry when there's a new guy on the gate." She looked up, catching Dar gazing down at her with a half fearful, half hopeful expression. "Makes me feel like I really belong here."

Dar's lips twitched. "Would you like to? Live here...all the time?"

Woo. Kerry breathed out slowly. She had her hand lying lightly on Dar's stomach, and she could feel the short, tense breaths, and the rapid beating of her heart, despite the fact that her attitude was one of forced casualness. "That's a big step," she admitted softly.

"Well, just something to think about," Dar told her. "No rush." Her jaw clamped down on the almost stuttered word, hoping she hadn't moved too fast.

"Definitely." Kerry let the smile inside her come out, and she hugged her lover, feeling the tension relax a bit as she squeezed hard. "Thank you, Dar. I can't tell you what you asking me that means." A powerful hug back was her answer. "Mm…I wonder if being in love feels this good for everyone."

I don't know." Dar seemed to be having trouble swallowing. "But it's never been like this for me before…and I doubt it ever could be again, so I hope this lasts a long time." The words tumbled out in an uncharacteristic rush, and ended with a soft throat clearing.

"Mm. I hate to tell you this, Dar…" Kerry's eyes gentled. "But when I was eight, I think, I decided if I ever fell in love it would be one of those forever and ever things." She took a breath, as she felt Dar stop breathing entirely. "I know that sounds really…um…"

"Perfect," Dar blurted. "It sounds…perfect. Forever and ever sounds…just fine with me."

Forever. Something inside Kerry smiled contentedly.

Welcome home.

Kerry glanced up. "Did you say something?"

The blue eyes seemed to deepen a shade, and a faint hint of amusement tinged them. "Nothing you haven't heard before, just that I love you."

Kerry's brows knit. "I thought…" She tugged her ear. "Hearing things. I love you, too."

Chapter 3

The sun made Kerry wince as she turned westward onto the causeway and headed towards the airport. She flipped her sunglasses out of the Mustang's glove compartment and slipped them on, getting instant relief from the intense glare.

A Christmas album was playing merrily in her CD player, and she hummed along as she picked up the expressway towards the airport.

Traffic was surprisingly light, and she figured she got everyone between those that did a big Christmas lunch and were now half comatose in front of football, and those who had Christmas dinner and were making last minute preparations. Those people who eschewed the day altogether were probably at the beach, since just about everything else was closed.

The airport, on the other hand, was a royal mess. Kerry sighed and dodged a number of taxis as she entered the arrival lanes, finding tempers flaring in the heat. She pulled off into short-term parking and grabbed a ticket, hoping to get lucky.

And of course she didn't, ending up about as far away from the Northwest terminal as she could and still be in Miami, but she figured she was early, and the walk wouldn't hurt her any—not after that breakfast, at any rate.

Kerry ran a hand through her fair hair and got out, locking the Mustang and squaring her shoulders. She was really glad her siblings were coming, but the sense of guilt she felt for fracturing a good part of their lives was weighing heavily on her.

There was no one else to take the responsibility, after all. Even Dar had been shocked she'd released the damaging information on her father, and only the fact that the server sent the documents out anonymously had saved her ass when the recipients received them and the shit hit the fan.

How many times had she wished she'd recalled them.

Dar would have stood behind her, she knew. But resigning would have really been her only option; mixing the company up in business like that would have been something not even her powerful boss could have protected her from. It was bad enough she'd been called to testify by the Senate judiciary subcommittee investigating the matter.

One thing at least she didn't have to worry about was them finding any way she'd benefited from the nasty stuff. She'd been self-supporting since college, and she'd had Mark do a trace to make sure there were no hidden bank accounts with suspicious dollars in them under her name. But the press had been sniffing around anyway, and she'd been glad more than once that she worked in a secure building and spent most of her free time on a nice, inaccessible island in someone else's condo.

Kerry walked briskly across the parking lot, glad she'd chosen a light t-shirt tucked into faded jeans for the trip as she began to feel the heat. The concourse was invitingly cool, and she went inside with a feeling of relief, then she stopped, startled at the seemingly mindless chaos before her.

Bad weather in the rest of the country had forced hundreds of people to camp out in the airport, and there were bodies slumped everywhere, trying to get some rest. The restaurants were working overtime, and it looked like a multinational convention inside. "Wow." She headed off towards Terminal G, where Northwest was housed, and wandered over to a display to search for the flight. It was one of the few on time, she was glad to note, and due in approximately ten minutes. Kerry assured herself of the gate, then edged into a cappuccino bar and ordered herself a double as she sat down to wait.

She took a sip of her coffee and enjoyed the strong taste as it entered her system and perked her up. While she'd seen Angela at Thanksgiving, she hadn't seen her brother since the preceding holidays, and she wondered if he'd changed any. She knew she had; her hair was shorter and a lot more sun-streaked, and she was packing an additional fifteen pounds of what was mostly muscle on her slim frame, which had changed her shape and given her a completely different way of walking and moving.

That was all the swimming, diving, running, and climbing she'd been doing with Dar, which required a lot of time and energy, but which had made her feel really good about the way she looked and felt. Everyone looked at her when she walked into a room now, and she been shocked to realize she liked that, a bit of personal egotism she hadn't expected to find in herself.

Not that she had considered herself ugly, just sort of plain and unremarkable, and that part of her still cooed in wonder when she found Dar's eyes running over her with obvious attraction, still finding it hard to believe that, out of all the people the tall, gorgeous, incredibly sexy Dar Roberts could have picked, she'd been the one to catch those pretty baby blues.

Kerry sighed and hugged the feeling to her, hoping she never lost the wonder in it.

A crowd of people were heading out from the Northwest flights carrying overcoats, mufflers, scarves, and heavy winter sweaters. Kerry sincerely hoped they'd all take them off before the walked out the front doors so they wouldn't cause a traffic jam when they passed out from heatstroke. She spotted her sister and brother as they headed towards the exit, and she stood up, draining her cappuccino and heading towards them, catching Angela's eye as she approached.

Her sister plucked Michael's sleeve, and pointed, and Kerry had to muffle a smile as her brother caught sight of her and his dark eyebrows jerked up as his eyes widened. *Guess I do look different,* she decided, as she closed with them. "Hey! Merry Christmas!"

Michael hugged her, before he stepped back, and held her at arm's length. "Holy shit, Kerry, do I know you?" Her brother was slightly shorter than she was, and had disheveled brown hair and hazel eyes. He was lightly built, and had a perpetual look of wonderment about him. "Check you out."

Angela chuckled and shook her head. She was taller than Kerry and had the same light brown hair as Michael, though slightly curly and longer and framing an oval face that bore little resemblance to her sister's.

"This isn't a library," Kerry answered wryly, before she shook herself loose from his grip and hugged Angela. "Good to see you guys, even if the cause is pretty bad." She exchanged looks with them. "How was the flight?"

"Given the weather everywhere else, it really wasn't bad," Angela told her. "The change in Detroit was on time for once, and even though it was bumpy most of the way, once we'd crossed into Florida, it was beautiful." She glanced around. "This place is a zoo."

"No, that's further south," Kerry replied solemnly. "Actually, everyone's pretty much stuck here, because the weather's so bad up in the Northeast and the Midwest." She tugged their sleeves. "C'mon. Do you guys have any baggage? Hope not."

Michael shook his head. "Nope, just these carryons. We figured one change of clothes would be enough to get us through tonight. We've got a noon flight back tomorrow. Angela's supposed to pick up Sally at five, and I have a flight out to school at seven."

Kerry deftly guided them through the concourse and towards the doors. "But first, take your coats off," she warned.

"We'll be fine," Angela laughed.

"Okay…" Kerry hit the floor plate to open the doors, and they went from 72 degree humidity-controlled air conditioning into 88 degree 98 percent mostly soup masquerading as air.

"Whoa." Angela stopped. "Gotcha. Coats gotta come off." She stripped out of her heavy jacket and draped it over one arm while Michael did the same, also pulling off his heavy sweater. "Good grief, it's green," she commented, glancing around. "It's so weird."

Kerry smiled. "You get used to it after a while. Come on. I'm parked out in south nowhere." She started across the parking lot, and her siblings followed, with Angela catching up to her quickly. "How much does he know?" Kerry asked softly.

"Well, he knows about, um…you." Angela answered in a whisper. "And about Dar."

"Darn good thing, since we're going over to her place," Kerry replied wryly.

"Really?" Angie gazed at her. "I thought…" She broke off at Kerry's expression, and smiled instead. "I bet it's nice there, huh?"

"Definitely is," Kerry agreed. "So he knows about us, huh?"

Angie accepted the subject change. "Yeah, but he doesn't know about me and Brian, and he's, um…he's got the idea that he's going to make sure Dar can, um, as he put it, 'take care of my sister.'"

"Oh boy." Kerry burst into laughter, quickly muffled. "Well, no problems there. Wait till he sees her place." She shot a glance at her brother, who was staring around with interest at the thick foliage.

"How's Dar, anyway? I forgot to ask you before," Angela asked casually. "You guys are still together and everything, right?"

"Of course we are." Kerry smiled. "She's fine. We just opened our presents to each other. Jesus, did we ever go nuts," she confided. "And it's her birthday today, too, so…" She glanced at her sister. "How's the baby coming along?"

Angie put a hand over her stomach, a barely visible three months pregnant. "Not bad… a little easier than the last one, really. I haven't been as sick." She exhaled. "Richard is convincing himself it's a boy." Richard was Angie's husband, a stockbroker whose family was close with Kerry's parents. "Brian says he doesn't care, but he hopes the baby looks like me."

Brian, on the other hand, Kerry's ex-fiancé, was the father of Angie's unborn child. "You know, I never expected our family to qualify for a TV movie of the week," Kerry sighed. "We're Republicans, for God's sake."

Angela had to laugh, though a bit wryly. "I know. I was thinking of writing my memoirs…think there'd be a market for them?"

"Are you kidding? You'll be on the bestseller list," Kerry assured her, as Michael trotted back over to them. "So how's school?" she asked her brother.

"A pain in the ass," Michael replied sourly. "I had to tell my statistics professor off the other day." He kicked a rock, an oddly adolescent behavior considering his age. "It didn't help; he failed me anyway."

Kerry sighed. "Uh oh. Are you in trouble?" She gave him a knowing look. School had never been Michael's strong point. In fact, she wasn't sure what was his strong point, or if he even had one.

"Yeah." He peered at her sheepishly. "In fact, I owe you a big one, sis: if it hadn't been for you shaking up the world, I'd have had to tell 'em I flunked out this semester again, and they'd have cared," he admitted, as they approached Kerry's car. "Hey, that hotrod yours?"

"Yes—and no, you can't drive it." Kerry hit the automatic keylock and popped the trunk for their luggage. "I like my insurance low, thanks." She waited for them to put their stuff in, then closed the hatch and opened the doors. "You'll get to meet some of my friends and coworkers tonight. We had a party planned, so…"

"Great." Michael gallantly got into the back seat and allowed Angela the privilege of riding up front. "I wanna meet this Dar person, though; you should hear dad talk about her."

Kerry started the car, and put it into gear. "Don't worry, you will," she promised, pulling carefully out of the parking lot and heading for the toll booth. "And Mike…don't try anything with her, okay? She's out of your league."

Her brother snorted. "I'm wounded. Like I would make a move on my sister's sweetie… yeah, right!" He gave Kerry a rakish grin. "I can't help it if girls think I'm cute, though—and what exactly do you mean, out of my league?"

Kerry didn't answer, as she was busy paying for her parking and navigating the exit roads to catch the right highway out of the airport. They talked about inconsequential topics on the trip back, and Kerry pointed out a few landmarks as they hit the causeway, including the Port of Miami. "The cruise ships go out of there…it's quite a sight on Sunday mornings." She pulled into the ferry terminal. "You have to ride a boat out to Dar's place."

"Whooo, now that's privacy," Michael stated approvingly.

Kerry almost pulled into the guest's lane, then she remembered at the last moment, and diverted smoothly into the special row for residents, getting a smile and wave from the security guard.

Angela glanced at the sign, then at her. "Resident's Lane, huh?" she asked, one eyebrow lifting. "Looks like they know you pretty well here."

"Hi Carlos," Kerry greeted the deckhand. "Merry Christmas."

"Feliz Navidad, Ms. Kerry." The man waved, then pointed at her new sticker and gave her a thumbs up as he crossed the deck of the ferry and secured the ramp.

Kerry was aware of the looks she was getting from her siblings, but she waited for the ferry to undock and start its way across the cut before she glanced at them.

"So you live here too?" Michael asked, curiously.

"Pretty much, yeah," Kerry replied. "Dar's got a big place, five bedrooms; there's plenty of breathing space there. She asked me after Thanksgiving if I wanted to move in part time, and I said yes." She was aware of the awkward silence. "She inherited the condo from an aunt of hers, pretty much rent free. We share expenses otherwise, though."

"Oh, like roommates," Angela answered, slowly. "Doesn't that mess you up at work?"

"Not really," Kerry replied, leaning back, and propping her knee up against the steering wheel. "We don't mention it at work, and we pretty much just do our jobs there." A shrug. "Then we go home. I was staying at my place most of the week, but that's getting pretty pointless."

Another really awkward silence. "So...this is, like, really serious, isn't it?" Michael finally asked slowly. "You two are, like, living to-gether, right?"

Kerry turned her head to regard him. "Yes. This isn't one of your flings of the week, Mike." She felt her temper prickling a little. "Or did you think I was just literally kissing my boss's ass?" She shocked both of them, she could tell, and she almost laughed at the expressions on their faces. "Sorry, that was pretty crude."

Michael scrubbed his head. "Um...it's going to take a little bit to get used to this, y'now? I mean, Jesus, Kerry, of course I didn't think you were just playing around, or anything; it just happened so fast."

She snorted. "I remember you going through six girlfriends in four months last year; give me a break." She gave him a look. "Double standards, huh?"

"Well, no, it's not that," he protested. "I mean, that's me, Ker; I've always been a freaking flirt, and we all know it. I had three dates for my senior prom, for Christ's sake." He leaned on the seat and put a hand on her shoulder. "But you always said when you fell in love, it'd be just the one time, remember?" A smile. "So..."

Kerry gazed at him, crossing her arms over her chest. "It's the one time," she replied evenly.

They both stared at her. "Really?" Michael asked.

"Yep," Kerry answered with a smile. "She's it."

He digested this. "Well, all I can say is, she'd better be worth it, then." His lip poked out pugnaciously. "She'd better be good enough for my sister."

Kerry bit off a wry grin and started the car as they docked. "You can judge for yourself in a few minutes." She directed the Mustang up the ramp and through the courtesy spray, turning left and heading towards the condo. They were both quiet while she parked next to Dar's Lexus. "Okay, here we are." She popped the hatch and got out, hearing the door on the condo open as they walked around to get the bags out.

"Hey." Dar's voice, tinged with amusement floated over them. "Clemente just called and wanted to know if you wanted dark chocolate or milk chocolate mousse."

Kerry looked up, to see her lover leaning on the stair balcony, dressed casually in faded cutoff denim shorts with a bright red polo shirt tucked into them. "Ah." She grinned. "I'll call him back." She noticed her siblings' glances. "You know Angela; this is my brother, Michael." She gave him a poke. "Mike, this is Dar. Say hello, and stop staring like a tourist."

"I am a tourist," her brother protested, then summoned up a bright smile. "Hello, Dar, it's nice to meet you."

One dark brow lifted along with the corner of Dar's mouth on that side. "Nice to meet you too," she replied politely. "Hello, Angela, welcome to Miami."

The chestnut-haired woman returned the polite nod. "Nice to see you again, Dar." She looked around. "It's lovely here."

"Thanks. Come on up." Dar motioned them forward.

Kerry prodded them both up the stairs and into the condo, exhaling as she felt Dar's hand patting her back in comfort as the dark-haired woman followed them in. "Let me call Clemente. You guys want something to drink?"

They were both glancing around the condo. "That would be great," Angela said. "Flying always makes me thirsty."

Kerry disappeared into the kitchen, leaving the three of them alone. Dar finally cleared her throat. "Would you like to sit down?" she asked politely, indicating the couch. Families, she reflected, were tough. "Nice flight?"

Angela put her bag down and seated herself, glaring at Michael until he did the same with an abashed look. He'd been studying the painting over the couch in fascination. "It was a good flight, yes," the woman started. "The weather's causing a lot of congestion at the airports, but we didn't have any problem."

Dar was about to answer when she heard the sound of glasses being fumbled in the kitchen. "Excuse me a minute." She produced a brief smile, then escaped to where Kerry was retrieving an errant tumbler. "Hi."

"Hi." The blond woman set the glass down on the counter and got a pitcher of peach-flavored iced tea from the refrigerator.

"You okay?" Dar asked mildly, as she came up behind her lover and rubbed her shoulders, feeling the tension in them.

Kerry poured two glasses, then set the pitcher down, and sighed. "They're being weird." She turned and looked up at Dar. "It's just so strange... I feel like I should be apologizing to them half the time, and the other half I'm mad because I feel like they're passing judgment on me."

"Well." Dar nibbled her lower lip. "I don't have any experience in the sibling scene, but I think they're actually passing judgment on me, not on you." She fondly ran her hands through Kerry's hair. "Give 'em time. They'll loosen up, and if they don't, I'll take 'em on a tour and shake 'em up a little."

That got a laugh from her companion. "Jesus, they're just my brother and sister, but I feel like a first time debater at the nationals." She picked up the glasses. "Come on, let's go face the inquisition."

🐾 🐾 🐾

"I'll get that." Dar eased up from her seat and ambled towards the door, glad of the distraction after two hours of desperately clever conversation with her lover's family. She pulled the door open, giving Colleen an amiable grin. "Hello, Colleen."

The redhead nodded back. "Merry Christmas, Dar. This is some island you've got here."

The taller woman chuckled. "Thanks. C'mon in. Kerry's brother and sister came down; we're just getting to know each other." She'd gotten a touch friendlier with Colleen the last week or so at the classes she taught at the gym, but there was still a reserve between them, and she suspected Colleen still harbored some doubts about Kerry's judgement in getting involved with her boss.

"Ooo..." Colleen hid a grimace. "Families—gotta love 'em. Be glad it's not mine." She stepped inside and moved past Dar, who kept the door open, spotting the catering crew headed her way.

"Hello, Clemente. Merry Christmas," Dar greeted the first of them.

"Feliz Navidad, Ms. Roberts." The sweating hospitality manager wiped his brow. "My people will bring in the tables and do the setup now, if that is okay with you."

"Great, go ahead." Dar cocked an ear inside, where Colleen's rich tones had been added to the conversation and things seemed to be loosening up a bit. It was curiously exhausting, dealing with people on this kind of emotional level, she mused, seating herself on the railing and watching as the uniformed busboys and porters brought folding tables, linen, and chafing dishes inside. It was much easier to stand in a boardroom among business adversaries, because that never touched you, not on the inside, where it counted.

It had been a long time since she'd had any family, and even then.... Dar gazed out over the neatly landscaped area. Her father, Andrew, had been career Navy, and her childhood had been spent moving from place to place, though his longest postings had been here in South Florida and Dar had always considered Miami her home town. Her father's family had shunned him after his marriage to her mother, whose eclectic tastes and odd ways were as alien to them as a Martian's. A wealthy northerner, liberal in her politics, esoteric in her religion, and an artist by nature, Cecilia Roberts had seemed ill-suited to her admittedly redneck, conservative husband with his mostly poor, Alabama-based extended clan.

Somehow, they'd gotten past that, though. That was what gave Dar hope in her own relationship with Kerry, because as different as they were, they were nowhere in that league. Dar sighed, hoping again she hadn't pushed things too fast with the decal. As much as she wanted the security that Kerry moving in would bring, she didn't want to seem like she was forcing the younger woman into a decision. "She looked pretty happy about it, though," she commented to the thin air, feeling a bit of optimism rise at that. Curiously, she got up and peered over the railing at Kerry's Mustang, smiling when she spotted the new decal firmly in place. "Guess she was."

Dar watched as a waiter walked by carrying a beautiful centerpiece, bathing her with a sweet, floral scent. She reached out and plucked a small, tightly budded rose from the arrangement and twirled it between her fingers, sniffing it idly before she girded her loins, as it were, and returned to the living room.

Kerry was seated on the love seat, still looking uncomfortable and facing the couch where her brother and sister were perched. Colleen had captured the chair next to her. Dar stepped around the end of the love seat and settled into place next to her lover, catching her eye and handing her the rose.

It threw Kerry off balance, and she gave Dar a near breathless, startled look as she took the bloom, bringing it to her nose in pure reflex as the taller woman relaxed and extended her long legs, crossing them at the ankles. "Thanks." Kerry smiled, forgetting their guests for a long moment.

Dar winked at her, then turned her attention to the raptly watching trio. "Is there a problem?" she asked, in her best boardroom no-nonsense voice, one eyebrow lifting up in question.

"Uh…" Colleen fished for a conversation starter.

"You know." Michael folded his arms across his chest and grabbed the bull by the horns. "Outside the movies, I've never actually seen one human being give another human being a rose before." He cocked his head at Dar. "That is obnoxiously romantic."

Everyone froze, waiting for Dar's reaction. She let them wait a beat, then smiled lazily. "My father taught me to do that," she replied simply.

"What, to give people flowers?" Colleen asked, curiously.

"To let my actions speak louder than words," Dar answered, feeling the ice breaking a little as grins spread around the room. Kerry moved closer and leaned against her shoulder, tucking her legs up and relaxing. "Now would someone explain to me the candles in the little paper bags I saw everywhere last time I was up north?"

"Well…" Michael rubbed his hands together. "There's this tradition…."

Kerry regarded her lover's profile, feeling a warm wash of affection as she reflected on Dar's quiet sacrifice, her giving up of a tiny bit of her cool reserve to smooth the way for Kerry's own comfort. She lifted her rose and sniffed it appreciatively.

Nice.

🐃🐃 🐃🐃 🐃🐃

Dar leaned back against the sliding glass door, sipping on a glass of very spiked eggnog and listening to Duks relate a story of his last vacation in Germany. The party was in full swing, and after the initial shock of having so many people in her usually peaceful condo, she'd actually started having an acceptably good time.

Most of the invites had been from work. Louis "Duks" Draefus, ILS's Finance VP, and Mariana Delgado, ditto for Personnel, were friends of Dar's. Mark and his fiancée Barbara often joined them socially outside of work, and Maria was Dar's longtime assistant. Colleen and Kerry's siblings rounded out the group.

Mariana and Mark were seated on the couch with Kerry, Angela and Michael occupied the loveseat, and all five were arguing about the appropriateness of sports salaries. Dar chuckled as Mark predictably supported the "pay 'em anything as long as they score" view, and Mariana insisted the money could be better used to feed orphans in underdeveloped countries.

Everyone had brought presents, and Dar had, using verbal and almost physical strongarm tactics, insisted on their placement under the to be tree and opened at an unspecified "later." "I haven't opened presents at a birthday party since I was five years old, damn it," she'd told Kerry. "I'm not starting up again at 30."

Colleen was sitting with Duks, Barbara, and an interested but mostly very quiet Maria. Dar had been surprised that Kerry had invited her and even more surprised that her assistant had attended, but she was glad, and she'd spent a few minutes giving the woman a tour around the apartment—mostly to convince her that Dar really, truly, didn't live in her Lexus.

"Dar?"

"Hmm?" She glanced down, startled, as her name was called. "Sorry… just thinking."

"You've been to the Netherlands, haven't you?" Duks asked. "Tell them: is it not true things are so much more relaxed in Europe?"

"Well…" Dar slipped into the armchair she'd been leaning against and considered. "Yes and no; they're different cultures, and they all have things that they're very strict about, the French about language, for instance. They hate Americanisms creeping into their speech, and we get into trouble with that a lot because it's so damn hard to translate a lot of the technological terms."

"Sí," Maria interrupted shyly. "When I'm having to order things for you, it's hard," she stated. "It is me speaking Spanish, and our salesman speaking Spanish, and we are every third word going to English for 'buses' and 'gigapets.'"

"Gigabytes," Colleen and Duks corrected simultaneously.

Dar nodded. "Right, and you have to be careful of the cultural bias, especially in the Pac Rim countries if you're a woman. I would say that in Europe they're certainly a whole lot more relaxed about sex."

They all laughed, and Maria blushed. "Um," Dar laughed herself, "that came out wrong. What I mean is, take the Clinton scandal. The French look at us and say 'you must be kidding—you're spending how much on WHAT?'" She waited for the laughter to die down. "Because there, of course, mistresses are paid for as a matter of course in the government; no one cares about that. They do care if the person does their job, so they think we're very hung up on sex, and frankly, it doesn't make much sense to them."

"Right, that's true," Duks agreed. "And Americans can be the biggest a—" His eyes flicked to Maria. "Ah...the most obnoxious people overseas; we do ourselves no favors a lot of times, and that makes the people view the entire country in a certain way."

Dar smiled and sipped her eggnog. "There are places overseas where I refuse to speak English when I'm out and about casually."

Duks rattled off a question in German, and she answered it in kind with a tolerant smile. "Not bad," he chuckled. "You've even got the accent right."

They all laughed.

Kerry peeked over and smiled as she saw Dar lean back and take a casual swallow of her drink. The party was working out better than she'd planned, and she was even having a good time catching up with her brother and sister and trading techie horror stories with Mark. The caterers had brought in eight chafing dishes full of things she knew Dar liked, along with a polite bartender who was behind a well-stocked mini bar they'd rolled in for the party. Everyone had done the buffet justice, and now they just had to get through the cake and she could claim a success.

A soft knock came at the door, and she looked up to see it open and Jack poke his crew-cutted head in. He spotted her, grinned, and stuck a hand inside, curling a finger at her before putting it to his lips.

Kerry darted a glance towards Dar, who hadn't noticed. She trotted across the apartment and reached the door. "Hi Jack, c'mon in."

"Shh...c'mere." He tugged her outside. "I've got a present, but if I give it to her, she's gonna say no," he whispered, "but if you're holding it, I bet she says yes."

Kerry's brows knit. "What?" She muffled a laugh. "Aw, come on, Jack, I know she'll love whatever..." She stopped speaking as he produced the present, a cream-colored puppy wearing a tiny Navy sweatshirt. "Oh my god...."

"Isn't she cute?" Jack whispered. "She rode all the way in my back seat, and she was such a good girl..." He held the puppy out. "Say hello."

Kerry took the animal, who squirmed and sniffed her hair, making a small whining sound. "Jack, Dar's going to go bananas, you know that." She stroked the puppy's soft fur and felt its silky ears. "I don't know if she'll go for this."

"Listen, I got a 'maybe' out of her when she was up by us, and she really likes Alabaster, the puppy's mother. They're great dogs."

"Oh, I know, I know." Kerry scratched the puppy's chest and it licked her, finding some errant sauce on her chin and searching enthusiastically for more. "But it's a lot of responsibility, and she's not home most of the day. I don't know if that's fair."

Jacks' shoulders sagged. "You should have seen her face when she was playing with them. I know she really wants one, and they're great companions. You know, she could go running with Dar in the morning and all…" He looked at Kerry's face. "No, huh?"

Kerry sighed, gazing at the warm brown eyes that seemed to radiate love. "It's not my decision." She remembered her cocker spaniel, Susie, who had looked at her with that same trusting gaze. "Hey sweetie," she whispered, reliving the memory of that last morning, when she'd said goodbye to her friend, and felt the hurt all over again. She'd never gotten attached to a pet since, for what she thought was good reason. "I don't…."

The door opened, spilling light out onto the porch, and a pair of sharp, blue eyes captured them. "What on earth is going on out here?" Dar asked, glancing at Jack as Kerry turned to face her. "What are you two…." A pause. "Oh. I see." Her eyes went from the puppy to her lover, then back to the puppy. "What have we here?"

Jack put on his most innocent expression. "You said I could bring her."

"I what?" Dar's brows shot up. "When was this?"

"When I talk to you today, I asked if I could bring a special present, and you said 'Yeah.'" Jack put his hands behind his back and rocked on his heels smugly. "So I did."

"Um…" Kerry shifted the puppy and tried to keep it from chewing on her earlobe. "I…he called me out here, and I um…ooo, stop that…" She lifted her eyes to Dar's in appeal. "I told him it'd be kinda tough for you to handle a pet."

"Ah." Dar eyed them both. "I get it; he called you out here, trying to get you on his side, because he knew if you asked me if I wanted to keep the puppy, I'd probably say yes. Right?"

Jack studied his flight boots, then glanced up through blond eye-lashes. "It was a plan."

"Uh huh. And what do you think of this plan, Kerry?" Dar in-quired, a gentle twinkle in her eyes.

"Oh, well, I, um…" Kerry watched as the puppy yawned and put her fuzzy head down on the blond woman's shoulder. "I mean, I told him I didn't think you'd go for it. I mean, you're not here a lot, and a dog's a lot of responsibility, and all that." She stroked the animal's fur. "She's really cute though, huh?" The puppy nuzzled her. "Maybe I could, um…" She let the thought trail off. "Find someplace, or maybe I could…um… but I don't think my complex takes pets. I…" A small tongue licked her cheek. "Aww…uh…"

The puppy turned its head and gazed at her. Kerry gazed back at her. Jack gazed at them both.

Dar burst out laughing. "Well, to be honest, you just beat me to it, Jack," she informed her pilot friend. "I was actually working on getting a puppy." Her eyes dropped to Kerry's surprised ones. "A cocker span-iel, as a matter of fact, but I suppose a Labrador will do." She gave Kerry a shy, somewhat hopeful look. "I figured between the two of us we could…I mean, I thought maybe a puppy would be a good Christ-mas present for you."

Kerry's jaw dropped as she saw the smile on Dar's face. "Wait—you mean it's for me?"

Dar nodded slightly.

"Son of a…" She turned to look at Jack. "You…"

He chuckled. "Merry Christmas, Kerry." His face crinkled into a smile. "When Alabaster heard what happened to you when you were a kid, she insisted on personally sending a little gift down for you."

Kerry had to stop and think a minute. Her heart was beating so fast she could hardly distinguish the beats. This was more than a puppy. It was a commitment, on Dar's part, to her. To them. Kerry took a deep breath, and looked up at her lover. "I guess with two people maybe it won't be so hard." She hugged the puppy a little, and it licked her neck. "Ooo, that tickles!" Her eyes lifted to Dar's. "Thank you."

Dar looked exceedingly pleased with herself. "You're welcome." She turned her head. "Jack, you hungry? We've got enough food in here to feed half of Miami." She opened the door and stood aside to let him enter. "Go on, there's a bar in the back. You can stay over until tomorrow, right?"

Jack hugged her. "Yep. Otherwise I'd have to stick to club soda, and what a waste of your birthday party that would be." He grinned and moved past her, leaving them alone on the porch.

Dar let the door close behind him and leaned on the railing, taking a breath of the cool air and letting it out. "Picked a name yet?"

Kerry walked over and perched next to her. "My brain hasn't stopped spinning yet, are you kidding? Dar…" She stroked the puppy. "I don't know what to say. I never thought you'd even consider allowing something so much trouble as this into your day to day life."

Dar scratched the puppy's chin, then crossed her arms over her chest and leaned back. "I've wanted a dog for a long time," she answered quietly. "My mother was badly allergic to fur, and we never had one when I was growing up, but when I went to college, I found this mutt and I adopted him. Damn thing followed me everywhere, waited for me outside my classrooms…"

Kerry just waited.

"Day after I graduated, he got hit by a car." Dar's voice was steady, and almost resigned. "I spent the whole day at the vet's office, but in the end, there was nothing they could do… I just held him while they put him down." She shook her head. "It's incredible how much you can become attached to an animal. It felt like it was family that was dying."

"Dar…" Kerry's voice ached.

"My father said it's because animals give you something humans never do: unconditional love," the dark-haired woman concluded quietly. "They don't care how rich you are, or who your parents are, or what you do; it doesn't matter to them." She looked up at Kerry. "It's no trouble, Kerry. We'll find a way to work it out. The worst problem is going to be sucking up all the little bitty Labrador hairs or we're going to end up wearing a lot of tweed to work."

"Hmm." Kerry regarded the puppy, who yawned and licked her face again. "I like tweed."

"I hate it," Dar replied cheerfully. "C'mon, let's go introduce our new friend to the crowd." She reached for the door and circled Kerry's shoulders with her other arm. "What are we going to call her?"

"You're going to have to give me a little while to think about that, Dar." The blond woman advised her, as they entered the condo. "Wait, she's so creamy colored…how about Cappuccino?"

Dar laughed. "Cappuccino it is. Hey everyone," she called. "C'mere and meet Kerry's Christmas present: Cappuccino."

"Oh, Calinde…" Maria quickly came over, cooing at the puppy, who woke up and looked around in bewildered alarm at the sudden sea of faces.

Dar stepped back, capturing a miniature shish kebab from one of the chafing dishes and nibbling on it as she watched everyone fuss over her lover and the puppy. Kerry was steadily becoming more animated, and she quickly sat down on the tile and let the puppy run around, laughing at its antics. The animal decided her shoelace was appropriate prey and tugged it, growling and scrabbling on the slick surface.

"I think I can report back to Alabaster that her daughter has a good home," Jack commented, balancing his full plate on one hand and attacking forkfuls of its contents with the other. "She'll be happy as hell."

"Yeah." Dar snagged a coconut shrimp and bit it in half. "Thanks, Jack; I owe you another one." She looked at her friend in quiet gratitude.

"No problem," the aviator grinned. "I got me a good plate of chow, a way comfortable looking couch for the night, the company of two lovely ladies, and a damn fine home for one of Alabaster's puppies. Can't ask for better than that."

Dar smiled contentedly in silent agreement.

"Close the door."

Kerry took one more quick look around the now quiet and mostly dark condo. Jack was snugged down on the couch, and she'd settled Angela and Michael upstairs, her sister in her room and her brother in the spare room on the other side of her newly converted office. She shut the door to Dar's bedroom firmly, then turned and regarded her lover, who was sprawled on the waterbed, eyes closed.

"Whew." Kerry yawned, rubbing her eyes. "I can't believe it's 3 a.m. I haven't talked that much since the debating finals in college."

"Mm," Dar nodded. "It was nice, though…good party."

Kerry perched on the edge of the waterbed. "Yeah? You had fun?"

One blue eye eased open. "Yes, I did." Dar sounded faintly surprised. "I think everyone did, and the picture you got of Duks falling asleep on the chair with that puppy is some of the best blackmail material I've seen in years," she remarked, lifting her arms over her head and stretching. "Killer dessert."

The blond woman's eyes lit up. She'd personally constructed it, a cake with one layer of dark chocolate mousse and a second layer of chocolate chip cheesecake separated by crushed Oreo cookies, and covered in a crispy, hard milk chocolate shell. "You should know, you had four pieces," she teased. "And I saved you some in the refrigerator."

Dar's eyes brightened. "Really?" She started to get up, only to have Kerry catch her shoulder and stop her.

"You're going to be sick to your stomach, Dar, come on now," she laughed. "And you'll wake up Jack and the puppy."

The dark-haired woman settled back down. "Yeah, you're right," she agreed reluctantly. "There's always breakfast."

"Augh." Kerry covered her eyes and winced.

"What? I'll have orange juice with it if it makes you happier," Dar teased, then patted her leg. "Just kidding. We'll have it tomorrow night, after everyone leaves," she relented. "Did you type up the recipe for everyone? I think Maria wants to put it on the company bulletin board. I hope she calls it something other than my birthday cake, though."

Kerry laughed, then let herself slide into the waterbed, resting her head on Dar's chest as she gazed up at the ceiling. "I think my brother has a crush on you."

"Ah, is that why he was babbling," the executive mused. "Is he prone to those?"

"Oh yeah," the blond woman snorted. "No offense to you or anything, but he goes gaga over just about every pretty woman he sees." She glanced up at Dar. "And you definitely qualify."

The blue eyes warmed as Dar smiled back at her. "He's sort of sweet, and your sister and I managed to have a nice conversation about the Miami area...she's funny."

"Mm...she likes you." Kerry found herself a little surprised by that. "I wasn't sure if...Angie tends to be a little on the conservative side."

Dar rolled her head to one side. "But you said she knew about you, right?"

"I said conservative, not blind or stupid," the smaller woman replied dryly. "Just because someone doesn't want to see something, doesn't mean they can't."

"Ah." Dar lowered a hand, and gently rubbed Kerry's belly, eliciting a contented murmur from her. "Thanks for the party."

A green eye rotated up and gazed at her. "Does that mean I can do it again?" Kerry inquired.

"As many times as you like," the dark-haired woman assured her.

Kerry rolled over so she could look up at Dar. "That's a lot of birthday parties."

That got a contented smile from her lover.

They gazed at each other in peaceful silence for a moment or two. "I think Maria knows about us," Kerry finally commented, surprised when Dar started laughing.

"Maria knew about us before I did," the taller woman admitted. "I should have realized when she asked me if I wanted one set of tickets or two for Thanksgiving, and whether to put us in separate rooms at Disney."

"Really?" Kerry almost sat up in amazement. "She did that? No wonder she went along with me on—uh…."

A low, sensual chuckle. "On getting us to stay in the park?" Dar's eyes sparkled wickedly. "C'mon, Kerry, I'd figured *that* one out at least." She gave the smaller woman a gentle poke.

Kerry blushed. "I was trying to get you to relax," she complained feebly. "If you'd figured it out, why'd you go along with it?" She glanced up at Dar. "You could have stopped it."

Gentle blue eyes regarded her. "I know. But I didn't want to."

"Oh," Kerry murmured. "Well, I'm glad you didn't." She smiled up at Dar. "Because I really like where it's taken us."

"You do, huh?" The dark-haired woman idly traced a finger across Kerry's face.

"Yes, I do," her lover replied softly. She wrapped her fingers around Dar's and lifted her hand up, pressing her lips against the back of it and tucking it against her heart. "Thank you for the puppy."

Dar grinned wholeheartedly, then sobered. "Listen, I didn't want you to think I just got that puppy so…" She paused. "I mean, it wasn't to pressure you into moving in here or anything."

"Oh." Kerry tilted her head to one side. "That's too bad; I was hoping that was part of the reason." She felt a tiny, mischievous smile appear on her face at the look of startlement on Dar's.

"You…but…" Dar scowled engagingly. "I was trying to be serious here."

"Me too. I'm seriously glad you felt comfortable enough to make the offer, Dar," Kerry reassured her. "In fact, I think I'd like to give it a try."

Blue eyes widened in delight. "Really?" Dar watched Kerry nod.

"Great." She smiled in relief. "Guess we've got some work to do this week then, huh?"

"Yeah." Kerry inched forward and kissed her. "First things first though...guess we'd better get undressed."

"Oh, sure," Dar replied agreeably, sliding her hands up over Kerry's hips and unbuckling the thin leather belt around her waist. "No problem."

"Well, that wasn't what I had in mind but..." Kerry unbuttoned the top button on Dar's cotton shirt with her teeth. "But I guess it'll serve the right purpose." She felt the cool of the air conditioning on her skin as her pants were eased off and Dar's familiar touch circled her thighs, then traveled up to start unbuttoning her shirt.

"Mm..." She had Dar's blouse open now, and the taller woman lifted her body up a little, letting her slip the fabric off over her tanned shoulders. Kerry let her hands go flat against the tensed abdominal muscles, leaning lightly against them as she nuzzled Dar's bare neck, then lowering herself down as the taller woman did, letting their bodies touch and slide against each other.

She shrugged out of her shirt and a trail of warmth followed Dar's hands across her skin, sliding across her shoulderblades and down her sides, then gently gripping her hips as they shifted, rolling over and tangling their limbs as she forgot the long day and the fatigue that faded before the insistent nibbling along her neck that dipped to her collarbone and beyond.

It was, Kerry decided, the perfect end to a darn near perfect day.

The quiet afternoon sunlight drifted gently into the apartment as quiet finally descended. Dar hitched one leg over the arm of the chair she was sprawled on and leaned back as Kerry walked in carrying their new puppy. "Everyone's safely headed home, finally," she remarked as the blond woman perched on the chair arm, letting Cappuccino chew on her fingers.

"Finally," Kerry agreed. "I thought I'd never get my brother to shut up. Did you have to come sauntering in this morning practically in your underwear?"

Dar gave her a look. "It's not underwear, it's what I run in," she objected. "This is Miami, remember? Running in a sweatsuit is an invitation to heatstroke." She let her head rest against the back of the chair.

"Damn...I have sixteen pages of e-mail I have to go through before tomorrow morning."

"Don't remind me," Kerry sighed. "I have position status reports on two different accounts due tomorrow at the 9 a.m. staff meeting, and I haven't even started yet." She cuddled the puppy closer to her. "Guess we'd better get started; we have a ton of leftovers for dinner, unless that really bugs you."

"Nah, that's fine." Dar lifted a hand and stroked the backs of her knuckles against Kerry's bare thigh. The blond woman was wearing a pair of cutoff denim shorts and a t-shirt, and Dar could smell the remnants of sun tan lotion clinging to her skin. "I really don't feel like looking at that goddamned mail," she finally admitted.

"Mm. Well, I don't feel like doing those reports, so I guess we're even," Kerry told her. "We could be like everyone else and do our work when we're actually supposed to be working," she reasoned. "As a matter of fact, I can't believe we haven't had a major problem this weekend; that's a first."

"Shhh, don't invoke any," Dar implored her. "Please. I don't feel like having to scream at people tonight." She tickled the sleepy puppy. "Hey, there girl." A smile crossed her face. "She's really a cutie, huh?"

"Yeah," Kerry smiled. "She was fiercely defending the kitchen from the broom earlier," she chuckled. "Tell you what; let's play with her for a little while, then eat dinner, then maybe we'll be in the mood for work."

"Okay." Dar moved over and allowed Kerry to join her on the couch, as she pensively played with Chino's fuzzy ears.

Kerry stroked the animal for a moment, then glanced at her face. "Something wrong?"

Dar's lips tightened. "No, not really... I was just thinking."

"About what?" Kerry tucked her feet up under her. "You're not having second thoughts about the puppy, are you? I mean, we can find someone..."

"No, no." Dar shook her head, surprised at the surfacing memories. "I was just...imagining how much my father would have loved to meet her." She felt a comforting hand circle her arm. "I wish he could have."

Kerry pursed her lips. "I wish I could have met him; he sounds like a wonderful person."

Dar nodded faintly. "He was..." She exhaled. "I think I just miss him more on my birthday. No matter what was going on, he'd always try to be home for that."

"Oh, Dar…" Kerry was dismayed.

"Yeah," Dar acknowledged the emotion. "Anyway…that's the other reason I didn't do much to celebrate after that. It was easier to pretend I didn't have a birthday."

"I'm sorry," the smaller woman murmured. "I wish you'd told me… Dar, I would never have…"

"It's okay," she was told firmly. "I'm glad we did this. I had a good time, and I know… if my dad was here, he'd kick my ass if I'd told you no." She looked up at Kerry. "It's time I took that day back."

"Mm."

Dar looked at her. "I wish you could have met him too. I think you two would have hit it off." She managed a smile as Kerry hugged her. "Anyway… um, did you say you had some of that cake left?" Time for a subject change. "I bet it goes good with ice cream, huh?"

"Yeah," Kerry murmured softly. "I bet it does."

🐾   🐾   🐾

The office was very quiet as a late afternoon sun filtered inside, dusting the maroon carpet with soft, golden motes. It was empty, as though waiting for something to happen, the PC on the desk showing slowly pacing panthers, and a small tank on the wooden surface holding two Siamese fighting fish circling each other.

The door slammed open, breaking the silence, and Dar strode in, carrying a stack of printouts that she tossed on the desk, circling it and claiming the chair with an air of impatient disgust. "Stupid pieces of half-assed useless…"

It had been a tough day. Two meetings, and the last one had been mostly her yelling at a table full of gloomy department heads who were weeks behind in closing their budgets.

Dar closed her eyes and rested her head in her hand for a moment, then straightened and pulled the folders over, flipping the first one open and looking at the contents. She read for a long moment, then reached over without looking up and dialed a number on her speakerphone.

"Sales Executive, good afternoon," a precise, Hispanic-accented voice answered.

"Put José on the line," Dar snarled.

"Uno momento, Señora." The line went to Muzak.

"I'm not a señora, arroz-for-brains," Dar muttered at it, riffling through the pages irritatedly.

The inner door opened, and Kerry poked her blond head in. "Hi."

Dar waved and pointed at the speakerphone. Kerry entered, moving across the carpeted floor silently and kneeling at her side. She picked up Dar's pencil and pad and started writing. "What do you want, Dar?" José Guiterrez's voice abruptly broke the peaceful quiet.

"Competence," Dar shot back. "But I'm not likely to get it from Sales anytime soon, so I'll settle for the damn budget numbers, like I've been asking for the last two weeks."

Kerry peeked up at her, then went back to her scribbling.

"You got them yesterday!" José barked back. "It's not my fault if you can't find your damn inbox."

Dar peered over at the tray, which contained precisely two small, flat pieces of paper. She stood and picked them up, flipping them over and studying them. "Oh, right," she snorted. "Yeah, the bathroom supply requisition—yeah, I can see where you'd confuse your budget with that."

"What the hell are you talking about?"

"The only thing in my inbox is the goddamned toilet paper bill, José. So unless you're submitting that, try again."

"Jesú...Marta, como esta venta numerales?"

"Painted on your butt, probably," Dar muttered under her breath. She could hear the secretary scrambling on the other end, then a rapid exchange of frenetic Spanish. "I'm waiting," she yelled. "I've got four days to close the books, José. Either get me those damned numbers now, or I'll submit the budget without them!" She slapped the release on the phone, and tossed the top folder in the in box. "Jerk."

"Well." Kerry nibbled her pencil. "I was going to write you a note saying I was running by the apartment after work to pick up some stuff to bring over."

"Mmph." Dar propped her head up on one hand. "I'd help, except I've got a client briefing at six, and that won't let out until after eight, probably."

"That's okay," Kerry told her. "Meet you at the gym at eight-thirty then?" Ken said he was looking forward to trying that new stuff with you tonight."

Dar leaned back in her chair, and exhaled. "Boy, I'll be ready for a sparring session tonight, that's for sure." She gave Kerry a wry look. "Can I go back to last weekend?"

Kerry peeked at the door, then leaned over and kissed her knee. "It's a short week, Dar. We've got New Year's coming up, and another long weekend…hang in there."

"Grumph." Dar allowed herself the luxury of indulging in a riffling of Kerry's hair, scratching the back of her neck and watching her lover drop her head forward and release a tiny moan of pleasure. "Thanks for reminding me. Things going okay over by you?"

Kerry straightened. "Yes—well, mostly," she amended. "Eleanor roped me into a meeting at four, but other than that, the day's gone fine." A sigh. "I think she wants to bitch about you, and frankly, Dar, I'm not in the mood for it today."

"Sorry," Dar apologized. "I had a run-in with her this morning at the 8 a.m. meeting and told her she wasn't getting her extra personnel allocations this year." Dar lifted a page and reviewed it. "Two of the marketing campaigns flopped big time."

"Ouch." Kerry winced. "Did you get lunch?"

Blue eyes peeked guiltily at her.

"No wonder you're so grumpy." Kerry got to her feet. "I've got half a sandwich at my desk; let me bring it over."

"I am not a slave to my biology," Dar protested, scowling. "I'm perfectly capable of being a rampaging bastard even on a full stomach."

"Okay, boss." Kerry tweaked her ear tolerantly. "I'll be right back."

Dar watched her disappear, enjoying the warm wash of sensuality brought on by the gentle swagger in Kerry's walk. The door closed and she sighed. "Down, slave," she chastised her rebellious body and swiveled around, pulling over the next folder.

🐾   🐾   🐾

"Hey, Kerry." Elaine Costas was standing in the kitchen getting herself a cup of cappuccino. "How was your Christmas?"

"Nice." Kerry went to the cabinet and removed her personal tea jar, then selected two bags and set up two cups to steep. "How about yours?"

The accounting assistant glanced at the cups, but didn't comment on them. "Pain in my ass…my damn cat got into the tree ornaments and pulled half the damn thing down on top of her, and she got tangled in the tinsel."

Kerry laughed. "Well, I got a puppy," she admitted, figuring that was pretty safe. "A Labrador Retriever."

"Really?" Elaine gave her a surprised look. "Wow, I didn't think your complex allowed dogs; my sister's cousin lives there."

Oh, turtle turds. Kerry drew in a breath. "They know I'm thinking of moving, so they didn't make a big deal out of it."

"Oh." Elaine nodded. "Yeah, they'll sometimes do that; depends on who you get to talk to. So, boy or girl?"

Phew. "Girl. I named her Cappuccino. She's a really creamy white color." Kerry smiled. "I'll bring in pictures. She's really cute." Kerry added some cream and a good sized dose of honey to the tea and stirred both cups. "See you at the gym tonight?"

"You bet," Elaine agreed. "I musta put on ten pounds over the weekend; my mother just kept stuffing me like a turkey." She took her cup, then waited for Kerry to walk out before her carrying her two cups. "Want me to get your office door?" She walked alongside the shorter woman and held the heavy door open. "There you go."

"Thanks." Kerry smiled as she pushed the door inward. "See ya later." She walked across the carpet and set her cup down, then picked up the half sandwich she'd promised Dar and took the other cup of tea down the back hallway. She could hear Dar's voice as she got closer, and she winced at the raw anger in it.

She pushed the inner door open and peeked inside. Dar was standing with her back to Kerry, leaning on her desk and yelling into the phone. There was a hoarse note in her boss's usually smooth voice that usually meant she'd spent too much time hollering.

Tea was good for that, Kerry reasoned as she eased across the floor and came up next to her lover.

"That's it, Rory. Either you people complete those circuits by tomorrow night, or I'll find another provider," Dar stated flatly. "Do I make myself clear?"

"But Dar…"

"Don't 'but Dar' me," she interrupted. "We put this order in two months ago, and I've got a live New Year's Eve broadcast to support from London. It's a firm deadline."

A sigh. "I'll get right back to you."

Dar hung up and sat down. "I swear, Kerry, sometimes I feel like I'm an Eskimo sled dog dragging half the continent behind me."

Kerry took hold of her jaw, and turned her head, examining her face intently. "Well, you've got the eyes for it, that's for sure; they look like a Husky's." She handed her the sandwich. "Here, munch on this, and I brought you some tea."

"I hate tea," Dar sighed, unwrapping the chicken sandwich and taking a bite.

"I know, but your voice sounds like you can use it, it doesn't have caffeine in it, and I put enough honey and cream in so that you won't even realize it's tea. Try it." Kerry nudged the mug over. "I'm going to my meeting; wish me luck."

"Goff lockf." Dar swallowed, then gave her a look. "Thanks."

Kerry waggled her fingers and left.

Dar stared evilly at the steaming mug, then cautiously sniffed it. "Mm." An eyebrow lifted as she picked the cup up and took a sip, mouthing the substance a little before she swallowed it. "Hmph."

Kerry walked into the marketing department's meeting room and set down her mug, giving the two junior clerks there a brief smile as she took her seat. "Afternoon."

"Hey, Kerry." Candy leaned forward. "I heard some gossip…I bet you can tell me if it's true or not."

"I can try," Kerry answered warily. "What is it?"

"A little bird told me it was the Ice Queen's birthday this past weekend…true?"

It was always a question as to what was safe to admit knowing. Kerry figured this was relatively harmless. "You mean Dar? Yeah, as a matter of fact it was," Kerry told them. "Why?"

"Just curious." Candy sat back, tapping her lips with her pen. "Did she have a party?"

Kerry wished she'd talked to Dar about how much to say about it. She made a quick decision. "Yeah, a couple of us went over to her place had a little get together. Me, Duks, Mari, Mark; you know."

"Ah." Candy nodded. "So you know where she lives then?" The other woman was watching her closely.

"No. We were all blindfolded and put in the back of a bus, then knocked out with nerve gas before we got there," Kerry told them seriously. "I have no idea where it is."

Fortunately, Eleanor chose that moment to enter with her favorite assistant Peter. "Hello, hello… good afternoon, Kerry, how are you?" She put her papers down and straightened the wool suit she was wearing, a thick rust red color that reminded Kerry of dried blood. "Hope you had a good holiday?"

"Great, thanks," Kerry replied. "And you?"

"We had Justin's whole family over, and everyone had a lovely time," the Marketing VP assured her. "Did you get to go home?"

It stung. "No; I stayed here and spent the time with friends."

"She went to Dar's birthday party," Candy interrupted.

"Really?" Eleanor lifted an eyebrow. "That must have been a treat. I heard her royal highness admitted to a birthday…which one was it?"

They all looked knowingly at Kerry, who suddenly felt very conspicuous. "I didn't count the candles," she remarked dryly. "Did we have an actual subject for this meeting, or is it just a general gossipfest?" Her head tilted in question. "Honestly, I have no idea, and I'm not really sure why everyone is so interested in it, but if you are, why not just ask Dar?"

Eleanor smirked. "Well, let's get down to business, shall we? But Kerry, it's so adorable the way you stand up for the old monster. It warms the cockles of my heart."

Kerry scratched her ear. "If you say so." She indicated amused condescension. "All right—I think the first topic on the list is the plans for expansion in the Northwest next year…"

"Dar," Maria's voice crackled through the speakerphone.

Now what? Dar put her pen down and glared at the instrument. "Yes?"

"There is a Mr… pardonamente, a Mr. Fabaracini here to see you."

Dar sat back and scowled. Steve Fabricini was the newly hired assistant of José Guiterrez, the VP of Sales for ILS. He was also an old…acquaintance of Dar's, and she suspected José had hired him specifically because of that. "All right." She sighed. No sense in putting it off any longer. "Send him in. "

The door opened seconds later, and a tall, good-looking man in a very well-tailored suit entered. Hello, Steven." Dar stood quietly behind her desk, her hands resting on the surface.

"Well, well, well…look at what we have here. If it isn't my old and best buddy, Dar Roberts." Steven sauntered in; shutting the door behind him as he crossed the room towards her. His hazel eyes made no bones about studying her as he came forward, and that slick, toothy smile creased his face as he held a hand out. "Been a while, hasn't it?"

Not nearly long enough, Dar almost answered as she reluctantly took his grip and returned the strong handshake with one of her own. "Certainly has," she replied evenly. "I believe the last time I saw you was right after you were thrown out of school that last semester."

Steve comfortably took a seat. "Mm...yes, and you enjoyed engineering that, didn't you?" he chuckled. "That's okay, no hard feelings...after all, things turned out all right, didn't they? Here we both are." He spread his arms out. "My office isn't as nice as this one, but..." Now he turned his eyes on her. "Maybe that'll change soon."

Dar merely lifted an eyebrow and refused to take the bait. "Well, best of luck to you," she said, keeping a neutral expression. "I know José could use the help."

Steve studied her with lazy eyes. "Thanks." A smile. "Just thought I'd stop by and say hello."

"So I see." Dar resumed her seat, and pulled over a stack of papers. "Well, I'd love to chat, but it's a busy day."

A knock came on the inner door. "Come," Dar called out, half turning her head to watch as Kerry entered.

The blond woman passed through the sunlight pouring in her window, burnishing her pale hair and highlighting her graceful physique. "I've got those reports," she said, giving Steven a curious look, then turning her attention to Dar. "That New York center is going to be almost impossible to complete. Nynex is projecting sixty days to pull the circuits."

"Not good enough," Dar said tersely. "I'll see what I can do." She turned to where Steven was watching interestedly. "Kerry, this is Steven Fabricini, José's new AVP," she stated. "This is Kerry Stuart, my right hand."

Kerry almost, almost, smiled at that. Dar had seen the crinkling of the skin around her eyes as she extended a courteous hand to Steven. "Pleased to meet you."

"Likewise, I'm sure," he said lazily, giving her a charming smile. "We'll be working very closely together, I can see that."

Kerry merely nodded, then turned and slipped out, leaving them alone again.

"Well, well. Dar, you old whore, your taste certainly has improved," Steven laughed. "That's a nice piece of ass."

Dar only just put a lid on her temper as she realized almost too late he was trying to get under her skin. "This is an EEOC company, Steven, and we take that seriously. I'd keep those kinds of comments shoved up your behind, where they belong."

"Ah, now Dar." He stood up, that obnoxious smile sliding onto his face. "You've got everyone here so blinded by that kiss my ass attitude…but I know you better."

Dar looked at him coolly. "Steven, I'm not the person you knew way back when. Don't make that mistake."

He laughed softly. "I'll be seeing you, Dar."

She kept her eyes on her reports until she heard the door close, then picked up her pen and nibbled the end of it as she studied the now blissfully empty space.

This was going to be trouble. She could just feel it. Dar shook her head and went back to work.

Chapter 4

"No, No, NO, NO, NO." Dar spoke in ever increasing increments of volume, scratching out items with her green pen. "I am not moving allocations from Houston to Boston just so you can sell an account to your brother's uncle's cousin at half rate, José. I'm just not going to do it."

"Excuse me, Dar?" A polite Hispanic voice interrupted her dark muttering.

Dar lifted pale blue eyes to the door and slumped into her chair. "Sorry, what is it?" She propped her head up on one fist and sighed. It was late, and she was tired and admittedly cranky. It was Thursday afternoon, and the week had been a long one despite its shortened nature. She was glad it was ending, though, and she was looking forward to the coming weekend.

Maria gave her an understanding smile. "Kerrisita left a message for you. She said she was leaving, and was going to the Bayside and the shopping."

Rats. Dar rubbed her eyes and nodded. "Yeah, I was supposed to…ah, I mean, I got stuck in that meeting longer than I thought." She stared at the stack of reports. "Listen, why don't you get out of here?"

"You too should go home, Dar," Maria chided her. "Is late; so many people are gone."

Dar sighed and leaned back in her chair. She had a stack of things left undone in her inbox and a half a dozen matters still up in the air. But Maria was right; getting things done when the rest of the world was on vacation was pretty damn useless.

"Yeah, I…" A pressure around her wrist made her look down. "Oh, that's what I was supposed to do, damn it. I have to get this fixed." She stood up. "All right, that's it. I'm out of here. This stuff can wait until next year." She flipped off her PC and stood, grabbing her car keys and thumping the stack of reports into her inbox. "C'mon Maria, I'll walk you out."

The elevator and hallways were mostly empty, and they rode down in companionable silence until almost the bottom floor. "Dar?"

"Hmm?" Dar glanced at Maria.

"I am hearing the whispers again." Maria looked apologetic. "About you and Kerrisita."

Dar closed her eyes and blew out a breath. "Yeah, Duks told me the same thing." She waited for the doors to open and walked out with Maria at her side. "I don't know what we can do about it though; we don't even have lunch together anymore." Dar felt bad about that. She'd enjoyed taking a break in the middle of the day and spending it with Kerry, but that was so out of her normal routine it had made the gossip rounds immediately.

"Is stupid." Maria frowned. "They hear she went to your party, and it's a big thing."

Dar shrugged wearily. "Let them talk, Maria. It's not the worst thing I've had said about me around here."

They walked outside and Dar got in her car with a strange feeling of freedom. An afternoon free was a rare occurrence for her, and she stretched as she settled into the leather seat, adjusting the rearview mirror before starting the Lexus and pulling out of the parking lot.

🐺   🐺   🐺

"What do you think of these?" Kerry inquired, running a hand over a soft, silky piece of fabric.

Colleen peered over her shoulder. "I think it's a kite, kiddo; where are you gonna fly it?"

"Oh, I don't know." Kerry held out the beautiful construct, a shimmering rainbow of colors that fluttered in the breeze coming off the water. "We've got that golf course in the center of the island; I bet I could fly it in there." She grinned recklessly and folded the item up, handing it to the stall's owner along with her credit card. "You going over to your mom's house for New Year's?"

"Ehhh, I don't know. I'm still deciding," Colleen sighed. "They're having a party at the complex, but Ramon's bragging he's making the drinks, and you know what happened the last time he did that. What about you? I didn't hear your plans."

Kerry looked down at the ground, then visibly inhaled. "Well, I…" She turned and looked at Colleen. "I was hoping you'd help me move some of my stuff."

The redhead gazed at her. "Oh…wow." Glancing around, she steered Kerry to a table at the small café they'd just been passing. "Here, siddown."

They looked at each other. "So…you're doing it, then," Colleen murmured. "I thought you were going to see how it worked out."

The blond woman toyed with the table tent. "I did. I mean…" She glanced up the perky waitress who approached. "Lemonade, please."

"Same," Colleen added, absently, shooing the woman off. "Kerry…"

"I know, I know." Kerry rested her arms on the table and turned her head to gaze out over Biscayne Bay. "I said I wanted time, I said I didn't want to rush into anything…"

"And? So what's this then?" Her friend asked.

Kerry propped her chin up on her fists and produced a wry smile. "Colleen, I really like being with her, around her, I'm miserable on the days we're not together." She accepted the glass from the waitress and poked her straw in, slurping up a bit before she went on. "We talked the other day, and she gave me my resident's decal. She asked me if I wanted to make it permanent."

Colleen sighed. "Ker, I'm glad for that, honest I am."

A little silence fell. "But you think I'm making a mistake," the blond woman stated softly. "Don't you?"

Her friend sipped at her drink for a moment. "You're really stuck on her, aren't you?"

Kerry sucked in a breath of the cool, salty air. "Yeah, I sure am," she admitted. "I feel really comfortable around her, too. The other night we just sat out on the porch with our arms around each other, and made patterns out of the stars." She paused thoughtfully. "It's like I've known her all my life."

Colleen sighed. "Well, I'm gonna miss you." She gave Kerry a wry smile. "And for the record, no, I don't think you're making a mistake. I just worry about you isolating yourself out there." She put a hand on Kerry's. "At least with you at the apartment most of the week, we can get together, you see your other friends. It's not that I have anything against Dar, I just don't want you to forget about the rest of us."

Kerry considered that, acknowledging that it would be very easy to do. "You're right, I need to make sure I get out and do things with other people; that place does tend to suck you in." She smiled at Colleen. "Hey, maybe I can change Dar from being a recluse to a party animal—what do you think?"

The redhead rolled her eyes and chuckled. "Well, that Christmas party was a lot of fun; maybe you can." She agreed. "How about New Years' Eve, for instance?"

Oh, if she only could. Kerry sighed inwardly. "Ah, well, the company's having a get-together out at Sonesta Beach on the Key; it's a formal dance kinda thing," she explained. "Neither of us really wants to go, but Dar says if she doesn't show up for at least a while, she'll get all kinds of grief."

"Oooo, a formal? You got a dress?" Colleen asked, then plucked Kerry's crisply pressed cotton shirt. "One that fits you now that you aren't skin and bones anymore?"

Kerry blinked, then chewed her lip. "Holy crap. Well, yeah, I've got two or three I could get away with…." She almost slapped herself. "I can't believe I didn't think of that, though. Wow…well, I'll figure out something tonight, I guess."

"Nuh uh. C'mon. Castellano's is right over there, honey. Let's get you a snazzy Cuban dress to wear to your dance. You gonna dance with Dar?" the redhead teased.

"Uh," Kerry blushed, "no, I …that would be a little too much, I think." She gave her friend a wry look. "But you know, a new dress isn't a bad idea…maybe they'll have something more up to date than what I wore to that Viscaya thing last year."

Colleen made a face. "Kerry, you make darn near everything look good, child, but that…that you had to really work at, ya know?" She put a hand on Kerry's back and steered her towards the store, an understated place which disgorged the smell of silk, starch, and money as they opened the door and entered.

🦋　🦋　🦋

Dar strolled around the inside the mall, waiting for her watch to be repaired. She stopped and got some cinnamon roasted nuts and nibbled them as she walked, eyeing the trendy fashions with a jaundiced eye. "Bellbottoms...never liked those the first time around," she muttered disapprovingly, noting that the passing teenagers were dressed in them, along with elevator sneakers and thin, pastel tank tops.

"Yech." Dar preferred her navy polo tucked into pressed Dockers. "My father would have lassoed me before I could have left the house looking like that." She went over the words in her head, then chuckled ruefully. "Dar, you're getting old." Her eyes flicked to the right and she slowed to study the baubles in the window of Mayor's jewelers. "Mm...nice."

A voice sounded behind her. "Ah, Ms. Roberts! Been a long time."

Dar stopped and turned. "Hello, Richard. Yes, it has," she politely greeted the salesman. "How've you been?"

"Fine, fine thanks. You're looking well." The tall, immaculately dressed man smiled at her. "I've got some nice earrings; can I show them to you?"

Dar sighed, then figured she had plenty of time, and she'd just lost one half of a favorite pair of studs anyway. "Sure," she agreed, following him inside the marbled doorway and into the jewelry shop.

🦋　🦋　🦋

"Let's see." Colleen held out a long dress with frilly lace twirls near the neckline, and a bustle. "What do you think?"

Kerry burst into laughter. "I'd look like Carmen Miranda is what I think. Get out of here, Col!" She shook her head, and browsed the selection, moving more towards some understated, sedately dark gowns with conservative necklines. "This is more the company's speed, I think."

"Oh god." Colleen rolled her eyes. "What's Dar wearing?"

Kerry's brows knit. "A strapless black thing, very simple, very drapy, made me drool...why?"

Colleen giggled. "Oh." She gave her friend a look. "She's certainly loosened you up in some ways."

"Huh?" Kerry peered at her, then blushed hotly. "Oh…um…eyah. I guess she has."

She distracted herself by burrowing deeper in the racks of dresses, then stopped, as her hands touched a soft, deep green silken one. "Ooo."

Colleen was immediately there, peering over her shoulder. "Mmm…." She lifted the gown out and examined it. It had one shoulder, leaving the other bare, and most of the back and one side was cut out, with a soft gathering at the hip then a straight fall to an uneven, edgy hem. "That's nice, Ker." She nudged her friend. "Try it on."

Kerry hesitated, then grinned. "Okay." She smiled at the hovering attendant, who showed her into a fitting room.

"Okay." She reviewed herself in the mirror for a moment, then took the dress off the hanger and slipped into it, allowing the silky folds to warm against her skin as she adjusted the fabric. "Hmm."

She blinked, turning a little and watching the gown's conspicuous gaps reveal her toned body. "Oo…not bad, Stuart, not bad at all." She grinned unrepentantly at herself for a moment then she exhaled and opened the door, assuming a more serious expression. "What do you think, Col?"

Colleen looked up from where she was leafing through a catalog, and stared, letting a low whistle escape. "Holy Mary, mother of God, Kerry!" she chortled. "That looks fantastic! You should wear your hair up, too."

Obligingly, Kerry lifted her pale locks and pulled them back, exposing the line of her neck. "Think so?" She glanced sideways, and caught her reflection in the mirror, surprised at its sophistication. "Mm, I think you're right."

The redhead closed in and adjusted the shoulder a bit. "Definitely a good choice. You can wear that old silver necklace you've got, the one with the emerald?"

Kerry nodded. "Yeah, that'd go perfect. Okay." She gave the saleswoman a nod. "I'll take it, thanks." She ducked back into the fitting room and carefully removed the dress. "Think you'll like that, Dar?" she murmured to her reflection, whose eyes twinkled mischievously back at her.

"Here…they're blue diamonds."

Dar took the black display pad and examined them. "Huh, never seen any like that before." She studied the earrings, lacy platinum surrounding a carat-sized diamond in a conspicuous blue shade. "Nice."

"Mm. I thought of you when I saw them…they come close to matching your eyes." The salesman smiled. "I was going to call you, but it's been so busy."

Dar nodded, debating with herself. They were expensive, but how often did she ever buy stuff like this for herself? She imagined Kerry's reaction to them, and that put a grin on her face. "I'll take them." She pushed the pad back towards the delighted salesman and let her eyes roam around the display case. "Box them up…in fact, I've got a company event I have to go to tomorrow night; that'll work."

She got up and roamed around as he processed the purchase and found herself looking down at a neat display of rings.

Rings. She wasn't fond of rings, really. She'd tried wearing one or two on occasion, but with her typing all the time, they tended to annoy her, making her take them off and promptly lose them.

"Would you like to see anything, ma'am?" the girl behind the counter asked politely. "We've got some new ones in."

Before Dar could answer, she disappeared and came back with a velvet-lined box, which she opened on top of the counter and turned around to face Dar. "We haven't even had time to really catalog these, but…"

Dar found her eyes drawn to the center of the box, where a brilliant stone was winking. She leaned over and blinked, then gently picked up the small rest the ring was on.

It gathered the light in and twinkled at her, a brilliant cut diamond at least two carats that had a definite hint of rose to it. The setting was appropriate, an exquisite tracing of rich gold shaped into a nest of rose petals that cradled the stone, and two smaller stones on either side.

"It's beautiful, isn't it?" the woman asked hesitantly.

"Yes, it is," Dar murmured, suddenly grabbed with an insane impulse. "I'll take it."

Dead silence.

Dar looked up, to see the clerk's jaw hanging open. "It's for sale, right?"

"Uh, yes, um…um…" She looked over to her boss, who was busy at the register. "Richard? Mr. Ellis?"

"Just a moment, Judy," the manager murmured, holding a finger up.

The girl licked her lips. "We can…um…I think the jeweler is here now, we can have it sized…for you, ma'am."

Dar shook her head absently, still gazing at the ring. "No, it's not for me. It's for someone who's about a different from me as you can get and still be a human being."

As if she'd ever, ever have the guts to give it to her. Right. Dar exhaled quietly. It didn't really matter; just by her getting this, she'd know, in her own heart, what it meant, even if she never gathered up the courage to admit that to Kerry.

But wait. "Um, size…" Dar chewed her lip, then dug out her cell phone and dialed. It only rang three times. "Hey."

"Oh. Hey!" Kerry's voice sounded surprised. "Where are you? I just tried to call the office but I got the voice mail."

"I left early, had to go get my watch fixed," Dar told her. "And I ah…I met up with that guy who's doing the new handheld inventory counter for the warehouses. You remember, I told you about it?"

There was a pause. "Oh…oh, right, yes, I do…they wear it on their hands and just click, yeah." Kerry answered. "So?"

"Oh…well, we were just spec'ing it out here. He needs a size range to give the engineers, and…ah…well, my hand's not a good example for the women…what ring size are you?"

Dead silence. "Uh, oh, yeah, that's true, yeah; mine's a seven, a bunch smaller than yours, huh?" Kerry told her.

"About three sizes," Dar acknowledged wryly. "Great, thanks, Ker. Where are you, anyway?"

"Bayside. Col and I are just browsing. I got a kite and something to wear tomorrow night."

"Oh yeah? Can't wait to see it," the executive replied blithely. "Thanks, Kerry; talk to you later." She disconnected and looked up at the bemused clerk. "Tell him a size seven."

The manager walked over, and peered over the clerk's shoulder. "What do we have here?"

"She's, um…she bought this," the clerk squeaked.

Richard took the ring, and cradled it in one hand. "Um…Ms. Roberts…I um…well, that's spectacular. I'm thrilled, but um. This is a unique cut stone, and I…"

"Shh." Dar held up a hand. "Don't tell me how much it is. I don't care." She handed over a different card. "This'll cover it, won't it?"

The manager took the platinum American Express card and glanced at it. "Well, I had someone who put a Jaguar on one the other day, so I suppose it will…" He cleared his throat. "Let me have Michael come out and size it for you; I…"

"She wants it done a seven," the clerk supplied promptly.

"Can I get something engraved on it, while he's at it?" Dar asked, suddenly. "Will that take long?" She brought out a scrap of paper and scribbled on it, then handed it to him.

He stared at the words, then at her. "No, no, a few minutes, certainly… Ms. Roberts, can I get you a cup of coffee or something while you wait?" Richard asked anxiously.

Blue eyes glanced up. "No, not unless the coffee shop has double chocolate chunk ice cream; that's where I was headed."

The manager gave the clerk a significant look and shooed her towards the door with an almost frantic gesture. "Well, let me just go get Michael to take care of this for you right away." He disappeared along with the clerk, leaving Dar completely alone in the store.

She rested her chin on her fist, and regarded her reflection in the small mirror resting on the counter, watching the tiny tugs of emotion at the corners of her lips.

🐾   🐾   🐾

"Here you go, ma'am, all ready." The watch clerk handed Dar her watch back. "We had a heck of a time with it; what was in that water?"

"Puppy saliva," Dar responded, straight-faced, as she took the package. "Thanks." She left the store and headed for her car, feeling the pavement under her shoes oddly far away.

She slid into the leather seat, setting her packages down on the other seat and starting the car. Then she sat there for a long moment, letting the air conditioning blow against her face, and considering what she'd just done.

Heck. It was just a ring. Just a piece of metal and stone, with a couple of words engraved in it.

And yet, in a way, it stood for something far more profound, to her. It was, even if in her own mind only, crossing the line into a commitment she'd once promised herself she'd never offer again. She took out the ring and opened the box, staring at the glittering stone that winked back at her.

She hoped she'd have the courage, someday, to hand it to Kerry. But for now, she merely tucked it back into its box and put it away for the future.

🐾   🐾   🐾

Kerry stepped out of the bathroom, the air-conditioned atmosphere a little bracing after the apricot-scented steam bath her shower had created. The late afternoon sun cast her balcony in shadow as she studied her reflection in the dresser mirror.

"Ew." She raked her fingers through her hair, which was damp and sticking out all over the place. "ChiaKerry." She smiled, turning to glance around the room, her room now, and nodded a little at the familiar bedspread and the throw over the overstuffed chair in one corner. It wasn't much, but it was a start, this slow process of making this space hers.

She walked over to the huge walk in closet and pulled out her new dress, still sheathed in protective plastic. She hung it up on the door hook where its neatly draped folds shimmered softly in the light, and she found herself grinning a little as she pictured herself wearing it. It occurred to her, suddenly, that her coworkers, and Dar for that matter, had only ever seen her in casual or business clothing.

Or, of course, in Dar's case, no clothing, Kerry giggled to herself. No one had seen her really dressed, as she was accustomed to do around her father's complicated professional requirements. "Should be interesting," she informed the figure regarding her in the mirror.

Her underthings were already laid out on the bed, and she wriggled into the lacy, strapless bra, a pair of natural toned panty hose and the silk half slip, which warmed against her skin as she walked towards the mirror again and turned, checking the line of the soft fabric. "So far so good."

A bit of perfume next as she touched the backs of her ears and her pulse point before slipping on the dress, fastening the catches and twitching the rich, green fabric to lay neatly across her curves.

Slowly, she lifted her eyes to the mirror and studied the results, pleased with the overall look of poised sophistication. Then she stuck her tongue out and grinned before ambling forward and rooting around her jewelry box. The gorgeous jade and pearl earrings Dar had surprised her with at the very end of Christmas winked shyly from her earlobes as she picked up the antique necklace her aunt had given her, fastening it around her neck and allowing the clear, mossy green stone to nestle in the hollow of her throat.

The necklace glinted softly, its age-darkened silver contrasting with her tanned skin. Kerry padded into the bathroom and applied her makeup, a touch more than her usual. She dusted her face with a little powder and composed herself before wiggling her feet into her medium height heels and heading for the steps.

She paused on the landing, peering down into the condo. Dar was standing near the sliding glass doors, gazing out at the sea, and she had a moment just to look at her.

Wow.

Dar was wearing a simple, strapless black sheath in a matte silk that clung to her body and outlined its athletic grace with beautiful clarity. She had her hair loose, its neatly layered glossiness crackling around her head and matching the dress almost exactly.

Kerry cleared her throat and fastened her eyes on Dar's face as she turned and looked up, reading everything she'd hoped for in the widening baby blues and the dark, lifting eyebrows. "What do you think?" she asked diffidently, lifting her arms a little and indicating her outfit.

Dar walked slowly towards her, a frank, appreciative grin spreading across her face. "I think I'm in deep trouble." She crooked a finger at Kerry. "C'mere."

Her ego smirking contentedly, Kerry complied. She eased down off the last stair and stood quietly as Dar stepped forward, circling around her like a tall, nice-smelling jungle cat sniffing its prey. "Oh yeah." The dark-haired woman sighed. "I'm in big time trouble." She leaned over and sniffed Kerry's neck, then nibbled it lightly. "You look gorgeous."

"Thank you." Kerry felt the goosebumps spread across her skin. "But why are you in trouble?" She watched Dar slide around to face her, and take her by the waist, her fingers slipping under the fabric and exploring her bare skin.

"Because I have to be your goddamned boss tonight," Dar whispered, "and I don't want to be."

Kerry exhaled, running her hands up Dar's body and feeling the warm skin under the cool fabric. "Oh." She felt a distinct sense of disappointment. "I wish you didn't have to be either." She lifted her eyes. "You look wonderful, by the way." She tilted her head. "Ooh, nice. Are those new?"

Brilliant, soft blue stones glinted from Dar's earlobes. "Yeah." Dar lifted a hand and touched one ear. "You like them?"

Kerry stood on her tiptoes and examined them. "They're fantastic…they match your eyes, Dar; wow."

Her lover smiled, then laid a finger on the necklace Kerry was wearing. "This matches yours." She brushed the soft, errant hairs near Kerry's ear that had escaped her knot. "I like your hair up."

They gazed at each other. "Tell you what," Kerry suddenly blurted. "We go to the company party, then maybe we can go out someplace else?" She watched the interested look appear on Dar's face. "Someplace really nice?"

White teeth flashed in a delighted smile. "You're on," Dar agreed readily. "Listen…how attached to that lipstick are you?"

"Um, well, I'm not but…" Kerry thoroughly enjoyed the kiss, the wonderful scent of powder and Dar's perfume, and the soft feel of silk under her fingertips. They paused, and she sighed, resisting the urge to go further, party be damned. "I think I'm in trouble too." Her hands outlined the familiar curves under the fabric. "But everyone thinks I have a crush on you anyway, so…."

Dar chuckled wryly. "C'mon. Let's get this over with." She bent her head for another kiss, though, and they moved together in a wash of crimson light from the window, bodies easing against each other exchanging light touches that left them both breathing hard. "Oh boy." Dar released a ragged breath.

"Mm." Kerry forced her hands to stop their restless searching. "When does this stupid thing start?" Dar's fingers were still lightly stroking her ribs, and her body growled softly in frustration, wanting much more. "Hey, Dar?"

"Huh?" Dar was exploring the edge of her ear with tantalizing nibbles.

"If you don't want to be wearing a black lace doily," Kerry said between labored breaths, "you'd better cut that out."

"You want me to stop?" the voice whispered into her ear, every touch stoking the growing fire in Kerry's guts.

"No," she found herself answering helplessly as her body slipped disobediently out of her control and rubbed up against Dar's in an explosion of sensation. "But we're going to be late."

Dar moved around to the other side, nibbling across her throat. "Do you care?"

Kerry lost track of the question for a moment. "No," she finally replied softly.

A loud noise startled both of them and they jumped. "Wha—?" Dar glanced around dazedly before realizing it was coming from the dining room table. "Son of a bitch," she groaned feelingly as she iden- tified the sound as both of their pagers going off in tandem, rattling on the wood and skittering across its surface. "I'm gonna throw those things in the goddamned Atlantic Ocean right bloody now."

Kerry caught her breath. "They'd just get you another one." She patted Dar's side, then gave her a little hug. "We'll have plenty of time later to snuggle."

"Grumph." Dar looked definitely unhappy. "Bite me."

Kerry complied, getting a muffled scream from her lover. "Whoops…little sensitive there, huh?" She gave Dar an apologetic look. "Sorry."

Dar started laughing weakly. "My own fault."

Kerry gave her a last hug then went over to the table and compared both pager displays. "Ops." She glanced at Dar. "I doubt they're paging us to wish us a Happy New Year." She reached for the condo phone, then paused. "Damn, I keep forgetting that." She fished her cell phone out of her briefcase and dialed the Ops number. "Hi, it's Kerry Stuart…"

Dar leaned against the couch, folding her arms over her chest, trying to beat down the annoyance that was creeping up and putting her in a bad mood. Part of it was, she wryly admitted, her subverted libido. But the other part of it was a feeling of irritation that she and Kerry had to keep so much of their lives hidden, to the point where Kerry didn't dare use the condo phone to call work because the caller ID would immediately identify where she was calling from.

She could block it, of course, but that led to other questions. Dar sighed. "What's up?"

Kerry covered the receiver. "Some kind of glitch in the main backup systems," she mouthed. "Yes," she added, into the phone. "No, I haven't…have you tried her at home?" She glanced at Dar and rolled her eyes. "I know, but…oh. I see." She covered the receiver. "You wrote the program that runs it?"

Dar nodded. "Yeah." She reached for the wireless phone. "I'll call 'em; they probably did a core dump again." She dialed the same number Kerry was talking to.

"Okay, well, let me know if there's anything I can do," Kerry spoke reassuringly. "Bye." She closed her phone. "He had another line ring- ing; imagine that."

Dar smirked. "Yeah?" she barked into the phone.

Kerry walked over and rubbed her back, leaning her forehead against

Dar's shoulder for a brief instant. Then she straightened, and picked up her purse, clipping her pager and phone to the strap and holding her keys up where Dar could see them. "Meet you there?" she mouthed.

Dar looked decidedly unhappy, and answered with a shrug. "I guess," she whispered back. "Drive careful, okay?"

Kerry patted her leg and nodded, then headed for the door.

"Wonder where the Ice Princess is?"

"She's probably too busy screwing someone over to show up. We'll hear about it Monday."

Kerry held her temper—and her tongue—with difficulty.

"Screwing someone over, or screwing someone...didn't she have a meeting with that new account executive from Aldax?"

"The redhead? Yeah, that's her type all right."

Breathe. Kerry sipped her drink grimly, and tried to pay attention to what Mark was saying. "Sorry...did you say they were putting in a hundred megabit there?"

"Yeah." The MIS Chief, resplendent in a neat suit and tie, nodded. "Alan says he heard they were going to petition the account team to go to DS3's there, but I dunno."

"Means new substructure." Kerry shook her head. "They're gonna have to pay for it."

"Mm. Hey," Mark changed the subject. "Have I told you that's a killer dress?"

"Twice." Kerry smiled at him. "But thank you. I appreciate the compliment."

Mark smiled back. "No problem. Uh..." He moved closer, conscious of the three or four other employees around them. "Do you know if the boss is gonna show?"

"I think so," Kerry answered carefully, seeing ears perk around her. "She said she was on Thursday, but you know how it is. I got paged from Ops right before I left; they were trying to get a hold of her for the backup systems."

"Shit." Mark scowled. "Yeah, she wrote the damn thing, so they always call her when it crashes." He set his drink down. "Lemme go call, see what's going on." He walked to a more secluded spot and pulled out his cell phone, leaving Kerry to observe the slowly filling room.

The ballroom was large and colorfully decorated with balloons knotted in cheerful clusters and glitter scattered everywhere. Each table had a festive centerpiece, and the dance floor was large, though at the moment mostly empty. The celebrants were trickling in steadily, however, wearing an intriguing collection of formal wear.

"Well, good evening, Kerry." Eleanor wafted up in an elegant silver gown with a plunging neckline. "Don't you look wonderful." She turned. "Have you met my husband? Justin, darling, this is Kerry Stuart, the new staff member I've been telling you about."

"Pleased to meet you." Kerry extended a hand to the tall, urbane, gray-haired man.

"Same here." The man eyed her with interest. "You're Roger Stuart's kid, aren't you?" he asked. "One of 'em?"

Kerry swallowed the bitter taste in her mouth. "Yes," she admitted. "His oldest daughter."

The man was about to answer when Eleanor made a sound between a snort and a sneeze. "Well, look who's gracing us with her presence."

They all turned and watched as Dar entered, greeting the two or three people closest to the door as she made her way into the room.

All her defenses were up, Kerry could tell, seeing the cold, almost arrogant attitude as her lover swept the room with her pale blue eyes, ignoring the stares coming her direction ranging from curious, to lustful, to disgusted. For a brief instant, their eyes met, and she saw the flash of sudden warmth sweep over Dar's features, disappearing immediately as she angled her steps towards the bar.

Everyone was watching her. Dar's powerful stride and striking good looks drew the eye like a large, animate magnet, and you couldn't help but get caught up in that aura of attractive danger. Kerry watched along with the rest of them, then dropped her gaze as Eleanor started sniping.

"I have no idea why everyone thinks she's so good looking."

"Because she is." Kerry heard the words and kept herself from looking around to see who said them when her brain acknowledged that she had. She managed to keep her composure as Eleanor turned sharp eyes on her. "C'mon, Eleanor. You don't have to like her, but you can't say she's ugly."

Her husband laughed. "Pinned her correctly, Ms. Stuart." He was watching Dar as well. "El, she's a bitch by your lights, but she's a damn fine looking one by mine."

Miffed, Eleanor stalked off, dragging her spouse with her. Mark came back. "Looks like everything's okay," he reported, then looked where Kerry was pointing. "Huh…Oh!" A low whistle sounded. "Wow…"

Kerry smiled wistfully as Dar accepted the drink she'd gotten from the bartender and started working her way around the edge of the room. "Yeah," she murmured.

"Hey, Kerry?" Mark edged closer and lowered his voice.

"Mm?"

"She dance?"

Kerry smiled. "Why don't you ask her?"

"Yeah?"

The blond woman nodded. "Wish I could," she admitted.

Mark studied her, then glanced around the room. "This must suck for you, huh?" he sympathized. "If you guys so much as go to the bathroom together, I'll hear about it on Monday." He watched Kerry's jaw tighten. "Sorry."

"Not your fault," Kerry replied quietly. "It's true. I heard yesterday that a story's going around about how I bring Dar's coffee to her every afternoon." She rubbed her temple lightly. "I bring her tea, once—once, Mark—and that's what happens."

Mark wisely remained silent and cast his eyes on the floor.

"Ooh, look what the cat dragged in," the voice drifted over. "Guess she didn't bring her little redheaded friend with her."

Kerry ground her teeth.

"Good evening, Dar." Duks straightened his snug bow tie and made her a half bow. "You are looking very well tonight."

Dar took a long swallow of her very alcoholic beverage and cocked her head at him. "You too." She glanced around the room. "Late start—got caught on a call with the office."

"Heavy traffic coming up Biscayne," Duks explained. "You didn't hit it because you come over from the beach; anyone coming from Kendall or south is sitting twiddling their whatevers." He scratched his jaw. "Except Kerry, of course."

Dar glanced at him warily. "Maybe she found a better route."

Duks chuckled. "She should hire out to the Department of Transportation in that case." He put his hands behind him and rocked on his heels. "I would venture to say the Operations division is beautifully represented this evening, in any event." His eyes drifted over to where Kerry was standing next to Mark.

Dar peeked. "Hmm." She hid a smirk behind her glass. In the sea of glamorous dresses, Kerry's simple elegance stood out clearly, and her boss noticed more than one envious glance tossed her way. "Yes it is," she agreed. "You interested in the buffet?"

"Certainly," Duks assented gravely. "I intend to have one of every-thing before Mari gets here and makes me stick to bits of white fish and broccoli." He gestured. "After you, madame."

Dar finished her drink and set it down on a nearby bus tray, then proceeded across the dance floor to where the food tables were attract-ing a growing crowd. She picked up a plate and reviewed her choices, then was suddenly aware of a warm presence at her elbow. Her sense of smell told her who it was before she looked, and she only barely kept an uncharacteristic smile from crossing her face. "Evening, Kerry."

"Hi there," Kerry answered amiably. "How's the backup system?"

"Working." Dar held her plate out for some sliced roast beef, then added a large scoop of mashed potatoes, blithely ignoring the subtle throat clearing next to her. "They connected up the new servers in the print room and the algorithms didn't recognize them." She plopped two biscuits and a bunch of grapes on her plate, then wandered along the rest of the display, marking several things to go back for. She was aware of Duks coming up behind her with a plate of his own. "Pick your own seat, or did they do assigned seating again this year?"

"Assigned." Duks nudged her with an elbow. "Number twelve is ours; Mari did the seating, so you should have a peaceful dinner, at least."

Dar claimed a chair and seated herself, noting the small list on the table. Herself, Duks, Mariana, Mark and his fiancée Barbara, Maria and her husband Tomas, and, of course, Kerry. Mark was leading Barbara over, and Maria had just entered.

Dar looked up to see Kerry approaching, and she smiled grimly as the blond woman hesitated, trying to pick a politically correct place to sit. "Hey, Kerry." She indicated the seat next to her. "Save everyone else the trouble of finding an excuse not to."

"Why?" Kerry put her plate down anyway, and took the seat next to her boss. "Do you throw your food or something?"

That caused a chuckle.

"Ever see me at a meeting? Only one with two empty chairs on either side of me." Dar gazed around the table sardonically. "You'd think I had spikes."

"You do," Duks replied seriously. "Those damned pencils you use... how many times have you poked me with them? I go across the table, thank you very much."

Another chuckle.

"Hi, Maria." Kerry smiled warmly at the older woman as she approached. She stood and extended a hand to the short, owlish man with her. "You must be Tomas; I've heard so much about you. I'm Kerry Stuart."

Tomas took her hand and shook it vigorously. "Yes, Maria has told me much about you as well; it is good to meet you finally." He gave Dar a timid look. "Hello, Ms. Roberts, it is nice to see you again."

"Evening, Tomas..." Dar waved a fork at him. "I think I remember asking you to call me Dar last time we met though; wasn't it at the picnic?"

"Sí." He gave her a mildly abashed look. "Pardon, Dar."

"They've got some nice things on the buffet, Maria," Kerry advised her. "Nice, fresh green beans." She forked one and held it up.

Dar sniffed at it. "Looks dangerous to me." She went back to her pile of mashed potatoes, puddling the little well of butter she'd melted in the center.

"How would you know?" Kerry felt herself relaxing a little, now that she was in a circle of friendly faces. "The last green thing I saw you eat was that lime Jell-O we had in the cafeteria the other day."

Everyone laughed. "Dios Mío, Dar..." Maria peered at her boss's plate. "I think that is half of the bull you have there."

"I will not comment on Dar and bulls," Duks intoned soberly. "It is not something we discuss in public."

"Hey!" Dar gave them all a dire look. "If I wanted abuse over dinner, I'd have gone over and sat next to José." She pointed across the room, where José was holding court at his own table, accompanied by both Eleanor, and a smiling Steve Fabricini.

Abashed faces quickly reddened, and an awkward silence fell. "Pardon, Dar," Maria said softly. "I did not mean any trouble."

Dar glanced around. Kerry was staring at her plate, and Duks fiddled with his fork. "I was joking," the dark-haired woman told them quietly. "It's okay to give me grief about my eating habits, really." A pause. "I started it, remember?"

Everyone relaxed a little, and Dar sighed inwardly.

"I think we are all just jealous, my friend," Duks admitted, regaining some of his cheerfulness. "We all wish we could eat like you do, and still look like you do."

Dar accepted the compliment and the change of subject with a graceful nod of her head. "You want to borrow my dress, Duks?" she inquired, a brow lifting. "Is that what you're getting at?"

Her friend rose to the occasion. "Tch. You know black is not my color. Now, that red thing you wore last year…"

Everyone let out a relieved laugh and went back to getting their food and settling at the table. Kerry was still quiet though, sitting erect in her chair and eating with natural but impeccable manners. Dar put her fork down and reached for a glass, using her motion to cover her other hand slipping under the tablecloth and closing her fingers around Kerry's knee.

A faint smile tugged at Kerry's lips, and she visibly relaxed. She gave a very quick look around, then surreptitiously snuck a green bean onto Dar's plate, and dared her not to eat the evidence.

The pale blue eyes narrowed a trifle, but Dar speared the intruder and smothered it in buttered potatoes before popping it into her mouth, chewing quickly and swallowing, then winking at her.

Kerry sighed and chewed on her forkful of fish filet, adding a bit of steamed cauliflower to the mouthful. When she looked back down at her plate, she was very surprised to see a mound of mashed potatoes nestling next to her fish, and she gave Dar a startled look.

"I don't know, Dukky; that account's never going to consolidate if they don't start integrating their systems with ours," Dar was saying, pointing her fork at the Finance VP.

"Oh Dar, can we talk about the weather instead of business?" Mariana broke in as she arrived and seated herself next to Duks with a filled plate. "Seen any good movies lately?" She paused and smiled at Kerry. "Hello, Kerry, how are you liking your first formal ILS party?"

Kerry was caught with a mouthful of potatoes, which she'd been enjoying. She swallowed them hastily and wiped her lips. "Very nice, thanks, and the last movie I saw was *Like Water for Chocolate*…it was really interesting."

"I saw that," Mari agreed. "Good performances."

"I'm going back up, anyone want anything ?" Dar asked, getting to her feet. "No?" She shrugged and stepped around the table, heading back for the buffet.

Mari leaned over past Duks. "Kerry, how in the hell does she get away with that?"

Kerry sighed, and lowered her voice. "A lot of hard work, if you mean her figure. What gets me pissed off is that her cholesterol and blood pressure are lower than mine," she complained. "Is that fair?" She held up a piece of cauliflower.

Duks and Mari chuckled. "No, it's not," Mari agreed. "But you've been sharing her gym time, I see." She indicated Kerry's muscular arms. "Good for you. I wish I had either the energy or the willpower."

Kerry smiled to acknowledge the compliment. "Actually, it's a lot of fun, and I found that the more you do it, the more energy you have." She pushed her chair back. "Excuse me." She drained her water down, then headed outside for the restroom.

She pushed the door open, and slowed, as a small group inside turned, voices cutting off in mid-syllable. *Wonder who they were talking about.* "Hi."

"Oh, hi, Kerry." One of the marketing executives smiled sweetly at her. "Having fun?"

Bite my left kneecap. "Sure; it's a nice party," Kerry replied. "How about you?"

"Great." A second woman also smiled. She was an outside sales agent, Kerry remembered. "Pretty dress…that color looks good on you."

"Thanks." Kerry easily handled the false banter. "I love that purse. Did you get it to match your shoes?"

"Yeah, Macy's…well, gotta go." The two women left hastily with their two companions following them. Kerry watched them go and sighed, then shook her head and used the facilities, deciding that she still hated panty hose and they still made her itch in inappropriate places. She stood at the mirror when she was done, washing her hands, and glanced into the reflection as the door opened behind her.

Beautiful blue eyes appeared.

"Do you have any aspirin?" Kerry asked plaintively.

Dar entered and let the door close, then eyed the stalls to check for other occupants. "Yes, I do." She came up behind Kerry and put both hands on her bare neck, massaging it with sure, powerful fingers. "How are you doing?"

"If I had a two by four, you'd have a lot of paperwork to sign and Mariana would be very, very, very pissed off at me," Kerry growled. "Don't these people have anything better to do with their time than trash other employees?"

Dar shrugged. "To each their own entertainment." She placed a daring kiss on Kerry's neck, just under her ear. "I prefer mine."

Kerry inhaled sharply. "Dar, if you start that, and then make me go out there and pretend not to know you as anything but my boss, my brain is going to explode." She got an impish look, but Dar ceased her nibbling and scratched Kerry's neck lightly with her fingertips instead. "C'mon, I've got some pills in my purse."

The door swung open abruptly, almost hitting them, and Eleanor stalked in, obviously miffed. She stopped short when she spotted the two of them standing there, though Dar had dropped her hands to her sides at the first sound of the hinges.

"Problem?" Dar lifted an eyebrow.

"Strategy session?" Eleanor asked, with acid sweetness. "Don't let me interrupt." She turned and entered a stall, closing the door with a sharp snick of the lock.

Dar and Kerry exchanged wry looks. Dar patted Kerry's back and indicated the door. "Like I was saying, Kerry…sometimes you can just ping and ping, and you never get a valid response."

"Sometimes what you're pinging doesn't even have an address," her assistant remarked. "It's just a dummy device."

Dar snickered as the door rattled. "Ring in, but no ring out."

"Sixty megahertz card in a hundred megahertz bus."

"A SIMM short of a bank."

"A SCSI chain with no terminator."

Eleanor emerged, jerking her clothing straight. "You know, one of the biggest problems we have is that only a few people in our company speak normal ENGLISH." She stomped out, leaving the two nerds in momentary peace. Dar chuckled, then sighed and gestured towards the door. "We've had our fun. C'mon, let's go back out before everyone thinks I'm planning a hostile takeover in here."

Kerry pulled the door open and followed Dar out, watching eyes in the lobby flick to them in interest. "I should carry my palm pilot around and pretend to be taking notes on everything you say," she muttered, giving two of the fourth floor art designers a smile as they passed.

"Think they could get any closer to each other?"

The whisper carried in a moment of broken sound to Kerry's ears, and she glanced at Dar, puzzled. She wasn't that close to her, no closer than she...

With a sigh, she dropped back a pace. Yes, they were that close. Inside each other's personal space as a matter of fact, far cozier than the normally very standoffish Dar would have allowed anyone else to be.

She wondered if Dar even realized it.

"Ah, what do we have here?" Steve Fabricini inserted himself into their path. "Dar, just the person I was looking for."

"Why?" Dar asked bluntly. "Can't figure out how to work your pager again?"

Kerry winced.

"You're such a sweetheart," Steve replied. "Actually, I wanted to see if you'd join me on the dance floor."

Dar's eyebrow lifted sharply. "What would be the point in that?" She watched him as he circled her once.

"C'mon, Dar. Loosen up." Steve laughed. "It's a party, you're a good looking woman, I'm a good looking guy... Who are you waiting to ask, Lou Draefus?"

"At least he has a personality and a brain." Dar smiled at him. "But if you want, sure. Let's go." She gestured towards the dance floor. "Better stand on your tiptoes, though."

He chuckled, then suddenly turned to Kerry, as though noticing her for the first time. "Oh, sorry. Do you mind if I dance with Dar?" He smiled sweetly. "It won't look bad for you, will it?"

Kerry felt warning bells go off. "Aesthetically, you mean?" she replied. "No, that's a pretty acceptable tuxedo. You might want to give the cummerbund a miss next time, though. I haven't seen one of those since I was in high school." She added a very pleasant smile.

"Thanks." Steve gave her back a thin-lipped smile. "Glad to know we have a fashion consultant on the fifteenth floor if we ever need one." He turned and raised an eyebrow at Dar. "Well?"

If looks could kill, the old saying went, Steve Fabricini would have exploded messily all over the ballroom, leaving tatters of black and white fabric behind him and not much else. "Let's go." Dar sighed, leading the way back towards the party.

It was going to be a very long night. Kerry paused for a moment, watching Dar and Steve step onto the dance floor. The very idea that a snake like that could do what he was doing and she couldn't burned her guts. *Why that little...*

"Hey, Ker?" Mark's voice broke into her seething thoughts. "I see the boss got hijacked. Wanna dance?"

Kerry gave the stocky, dark-haired man a wry grin. "Sure." She took Mark's hand and they started towards the parquet floor. "Why not?"

🐾   🐾   🐾

"Ugh." Kerry leaned against the door, flexing her tired toes as Dar keyed the code into the condo's lock. She'd followed her boss home after the dinner had ended, and a few rounds of dancing had left her with sore feet and an abiding distaste for fruity men's cologne. "Ever consider company-wide dancing lessons?"

Dar smiled, and held the door for her. "At least you got to practice," she remarked, having spent the rest of the evening mostly watching and exchanging brief comments with the few people brave enough to approach her. "Mark's not bad."

"No." Kerry kicked off her heels and sighed in relief. "I'm not used to these anymore. I used to have to suffer through this stuff once a week when I was younger."

"You're a good dancer," Dar complimented her. "A lot better than I am, anyway. I thoroughly enjoyed stepping on Steve's feet." She grinned evilly and continued on into the living room, removing her own shoes and stretching a kink out of her back. "Went better than last year, though; I ended up in a screamfest with José outside the men's room that time. Ugly." She went over to the glass doors and peered out. "It's early yet; you interested in going over to the Mansion? Looks like they've got a nice party going over there."

Kerry joined her, looking out at the well-lit old house where the courtyard outside had been transformed into a dance floor under the bright stars. She could see tuxedoed and gowned forms dancing together, and attractive as the sight was, she was suddenly reluctant to go again into the limelight, under the eyes of all those people. With a sigh, she rested her head against Dar's arm.

The dark-haired woman glanced down. "Tired?"

Kerry gave her an apologetic look. "Dealing with all those people was exhausting." She kissed Dar's shoulder. "Could I interest you in some music, some good champagne, and a few waltzes right here? The living room's big enough."

Dar smiled. "Sure." She leaned closer. "I may be able to find some chocolate-covered strawberries to go with that champagne."

"Oo."

"Besides, I'm honestly not a good dancer, Kerry. I'm really kinda glad no one else asked me at that damn party." Dar leaned on the door frame. "I can't even remem…" She paused, thinking. "Anyway, just don't move too fast, huh?"

Kerry sensed her change of mood, and she turned, leaning against the glass so she could see Dar's face. "I won't… listen, you okay? We can just relax if you want, put on the Times Square thing, and watch the ball drop."

Dar folded her arms. "No, I'd like to share a few turns with you." She smiled at the blond woman. "I grew up fast when I was a kid. I was too tall for most of the guys to ask to dance."

"Their loss." Kerry took her hand. "I didn't have that problem. Everyone wanted to dance with me, but for none of the right reasons." She straightened and got closer to Dar, letting her hands rest on her lover's hips, as Dar circled her shoulders. "They were all looking out for themselves, wanting to catch my father's eye. I always felt like a dressed up stepladder."

Dar reached behind her and turned the sophisticated stereo system on, her own addition to the condo. A quiet melody emitted, and she smiled at Kerry, as they nestled closer together, swaying to the music. "I can't believe that, Kerry," Dar said. "How could anyone be this close to you and not notice how beautiful you are?"

"Well…" Kerry laid her cheek against Dar's shoulder. "I never thought of myself that way, and I don't think any of them did either. I always felt gawky; I wasn't very coordinated and I was always worried about doing something wrong and getting yelled at by my parents." She moved in a little circle, and Dar followed her lead. "You can't tell me with your body control and reflexes that you're not a good dancer, Dar, I just won't believe it."

"Mm." Dar slid closer and found the rhythm of the music. "Let's just say a naval base isn't a place where you learn refined skills like dancing, at least…" A wry chuckle. "Not this kind. I can do a mean break dance if you force me to it."

Kerry stopped dead. "You mean that spinning on your head stuff?" She peered up at her lover incredulously. "You're kidding."

"Nope." Dar pulled her close again. "I'm sure if we'd met as high schoolers, you wouldn't have looked twice at me."

Kerry thought about that as they made the music louder and swayed across the marble floor. She tried to imagine Dar coming to her Christian high school, set down in a world that would have been as alien to her as a military base would have been to Kerry.

She remembered how she felt then, just coming out of puberty, just becoming aware of who her father was, and how her family was viewed, her friends so carefully picked, her activities strictly regulated.

What if Dar had walked into her life at just that moment? "You're wrong," she murmured softly.

"About what?" Dar had her eyes closed, and was simply enjoying the closeness.

"I would have been drawn to you like a iron plate and a magnet," Kerry told her. "For one thing, your intelligence would have reassured me that I wasn't a freak." She inhaled. "I would have been totally fascinated by you."

Dar thought about that, as they moved in a lazy circle. "Think we would have been friends?" She sounded surprised.

Kerry smiled. "You would have been the friend they couldn't run off—and who wouldn't have deserted me."

Dar kissed her. "Your folks would have hated my guts." She gazed into Kerry's eyes. "But you're right."

They kissed again, then slid together as fireworks off the shoreline arced upwards, leaving a faintly heard whistle and pop behind them.

"Happy New Year, Dar."

"It already is."

Chapter 5

 The office was mostly silent, save the faint scratching of a pen on paper and the soft, distinctive hum of the computer on the desk. It was a room filled with warm mahogany wood, a small conference table on one side surrounded by chairs on one side, a discreet credenza containing a pitcher of water and a set of glasses on the other, and the desk in the rear center, its back facing a large, floor to ceiling window which afforded a horizon view of a choppy, greenish blue Atlantic Ocean.

Dar was seated at her desk dressed in a conservative gray skirt and white silk shirt, the sleeves of which were rolled up past her elbows, exposing tanned, muscular forearms. Draped over the back of the chair was a gray blazer, and her dark head was propped up on one fist while the other hand curled about a busily moving pen. One paper was completed and then it was turned over, coming to rest next to a small aquarium where the two suspicious Siamese fighting fish swam languidly, sparing occasional goggling eyes for the desk's tenant.

"Twelve down, eighteen to go," Dar sighed, scratching her jaw with the edge of the pen. "You'd think we'd have gotten our staff evaluations on computer by now." She paused, and then punched a button on the large console phone on her desk. "Mari?"

"Hello, Dar. Good afternoon." The Personnel Director's voice was relaxed and friendly.

"Mind if I ask why one of the largest goddamn IS companies in the world can't put its evals on the intranet?" Dar asked testily. "Do you know how much faster it would be?"

"Ah, Dar." Mariana sighed, as though she'd been answering that very question all day long. Which she had. "If we did that, how would we comply with the regulation that dictates we ensure all our senior staff know how to write longhand?" she inquired lightly. "Now, now, you shouldn't complain; you only have thirty people you're directly responsible for. Think how José must feel—he has two hundred."

Dar considered this, chewing the end of her pen. "You're right. That put me in a much better mood." She chuckled. "He must be tearing out what's left of his hair."

"You're not kidding," Mari sighed. "Actually, the reason they're not e-forms is because there were some concerns about employee security: the e-forms might be accessible by people on the intranet that really shouldn't be able to read them."

"Oh." Dar thought about that. "So I probably shouldn't tell you that I just passed by the main printer room and saw all of José's completed forms printing out, right?"

Mari sighed aggrievedly.

"It was like a feeding frenzy in there." Dar grinned at the phone. "Everyone was peeking."

"And you didn't stop it? Come on, Dar, you're supposed to be responsible management up there." The personnel director sounded peeved.

"Hey… how was I supposed to know that wasn't a new sales incentive of his?" Dar asked reasonably. "After all, I fill out mine longhand."

"Jesú. All right, I could use a cup of coffee anyway. I'll wander down there," Mariana exhaled. "How are you doing?"

"'Bout halfway," Dar lied.

"Uh huh." Mariana sounded supremely unconvinced. "Why do you all have to wait until the last minute?"

"Because it's such a pain in the ass, Mari!" Dar responded, exasperatedly. "Tell Houston to get their anal pusses into the 21st century with the rest of us and put these damn things online! If they'd migrate to IIS4, security wouldn't be a goddamned problem!"

"Can you spell that phonetically, Dar? I'm sending them a carrier pigeon," Mariana responded in a serious voice. "All right, I'll put in a recommendation—again—for the forms to be changed to e-forms."

"Thanks," Dar grumped. "Gotta go." She hung up and resumed the onerous task. Each form had fifty categories in which she had to grade her employees, and a comments section which, by regulation, had to be filled in. "Jesus Christ," she moaned, riffling through the stack. "Can't I just send in a slip of paper that says 'If they're not fired, they're fine?'" she complained to the fish, who wiggled their fins at her.

"No, huh." She bent her head to the paper, reaching out and snagging a piece of dried fruit from a cobalt blue dish on her desktop and nibbling it.

A tap at the outer door was a welcome interruption. "C'mon in," she called out, looking up to see her secretary poke her head in. "Maria, have we gotten the status reports from Marketing yet?"

The short, older woman shook her head. "Nada, and I have called that new facilitatoria there three times." She walked across the carpeted floor and put several folders into Dar's inbox. "Three new accounts; Kerrisita is going to be busy this week."

"Mm," Dar agreed, the mention of her assistant bringing an unconscious smile to her face. "Hang on." She punched a number into the phone. It rang twice, then a perky voice answered. "I need to talk to José," Dar stated crisply.

"I'm sorry, he's in conference right now," the voice answered.

"Tell him to get out of the john and onto the phone or he'll have me in there hunting him down in thirty seconds," Dar replied, pitching her voice lower.

Dead silence. "One moment, please."

Dar waited, checking her watch. Maria covered her mouth to keep a laugh from escaping. Twenty-seven seconds later, the phone picked up again.

"What the hell, Dar?" the Marketing VP snarled.

"I need those status reports," Dar snarled right back. "And I frankly don't have the time to have my goddamned staff running around the building chasing down your staff to get them."

In the silence, she could hear his heavy breathing. She waited, making a few more comments on the sheet in front of her and munching another piece of dried fruit. "I'm waiting," she commented crisply.

"Hold on." The line went to music and Dar hummed along, selecting a pecan from the dish and pushing it towards Maria. "Want some trail mix?"

The secretary accepted the offer, picking up a piece of apricot and putting it into her mouth, privately amused by her boss's sudden fondness for the relatively healthy snack, replacing her usual dish of chocolates.

"They'll be there in five minutes," José's voice came back on. "And stop scaring the shit out of my staff."

"If your staff did their jobs, I wouldn't have to be calling you, now would I?" Dar replied silkily before she disconnected. "Asshole," she muttered, shaking her head. "Okay, if you don't get those reports by the time you get out to your desk, lemme know."

"Sí. Dar, have you heard about Mr. José's new assistant?" Maria lowered her voice. "I'm not the one for to be talking in corners, but I hear twice today he is very sharp, and they are looking for him to, how you say, go against you."

Dar leaned on her elbows and fiddled with the pen in her hands, then looked up. "I've heard the same thing." Her pale, intense blue eyes regarded Maria. "Kerry's in a meeting with him and Eleanor right now, in fact; he called the facilities projections for this year into question."

"Dios Mío." The older woman's brow creased. "Is trouble, no?"

A slow nod. "Mr. Fabricini and I have met before," the executive remarked quietly. "In fact, we used to be friends." A pause. "We are not friends now," she told Maria frankly. "It could get very ugly, yes."

Maria sighed and frowned. "Why cannot everyone just come, do their work, go home, not spend all day making problems?" She exhaled. "Poor Kerrisita, stuck with those two."

A quiet smile edged Dar's face. "She's tough; she'll be fine, Maria," she reassured her secretary. "Listen, I know I've got a meeting after lunch with the executive committee, but did we reschedule that client briefing for tomorrow or is it still at four?"

"I'll check." Maria headed for the door. "And I'll let you know about those reports."

"Thanks." Dar let out a breath and went back to her task, concentrating for a minute, then dropping her pen down and leaning back, her eyes thoughtful.

So. Even Maria had heard it. Dar felt a familiar frustration rising in her, triggered by the secretary's plaintive question. Why couldn't everyone just show up and do their job? It had become obvious at their first encounter that Steven Fabricini had been hired specifically because he knew Dar, and José was hoping that knowledge could turn things to his advantage in the boardroom.

Not that he wasn't qualified, Dar mused. He was, moreso than José, in her honest opinion. But he was also less scrupulous than the blustery Cuban, more ruthless, and far more aggressively antagonistic.

Like her, if she wanted to view things very objectively, in which case José's choice hadn't been a bad one for his purposes.

Since they'd gotten back from the holidays, it had been one testing jab after another. The last thing had been a stack of contracts they'd processed, ones whose execution he'd questioned and called a grandstand meeting about. She knew Steven was looking to prove himself to José and use this as an opportunity to fence with her, so she'd reviewed the information—and sent Kerry to the meeting he'd demanded instead.

She wondered how it was going.

"I'm sorry, I'm not sure I understand the question," Kerry stated, turning her pencil in her hands and peering patiently across the table at José, Eleanor, and Steven. Kerry had the very uncomfortable sensation of being a rabbit in a cage with three hungry snakes.

Fortunately, rabbits did have claws, and teeth, and could use them when needed. "What do half a dozen prospective leads that haven't even gone to bid status have to do with projections from last year?"

Steven Fabricini had been very obviously miffed that Dar had sent her, Kerry realized, but she also understood why her boss had done so; she had the answers to their questions, and it prevented the meeting from appearing to be a forum where Dar would be pushed into the defensive, attacked by the three.

Now Steven stood, walking to the whiteboard. "Well, as I see it, if we can show that kind of potential, then Facilities has the obligation to add bandwidth so we have the ability to close the deals." He held his hands out. "What is there to understand?"

Kerry cocked her head. "That's like saying you're going to buy six hamburgers at McDonald's because you might get hungry," she stated. "Upping bandwidth on the network is done via a formula based on your department's past performance; if you want that changed, you need to close more contracts, because they're not going to acquire hard circuits on the possibility of leads." She consulted the information Dar had printed out for her. "According to the last five years' projections, Infrastructure is increasing the acquisition of circuits based on a new account rate of ten percent." She looked up. "Are you saying we're going to close more new accounts than that?"

"We have no idea!" José threw his hands up. "But we can't sell the accounts if we don't have the bandwidth to handle their demands immediately."

"Don't you see, Kerry?" Eleanor added smoothly, smiling at her. "We have to have a bargaining chip."

"Ah." Kerry folded her hands over the papers. "Okay, so what happens if we don't add that many accounts, and we end up with a negative balance we have to compensate for?"

"See? That's your problem, cupcake: you can't think like that, you have to think positive." Steven pointed the marker at her. "You're too conservative, and it's killing our potential to sign new business."

Kerry propped her chin up on one hand. "No, we're just following the written guidelines for new business, as set down by Corporate in Houston. If you have an issue with how the business case has to be structured, you need to address that with Alastair McLean, since it's his model." She neatly flipped the tables on him. "And those five accounts you tossed into this issue do not adhere that standard. In fact, two of them show significant potential for a loss on the overall account, despite the bonus you all will get for signing the new business." Her voice was gentle, and almost pleasant. "So, as you can see, I'm really not convinced we should go to Infrastructure on this and ask them to accelerate their program." She stood up. "Now, if you'll all excuse me, I have a lunch meeting I'm due at in twenty minutes."

José grabbed his papers and left with a disgusted look. Eleanor trailed him out, leaving Steven and Kerry in the room. He sauntered over to her. "You're pretty sharp."

Sea green eyes regarded him. "Thank you." She picked up her papers. "Excuse me."

"Hey, hey, hold on." Steven circled around and perched on the table. "I'm not going to bite you." He smiled. "Unless you want me to, of course." He flicked the papers. "No need to be hostile; we're on the same side, remember?"

"Are we?" Kerry asked. "Then why accuse our division of deliberately sabotaging yours?" She held up the printed mail. "Or didn't you write this?"

"Aw, c'mon," Steven chuckled. "It's just a game, loosen up." He slapped his folded papers against her arm lightly. "We're both pretty new here, right?"

"More or less," Kerry replied, purposely relaxing her pose.

"So we can talk. Look, I'm not here to make trouble, okay? I'm just trying my best to jump-start some sales here; it's to all our benefit, remember?" His brows lifted. "We can help each other. Things are kind of stagnating, and if we work together, maybe we can get things moving again."

Kerry studied him. He was charming, he knew it, and she could feel the allure of that engaging smile. "I'd be glad to help in any way I could," she answered carefully, "without compromising our standards."

He moved closer, in a casual way. "Ah, now, Kerry, would I ask you to compromise your standards?" he grinned. "I heard you say you have a lunch meeting; maybe tomorrow we could grab a bite in the cafeteria and chat—how about it?" Steven captured her eyes, and his lips twitched a little.

"All right," the blond woman said quietly, "we can do that." She shifted papers. "I have to go or I'll be late for my meeting."

He winked. "Go on, cupcake, see you later." He watched her leave, then smiled to himself, letting out a low, soft chuckle.

🐮🐮   🐮🐮   🐮🐮

The cafeteria was crowded with the early lunch crowd, staff who came in before eight and by noon were more than ready to eat. Kerry picked up her tray and wound her way through the room, spotting Maria and several other older women seated near the back where a window allowed a view of the water. "Hi," she greeted them, putting her tray down by an empty chair. "Looks like we're going to get some rain."

"Sí," Maria agreed, looking out at the threatening clouds. "How are you, Kerrisita? Did your meeting go all right?"

Kerry seated herself, and picked up her silverware. "More or less." She took a sip of her iced tea and speared a piece of lettuce. "We agreed to disagree; you know, the usual." She gave the older woman a wry look, then glanced around casually. "Boss get stuck again?"

Maria nodded. "Sí, a conference call from France. She asked me to bring her up a sandwich."

Kerry clucked and shook her head. The table talk turned to the latest episode of a favorite TV show, and she joined in cheerfully.

"Guess that honeymoon ended fast." The faintly sarcastic remark made Duks raise his head and regard the speaker coolly.

"Excuse me?"

Comptroller Selene Advosan leaned closer. "C'mon, Duks; when she first started, her and the ice princess were tighter than a champagne cork in a bottle, but I haven't even seen them eat lunch together since the New Year. I guess the novelty wore off."

The Financial VP chewed his corned beef sandwich thoughtfully. "Never noticed," he said noncommittally, then glanced over at Kerry, who appeared perfectly at home with her tablemates and was laughing at something Maria had said. "Maybe they're just busy. Dar never did lunch much anyway, and they seem friendly enough."

"Yeah, but I thought we had a juicy one going there for a little while," Selene sighed. "I should have known better; Dar's way out of her league."

"Mm." Duks dismissed the subject and concentrated on his lunch.

Kerry put her tray away and joined Maria as the secretary ordered a sandwich for their boss. The older woman checked the available options, then glanced sideways. "What you think, chicken salad?" she inquired, her brow creasing.

"Tuna melt on raisin toast," Kerry murmured, "with french fries."

"Aie." Maria winced and gave her an appalled look. The blond woman shrugged and smiled. "Dios Mío. All right." She ordered the sandwich and gathered some napkins as it was being made. She took the bag the counterman handed her and clucked, then followed Kerry to the elevator. At the last minute, running footsteps and a hand between the door delayed them as Steven Fabricini oozed in.

"Well, hello there." He picked his way through the mailman and two administrative assistants, choosing to lean against the same wall Kerry was. "How was lunch?"

"Fine, thanks," the blond woman replied readily. "This cafeteria's really not bad; it's better than most of the restaurants around here."

"Ah." He watched as the doors opened, and one woman left. "You live in the area?"

"Kendall," Kerry answered amiably.

"Hey, me too." Steven smiled. "Seems like most of the building does, either that, or up in Miramar." He glanced up as the mailman and the other woman left. "Guess we're headed to the same place," he noted, seeing the fifteen button the only one left lit.

"Guess we are." Kerry eyed him. "Where in Kendall did you end up?"

He told her, crossing his arms. "It's a nice little complex, got a clubhouse and all that."

"That's not too far from where I am. I like the area. We go rollerblading down to that little bakery on the corner near the mall all the time," the blond woman commented.

"Hey, I blade all the time." Steven smiled. "Maybe we'll bump into each other sometime down there. I like that little place." The door opened and he gestured. "Ladies first."

Kerry followed Maria out, seeing the stiff set of the secretary's back and biting off a tiny smile. Steven accompanied them down the hall and into Dar's outer office, where the executive's distinctive, vibrant voice could be heard growling through the thick wood paneling. "Aie, what now?" Maria sighed.

Steven chuckled. "Dar never needed a reason to be rude, crude and obnoxious." He brushed by them and walked into the dark-haired woman's office, closing the door behind him.

Kerry and Maria exchanged glances, then Kerry picked up the paper bag. "I'll drop this off." She paused with a hand on the doorknob, then opened the inner office door and stepped inside.

"Mike, I don't give a goddamn what they're telling you, it's bullshit." Dar punctuated her words by slamming her pencil on the desk. "I'm not going to accept sixty days to pull a lousy circuit, so they better come up with something else."

"Look, Dar, we've been going around and around with them for two months. They won't budge," the man's voice replied, sounding tired. "They've got unions to deal with up there, and facilities that are older than my damn mother."

Dar looked up as the door opened, and her nostrils flared a bit as Steven walked brazenly into her office. "Hang on a minute." She hit the hold button. "People knock before they come into this office."

Steven clucked, and dropped into a chair. "Get your panties out of a wad, Dar."

"What do you want? I'm in the middle of something," the dark-haired woman snapped back.

Steven leaned back, glancing up as the outer door opened and Kerry slipped in. "Thought people knocked first?" he asked mockingly, smiling at Dar.

"She doesn't have to knock. She works here," Dar replied. "You've got ten seconds. Talk, or get out."

Kerry paced quietly across the carpet and deposited the bag on Dar's desk. "Lunch," she murmured, then headed for the inner door that lead down a service corridor to her own office.

"Thanks." Dar spared her a brief glance. "Hold on a second, I have some contracts to turn over to you." Then she focused back on her unwelcome guest. "What is it?"

"I want a task force." He leaned forward abruptly. "I want two people from your staff so I can figure out what the hell you're trying to accomplish around here, and see if I can straighten it out." He pointed. "I want her, and whoever else you have, assigned over to me for a period of two months, starting tomorrow."

Silence fell. Dar folded her hands over her desk, and blinked at him. "That's what you want?" she inquired mildly.

"That's what I want." He smiled.

One long, powerful finger pointed at the door. "What I want is you out of my office," she stated flatly. "I don't have the time or the people to dedicate to you for your wild goose chase. If you want to bring in temps to play with files, talk to Mariana."

"Afraid of what I'll find, Dar?" He crossed his legs, and smiled at her, as he glanced sideways at the quietly waiting Kerry. "You can't hide it forever."

Dar merely stared steadily at him.

"Fine." He stood up and brushed his pants off. "I'll just make it a formal request up the line. I'll get what I want, and everyone will know it. Sorry, Dar; I was trying to spare you that for old time's sake." He winked at Kerry and left, the door closing behind him with a bang.

A silence settled, then Kerry cleared her throat. "You know what I want?"

Dar raised an eyebrow at her.

The blond woman walked over and settled on the corner of Dar's desk. "I want a shower." She pointed. "Right in that corner, so every time I have to talk to that sneaky little piece of pig manure I can go and hose myself off." She made a face and gagged. "He makes me feel so slimy!" She shuddered. "Ugh! Gag! Gross! Yuck!"

That got a weary chuckle from the taller woman, who shook her head and sighed. "He's a piece of work, that's for sure." She punched the phone button. "Mike, you still there?"

"Yeah," a muffled voice answered. "Just eating my lunch."

"All right, gimme the name of someone up in their chain. I'll see what I can do to shove things along a little." Dar propped her head up on one hand. "Sixty days. My dog could pull a circuit in less than sixty days."

"Probably do a neater job of it, too," Mike agreed. "I'll e-mail you with some names. Thanks, Dar."

"Yeah, yeah," Dar sighed as she disconnected and turned to face Kerry. "Hey."

Kerry cocked her head and smiled. "Hey." She indicated the bag. "Tuna on raisin… better eat the french fries before they soak through the bag."

Dar's expression gentled, and she captured Kerry's hand, squeezing it. "Thanks. How'd the meeting go? You must have made an impression or he wouldn't be asking for you."

Kerry rolled her sea green eyes. "I think he's just bound and determined to screw you over. He went from being condescending and antagonistic to hitting on me." She made a face. "He wants to do lunch tomorrow." She watched Dar's right eyebrow lift. "Here, just in the cafeteria," she amended with a gentle twinkle. The eyebrow remained where it was. "Ooo, do I sense some territoriality raising its head?"

"Hmph." Dar snorted softly. "No… that's not… you can go to lunch with whoever you want to, Kerry, I'm not, um…"

A hand cupped her cheek unexpectedly. "I'm flattered," Kerry whispered.

Dar fell silent, then chuckled a little. "I do have a pronounced possessive streak," she admitted, shame-faced. "But be careful, all right? He's very sharp."

The blond woman leaned closer. "Not as sharp as you are," she murmured softly, "even though he thinks he is. What is his problem with you, anyway?"

Dar sighed. "We went to school together, and we were pretty good friends. We were both in the martial arts together, hung out with some of the same crowd. The trouble started when I beat him in the nationals that year."

"Ah." Kerry lifted a hand. "I get it…let me guess, he was god's gift to karate?"

"No," Dar replied, surprisingly. "He wasn't really that good, and maybe that was the problem. He never made it past the preliminary rounds, and I was the one that kicked him into the loser's bracket, purely by chance." She exhaled, remembering. "He felt I should have helped him get further because he was trying to impress this girl on the opposing team he'd been after for years; it was why he got involved in the stuff to begin with."

"That doesn't make sense; why would you have taken a dive for him?" Kerry inquired. "I can't see you doing that in any case."

Pale blue eyes winked at her from under long, dark lashes. "It was complicated; he thought I owed him the favor, but at any rate, I didn't, and he lost, and he dropped out of the karate program after that." She paused, ordering her thoughts. "He was majoring in systems design, and through a chance routine I was running, I discovered he'd stolen his entire senior's design matrix from someone else."

"Uh oh." Kerry winced.

"Yeah. Well, me being a moral and upright bastard in the old days, I had to go running to the department head with it, and he was tossed out of school," Dar sighed. "Our last meeting wasn't very pleasant; he told me he'd get back at me someday, and now here he is trying."

"Jesus, he should get a life. What was that, ten years ago? What a waste of time." Kerry folded her arms across her chest. "He gives me the creeps."

"Mm." Dar agreed. "Well, we have to deal with him. If he keeps pushing you, you can tell him you're not interested or that you're involved with someone."

"Both of which are completely true," Kerry agreed. "Your sandwich is getting cold." She gave her boss a not so subtle nudge.

The dark-haired woman smiled and opened the bag, tugging out the sandwich and munching on a fry. "Mm…bet Maria made a face at you for this." She bit into the gooey sandwich happily. "She usually brings me chicken salad on pita."

Kerry watched her indulgently for a minute, then stood up. "Yes, she did, but not nearly as nasty a face as when old Stevie Snake was flirting with me." She touched Dar's shoulder. "I think she has a protective streak, too."

"Mm hmm," Dar nodded, with her mouth full. "She thinks you're a manifestation of the Blessed Virgin for getting me to eat trail mix instead of malted milk balls."

Kerry snorted softly. "That didn't take much effort at all. C'mon, anyone could have done it."

Dar studied her sandwich for a moment, before taking a bite of it. "No one else ever tried," she remarked casually as she chewed the mouthful, enjoying the gentle tang of the raisins in the bread. "Even my mother gave up on me."

"Well." Kerry reached over and gently pushed an errant lock out of Dar's eyes. "I'm pretty stubborn." She smiled. "Not to mention a little on the possessive side myself," she confessed. "Was your mother into greens?"

"Vegetarian," Dar confirmed, wiping her mouth. "She tried, but my father told me even as a baby I used to chuck up the strained peas and go after his hamburger. Must have driven her nuts." She finished off her fries and neatly disposed of the bag. "Thank you. Now I have just enough time to review this damn status report before the executive committee meeting, and I'm stuck with a new client briefing at four; I won't get out of here before seven."

Kerry nodded. "I'm meeting a few folks over at the gym for a climbing session at six; will you be over for our class?"

"Oh yeah," Dar responded positively. "I'll be ready for that. It's been a long, aggravating day, and it's only lunchtime."

"Yikes." Kerry's hands had found their way across her boss's neck, feeling the tension in her shoulders. She stood up and went behind the chair, reaching over and giving her a gentle massage, enjoying the warm feel of Dar's skin under the cool silk of her blouse. "You're all wound up, huh?"

"Mm." Dar closed her eyes and dropped her head forward, submitting to her companion's touch gratefully. "Yeah. Ow…oh…damn, that feels good." It was such a nice feeling, she reflected. Not just the massage, which was relaxing her, but the warmth and caring she could practically feel emanating from Kerry. She finally leaned back and looked up at her. "Thanks."

Kerry smiled back. "You're welcome. I'd better get going. Did you actually have stuff to give me, or was that just a reason for me not to leave?"

A soft chuckle. "I'm not that bad. Here." Dar handed her the three folders. "Three new ones, and in case I didn't say it before, the two you structured last week were very well done." She meant it, too; the business plans had been very well thought out, and the start-up schedules were efficient. "I got a note from Eleanor regarding the New England Power meeting. She was very impressed with how you handled it."

Kerry positively beamed. A big, sunny grin covered her face and her eyes sparkled as she drank in the compliments. "Wow, thanks." Somehow, when Dar discussed business with her, she managed to forget their relationship and simply react as anyone else would in getting praised by their boss. It was a weird sensation, almost like she and Dar were two different people, the ones who worked together, and the ones who lived together. "Glad I did good."

Dar's phone buzzed. "Dar?" Maria sounded resigned.

"Yes?" The executive answered, leaning on an elbow.

"Personnel, line numero uno."

"I bet I know what this is." Dar sighed. "Thanks." She hit the button. "Dar Roberts."

"You are such the troublemaker, you know that?" Mariana's voice sounded halfway between irritation and wry amusement. "Are you trying to set some record for complaints against one employee?"

Dar lifted her hands and let them fall on the desk. "What did I do?"

"Oh, let's see…" A rustle of paper. "Being rude, obstructionist, uncooperative, detrimental to the progress of business…"

"She really wasn't, Mari." Kerry spoke over her boss's shoulder. "I was here. She was really polite, as a matter of fact."

Mariana sighed. "What did he want?"

"Me," Kerry replied. "He wanted me and another staff member assigned to him personally for two months, while he, as he put it, 'straightened us out.'"

A soft curse in a fluid language followed. "And you told him no, I take it?"

"I told him I had neither the time nor the staff to go on wild goose chases and that if he wanted dogsbodies to hunt stuff down to go see you," Dar replied. "I'm not assigning one of my staff, not even mentioning my very valuable and very efficient assistant, to that horse's ass."

"Mm, I see," the Personnel VP sighed. "Well, he kicked a copy of this up to Alastair, along with a bunch of statistics. It looks pretty nasty, Dar. I'll forward you a copy."

Dar drummed her fingers on her desk. "Did he copy José?"

A moment's silence. "Um…now that you mention it, no," Mariana replied, puzzled.

Dar smiled. "Okay, thanks. I'll handle Alastair if he decides to get involved." She pulled a folder over to her. "Meet you in the conference room?"

"You got it," Mariana agreed, and hung up.

"What does he hope to accomplish, Dar?" Kerry asked.

"Bottom line?" Dar rubbed a hand over her face. "He wants José's job and my head. If he can prove we lost money because of something I did, he's got a good chance of both."

Kerry blinked. "But how can he prove that? You know nothing like that happened."

"No one's perfect, Kerry. It's possible he could dig up something where we could have done our jobs better and we lost out because of it. We've got so many things going on at once, and so much of it involves making decisions based on the best information available at the time…it can happen." She settled her hands on her knee. "But I've got a pretty good batting average; he'd have to find something really major, and I'm not really worried about that."

"So what are you really worried about?" Kerry prodded gently. "Is it because he's made it so personal?"

Dar thought about that. "Maybe," she acknowledged. "Or maybe it's because he's sniffing after you." She let rueful grin cross her face. "And if he does find out about us, he will most certainly make an issue of it."

"Mmph." Kerry rolled her head to one side, smiling gently. "Well, we just have to make sure that doesn't happen…right?"

"Yeah," Dar said glumly. Hiding their relationship was difficult enough without this additional threat. But she had to protect Kerry.

"He sounds like he really means to make a case out of this, Dar," Kerry stated quietly, her brow creasing in concern. "Would it be easier if we just went along with it? I mean, it's not like he's going to actually find anything if he investigates our area."

The pale blue eyes thoughtfully roamed the room, settling on Kerry's face with quiet intensity. "Yes, it would be easier," she stated flatly, "but I'm not gonna do it." The ferocity in her voice surprised Kerry. "He wants a fight? He'll get one."

"So how'd a sharp girl like you end up in a rat's nest like this?"

The smile was meant to make her understand it was all in good fun. Kerry reflected, taking a thoughtful sip of her peach iced tea. "I submitted a resume, and it was accepted," she replied dryly, "and I happen to like it very much." It had been a slow morning, unfortunately, and no crises had developed that might have excused her lunch invitation from Steve Fabricini, although Dar had volunteered to create one if she really didn't want to go. "You do, huh?" Steve chuckled, scooping up a spoonful of yogurt. "That's hard to believe, considering who you work for."

Kerry shrugged. "You know, people say that a lot, but I've really enjoyed working for Dar. She's smart, she knows her stuff, she gives credit where credit's due, and she stands up for her staff," she said honestly. "If you know what you're doing, you have no problem with her." Just like Mark Polenti had told her at their first meeting. "Of course, if you don't…" She let the thought hang.

He laughed. "You poor little thing; wait until you get thrown to the fire as a sacrifice the first time she has to take the blame for something. You can't really be that naïve, can you?" He leaned forward. "Listen, cupcake, I know her, all right? You don't. She will turn on you like a rabid dog at the first opportunity."

"Really." The blond woman nibbled on her sandwich. "Well, thanks for the warning."

"Anytime." Fabricini smiled, then lowered his voice. "Listen, there's no reason we can't work together, all right? My job here is to try and punch through these roadblocks we seem to be coming up against, and if I do it, the whole company benefits. Don't get caught on the wrong side of that, hmm?" He put a hand on her wrist. "You're a sharp kid, everyone says so, and when this all shakes out, there could be opportunity for you, if you know what I mean."

Kerry smiled kindly at him. "You mean, if you dig up enough things to force Dar out, I might get her job."

He smiled back. "I said you were sharp." A dangerous glint entered his eyes. "Stick with me, cupcake."

The blond woman wiped her lips with her napkin, and set it down neatly on her plate. "There's just a few things I'd like to get squared away first."

"What's that?" He smiled, a triumphant look on his face.

"One, you need to let go of my wrist before I sink my fork into the back of your hand," Kerry responded mildly. "Two, if you call me cupcake again, I'm going to be forced to file sexual harassment papers." She smiled right into his eyes, enjoying the shock. "And three, where Dar goes, I go." She stood and picked up her tray as he let go of her. "Have a nice day."

She left him sitting there as she counted to twenty under her breath, waiting for her heart to stop hammering in her ears. "Stupid goddamned piece of—oh. Sorry." She'd collided with Mark Polenti, who glanced behind her.

"You okay?" he asked, having heard her growling. "Hey, what did you do to puss face over there? He looks like he's been hit in the head with an obsolete mainframe."

Kerry took several calming breaths. "He is such a pig." She put her tray down in the washing area. "He wanted me to work with him to find dirt on Dar, and then had the balls to say if I did, he'd see if he could get me her job when it was all over."

Mark burst into laughter. "Boy, did he ever get his lines crossed." He patted Kerry's shoulder. "Guess he picked on you because you're the newest, figured the rest of us had our loyalties set by now." He put his own tray down. "So what'd you tell him?"

"To kiss my ass," Kerry replied, with a hint of a blush. "Only more politely."

They both watched as their subject sauntered up, his neck still red from anger, and deposited his tray. "My mistake." He oozed savage politeness to Kerry. "Your loss." He left, giving them a disgusted look.

Mark and Kerry eyed each other. "Asshole," they said in sync. Kerry sighed. "Well, at least I won't have to worry about him asking me out on a date now," she remarked wryly.

"Yeah, but he could get nasty that way," Mark replied, snagging two large chocolate chip cookies and offering her one. "You know how rumors are."

"Been there, done that." Kerry bit into her cookie. "I think everyone's over that one already." Meaning the whispers about her and Dar, which had subsided dramatically since the new year had started. They'd been careful not to hang around each other at work, going to far as to not even have lunch together, and it seemed to have cooled the rumor mill to the point where everyone had gone on to something more interesting.

"Yeah, but be careful," the MIS chief warned as they headed for the elevator.

Kerry sighed and punched the button for the fifteenth floor, then held the door as she heard footsteps approach. She couldn't see outside from where she was, but somehow… A smile was already pulling at her lips as Dar stepped inside, moving to the rear of the car and leaning against it. "Speak of the devil," Kerry commented, as the doors slid shut. "I just pretty much blew up my lunch meeting."

"Oh really?" Dar leaned against the elevator wall. "Great; I've got a meeting scheduled with him, José, and Mariana in twenty minutes. What happened?"

"He asked me to help him screw you and I told him to go to hell," Kerry replied.

Dar rubbed her temples. "It might have been better if you'd agreed."

Kerry and Mark both stared at her. "What?" they asked simultaneously.

The doors opened onto the fifteenth floor. "Then he'd have told you what his plan was." Dar exited, blowing the hair out of her eyes with an impatient breath. Mark made a quick getaway towards his lair with a significant backwards glance at Kerry.

Dar headed into her office with Kerry following her and waved at Maria as she continued through the inner door. Kerry waited until she was seated behind her desk before coming closer, sitting in the left hand side visitor's chair. "Are you serious?"

Dar propped her head up on one fist, visibly frazzled. "No, that was just my frustration talking," she admitted. "I'm not looking forward to dealing with him, and I wish I had a way to avoid it."

"Mm." Kerry grimaced. "Sorry, I think I just made it worse." She gave Dar an apologetic look. "Maybe I should go stick my head in my monitor and do something useful."

"Ah ah." Dar shook a finger at her. "Don't start with that stuff. He's the asshole, Kerry, not you."

A faint smile. "Whatever you say, boss." Kerry stood and sighed. "Good luck," she called back as she left.

Dar watched the empty space in front of her for a minute, then rubbed her eyes and took a sip of the cold coffee from her mug, her mind already turning toward the meeting ahead.

It was dark out before she got back to her desk and slumped into her chair. She pulled a vial from her top drawer and tipped out several pills, which she tossed into her mouth and washed down with a little soda from the can she'd carried in with her.

She gave her trackball a spin, bringing up her e-mail. Her inbox was a solid black mass of new messages, and just looking at the number of 'urgent' flags made her already aching head pound even worse. "Shit."

A soft knock came on the inner door, and she looked up in surprise. "Yeah?"

It opened, and Kerry entered, her silk shirt sleeves pushed all the way up and her jacket off. "Hey."

Dar smiled for the first time in hours. "Hi…thought you'd have gone home by now."

Kerry shook her head, walking over and perching on the edge of Dar's desk. "I've got a major restructuring of that new account I'm working on, and we lost two processors in Kansas, so…"

"Ah."

"And I was waiting for you," Kerry admitted with a tiny smile. "I heard you walked out of the meeting with Mari." She sighed heavily. "I had a visit from our friend Steve, saying he wanted to start over and really get a working relationship going with me."

"Ugh." Dar put her head back and closed her eyes. "Yes, I walked out. I told them both to grow up and start acting like corporate executives instead of kindergarteners." She opened a blue eye and regarded Kerry wryly. "Then I had to go to a marketing projection session with Eleanor and explain to her why spending money on television advertising doesn't do a thing for an international IS company."

The phone buzzed, and Dar put a finger to her lips before she answered it on speakerphone. "Yeah?"

"Well, good evening to you, too, Dar." Alastair's voice sounded less chipper than usual. "Thought I'd still find you there. Got a minute?"

Dar exhaled, and let the tip of her tongue protrude for a second. "Sure, Alastair, what's on your mind?" she asked the CEO.

"Well, I had a meeting with the sales leadership today." Alastair paused. "They're projecting a slowdown in the next two quarters, and frankly, that's not going to wash with the board."

"And?" Dar rubbed her temples.

"I asked them for an explanation and I was told they can't project any better because you're deliberately putting a hold on them…now," Alastair held up a verbal finger to forestall her objections. "I realize that's probably mostly bullshit, but what's the deal, Dar?"

Dar lifted her hands, and let them fall on the chair arms. "Alastair, the problem is they can't substantiate enough new accounts for me to increase infrastructure, period." A pause. "They're projecting twenty new accounts a quarter, they want me to provision for fifty, and I'm not gonna do it! I am not going to sit there at the end of the year and explain to you why Ops is over budget three hundred percent while they're sitting over there, fat and happy with what sales they did make."

Alastair sighed. "This is one of those cart and horse things."

"I can't help that," Dar replied. "Hell, if it were up to me, I'd rebuild the entire goddamned network from start to finish and give them a thousand times more bandwidth, but the executive committee won't give me the discretionary funds to even back up the frigging NetOps positions we do have."

"Hmm."

"They're full of shit."

"Dar, you have to stop repressing this stuff. Let me hear how you really feel," Alastair remarked dryly. "I get the picture. Now, second subject." He cleared his throat. "Rumor has it you've gotten involved with someone."

Kerry's eyebrows lifted in silent astonishment.

"Did that make it on the board agenda?" Dar answered acidly. "Whose damn business is it?"

"Ah—so it's true then?"

Dar weighted her options quickly. "Yes," she replied. "Got a problem with that?"

"Not unless you do," Alastair replied soothingly. "Relax, Dar; there was just a comment made that you weren't around the office as much, and Beatrice said the scuttlebutt was you'd started seeing someone."

Dar couldn't deny it, and she didn't see any point in trying. "Yeah, I got a life. You holding that against me?" But she consciously softened her voice a little.

"Nah. I never have before, have I?"

"No."

"Hope you have better luck this time. I'm glad for you, but be careful, willya, Dar?"

Dar steepled her fingers, the lamplight casting most of her face in shadow. "I will. Thanks, Alastair."

"Well, I'll see what I can do with those sales projections. We might have to compromise a little, though, Dar; can you get three, four percent more out of Infrastructure if I need it?"

"Oh, so you get to be the hero, huh?" Dar remarked. "Everyone's screaming, and Alastair the Brave uses his legendary negotiating skills to coax more lines out of that bastard Roberts in Ops."

Alastair cleared his throat. "That's not…"

Dar chuckled. "Yeah, if it's that desperate, I'll get you what you need, Alastair; just don't make it too easy, okay?"

A sigh. "Thanks, Dar. Have a good night, willya? Go home."

"'Night, Alastair." Dar hung up the phone and leaned back, meeting Kerry's eyes. "Good old Beatrice."

The blond woman got off the desk and knelt at her side, resting a hand on her knee for balance. "Are we in trouble? Good grief, Dar, just because you've been leaving work a little early people start rumors?"

"A little?" Dar smiled wearily. "Kerrison, before you and I met, ten p.m. was an early night for me." She chuckled at Kerry's shocked expression. "I'm not surprised someone noticed; don't worry about it." She patted Kerry's shoulder. "Besides, I got myself an assistant, remember? So I wouldn't have to work that hard anymore."

Kerry reached out and clasped her hand. "In that case, can I take you out to dinner? I hear a little Thai place calling our names." She kissed the fingers tangled with hers lightly. "I'll drive."

Dar got up and flipped off her screen without a second thought. "Lead on."

Chapter 6

Mariana was waiting in front of Dar's office door the next morning. "Uh oh," the executive murmured to herself. "That doesn't look good."

"Dar, I need to talk to you," Mari said as she approached. "You're not going to believe what they just dumped on us."

"Oh, I'll believe anything…once." Dar gestured towards the door. "C'mon." She led the way into her office. "Maria, book me for 1 p.m. at a meeting, and cancel the briefing conference call, please."

"Sí." Her secretary looked up from the phone. "Dar, your little puppy called."

"Thanks," Dar said absently before stopping short, causing Mariana to crash into her. "Wait a minute, what?" She turned. "Sorry." She poked her head back out. "Maria, who did you say called?"

The older woman smiled. "Sí, the puppy. I got a call, I picked up, is nothing. I said, 'hello, hello,' and then, 'buenos dias,' but nothing. I almost hang up, and I hear…" She made little whining noises. "I check caller ID, is your house."

Dar blinked, ignoring the muffled laugh from behind her. "She must have gotten out and knocked the phone off the hook in the living room. Do me a favor, call resident services out there and have them go check, will you?" She shook her head and ducked back in the office. "Great… my luck, she went and called Singapore while she was at it," she muttered as she closed the door. "All right, what's up?"

Mariana threw a packet on her desk for an answer. "Before you start screaming, I've already been on the phone with Alastair, twice, and he's not backing down."

Dar circled her desk and sat down, picking up the packet. Her eyes scanned it, and she looked up. "You're joking."

A shake of Mariana's head. "Nope. It's an executive retreat, with a program specifically for 'team building.' They have a reservation for twelve of us starting Friday afternoon. They're sending a bus to pick us up." She crossed her arms. "Alastair says they've been using a very similar program out in Texas for three months and it's worked great for them."

Dar covered her eyes. "Let me see if I understand this," she said incredulously. "He wants to send us all on a bus out into the wilderness to climb over rocks and trees and live in a cabin, and that's going to help us get along?"

"That's essentially it, yes." Mari nodded. "For the record, I've read up on this stuff, since I was trying to find some kind of help here, and it's got it's merits, Dar, but it depends on the participants."

"In our case, it depends on the participants not KILLING EACH OTHER," the dark-haired woman ending up yelling, her voice bouncing off the walls. "Is he NUTS?" She punched the phone. "Beatrice, is he there?" Then she drummed her fingers until the line opened.

"Now Dar, before you say anything, let me get my spiel in." Alastair's voice was cheerful, as usual. "Okay?"

Dar folded her hands on her desk. "Okay," she responded quietly.

"I got that e-mail yesterday, and to be honest, it concerned me," the CEO stated. "Not because I thought it was true, although you can be a stubborn obstructionist when you need to be, Dar, but it's always been in our best interests when you have."

"Uh huh," Dar grunted.

"I see it as an overall problem company-wide, and that's why we've been using these seminars. They're wonderful! You'll love it. Listen, it's just a weekend out in the middle of nowhere, no cell phones, no computers, the food's pretty good, and we found the damn things really do work, to help people get to know each other better."

"Uh huh."

"So, I'm sure if this new guy, and you, get to know each other, things will smooth out, and besides, the rest of the group needs a little team building. I've been getting a bunch of grumpies from that office lately."

"Alastair?"

"Yes? You can go off on me now, Dar."

"The problem with me and Steve Fabricini is that we do know each other—I got him thrown out of school for plagiarism ten years ago and he's kept a grudge." Dar paused. "You think sending us both out into the woods is a good idea?"

Long pause. "Ah." Alastair muttered. "I see…wish I'd known that."

"Can we cancel this now?" Dar asked, hopefully.

"Well, see, it's prepaid, and we've already transmitted the payment," the CEO sighed. "And if we cancel, we lose all that money…" He thought. "Let's do it anyway, Dar, and I'm counting on you to set an example and bring everyone back with at least a little more team spirit."

Dar sighed. "Alastair, I really don't have time for this, and you're tossing my top ops staff out incommunicado. What if something goes wrong over the weekend?" Her last trump card.

Alastair chuckled. "Dar, we both know you pick the kind of people who won't screw you over in a pinch; your staff can cover things. Go on, have a good time and loosen up a little. I went on one of these things and I had the time of my life, trust me." He heard the repeated sigh on the other end. "You're mad at me, huh?"

"If I thought this was going to do a damn bit of good, I wouldn't be," Dar snapped back.

"Ah ah, keep an open mind, Dar, you never know what can happen. You all could come back the best of friends," Alastair chuckled. "And, by the way, I just processed your year-end bonus. I know I forgot to send you a birthday card, but see if that's an acceptable substitute."

"Alastair…"

"Gotta go, the chairman of IBM is here; we're going to swap lies and exaggerations over rubber chicken," Alastair told her. "Just do it, Dar. When you get back, if it was that awful, I'll make it up to you."

"How?" Dar inquired sourly.

A slight pause. "We'll talk about resolving the issues in a more direct way."

Dar's dark eyebrows lifted. "All right," she agreed quietly. "That's worth a weekend."

Alastair chuckled. "That's my Dar...try to have a good time, huh?" He hung up.

Mari shifted in her chair, and shook her head. "You have such an interesting relationship with him," she sighed. "You're one of the few people I can say for sure he really, really likes."

"Well, I tried." Dar gave her a pointed look. "This is going to be a nightmare, Mariana."

"I know," the personnel VP agreed. "You and me, Duks, Kerry, José, Steve, Mark, his second, Eleanor, Duks, and El's assistant, and my assistant, Mary Lou." She paused. "You know what your biggest problem is going to be, don't you?"

"Besides not killing Steve?" Dar played with a pencil. "Yeah. I do."

"You two have such a cute little chemistry when you're around each other," Mari told her impishly. "That's going to be tough to hide out there in the wilderness with nothing to do but talk to each other and roast marshmallows." She stood up. "Thanks for trying, my friend; it was a good fight, and you'd have had him if we hadn't already coughed up the bucks."

"Yeah." Dar leaned back, exhaling. "I should have just offered him my bonus back to cover it," she told her friend wryly. "It would be worth the money."

Mari chuckled as she turned to leave. "It's just two days, Dar. We'll be back in Miami on Sunday afternoon. I'm sure we'll survive."

Dar regarded her back as she left then threw her pencil down on the desk, leaning forward and studying the packet in consternation. A light tap on the inside door, however, put a tiny smile on her face. "C'mon in."

Kerry poked her head in, then entered. "Hey."

"Hey." Dar leaned back in her chair and folded her hands across her stomach.

"Are we in trouble?" the blond woman inquired curiously.

"We may be." Dar pushed the packet over to her. "Cancel your plans for the weekend." Actually, they hadn't had any concrete ones, just a vague plan that included diving, a trip to Bayside, and spending some quality time with Cappuccino.

Kerry took the packet and sat down in one of Dar's visitor chairs, studying it with interest. "Oh, I've heard of these." She glanced up with a smile. "This sounds interesting...it's upstate from here, isn't it?"

"Mm hmm," Dar acknowledged.

A shrug. "Sounds like it might even be fun, Dar. I mean, there are cabins, it's not like you're out foraging for bugs and rainwater or something."

Dar chuckled. "If it were just you and me, or just you, me, Duks and Mariana, and even throw Mark in there, I'd agree with you, but we're going to have Steve, José, Eleanor, and a couple other people with us."

"So?" Kerry peered at the agenda. "Oh, that's cool, they have obstacle courses, and you have to help each other through them." She looked up. "Who knows? Maybe it'll help, Dar."

The dark-haired woman gazed at her. "So you don't mind spending an entire weekend pretending not to know me?" she inquired mildly. "Other than as your boss?"

Kerry blinked. "Oh." She bit her lip. "Right. Hmm. You couldn't get us out of this?"

"I tried." Dar lifted her hands and let them fall. "Alastair had already paid for the damn thing; we're kind of stuck."

They looked at each other. "Ew," Kerry finally sighed. "Well, I'm sure we can do this; I mean, we manage pretty well during working hours anyway." She stood up and put the packet back down on Dar's desk, then circled around and perched on the edge next to Dar.

"We do huh?" The executive's lips twitched. "Well, I have to say you're the first assistant I've ever had who's made a habit of camping on my desk." She tweaked the edge of Kerry's skirt. "Most of them wouldn't get within ten feet of me."

Kerry's eyebrows lifted. "Their loss," she replied in a sultry tone, which brought a genuine smile to her boss's face. Reflexively, she reached out and touched Dar's cheek, letting her thumb trace the smile. "Two days, huh? This is going to be a bitch on wheels, Dar."

The smile widened, and the dark-haired woman curled a hand around Kerry's knee and gave it a gentle squeeze. "We'll survive." She glanced at her watch. "Let's go to the damn meeting. I want to see Stevie baby's face when he sees what his e-mail kicked off. What did he want from you, by the way?"

"Oh." Kerry stood, and backed to get out of Dar's way so she could stand up. "He wanted me to sell you out for the possibility of getting your job."

Dar paused in the middle of standing, then she slowly straightened and ran a hand through her hair. "Funny," she commented briefly. "That's the deal Elana took."

Kerry snorted at the mention of Dar's ex, whom they'd bumped into recently at a restaurant, where a snarky Elana had lost a very short food fight to a very protective Kerry. "I knew she was an idiot when I saw her. Trade you for this job? Give me a break!" She bumped Dar lightly. "Not for any job on earth…or anything else on earth for that matter, or anything on Mars, Jupiter, the moon…" Her litany was abruptly cut off by a pair of warm lips and a fierce hug. "Mm," Kerry murmured when they parted. "I'm not sure, but I think that might clue them in to our relationship, Dar." She leaned back in and ran her hands over the cool fabric of her lover's shirt and kissed her again.

"Yes it would, but thank you." The dark-haired woman caressed her cheek and pressed her lips against Kerry's forehead before she released her. "C'mon, we're going to be late."

🐄🐄   🐄🐄   🐄🐄

They could hear the yelling halfway down the corridor. "Oh, this sounds pleasant," Dar muttered, glancing at her companion, who pursed her lips in agreement and pulled the door to the conference room open and motioned Dar to precede her.

The loud voices ceased as her six-foot-plus frame cleared the door, and all eyes turned her way. Dar was aware of Kerry entering behind her, but she kept her attention on the group around the table and paused, putting her hands on her hips.

The silence went on for a long moment, then Dar lifted one elegant eyebrow. "Is there a problem?" she snapped, putting aggravation into her voice. "Or are you people just yelling at each other out of boredom?"

José stood up, or to be more accurate, stood further up, since he was already kneeling on one knee on his chair. He waved a familiar packet at her. "Have you seen this shit?" He slapped it on the table. "What is this crap?"

Dar's eyes went to Mariana, who was leaning with her fingertips on the table. "I take it you've filled everyone in?" She waited for the Personnel VP to nod.

"She certainly did." Eleanor tapped her pen on the table. "Good grief, Dar, surely they can't expect us to just pick up and go; we all have lives!" A sweet smile at the Operations VP. "At least most of us do, at any rate."

"Yeah, I'm not going along with this," Steve interjected. "It's senseless."

Dar sauntered around to the head of the table, which they'd left conspicuously empty, and leaned on the back of the chair there. "It's paid for. We're going," she stated bluntly. "It wasn't my idea, but Houston's insistent, and that's all there is to it."

A chorus of voices thundered at her. Dar put up with it for a moment before she straightened and sucked in a breath. "SHUT THE HELL UP!" she thundered, making the glasses on the sideboard rattle. Kerry's eyes widened and she slumped down in her chair a little in pure reaction as a conspicuous silence dropped over the room. Dar let that go on a minute before pointing at Steve. "Next time, be careful what you ask for." She pitched her voice low, and her eyes swept over Eleanor and José. "You people had to start this, now Houston's answered, and by god you're going to go to this stupid thing and not say another word about it, or I'm gonna take the charge for the course out of your goddamn paychecks!" Each word had gotten louder and more penetrating, until the last word barked out, making the glasses rattle again. "Understood?"

Silence.

"I'll, um, bring a deck of cards." Mark offered, hesitantly.

Steve snorted, and leaned back. "I'm not going," he stated, staring insolently at Dar.

"Jes, you are." José turned on him. "If I gotta do this, you gotta do this." The Sales VP gave the room a disgusted look. "Lemme go call my wife."

Mariana passed a packet out to each person. "There are instructions in here on what to bring and what not to bring. No electronics, no cell phones, that kind of thing. Four changes of comfortable clothing, sundries, and any prescription drugs you need. "

"Does that include tranquilizers?" Eleanor muttered, glancing at the glowering Dar. "I'll bring some extra."

Duks had been fiddling with the packet, reviewing it. He glanced at his assistant, a young, heavyset woman with short blond hair and thick glasses. "Sandy, you all right with this?"

She pushed her glasses up her nose. "Yes, I'll get mother to watch my cats; it'll be different, at least." She glanced sideways at Kerry. "Have you been on one of these before?"

"No." Kerry had been keeping an eye on her boss, who still had distinct waves of anger pouring from her. "I never have, but I'm sure it'll be a learning experience, if nothing else." She glanced at Steve, whose face had settled into a grim mask and whose eyes were fastened on Dar.

Duks rubbed his jaw as his glance followed Kerry's. "Oh yeah." He nodded solemnly. "We are going to learn something; of that, I'm certain."

🐾   🐾   🐾

Kerry debated between two different shirts, then finally chose one and stuffed it in her overnight bag, which hadn't gotten much use since she'd moved in with Dar. Her lover had taken Chino in the cart and was scooting off across the island to the small Italian café in the center to pick up two orders of pasta for dinner. She had protested that she could just make some, but Dar had told her they'd both might as well relax as much as possible, since it was even money the next couple of days were going to be just a bitch.

Despite her usual optimism, Kerry had to reluctantly agree about that, and besides, she had a craving for the trattoria's fettuccini alfredo, which was really tough to make from scratch.

She finished packing her bag, zipping it up and trotting down the stairs, stopping to review the chewed boot that Chino had gotten to after the clever little puppy had escaped from her utility room dwelling. "Ooo, you're a lucky little girl, Chino; this is an old one," she chuckled, turning it over and running a finger over the shredded heel. The puppy had pulled it out of Dar's closet after turning over the wastepaper basket and knocking the phone off the hook. A visit by the puppy sitter had returned her to her room, but now they had to figure out how she got out in the first place.

The back door opened as she passed through the kitchen, and Dar walked in carrying the puppy under one arm and a large, aromatic bag under the other.

"Mm…that smells good," Kerry smiled, taking the bag from her. "I can just imagine what we're going to get at the retreat; what do you think, beanie weenies?"

Dar sighed, and put Chino down. The puppy immediately went to her bowl and started to lap water. "Probably; from what the packet said, it's very 'rustic'—which usually means burgers and dogs…guess it could be worse."

"Oh yeah. They could have picked one that only served raw vegetables; they have those, you know. It combines a health food seminar with a corporate twist."

A low snort. "I'd have flown to Houston and beaten Alastair with a bag of celery until he screamed if he'd done that to me," the dark-haired woman muttered. "It's going to be bad enough as it is." She tugged the two containers out of the bag and pulled out a long, fragrant loaf of garlic bread stuffed with cheese. "You all packed?"

"Mm hmm." Kerry retrieved some silverware and a pair of napkins and tugged Dar towards the living room. "C'mon, Dar, it's not going to be that bad. I bet everyone gets so involved in either what we're doing or in how uncomfortable they are that they'll forget how much we all don't like each other." She opened her container of pasta and breathed in the rich scent.

"Maybe." Dar sighed, prodding at her own dinner, a large pile of angel hair bolognese. She split the garlic bread in half and gave Kerry her portion.

The blond woman tore off a chunk and dipped it in the alfredo sauce. "I mean, we are all adults, after all, and professionals, for goodness sake; surely we can get along for two days."

Dar chuckled. "You may be right, my friend, and I hope you are, or it's going to be a damned unpleasant weekend." She swallowed a mouthful. "Did you read all the way through that packet? They observe us, and a status report gets sent back to Houston." She gave Kerry a wry look as the blond woman flipped through the channels and settled on the History Channel. "That should kick start some cooperation; no one wants Alastair to know they acted like a cranky little baby."

Kerry licked her fingers. "Do you think he's really concerned about our office?" she asked. "You don't think he's buying into Steve's accusations, do you?"

Dar shrugged, as she plowed through a mouthful of her dinner. "Hard to say," she answered, after she swallowed. "How's your pasta?"

Kerry leaned over and kissed her gently. "Taste for yourself," she teased, then offered Dar a forkful.

"Uh uh." Dar evaded the fork and went for the source, running her tongue over Kerry's lips before she returned the kiss, putting her almost finished container down on the coffee table and freeing up her hands to stroke the blond woman's face, then travel down her shoulders. "Oh yeah…I like that," she breathed.

"Me too." Kerry put her own dish down, and turned her attention fully to her companion's body, which her hands were itching to feel. She loved the silky texture of Dar's skin, and her fingers slid beneath the cotton t-shirt eagerly as they spent a leisurely few minutes exploring each other. She nuzzled Dar's neck and tucked a playful touch under the waistband of her jeans, feeling the muscles contract, giving her easy passage. "Wanna give 'In Search of Ancient Mysteries' a miss?" she inquired softly.

"This qualifies, doesn't it?" Dar replied with a chuckle as she teased a shirt button loose.

"Who you calling ancient?" Kerry bit down on a tasty earlobe, feeling the laugh travel through Dar's body. "Hmm?" She tickled Dar's belly button, an area she'd discovered was very sensitive. "C'mon, I hear a nice, warm waterbed whispering my name." She nipped the soft skin on Dar's neck, then glanced up. "Hey!"

Dar reacted, her body shifting as she straightened up. "What in…oh." A soft laugh. "Chino, what do you think you're doing?"

The puppy was busted, tiny paws propped up on the low table, face covered in bolognese sauce, wide brown eyes fastened on them in a big canine "uh oh." A thin strand of spaghetti drooped from her mouth, and the pink tongue licked at it.

"Bad puppy!" Kerry scolded her sternly, getting a tail wag. "No, don't wag your little butt at me…bad girl!"

The small creamy ears drooped and she dropped off the table, sitting down and looking up at them through dark eyelashes. The effect was ruined by a satisfied lip lick, however. Both women laughed. "Oh, it's not funny," Dar sighed, "but I can't help it; look at that puss."

"Yeah, she's got a better pout than you do," Kerry replied with a faint giggle.

Both dark eyebrows lifted. "I most certainly do not have a pout," Dar stated sternly.

Kerry traced the warm coral lips with a delicate finger. "Yes, you do, when you want something you know is bad for you," she teased gently. "Like that cake I made for your birthday." The lips edged in a sheepish grin. "See?" She laughed. "I love that smile."

"Does that mean I get the cake?" Dar asked ingenuously. She reached down and tickled Chino's ears, and the puppy stumbled over, putting her paws up on the edge of the couch and licking Kerry's arm. "I bet you'd like some too, hmm?"

"No no no, no chocolate for her." Kerry rubbed the silky ears. "I'm glad Colleen agreed to come puppy sit. I'd feel really bad leaving her here with just the island people dropping in once in a while." She flicked a glance to Dar. "That is okay, right?"

"Mm hmm," Dar agreed. "That works. I was going to see if Clemente could have someone hang out in here, but Colleen's a better choice, even if she's not too sure about me." She tugged lightly on a lock of Kerry's hair.

Kerry sighed. "It's...she just worries about me, that's all. She thinks it's great we're together, but the work thing weirds her out," she admitted, slowly. "And it is sort of weird. I feel like I'm two different people sometimes."

"Yeah, me too," Dar agreed.

"And I feel so..." Kerry pushed a lock of Dar's hair back. "I get upset when you get so stressed, like when you were yelling at everyone at the meeting today, my guts hurt me," she admitted. "I got so mad at that creep today, I almost slapped him in the lunchroom, and it wasn't because I felt he was insulting my intelligence, it was just that he was doing something to get at you, and I just couldn't stand it."

Dar remained quiet, letting the puppy chew on her fingers while she considered Kerry's words. "Sorry," she finally muttered. "It's just the way I do things."

"I know." Kerry smiled a little. "It's just so..." She paused. "Your reputation is based on reality, and I forget that sometimes, because I know you mostly like this." She put a hand on Dar's cheek. "I forget most everyone else sees a different picture."

Dar exhaled. "You make me sound very schizophrenic." She made a face. "And unfortunately, you're going to have to live with Ms. Hyde this weekend. I'll apologize in advance."

Kerry laughed ruefully. "Probably better off that way or I'm liable to forget and start hugging you in front of everyone." She demonstrated, settling more comfortably as Dar returned the hug.

"How about we get rid of our plates and keep searching?" Dar rumbled, right into her ear, the warm breath sending a light, pleasant shiver down Kerry's back. "I don't want to think or talk about work any more tonight."

Kerry murmured agreement as she nipped her way along Dar's collarbone. She broke off reluctantly and turned to grab the containers, only to find a cream colored puppy with an Alfredo colored nose licking her chops. "Oh, poo, Dar, she's going to be sick to her stomach."

Dar lifted the pasta out of the puppy's reach and took it into the kitchen as Kerry slid up behind her, capturing her with a solid grip around her waist. "Whoa." The hands slipped up under her shirt and explored her skin, making her knees shiver and almost unlock, and she grabbed the counter momentarily for balance.

Then she turned and faced her relentless attacker, wrapping her fingers in Kerry's blond hair and ducking her head as the smaller woman pressed up against her, losing herself in the intense passion and letting the complications of her life drop away, fogging her awareness as her heart started pounding.

That must have been why she imagined she lifted Kerry up and carried her to the bedroom, because she knew she wasn't capable of doing that.

Right?

🐾　　🐾　　🐾

Kerry became aware of her surroundings when a sharp crack of thunder rattled the windows. She blinked her eyes open and glanced at the clock, realizing that though it was close to dawn, the weather was keeping it very dark outside.

Thunder rolled again, accompanied by several flashes of lightning. She peeked up to see the dim reflection of the clock's light against half open blue eyes. "Sounds nasty."

"Uh huh," Dar agreed.

"You're not considering going out and running in this, are you?"

"No," Dar snorted lightly, as she ran light fingertips across Kerry's bare ribs. "You think I'm nuts?"

"Just checking." Kerry nuzzled the soft breast she was resting on. "You've been very consistent lately."

Her lover snuggled closer, and made a soft noise deep in her throat. "Running's a good way to start the day out; kinda clears my head, gives me a little time to think." Thunder rumbled overhead. "However, this is perfect sleeping-in weather," she muttered.

Kerry eyed the rain lashing against the window, along with the almost constant flashes of lightning. "Yeah, it sure is." She slid a knee between Dar's thighs and went belly to belly with her, curling an arm around her back and exhaling contentedly. "Well, we have an hour or so before we have to get up, then."

"Mm hmm." Dar tugged the covers a little closer and let her eyes slide shut.

So of course the phone rang.

Dar cursed softly, and untangled one arm, reaching out and capturing the instrument. "Yeah?"

"Dar, it's Mark." The MIS chief sounded pissed.

"What's up?" Dar answered, stifling a yawn. "Meteor fall on Houston or something?"

"Worse—the overseas gateways are down. Exxon tanker dropped anchor in the wrong place going across the North Atlantic and snagged the cable. Took out three hundred pairs."

"Ugh." Dar winced. "Jesus, can we reroute?" She felt Kerry stir against her, and she stroked the woman's back lightly. "Oh shit—they've got a transatlantic sales meeting with four new British clients this morning!"

"I know," Mark replied, "that's why I'm calling. The shit's going to hit the fan in so many directions, we might as well set up a freaking stand and sell fertilizer." A soft sound of clicking keys came through the phone. "One of the pairs that was cut was the admin line; they can't tell who's up and who's down, and they can't reroute until they get some diagnostics over the cable…it could take hours, maybe all day."

"Can we buy transponder time and go via sat?" Kerry uttered, very softly.

Dar considered that for a minute.

"Did you say something, Dar?" Mark inquired. "Thought I heard something."

Tell him? What the hell, he knows she logs on from here all the time. "Kerry suggested a possibility: switch it to a sat conference and rent uplink time."

"Oh…tell her I said good morning." Mark's voice held a touch of triumphant amusement, despite the circumstances. "That's…well, they were going to do a multimedia real-time… I'm not sure the sat can handle that kind of bandwidth, but it's a thought. We'd have to reconfigure all the sets here, and there for the different network type. I'd have to put that on the fiber backbone."

"Is there any other possibility? Other than the reroute, which we have no reasonable ETA on?" Dar inquired.

"Not that I can see, boss; that's why I was calling you." Mark replied. "Got two for the price of one too; Kerry was next on my list of notifies."

"Please don't page me," Kerry mumbled. "I left it on vibrate, and it's on the dresser; it always scares the crap out of me when it goes off."

Dar muffled a laugh. "Okay, contact Intelsat, see if we can get one, no, get two transponders, and bring some of your people in early to go up and reconfigure the presentation system in the big conference room." She gave Kerry a hug. "Good work," she mouthed.

Kerry shrugged modestly. "I learned from the best," she mouthed back, resting her chin on Dar's breastbone with a contented sigh.

"Okay, will do." Mark replied, amid another clatter of keys and a rumble of thunder. "See ya in the office."

"I'll bring pastalitos," Dar promised, "and lots of Cuban coffee." She hung up and sighed as she regarded the dimly seen ceiling. "So much for sleeping in."

Kerry didn't let go of her. "Why? Is there anything you can do in the next hour there?" she asked reasonably. "It's going to take at least that long for Mark to get someone at Intelsat to answer him, considering they're in California and it's only quarter to six here." She started a slow, teasing rubbing up and down Dar's belly, running her fingers over the lightly rippled surface in little circles.

Dar hesitated, torn between a natural urge to pounce on the situation and her body's insidious desire to remain right where she was, in this nice, warm cuddle, where she could almost feel the affection surrounding her in the circle of Kerry's arms.

Shockingly, her body won out, and she capitulated, resettling her hold around her lover's body and exhaling softly. "You're right; no sense in going in there just to pace around the carpet." The gentle stroking was relaxing her and she felt her eyes flutter closed as she eased forward, finding Kerry's lips waiting for her.

They were both too sleepy to go too far, but they spent a very pleasant half an hour in nibbling and touching each other, until the reluctant gray light warned them of the growing dawn. Dar stretched and rolled out of bed, offering a hand down to her languidly watching lover. "I'm gonna go take a shower...the coffee should be ready."

"Y'know..." Kerry hopped out of the waterbed. "It would save time if we both showered at the same time."

Dar's dark brow lifted. "Oh it would, would it?" She laughed. "And save water, too…maybe," she agreed. "All right… let's go." She led the way into the bathroom, flipping on the light and ducking into the shower to start the water running.

"Mm." Kerry curled an arm around her, and nipped her waistline. "You know, Dar, I think the thought of not being able to touch you for two and a half days is making me… um…" She hesitated.

"Horny," Dar supplied, giving her a quick kiss. "That's all right." She smiled at the dull red flush that covered Kerry's neck and face. "C'mere." She drew the blond woman into the shower, and let the warm, pulsing water cascade over both of them. She squirted shower gel on a natural sponge and started scrubbing Kerry's body.

"Mmm." Kerry swayed a little, then captured her own bit of sponge and returned the service, rubbing the soft surface against Dar's tanned skin. She'd gotten halfway around her ribcage before she found herself sliding closer and replacing the sponge with her lips, unable to deny her body's cravings.

Dar responded, dropping soap-slick hands down over Kerry's hips, pulling her forward and into the intense flow from the shower head. She let herself forget the time as Kerry's hands slid up her thigh and they allowed a spiral of passion to take them over, building to a fiery intensity that left them both shaking as Dar leaned back against the water-warmed shower tile and managed to keep her legs from collapsing under her.

Kerry sucked in a breath that was half heated skin and half water, with the soft tang of their soap on the peripheries. "Oh…" She caught her breath, and bumped her head against Dar's arm. "Guess we're skipping breakfast this morning."

Dar chuckled, on an uneven breath. "Thought that was breakfast." They finished showering and got out, wrapping towels around each other and easing into the living room, where they could hear faint whines as Chino heard them moving. "Okay," Dar sighed, running her fingers through her damp hair. "Onward to Hell." She gave Kerry's blond head one last kiss. "Oh, Eleanor… you wish you had as much of a life as I do."

They both laughed.

Chapter 7

Kerry reached over and flicked her computer on as she sat down at her desk, glancing at her inbox and taking sip of fragrant, steaming coffee. She leaned back in her comfortable leather chair and smiled a little, resting her head against the soft surface as she waited for her computer to finish booting up. She was logging in when her phone rang. "Kerry Stuart."

"Hi, Kerry? It's John Brown in Charlotte." The man's voice sounded harried but friendly. He was a supervisor in the networking office, she recalled.

"Good morning, John, what can I do for you?" she answered cordially.

"Well, um, I got a request from your office, and I just wanted to check it out with someone; I don't want to do something then get my ass nailed, if you know what I mean. I tried Ms. Roberts's office first, but she's not there."

"She's just down the hall in MIS, but what's the problem?" Kerry inquired curiously. "What did we ask for?"

"It's the fractional T1 we use for the insurance division's data transfer; we got a request to turn their link off and reroute network traffic from your office to the London conference center," John replied. "They're gonna go bonkershits if we do that, so…"

Kerry's brow creased. "We asked for that? Wait, I mean, I know we've got a problem with the overseas links, but we found a way around that; who made the request?"

Ruffle of papers. "Someone named Fab…Fabarini or something," he muttered. "I didn't get the spelling; one of my guys took the call, and he gave it to me to check out." A pause. "You want me to go ahead?"

Kerry drummed her fingers on her desk. "No," she replied evenly. "In fact, don't do anything from this office unless you get it from Dar, Mark, or me."

A long pause. "Uh, okay," John replied, obviously confused. "I mean, usually I wouldn't question stuff like that; you guys ask for shuffling all the time, but this seemed a little drastic, you know?"

That stupid piece of… "Yes, I know, but, as a favor to me, just clear everything through Operations here first, okay?"

A shrug she could hear even through the phone. "Sure," John agreed amiably. "Better for me; that way I don't get my ass nailed from Insurance and Banking when they find out their pipe got taken down." He rattled a few keys. "Thanks, Kerry."

"No problem," the blond woman responded, and hung up. She stewed for a moment, then stood, about to head out the door to find Dar. The phone rang before she could move, however, and she punched the button again. "Kerry Stuart."

"This is José." The VP's voice sounded flustered. "We're having a meeting here, come down. I can't find Dar."

Green eyes regarded the phone warily. "Sure," Kerry replied. "Be right there." She circled her desk and strode out of her office, heading for the large conference room at the end of the hall. She opened the door, seeing a group of six or seven people inside, and walked on in.

"We were heading right for disaster!" Steve Fabricini was insisting, thumping a fist on the table. "Can you imagine the egg on our face?" He turned and saw Kerry approaching. "And you people didn't do a goddamned thing about it! This is disgraceful!" He threw his hands up.

"If I hadn't been here, I can only imagine what would have happened!" A pause. "Nice of you to show up, waltzing in here at nine o'clock."

Kerry paused and regarded him, then walked around to an empty chair and sat down, folding her hands on the table. "Mind starting at the beginning? I'm not sure what you're talking about."

José threw a pencil on the table. "We have a big goddamn conference with the overseas office in London and the lines are down."

Kerry nodded slowly. "The intercontinental trunks, yes. We were notified," she replied calmly, savoring what she knew was coming. "I was paged this morning." Well, not quite, but...

"And you did nothing," Steve fumed. "Well, I took care of it. I have the network office tying in some extra lines for us, so we'll be okay."

The blond woman cocked her head. "No, you don't," she replied calmly. "NetOps cleared it through us, and I told them not to do it."

"What?" José sat up. "Are you crazy, woman?"

"That's it! I knew it! You are trying to sabotage us," Fabricini accused smugly, leaning on his hands.

Kerry exhaled. "Those extra circuits belong to a live account, which you were going to take down without any prior notification, so yes, I told them not to do it." She stood and put her hands on her hips. "And it's not needed, because we already have an alternate link up."

Silence. "What?" José asked again, looking at Steve. "You said there was nothing." He looked back at Kerry. "No one was in your office—we called three times!"

The blond woman shrugged. "No one paged me," she replied simply, "or called my cell phone, or left me voice mail, or contacted Maria. Seems to me someone didn't try very hard to find out if we were doing something." She brushed a fleck of lint off her sleeve, then walked over to the presentation computer and accessed their intranetwork. A list of remote offices popped up, London conspicuously in the center. "There you go." She glanced up. "Is there anything else I can do? I've got a pretty big inbox to clear."

Steve wasn't finished. "Okay, so who did you steal lines from?" he asked sarcastically.

Kerry smiled at him, with no humor in her face. "No one. We bought sat time and used an uplink," she replied briefly. "And it was done before dawn, so I guess you can say I've been working for three hours longer than you have." She gave them all a look, then walked around the table and headed for the door.

"You should have let us know," José interrupted her. "You can't blame us for thinking we were high and dry, Ms. Stuart. I have a department and company to protect here."

Kerry turned at the door, and regarded him. "You're right," she told him, sincerely. "We should have paged you, but we were hoping to get the alternate route up before anyone even realized there was a problem. I apologize for that. I'll make sure you get notified the next time."

José fiddled with his tie. "Exactly, exactly, yes. Good." He nodded, then waved at his secretary. "Get this conference hooked up, will you?"

Kerry slipped out the door, glancing back briefly and seeing the hostile eyes watching her. She let the lock click behind her, leaning against the wall as she willed her body to stop shaking. She hated face-to-face conflict like that. All at once, her stomach rebelled, and she got to the ladies' room just in time to lose her breakfast, her body violently reacting to the sudden, unexpected stress. She leaned against the wall afterward, closing her eyes and hoping her stomach would settle. "Okay, Kerry, just relax; you've been in more tense situations that. What's up with you?" she asked herself silently. And it was true, she had—with her father, even with Dar, for heaven's sake, so why did this bastard get to her like this? She sighed and trudged to the sink, washing her mouth out and splashing water over her face, which felt overheated. She was just drying her face off with a paper towel when footsteps approached, and she glanced up as the door swung open and a familiar dark head poked in. "Oh, hi," She greeted Dar. "I was just coming to look for you."

Dar slipped inside and let the door close. "I was just coming to look for you, too." She peered at Kerry. "You okay?"

Embarrassed, Kerry nodded. "Yeah, yeah, I'm fine." She decided Dar didn't need any more stress of her own. "I was just making sure the conference went off. I logged on and confirmed the London servers were accessible from the big presentation room."

The blue eyes studied her in puzzled concern for a moment. "Good, good, I'm glad you did that." Dar glanced behind her then came closer, very gently touching Kerry's cheek. "You look really pale; you sure you're okay?"

Kerry also glanced around, conscious of how public a place they were in. "Yeah, I'm sure. Something disagreed with me, maybe that meat pastalito I had." She put a hand over her stomach. "But I'm fine now."

Dar stepped back, giving her a relieved nod. "Yeah, they were kinda greasy this morning," she commented. "Well, if that crisis is done, I've got another one for us to work on."

"What's up now?" She followed Dar outside and down the hall hearing the faint sounds of the presentation going on in the conference room.

"We took over a manufacturing plant's IS and we've got two mainframes down," Dar responded.

"And?" Kerry inquired. "That doesn't sound too tough."

"It's in Hong Kong," Dar replied dryly, "which now has a technology restriction and we can't get parts in to fix them."

"Oh." The blond chewed her lip. "That sucks."

"Mm."

"Smuggle the chips inside fortune cookies?"

Dar chuckled as they headed down the corridor.

🦋🦋   🦋🦋   🦋🦋

"Dar?" Maria's voice broke into her concentration as she pored over circuiting diagrams. Dar glanced up with a start, aware suddenly of the time.

"Yes?" she asked, checking her watch. Shit.

"Mariana just called. The bus is here," the secretary said. "She asks are you ready?"

Dar sat back, regarding the pile on her desk with a look of mild disgust. "No, but that's not going to stop this thing from happening, is it?" she muttered in response. "I've got a six inch stack of paper I need to go over and three reports due," she sighed, rubbing her temples. "Tell her I'll change and be down in the lobby in ten minutes. You might want to call Kerry and see if she's headed down."

"Not quite," a soft voice answered from the inner door.

Dar glanced up to see Kerry's head poking into her office. "Never mind on that last, Maria, she's right here."

"Okay, I will wrap things up here, Dar. Try to have a good weekend, okay?" Even Maria sounded doubtful, knowing what the situation was. "Good luck."

"Thanks," the dark-haired woman sighed. "You have a good weekend too, Maria." She glanced at Kerry. "You ready?"

Kerry entered, already changed into jeans and a sweatshirt. "As I ever will be." She gave Dar a concerned look. "I finished up everything

I could Dar, but there's still a lot of stuff pending. Next week's going to be a bitch."

"I know," Dar sighed, standing up and stretching and rolling her neck around to loosen it. "What a day. All right, let me go get out of this monkey suit and we'll head down." She stepped around the desk and held her arms out. "One for the road?"

No argument from Kerry. She slid into Dar's embrace, feeling the cool silk under her fingers that warmed as she closed her arms around the taller woman's body. "Mmm…." She sensed the pressure of lips against her head, and she let herself absorb the sweet feeling, wishing she could just stay like this and not have to get on that damned bus.

After a long moment, they parted reluctantly, and Dar let her fingers brush across Kerry's cheek. "I resent having to spend an entire weekend pretending not to be desperately in love with you," she stated, seriously. "I think I resent that more than having to go in the first place."

Kerry blushed a little. "I just hope I don't slip up and forget you're just my boss," she admitted. "You'd better stay far away from me at night." She gave Dar a pat. "Go change. I'll get my bag."

Dar sighed but complied, changing out of her suit and into a comfortable pair of jeans and a polo shirt. She ran a comb through her hair before she put her suit on a hanger and headed back to her office.

"Dar, it's cold out," Kerry scolded. "You need a sweater or something or you're going to catch a chill." She dug through her boss's bag and retrieved a soft fleece sweatshirt. "Put this on."

"Yes, mother," Dar chuckled, but did as she was told, slipping it over her head and adjusting the waistband. "Better?"

Kerry reviewed the rich, crimson color against Dar's tanned skin and dark hair and smiled. "I like that; you look really good in red." She shouldered her bag and exhaled. "Okay, let's go."

They went rode the elevator down in silence and exchanged one last significant look before the door opened.

The rest of the group was there waiting, and they collected several annoyed looks as they joined them. "Sorry," Dar briskly addressed the woman sent to collect them. "Just tying up loose ends."

The woman, a perky blond with an infectious smile, nodded. "Well, that's great, glad you could join us." She checked her clipboard. "You would be Roberts and Stuart, right?"

Dar nodded. "Yep."

"Excellent. My name's Skippy, and I'll be your guide during the seminar." She checked her list. "What we're going to do is get on board the bus and get started. The camp's about three and a half hours north of here, and on the way we'll have you fill out some questionnaires and pass out a little snack in case anyone gets hungry, okay?"

"A snack?" José objected. "Hey, come on now, most of us didn't get lunch." He glanced around, twitching his jacket closed. "It's almost six o'clock." Several other people nodded with him.

"All right." Skippy didn't miss a beat. "We also have some full dinners on board, so let's get going, and I'll explain more about the program when we're underway." She checked them over as they boarded the huge, chartered bus. "Now, no one has anything nasty like a computer or anything like that, right?" she reminded them. "We're trying to get your minds into a different space this weekend."

"I wonder how many people have asked her if she has any peanut butter," Duks joked in a low murmur, causing Dar to chuckle. "I cannot believe I am doing this, my friend, or that you are, for that matter."

Dar shrugged. "Won't hurt us," she replied laconically as she watched Kerry board, then stepped up after her, glad to leave the thick, diesel smell behind. The bus was plush, with two rows of seats going back on either side, spaced far enough apart to provide a decent amount of leg space. There was really no excuse to squeeze in, so Dar reluctantly went past the row Kerry had settled in, and slid into the row past her, pushing the arm between the two seats up and stretching out. If she leaned against the window, she could see Kerry's head doing the same and as she watched, the blond woman turned and peeked back through the opening at her.

Kerry stuck her tongue out, making Dar smile, which she quickly muffled as Steve settled in the seat across from her, his dark eyes regarding her coolly. Duks took the seat behind her, and Mariana took the one behind Steve, and she briefly kicked herself for not arranging to do the same with Kerry.

Great. Now she was stuck looking at Steve's obnoxious puss for three hours. With an aggrieved sigh, Dar propped one knee up and rested her arm against it as the bus pulled out of the parking lot in the fading twilight.

🐾 🐾 🐾

"Here you go." Skippy smiled at Kerry as she handed her a clipboard with a sheaf of papers on it. "Just fill everything out, and feel free to ask me if you have any questions."

Kerry took the papers. "What's this all for?" she asked, glancing at the forms.

Skippy put a hand on the seat back next to her. "Well, it's so we know you better so we can tailor the seminar more closely to your needs."

"Ah, wouldn't it have been more efficient to give us these before-hand?" the blond woman asked curiously. "I mean, it's not like you'll have much time to do any tinkering."

Skippy's perky smile became a little fixed. "Why, we'll stay up all night if we have to, don't you worry…if you'll just fill out that information."

Kerry pulled the cap off her pen and studied the papers. "If I didn't know better, I'd say this was just to keep us busy on the trip," she murmured, shaking of her head. "Because I don't know how much tailoring you're going to get done with a list of my favorite library books."

"Now, now, you just let us do our jobs. That information tells our analysts a lot about you," Skippy informed her as she escaped down the row, handing Dar her clipboard and leaning over to give Steve his. "There you go, any questions?"

"Yeah: do you have an assigned seat, or can you help me fill mine out?" Steve asked her, giving the young blond a smile.

Skippy beamed at him. "Well, let me pass out the rest of these, and I'll come back to give you a hand, okay?" She scuttled down the isle, making sure everyone had a clipboard. "Yes sir?" She leaned over where Duks was seated. "Did you need something? A pen?"

Duks held up one of his never-ending supply of mechanical pencils. "No, thank you."

"You must be an accountant." She smiled at him. "They always have those things."

Duks nodded gravely at her. "When you graduate from college with a financial degree, they give you a dozen cases of them," he assured her, "with your name on them." He held his up. "See?"

"Oh…yes." Skippy edged away from him, and turned a bright smile on Dar, who was neatly printing in her name. "And what are you?"

"Trouble," Dar replied, peering at her from under dark lashes with a faint smirk.

"Ah." Skippy backed off. "Well, how about some pop, huh? We've got cola, orange, and lime."

"Milk," Dar replied, intent on sucking as much enjoyment out of the weekend as she could. That included tormenting little blond girls who were far too perky for their own good.

"Milk…okay, I think we have some, let me go look." She escaped down the row towards the front of the bus, where Eleanor and her assistant were installed in regal splendor. The Marketing VP had a colorful woven throw tucked around her knees, and her assistant Peter, a tall, thin man with nervously blinking eyes and thick glasses, was hunched over the forms. Just about everyone else had chosen to wear jeans except for José, who was in a pair of neatly pressed chinos and a guyabera.

Dar tucked her knees up and rested her clipboard against them, chewing on her pen top as she studied the forms. They were a collection of questions meant to probe her innermost psyche, she reasoned; otherwise, why ask if she liked chicken instead of fish, or if she picked an aisle seat or a window in an airplane? She half believed Kerry was right, and this stuff was just to keep them occupied for a while until they got there or until the boredom of the trip set in and they fell asleep.

Skippy came back and handed Dar a small carton of milk, then sat down next to Steve and started going over the questions with him.

"Psst." A soft whisper caught her attention, and she glanced over at the back of the next seat. Kerry's green eyes were peering at her.

"Yeah?"

"Do we get points if we can answer more than ten percent of the questions with 'none of the above'?" the blond woman inquired. "I hate all those animals in question six."

"Hey!" José's voice rose. "What you mean here, relations with animals? What kind of people do you think we are?"

"Sir, that means pets." Skippy smiled perkily at him. "You know, like doggies and kitties. Do you have any loved pets?" Her smiled faded. "Not do you, uh, love pets, not in that way…um, we really don't…care to know about that."

"What about my python?" Duks commented dryly from his dark corner. "Do you consider the rats I feed her pets too?"

Dar covered her eyes and bit back a laugh.

"Um, well, no, because they're kind of um, transient, right? We mean permanent pets," Skippy replied. "Like that are there all the time."

"Like my Sweetiepie," Mariana mused, from her seat across from Dar. "She's the prettiest parrot."

Skippy smiled at her. "See? That's what I meant."

"Mm…. I loved her so much, I had her stuffed when she died," the Personnel VP added. "Now she's the most permanent thing in the house."

Dar clamped her jaw muscles tightly.

"You people are so disrespectful," Steve suddenly said, sharply. "This woman is here to do a job, and you all think it's a joke." He glared at them, and Skippy beamed gratefully at him. "The company takes this seriously, and you should too." He sat down, smiling at the guide as she eased into the seat next to him.

Dar sighed. It was going to be a long weekend.

The droning of the bus's tires finally changed, and Dar shifted, blinking her eyes and glancing out the window. It was pitch dark outside, only the very occasional lamp flicking by along with the requisite billboards. She glanced between the seats and spotted the gentle curve of Kerry's cheek as the blond woman dozed, her head resting against the window.

Across from her, Steve and Skippy were conversing in low tones, and everyone else seemed to have fallen asleep. Dar straightened and checked her watch, then stood and stretched the kink out of her back from the semi-comfortable seat. "Almost there?" she inquired quietly.

Skippy turned her head. "Yes, we just turned off the expressway but we've got a little bit to go yet," she replied cheerfully. "It's way, way out there; we wanted to get to where you couldn't even hear the traffic at all."

Dar leaned against her seat back and peered out the window. A billboard went by. "Aardvark Bail Bonds," she commented, "next right." Her head turned. "Guess you're not the only ones who wanted some privacy."

Skippy blinked at her. "What do you mean?"

Dar peered out again. "'Bill's Bail Haven,'" she enunciated. "'No waiting, six lines.'" Her blue eyes regarded her wryly. "We're out near Stark."

"Stark?" Steve asked, obviously disgruntled at having his discussion interrupted. "What are you talking about, Dar?"

"The federal penitentiary," came the dry response. "There's also a state jail out near here, if I'm not mistaken; no wonder it's empty."

"Oh, well, we're not going there," Skippy assured her. "It's a camp just west of here, really. We wouldn't take you to a prison."

"Oh, I don't know," Steve sniped. "I'd like to see that, myself."

Dar gazed at him. "Steve, you'd have a lot more to worry about than I would," she replied silkily.

He leaned back. "Oh, I don't think so. I think those women would knock that tough attitude of yours right off."

The dark-haired woman put her hands on her hips, and smiled at him. "At least my attitude has something to back it up," she replied meaningfully.

Skippy had been watching them, her head bobbing between them like an errant, blond ping-pong ball. "Oh...do you two know each other well?" she asked brightly.

Steve studied Dar's tall form speculatively. "C'mon, Dar, those days are long behind you. Cut the crap." He laughed. "When was the last time you even hit the mat?"

"Mat?" Skippy seemed to sense a fight, and dove into an attempt to divert it. "What kind of mats are those? Are you into aerobics? I am."

Dar decided to ignore them, and instead strolled off down the aisle, ending up in the back of the bus where there was a toilet and a small refrigerator. Dar explored that, finding a can of YooHoo to her muted delight. She also picked up a bag of pretzels and held on as the bus took a right turn and slowed drastically.

"Oh, we're almost there." Skippy stood up and went to her seat at the front, gathering up her stack of papers and peering out the front window. "Okay, folks, you'd better wake up." Her perky voice stirred the rest of the group, who struggled awake, peering around.

Dar made her way back to her seat and dropped into it, opening her soda and sucking at it in silence. A blond head appeared over the seat in front of her and she glanced up, only just barely keeping herself from giving Kerry a friendly smile. The green eyes, amber in the bus's low light, twinkled a little in acknowledgment, and instead she offered the blond woman some pretzels.

"Thanks," Kerry replied politely, selecting one and munching on it.

The bus passed through a set of stately gates and around a circular driveway, stopping with a soft jerk, and a hiss. Skippy stood up. "Here we are." She checked her clipboard. "Why don't you come on inside and we'll get everyone settled down for the evening. We've got hot drinks and some snacks if anyone's still hungry."

They shouldered their bags in silence and followed her off the bus, and in through two large, wooden doors into a large lodge type building. Dar glanced around, taking in the sedate décor. The lodge had a large sitting area near a fireplace, and a round table where two other of the retreat's staff were waiting. It reminded her vaguely of a good, if rural corporate hotel.

"Not bad," Duks remarked.

"Come right this way, ladies and gentlemen." Skippy led them over to the reception desk. "Now, this is how the retreat is set up. We've got rooms that were designed for two people. What we'd like to do is split you up first into men and women."

"Which do you qualify as, Dar?" Steve sniped. José snorted and shook his head in amusement.

Dar merely looked him up and down, then smirked. "As more woman than either of you can handle, that's for sure." She enjoyed the watching the veins appear on José's forehead. "Okay, everyone." Skippy had two bowls in her hands. "This is how this works, so it's nice and fair. Each of these has sets of pictures, folded up. Everyone picks one, and the people who have the matching pictures room together. Got it?"

"Why can't we have our own rooms?" Eleanor objected. "I'm very uncomfortable sharing quarters with people I hardly know." Her eyes, without question, rested on Dar. "Or those I know too well."

"Now, it's just for two nights," Skippy coaxed. "The rooms are nice-sized; you really have nothing to worry about. Part of the retreat is to let you break down some of the usual barriers with the people you work with, and this really helps. We used to have all the women in one room and all the men in another, but that didn't work out as well." She held up the dishes. "Okay, let's pick."

They picked.

"Now unfold your papers and hold them up."

They unfolded. Duks let out an almost imperceptible sigh. "Come along, José. I am hoping you do not snore too badly."

"Hey. My wife tells me I never do that," José replied, insulted.

Kerry peered at the small black star on her paper, then glanced up at the others. Her eyebrows lifted as she spotted the other star holder, a very innocent-looking Dar Roberts. "Fair's fair, I guess," Kerry commented, holding up her star.

"Lucky you," Eleanor muttered. "Snoring should be the least of your problems."

Dar let out a long breath. "You know, Eleanor, one of these days, I'm just going to get to the point where I'm over your bullshit," she told the Marketing VP crisply. "It's been a long day. Don't push me."

Eleanor stared at her, then she turned to Kerry. "There's five women, Kerry. Why don't you double up with Sandy over there, and let Miss Congeniality go by herself? Everyone'll be happier, I'm sure, and Sandy doesn't mind, do you?"

"I mind," Kerry replied. "It has been a long day, I'm tired, and I just want to get some rest. No offense to Sandy, but I'm perfectly happy rooming with Dar. She's housebroken, she puts the seat down, and she doesn't snore." She was aware of the faintly shocked looks. "You forget we travel together all the time," she added mildly.

"Well." Skippy put a determined smile on her face. "That brings me to our first little exercise." That got their attention. "Here are your keys. Your first task is to find your rooms." She exhaled. "Have a great night; we'll wake you for breakfast." She pointed at a credenza. "Coffee's there, if anyone needs it."

The retreat staff retreated, closing a plain, white door behind them.

They all looked at each other. Dar ran her hand through her hair and looked around. "Well, it's one building, so they can't be far."

Fabricini strolled around the edges of the big room. "Other than the front door, we've got two other possibilities. That door they went through and this locked grate."

"This is bullshit," José snapped. "What kind of stupid games are they playing? I'm not going to put up with this crap, I'm telling you." He glared at the walls. "I can sleep right here on the damned floor."

Kerry walked to where Fabricini was standing and examined the grate. It had a lock in it, and as he pulled against it, it sounded very solid. Kerry knelt and examined the lock curiously.

"You going to develop a useful skill, like picking those?" Steve asked with a chuckle.

"Dar, is that a Yale?" Kerry glanced over at her boss. "The key to the room, I mean?"

Blue eyes examined the item in question. "Yes."

"Let's all try our keys in here," Kerry suggested gently. "If this is the only way out, it would make sense one of our keys would open it."

Duks's did. He inserted his key after Dar and Steve tried theirs and it turned, making a solid click as the lock disengaged. Steve pulled the

door back to reveal a stairway leading up. "Good work, Kerry." The accountant patted her on the back. "One obstacle down. Shall we?"

They trudged upstairs and found another door at the top of the stairs, also locked. This time, it was Eleanor's key that worked, and they proceeded down a short hallway to where a wider spot featured an octagon of rooms, with all the doors facing inward around a central area containing a round table. Each room, instead of having a number, had a small animal plaque next to the door, and Dar peered at her key to see if something matched. "Tiger," she pointed with a wry look.

"Mine is the pig," Duks observed gravely.

"Half right."

Mariana nudged Dar in the ribs. "C'mon, be nice."

Dar glanced at her and raised a brow. "Why? No one else is." She stalked to the door and opened it, politely holding it as Kerry ventured past, then following the smaller woman inside before letting it shut.

"Urf." Mari rubbed her temples. "Gonna be a long weekend."

The sound of catty voices drifted through the door, which Kerry let close very firmly before she held up her paper. "Okay. How'd you do this? I didn't think you were into sleight of hand."

Dar smiled. "I have many skills." She glanced around the room, which was plainly decorated but comfortable. It looked very much like a hotel room, with a single dresser and mirror, two chairs, a small table, and a bed. A single, though quite large bed. "Damn good thing, too." She shook her head.

"Mm." Kerry was at her elbow. "One bed, huh? That must be giving them all fits."

Dar put an arm around her shoulders. "Yep," she smirked. "I can hear the screaming already."

"Breaking down barriers, huh?" Kerry mused. "Me waking up snuggling with Eleanor would certainly break down a barrier all right."

"Ew." Dar's nose wrinkled. "Well, if I have to put up with them during the day, at least the nights'll be pleasant." She inclined her head and kissed Kerry, who responded in like fashion.

"Uer...what if they're filming this or something?" Kerry darted a suspicious look at the room's innocuous-looking corners.

"Who, the retreat people?" Dar murmured, continuing her exploration of Kerry's face.

"Mm, to send back to Alastair or something."

Dar lifted her free hand and made a rude gesture towards any potential watching electronic eyes. Kerry chuckled. "You're such a bad girl." She felt the soft gust as Dar snarled against her lips, the faint vibration sending a little thrill down the length of her body. Dar rested her forehead against Kerry's and exhaled.

"So…how did you do it?" Kerry coaxed curiously.

A mischievous look took over Dar's face. "Would you believe me if I told you we just got lucky?" she admitted.

The blond brows lowered. "Knowing you? No."

A smile. "I watched Skippy Junior when she was folding them, memorized which ones went where, and made sure you and I picked first," Dar explained easily. "Remember, I got next to you? I saw which one you picked, and just made sure I got the same one."

Kerry absorbed this information respectfully. "Wow," she murmured. "Really?"

Dar laughed. "Well, we might as well get some sleep. I'm sure it's going to be a long, bitchy day tomorrow." She cocked her head, and they listened as irritated voices came through the thin walls around them. Eleanor's rose to a shout, then they heard a bang. "Bitchier for some than others, I guess."

"Well…" Kerry patted her gently to remove the sting. "You're not helping much, honey." She heard Dar sigh. "Not that I blame you, really; I feel like giving them all a sedative enema."

Dar set her bag down on the dresser and opened it, stifling a yawn as she pulled out her pajamas. "I know I shouldn't let it get to me, but lately…." She gave the familiar jersey a frown. "It's just rubbing me raw, and I'm not really sure why."

Kerry finished stripping out of her jeans and shirt, and tucking them away in her bag. "You seem a little…defensive." She paused, considering her words, aware of the stiffening of Dar's back. "I don't know, maybe it's just so different, work and what it's like after we leave the building. I feel it too."

"You do?" Dar didn't turn.

"That irresistible urge to bitch-slap people? Yeah." Kerry pulled her T-shirt over her head, and exhaled. "Especially when they say bad things about you. I just want to kill them."

Dar turned, and leaned against the dresser. "I thought you were a little snippier than usual with Eleanor." She smiled. "I put the seat down? Kerry, why the hell would I leave it up?"

"Grmpfh." The blond woman walked over and buried her face into Dar's shirt. "I did say that, didn't I? I don't know, she was just stomping all over my last nerve with those spike heels."

Dar reached over and flipped the light off, leaving them in stark, pitch darkness. The window outside was a blank square, the stars outside covered by clouds, and the city lights far, far away. Dar blinked and waited for her usually excellent night vision to adjust, but the air remained impenetrably dense. Ah. She edged closer and found the outline of Kerry's face by nibbling it. "Now, this is my kinda challenge." She felt an unexpected touch sneak up her thigh. "Mm."

"We could get in a lot of trouble this way," Kerry whispered, not really caring. "These are real thin walls, Dar."

Her lover's hands slid under the soft cotton shirt she was wearing, and eased it up, exploring her skin curiously. "Scream quietly," Dar advised, right into her ear. Kerry's nostrils flared. "Think of it as a character-building exercise."

🐾   🐾   🐾

A loud crack of thunder brought Kerry bolt upright, her heart thumping in reaction half at the noise, half from the dream she'd been shaken out of. A flash of lightning lit up the room, and she caught a brief glimpse of Dar lying asleep next to her, so still that Kerry reached out in unthinking reflex and touched her chest, only breathing herself when she felt the warm surface move under her hand.

"Buh." She rubbed her face with her other hand, trying to ease her brain into wakefulness and away from the shadows of her unconscious, and she was just aware of the musty, faintly antiseptic smell of the retreat's bedroom.

"Kerry?" A concerned voice came out of the darkness, and fingers closed over her hand. "What's up?"

"Just me." Kerry laid back down. "Bad dream."

"Mm, c'mere." Dar tugged her closer, and she curled her body up against the taller woman's with a sense of relief. "Listen to that thunder. What time is it?"

Kerry lifted her head a little. "Five. I think it was the noise that woke me up." She put her head back down on Dar's shoulder, and hugged her. "But I'm glad. I hate nightmares."

Dar rubbed her back lightly. "What was it about?"

The sting of tears was very unexpected. "Nothing intelligible,"

Kerry said, "just my subconscious doing some housecleaning." She listened to Dar's heartbeat, steady under her ear, and found it relaxed her. She allowed the familiar rhythm to lull her back into a light doze.

Dar gazed up at the unseen ceiling, now wide awake, her memory focusing on her own dreams, which had been far more peaceful, if a bit bizarre.

She'd been lying in the sun in a forest just next to a small spring. It had been cool, just enough to offset the warmth of the sunlight, and she'd been aware of being sleepy, and contented, half curled on her side with Kerry cuddled up next to her.

And then she'd realized the woman in her arms was pregnant, the gentle swelling prominent beneath her encircling arm. *What on earth was that all about?* Dar wondered in confusion. She felt Kerry snuggle closer, and release a breath that fluttered the cotton fabric across her chest, and warmed the skin underneath it. The blond woman's body was pressed against hers, and its slim, familiar contours certainly held no hint of impending motherhood, so…

Weird.

Dar had never really paid much attention to her dreams, never really remembered most of them, for that matter, leaving the studying of that stuff to her mother along with the rest of the esoterica. Now, she had very little hard data to go on in figuring out her puzzling vision.

A bizarre reaction to their deepening relationship?

Deeply hidden maternal instincts popping up?

A sudden need for a more traditional household?

Dar scratched the side of her nose. More likely a reaction to the two packages of moon pies she'd scarfed down on the bus trip. That'd been enough sugar to cause nightmares. And come to think of it, she'd shared her chocolate booty with Kerry, so that was probably the source of her friend's dream as well.

Satisfied, Dar closed her eyes and resolved to avoid re-experiencing the problem.

She'd only have one package next time.

Bong.

Bong.

Bong.

This time, Dar sat up straight, her eyes snapping wide open at the deep, sonorous chime that rattled the walls. "Son of a bitch."

The window had just started turning a pearl color from the dawn, and she could see the inside of the room outlined in a silvery glow, which quickly outlined Kerry's shifting form as she pushed herself up onto one elbow, blinking in utter confusion.

"Huh?"

Bong.

Bong.

Bong.

"Yow." Kerry covered her ear on one side. "What in the hell is that?"

A click answered her, then a cheerful female voice invaded their nest. "Good morning, everyone."

Dar pulled back the covers and got out of bed, moving towards her bag with single-minded intent.

"It's six-thirty, and time to get up. We're serving breakfast at seven-thirty, which you can find in the service area right outside your rooms. Please dress comfortably; we'll be inside this morning due to inclement weather."

The voice signed off with a satisfied click, and Dar, rummaging in her bag, found what she was looking for. She removed a tool kit, selected a set of diagonal cutters, and pushed her disheveled black hair out of her determined eyes and started a seek and destroy mission for the speakers.

"Dar."

"Shh. I can hear the residual hiss."

Kerry covered her face with her hands and scrubbed the skin, trying attain wakefulness. "God, you're such a nerd." She raked the covers back, then scrambled out of bed and dodged her hunting geek companion and trudged into the bathroom. "Bet you fixed the projector in high school, didn't you?" she called out.

"No, I substituted the films with porno," Dar muttered back absentmindedly. "Ah." She discovered the speakers hidden behind the air conditioning grill and retrieved a screwdriver with a chuckle of triumph. "Gotcha." She hopped up onto the small table and spent a moment removing the grill, then reached inside and clipped the wires with a satisfied snick. "Bong this."

"Nerd."

Dar replaced the grill and climbed down in a much better mood. "There." She put her tools away and removed her selection of clothing. "Wanna share a shower? Might as well get as much enjoyment out of the day as possible before the torture starts."

"Sure," Kerry agreed. "But you know, Dar, maybe it won't be so bad. Try not to go into it so negatively." She patted her friend on the stomach. "It might even help, you know?"

"I'll consider the weekend a success if we don't end up in litigation," Dar grumbled. "I know what today's gonna be like; they used to do these 'team building and sensitivity development' sessions in college. I hated them."

"Why?" Kerry unbuttoned Dar's shirt, and tugged her towards the shower. "It's just so people can get to know you better."

"I don't want people to know me better," the dark-haired woman replied, turning on the water and letting it warm. "I just want them to do their jobs…is that so unreasonable?"

They stepped under the water together, bare bodies tangling in a well-rehearsed dance of soap and chuckles. It didn't take long to finish washing, but Dar noticed the water was getting colder as they rinsed off and prepared to get out. "Huh." She joined a dripping Kerry outside the stall and stuck her hand under the water, now finding it cool, but not ice cold to the touch. "Only enough warm water for one set of showers; bet that's going to go over like a soggy pastalito."

"Hm." Kerry picked up a towel and started drying Dar off, admiring the taller woman's tanned form as she did so. "Guess that's to make people work together; you know, one takes the first shower one morning, the other takes it the second, right?"

"How unimaginative." Dar dried Kerry's hair, then ducked her head and nibbled on her friend's neck. "They could solve the problem like we did."

Kerry was about to answer when a knock came at the door. She jumped and grabbed for her towel, wrapping it around her body as Dar did the same. Her partner's towel, however, didn't cover an awful lot of her very tall frame. "Uh, Dar…"

"Go ahead and finish up. I'll see what that is," Dar offered, tucking the end of the towel under one arm and padding out of the bathroom towards the door. It sounded again as she turned the handle and opened it, finding José fuming on the other side of it. "Yes?"

"Dios Mío, Dar, put your clothes on!" the Cuban spluttered loudly.

Doors popped open on either side, and very curious heads poked out.

Dar smirked, perversely complimented. "Why? Do you shower with your clothes on, José? That explains a few things, gives your ring around the collar a whole new meaning." She leaned an arm against the doorjamb and lifted her eyebrows. "What do you want?" It was fun watching him try to look without looking, and she casually crossed one ankle over the other, aware of just how precariously the towel was covering her skin. "Well?"

José cleared his throat and stared fixedly at the wall. "You have taken the hot water!"

Dar pointed a finger at her own chest. "Me? What do I look like, a 160 pound sea sponge?" She snorted. "Twelve people taking showers at once, José, drains a hot water heater. Get a grip."

"Twelve people?" Steve eyed the towel-wrapped woman with a smirk. "Only six of us could at once…unless you and your friend in there are doubling up."

Everyone gazed at Dar with mixed looks of speculation. "At least she courteously assumed that we all shower," Duks broke the silence dryly.

Eleanor snorted. "'Dar' and 'courteous'? Not in your lifetime, bucko." She turned and pulled her head back inside and slammed the door. José walked off muttering and shoved past Duks into their room, leaving Steve and Dar facing each other in the awkward silence.

"Hit a nerve?" Steve smiled at her, making a show of glancing up and down her tall form.

"No." Dar gazed at him. "You're standing on one. Be careful." She turned and shut the door firmly behind her, but didn't slam it. "Shit." Kerry was brushing her damp hair out, perched demurely in a pair of jeans and a kelly green shirt neatly tucked into her waistband. "I think we were just busted."

Dar sighed, and removed her towel, ruffling her hair with it as she crossed to her bag and rooted out her own pair of jeans. "Yeah, I walked into that one, all right." She shook her head in disgust. "Jerk."

"Here." Kerry helpfully handed her a pair of cotton Dogbert briefs. "My little nerd."

Blue eyes glanced sideways at her, then Dar chuckled and relaxed. "C'mon. Let's go see what they've got for breakfast." She dressed quickly and raked a brush through her hair, then accompanied Kerry as they eased out the door and into the hallway. The rest of the group was already there, but most conversation stopped as they appeared, and only awkwardly restarted.

Ooo…guess who was the subject of that gossip. Kerry gave everyone a pleasant smile and picked up a plate, reviewing her options. "Morning." She selected a muffin and some marmalade, scooped herself some eggs and added several pieces of bacon, then took a seat between Duks and José. Everyone looked pretty grumpy, even the usually unflappable Duks, and she wondered how badly the rooming assignments really had been.

"Well, little Miss Sunshine." Steve was sitting across from her, pouring skim milk over a bowlful of what looked like Grape Nuts. "Sleep well?"

"Yes, I did." Kerry poured herself a cup of coffee, and added cream and sugar to it. "The storm woke me up once, but otherwise it was fine. How about you?"

"The floor was great." Steve gave Mark an acid smile.

"We flipped, you lost." The MIS chief took a big bite of biscuit.

"Sleeping on the floor is good for you," Eleanor declared primly. "Don't you agree, Mariana?"

"Oh yeah." The Personnel VP had her nose stuck in a cup of coffee.

Dar and Kerry exchanged glances. Dar rubbed a hand over her mouth to hide the smile that momentarily transformed her face. "I think I just figured out why Ops is the only division that works," she remarked, spearing a potato and popping it into her mouth. "What kind of idiots are you all? Those beds were big enough for the entire damned board of directors to sleep in together… just share them."

A moment of frozen silence greeted her words, broken by the appearance of Skippy.

"Well, good morning!" The retreat organizer took her place in the center of the breakfast display, perched on a stool in her crisp khakis and pressed blue shirt. "Did everyone sleep all right?"

"What was the purpose of only having one bed?" Eleanor snapped.

"Well…" Skippy took a breath. "I know it's a little awkward, but really, once you think about it, they're very large beds, and I'm sure you found a way to work things out so that you all were comfortable." Pause. "Right?"

Mostly hostile stares answered her.

"Oh dear."

Dar was busy munching. "Y'know, if you'd lay out the rules beforehand, you might get more cooperation."

"Dealing with the unexpected really does build team morale," Skippy disagreed. "Don't you think that's so, Ms. Roberts?"

Lazily amused blue eyes lifted to hers. "Lady, all we do all day long is deal with the unexpected. It never helped before, I doubt it will now."

Several snorts were audible around the table.

"That's pretty negative," Skippy mused.

"That's Dar: Ms. Negative," José sniped.

Dar waved her spoon at herself, then at Kerry. "We slept just fine last night, unlike the rest of you," she reminded them.

Skippy regrouped. "Well, that's great. Why don't you tell us how you did that?"

"Did what?" Kerry nibbled her muffin. "Went to sleep? We laid down, closed our eyes…you know."

"No, I mean, how did you work out sharing your space?" Skippy turned to Kerry, glad of a more pleasant victim. "Maybe some of the others can use the same techniques you used."

Kerry almost choked on her breakfast trying not to burst into helpless laughter. "Um…no, really, I don't think it'll work for anyone else. We really just didn't debate it." She took a sip of coffee. "It just didn't seem to be an issue—you're right, those beds are huge, and logically it made no sense to do anything other than just go to sleep." She was aware of the resentful looks and realized she was just making things worse. "But I think Dar's right; maybe if we knew what to expect, it would have been easier to deal with."

"Definitely," Duks grunted.

The rest of breakfast was consumed in a somewhat prickly silence.

"Okay." Skippy took her seat at the big round table with her twelve reluctant participants. They were seated alternating men and women, and had pads of paper, cups of water, boxes of crayons, and pensive looks to work with. "We're going to do some ice breaker exercises right now. I think we certainly can use those, don't you all agree?" She didn't wait for the answer that didn't come. "Right. Now, first, I'm going to go around the table, and I want each of you to tell me what your hobbies are." She turned to her right. "You first."

Steve gave her a pleasant smile. "I'm a marathon runner," he stated, with obvious satisfaction.

"Isn't that wonderful!" Skippy looked delighted. "So am I! We'll have to compare notes later." She gave Steve a warm smile. "Next?"

"I collect pencils," Duks deadpanned.

Skippy sighed.

"No, really, I do," the accountant objected. "My oldest one is from 1902. It's a very interesting subject, pencils."

"Absolutely," Skippy recovered. "And you?"

Eleanor's quiet assistant Peter cleared his throat. "Um...I raise tropical fish," he answered. "Salt water."

"Really?" Dar perked up her ears. "What size tank?"

"Three hundred gallons," Peter replied proudly. "Takes up my whole garage."

Even Dar's eyes popped. "That's not a tank, that's the Seaquarium," she pronounced. "Damn."

He looked very pleased with the response. "My family helps me take care of it. I've even got a baby nurse shark in there, but I had to segregate him because he was eating the rest of the fish and getting fat."

"Remarkable," Eleanor murmured, though it was not clear if she meant the fish, or the revelation that her assistant had a life outside work.

"Excellent," Skippy praised him. "Ms. Stuart?"

Everyone looked at Kerry curiously. "I write poetry," Kerry informed them with a brief grin, enjoying the expressions of mild surprise.

"Great." Skippy nodded. "Ms. Delgado?"

"I quilt."

"Mr. Guiterrez?"

"Dominos."

Skippy looked very pleased, then her eyes fell on Dar's daunting expression. "Ah. Ms. Roberts?"

"I collect shrunken heads," Dar remarked with a straight face.

Skippy sighed. Everyone else stared at Dar.

"Well, that's what you all expected, wasn't it?" the Ops VP queried sardonically. "Actually, I scuba dive," she relented, getting a prim smile from their counselor.

"Figures," Steve snorted. "You always were an unsocial loner."

"Steven." Mariana enunciated his name carefully. "That was uncalled for."

"Actually," Kerry spoke up. "You've got it wrong; the first rule of diving is never do it alone."

Eleanor leaned forward with sly interest. "Are you a diver as well, Kerry?"

Uh oh. Kerry hesitated, resisting the urge to look at her partner. Oh well, too late now. "Yes, I am," she smiled agreeably.

José looked like he was about to ask the obvious question when Skippy mercifully intervened. "Well, that's terrific. Okay..." She took a breath. "As you can see, our hobbies make us more well rounded people, and you all have such interesting hobbies, so I'm sure you're all very interesting people." She nodded briskly. "The next exercise we're going to do is to have you look at the person to your right, and tell me one good thing, and one bad thing about them." A bright smile. "Ready?"

Dar sighed and wished she were at the dentist's office.

🐃 🐃 🐃

After lunch, they moved into a different room with individual tables. Kerry watched Dar choose a table near the wall and seat herself behind it, her eyes cold and watchful. The exercises they'd gone through earlier hadn't worked particularly well, though it really hadn't been Dar's fault. She'd played along, and had even come up with something gracious to say about José, but when it was Eleanor's turn to speak on Dar...

Kerry sighed. The tension was giving her a headache, and she wished it was dinner they'd just eaten, not lunch, so she and Dar could escape back to their room and relax.

Skippy now had a partner named Dave. Dave was as relentlessly chipper as his blond partner, and he ambled from table to table putting down white cardboard boxes. "Okay, folks, here's how this works. I want you to pair up, and one member of the team opens this box and reads the instructions. You're not allowed to talk. After reading the instructions, you have to give the contents of the box to your partner, and instruct them on how to put together the parts inside without telling them what the end product is."

Dar rested her chin on one fist.

"Now, don't pair up with the person you're rooming with," Dave continued, "okay?"

Mariana gave Dar a wry look, then selected Duks as her partner, as

Mark and Elaine joined up, and José and Eleanor settled next to each other. Kerry gave Peter a grim smile as he proved discretion the better part of valor, and that left Steve to saunter over and perch on the chair next to Dar.

"I'll take that." Steve plucked the box from the table. "See how you like being told what to do for a change."

"We'll definitely fail, then," Dar remarked in kind, "since you couldn't direct someone out of a paper bag with instructions printed on the inside."

"Come on now, folks. Let's not get negative. It's so unproductive," Dave chided them.

"This weekend is unproductive," Dar responded edgily.

"Dar..." Mariana interjected.

"Dios Mío, finally!" José burst out. "We have something we agree on! Dar is right."

"I'm with you," Eleanor agreed.

"Well, you know your company sent you all here because they thought our program would do you some good." Skippy frowned. "But there's not much we can do if you're not willing to cooperate with us."

"These are child's games," José protested. "They mean nothing!"

"Actually, I think they do have a point," Kerry spoke up. "I think it's to try and get your thoughts away from what you usually have to think about, and, hopefully, to get you to see things a different way."

Skippy gave Kerry a very approving look. "Exactly."

"That's what I've been saying," Steve said. "It's what this company needs: a fresh perspective. So let's just give it a try, hmm?" He unfolded his instructions and read them with apparent interest.

"We're here—just make the best of it," Mariana stated, as she fingered the contents of her box. "Alastair wants this to work."

Dar snorted, but kept silent. Steve finished reading, then pushed the box over to her. "Okay, take the pieces out."

Dar obligingly dumped the box over, sending the wooden parts all over the table. She reviewed the bits, then lifted a hand and scooped them all towards her, ending up with them in a pile. One eyebrow lifted.

"All right, you got a long one there, take that, and the two shorter ones, and make a box."

"Boxes have four sides," Dar drawled.

"Take both long ones," Steve went on smoothly. "Then after you have a box, take the two flat pieces and put them on either side."

"There are four flat pieces. Two short, two long. Which ones do you mean?"

"Ms. Roberts, you're not supposed to ask questions." Dave hurried over. "Just do what he tells you to."

Dar's brows creased. "How can you define and solve a problem without asking questions?"

"Please. Just go with the program," the man told her. "And, Mr. Fabricini, you have to be more specific, like you were talking to a child."

Steve laughed. "That'll be a pleasure."

🐾 🐾 🐾

They all filed into dinner quietly, taking seats around the round table set with neat place settings, the center of the table filled with condiments and a basket of flowers. Kerry, who was right behind Dar coming into the room, reasoned by that fact she could sit next to her boss without causing much comment.

So she did.

Dar started playing with her napkin, and Kerry watched as she tore off a corner and started ripping it into tiny pieces. They'd gotten through the castle building exercise with less trouble than Kerry had frankly expected, and now they just had dinner to complete, and then they were free to spend their evening however they wished.

Of course, since there were no televisions, no books, no radios, and the nearest store, ten miles distant, was a 7-11, their options were very, very limited. Kerry suspected the retreat engineered this to encourage people to stay around the fire they'd built in the lodge sitting room and talk. And if everyone did, her disappearing with Dar upstairs would look odd, to say the least.

Kerry sighed, rubbing her temples to dispel the stress headache that had developed during the afternoon. She'd become aware that she was being watched, and it was making her very self-conscious, especially around Dar. She folded her hands in front of her and resisted glancing at her boss.

Skippy entered and took her seat. "Hi there! I hope you like what we're having for dinner. We've got a choice of chicken breast, fish filet, or meatloaf, and a couple of different side dishes. They'll be putting everything out shortly, and it's family style, so we'll all share."

"That sounds great," Mariana stated sincerely, "unless you're a vegetarian."

Skippy's face went still as she obviously hit a snag she'd not anticipated. "Is…anyone here a vegetarian?" she asked weakly.

They all shook their heads at her.

"Great," the blond woman sighed in relief, recovering her perk. "Okay… I thought I'd start the ball rolling tonight by having us all talk a little bit about our families and where we grew up." She smiled at the servers, who were putting down large platters and bowls. "Doesn't that smell great?" She took a breath. "Okay, I'll start. I'm from Kansas…"

"Have any pets when you grew up?" Dar asked, suddenly. "Little dog, maybe?"

"Dar." Mariana lifted a hand to hide a smirk.

"Um, no, I had rabbits," Skippy bravely went on. "My mother and father were farmers, and I grew up on a farm." She turned her head. "What about you?"

Steve finished serving himself some fish and a helping of steamed vegetables. "My dad's a stockbroker, and my mom's a real estate agent," he answered amiably. "I'm from Seattle." He handed a bowl of broccoli to Eleanor. "Next?"

"I can't see where it matters." The Marketing VP looked annoyed. "I'm from upstate New York, and my family owns several banks."

"This is sort of interesting," Kerry whispered to Dar.

"Gonna feel that way when it swings around to us?" Dar muttered back.

"Mm." Kerry glanced down, stung by the comment.

"Ms. Roberts?"

Dar's low voice answered, carefully noncommittal. "I grew up in South Dade at Homestead Air Force Base. My mother's an artist, my father was career Navy."

"You're a military brat? It figures." Steve's voice was amused. "That explains things."

"It certainly does," Eleanor smirked. "Maybe it's inherited. I hear you've got a friend in every port, isn't that true, Dar?"

Something snapped. Kerry realized later it was the wooden handle of the fork Dar had been holding. She glanced at her friend as Dar stood slowly, seeing the rage just under the surface of her calm features.

"You know, I have to work with you people. That's more than enough time wasted out of my life," Dar stated, then simply moved out from behind her chair and left the room.

"That was really uncalled for." Mariana gave Eleanor a look.

"Cmon, Mari, I was just joking. What the hell's the matter with her, all of a sudden?" Eleanor lifted her hands in righteous innocence.

"Getting a little touchy in her old age," Steve laughed.

"Actually," Kerry raised her voice, overriding them. "Dar's father died in Desert Storm."

They stared at her in surprise.

"They were very close, and it's something she feels very strongly about."

Eleanor had the grace to look uncomfortable. "Well, how in the hell was I supposed to know that?"

"How is it that you know all that?" Steve asked, swirling iced tea in his glass and watching Kerry closely.

"I asked," Kerry answered simply. "I took the time to get to know her, and I'm glad I did." She took a breath, then let it out. "And this constant fighting is one of the worst things about working here. I hate it." She lifted her eyes to Skippy's surprised face. "If you're writing it down, I'm from Michigan, and my parents are Senator and Mrs. Roger Stuart."

Now she shifted her glance to Eleanor. "Go ahead, make a catty comment about the hearings. It's par for your course."

Everyone was awkwardly silent, even Steve, who made a show of taking a drink of his tea. "Well, if you are going to spend time in this company, you had better learn to be less sensitive," José advised her. "We are all bastards here."

Skippy blinked. "Let's just leave our exercises for tomorrow, okay? I can see everyone's a little tense." She took a deep breath. "Maybe we can talk about something more neutral. Anyone into sports?"

Everyone relaxed a little as the discussion turned to current events. Kerry forced herself to join in, putting a firm hold on her desire to leave the room and go find Dar. After they finished, everyone moved towards the door and into the sitting area, and only then did Kerry allow herself to stay behind and corner Skippy. "I need a container."

The woman was caught off guard, and now Mariana came over, having noticed the exchange. "What's wrong, Kerry?"

"I'm going to bring Dar some dinner," Kerry said, as Skippy left to go find a box. "It's just been a really long day."

"Mm hmm," the older woman agreed. "I've never seen her go off like that. Is she not feeling well, or something?"

Kerry shrugged. "I don't think so; she just doesn't see much point in this, and frankly," She glanced around, "neither do I."

"Some good may yet come out of it," Mari disagreed. "You never know, but tell her to relax a little, will you?" She patted Kerry's arm. "I don't know how she rigged that room assignment, but I'm glad it worked out. I just hope our nights will be as peaceful." She made her way out the door, and Kerry had a moment to relax before Skippy brought her a takeout container. She took it and selected several pieces of meatloaf, then added mashed potatoes and a half ear of corn on the cob. A piece of chocolate cake just barely fit into the space remaining, but she managed, and picked up a set of silverware before she went out the other door and up the stairs.

It was very quiet near their rooms, and she paused a moment before she inserted her key into the door lock, and opened it. It was mostly dark inside, but she could make out Dar's form sprawled on the bed barely outlined in the light from the bathroom. She set her container on the desk and walked over, sitting down on the bed and meeting Dar's eyes. "Hi."

"Hi." A faintly hoarse response. "Sorry about that. I don't know what's gotten into me lately."

Kerry stroked her face tenderly. "Would it be supremely egotistical for me to say maybe it's my fault?" She smiled gently. "Don't worry about it. I brought you some meatloaf and potatoes." She retrieved the container, then sat back down. "Besides…they pushed a button they didn't even know was there. You have nothing to apologize for."

"Hm…yeah, I guess." Dar rolled over onto one side and propped her head up on her hand. "I've been thinking a lot about my father lately; I'm not really sure why." She watched as Kerry opened the foam lid and wielded her fork, cutting off a piece of meatloaf and scooping up some potatoes with it, offering it to Dar, who accepted it and chewed.

"I know you loved him a lot." Kerry offered another bite.

"Yes, I did." Dar swallowed. "I still do." She considered. "Maybe loving you just makes me remember that all the more clearly."

Kerry swallowed, caught by the simple emotion of the statement. She leaned over and rested her head against Dar's, finding a safe space in the chaos of the day. "I'm sure they're talking about us downstairs."

"I don't care." Dar reached out and curled her arms around Kerry's warm body.

"Me either." She dabbed a spot of potatoes on Dar's nose, then kissed it off, earning herself a smile. "Hell all day, Heaven at night."

Chapter 8

It was just getting light when Dar opened her eyes, momentarily disoriented before she remembered where they were. She and Kerry were lying tangled together in the center of the bed, bare bodies pressed against each other in a nest of warmth, and she could feel the gentle beat of her lover's heart tapping very lightly near her ribs. It almost made her forget they had another entire day to suffer through before they could go home. Dar considered the point as she slid an idle finger over Kerry's shoulder, admiring its firm curve. Maybe she could tell Skippy they both had something really contagious, and nasty and that they had to stay isolated in their room?

Let's see, what could they have… measles?

Nah.

Migraine?

Dar nibbled her lip. They weren't contagious, and the chances of both of them having one at the same time…probably not likely. Although… What usually caused them was stress, and they'd both been under the same stress, so it wasn't totally out of the question.

Chicken Pox?

Dar winced, having very vivid memories of her own bout with the disease, just after she'd gone from grade to middle school, one of the few of her childhood illnesses that had kept her in bed more than a day. Her mother, luckily, had already had it, but her father hadn't, and though he'd been scheduled to ship out the day she'd gotten sick, she remembered waking in a feverish sweat to find him at her bedside, where he'd stayed until she'd started to recover.

Good lord, he'd gotten so sick. Dar sighed. Two weeks of hospital, then they had to fly him out to his ship in a mail carrier. She smiled wistfully. No, they'd need a red magic marker for chicken pox, and all she had was black and purple.

Stomach flu?

Hmm. That had possibilities and didn't require any cosmetic work. She wondered if she could get Kerry to play along with her on it. No one wanted to hear details on that stuff anyway.

"Dar?"

"Hmm?" Dar looked down at the dim glints of light now reflecting off Kerry's open eyes. Well, halfway open, at any rate.

"You're up early." Her lover's voice was husky with sleep, and very distracting.

"Yeah. I was just thinking."

"'Bout what?" Kerry nuzzled her, one hand sliding up Dar's thigh.

"Upchucking."

Kerry paused, and tilted her head up in question. "Oh, that's romantic. Meatloaf didn't agree with you?"

"No, no, I'm fine," Dar laughed. "I was thinking of telling Skippy we both had the stomach flu so maybe they'd just leave us alone until it's time to leave."

"Ah ha. I see."

"It'd work; no one wants the stomach flu," Dar reasoned ingenuously. "I was thinking about faking chicken pox, but that could get messy."

"Ogh…. Don't even pronounce those words in my presence," Kerry groaned, holding up both hands with her index fingers crossed in a warding off gesture. "I had it in college."

"Ooo," Dar winced.

"I seriously thought I was going to die," Kerry murmured. "They kept me in an isolation chamber in the university hospital. I don't think I saw anyone but a single nurse for at least a week, and I was so sick."

Dar pulled her closer and hugged her.

"I remember one whole night, when all I wanted was water. I was so thirsty. I couldn't get up, there wasn't anything to drink in the room, and no way to call anyone." Kerry went on. "I was so miserable, I just started crying. "

"Why couldn't you get up?" Dar asked. "Were you dizzy from the fever?"

Kerry didn't answer for a moment. "They had my hands tied," she murmured. "So I wouldn't scratch and scar myself. I think my father asked them to do that."

Dar found herself staring up at the ceiling, caught between a sudden rage and the sobering personal knowledge that her own, however fractious childhood, had been unimaginably better than her lover's. "That was lousy."

A shrug. "It worked. I think I've only got one scar, on my knee." Kerry rolled over, studying her partner in the growing light. "What about you?"

Dar shook her head. "My father got a number ten can of naval issue calamine lotion and a paint brush and painted me from head to foot for three days until they quit itching."

"Aww, Dar, that is so sweet." Kerry smiled widely. "How old were you?"

"Eight."

Another big smile. "I bet you looked so cute."

"I bet I looked like an alien from outer space," Dar countered, but returned the grin. "Unfortunately for dad, he hadn't had the damn things yet."

"Oh." Kerry winced. "Didn't he know they were contagious?"

Dar felt a quiet sense of pride. "He knew."

Kerry sighed deeply. "I can't imagine either of my parents doing anything like that."

I think...I owe them both an apology, Dar thought to herself. Damn. She settled her arms more firmly around Kerry and relaxed, getting in a few more moments of peace before they had to start the day. "Weather cleared," she observed.

Kerry was facing the window, enjoying the hug very much. "So I see." Her head cocked to one side. "It's sunny out. We're supposed to go outside today, do some obstacle courses or something."

"Great." Dar closed her eyes. "I vote we rent a backhoe and just tunnel under everything."

"Dar, this is still Florida. We don't have our scuba gear."

Dar sighed.

"C'mon, Dar, maybe it'll be fun." Kerry nudged her. "Go into it with an open mind."

"I have an open mind," Dar disagreed. "I openly believe this is a crock of alligator crap in a seaside bucket."

"Paladar."

"Sorry." Dar shifted to a more comfortable position, pulling Kerry closer. "I'll be good, I promise. At least we're not going to be trying to build a bridge to Cuba using toothpicks," she acknowledged. "Maybe it'll be bearable this time."

"Atta girl." Kerry patted her. "Great attitude."

Dar snorted.

🐾   🐾   🐾

"Okay." Skippy appropriately skipped out ahead of them, walking backwards as they followed her across the pine needle strewn ground. "Wasn't breakfast good? I love those pancakes."

"Very nice," Mariana agreed, strolling along with her hands tucked behind her back.

"Did everyone have a, um, better night?" Skippy inquired, hopefully. Her eyes darted to Dar, who gazed placidly back at her.

Everyone exchanged glances. "We did improve circumstances, yes," Duks replied gravely. "The bolsters, you understand, they make very effective little blockades."

"Well, we commandeered a broom and used the shower curtain." Eleanor smirked. "Much more efficient."

"Not at blocking sound," Duks deadpanned.

"Hey, I told you, I do not snore," José complained.

"How would you know?" Kerry asked, curiously. "If you're sleeping?"

"My wife would tell me," the Cuban stoutly averred. "Would she not?"

No one answered. "So." Steve smiled at Kerry. "How about it: does Dar snore?"

Kerry met his gaze evenly. "I have no earthly idea. I could sleep through a 747 landing on the roof. She could have been up all night singing Christmas carols and I'd never know."

"I should be so damn lucky. You make more noise than a frigging dump truck," Mark told Steve. "Bet you don't have many girlfriends."

"Shut up," Steve muttered.

Dar smirked but kept quiet as they came around a bend in the wood chip-lined path, the sunlight scattered by the thick leaves overhead. It was cool out, a brisk wind blowing against them, and they found themselves facing a set of wooden structures.

Skippy folded her arms over her clipboard, her cheerfully yellow sweatshirt standing out vividly against the foliage. "Folks, this is the first of our two outdoor team-building exercises. This is our obstacle course." She turned and pointed. "We have our pit, our climbing wall, our ropes, and our tunnels. The objective is to get through the course."

Steve snorted, "No problem." He was wearing a thick t-shirt tucked into a pair of snug jeans, outlining a trimly muscular body.

"Ah ah." Skippy held up a finger. "The key is that everyone on your team has to get through, together," she told him. "You have to work together, because some things will be easy for some of you, and not for others, and you have to help each other out. Everyone understand?"

"Hold on." Eleanor held up a hand, palm out, eyebrows up. "Let me get this straight. You're asking us to climb over those things? Those wood things? And crawl on the ground?"

The counselor nodded. "That's right."

"Forget about it."

Mariana turned. "C'mon, Eleanor, it's not that hard…"

"No way." The Marketing VP shook her head. "I'm not gonna do it."

Dar turned and observed a bluebird hopping his way along a nearby branch. She listened to the squabbling behind her as Mari and Kerry tried to convince Eleanor to give the damn thing a try, while José complained loudly about the idiocy of the course.

"Yeah, you can't expect older folks to handle this," Steve stated helpfully. "It's not fair."

"Hey. I did not say I could not do this," José growled at him. "Keep your mouth to yourself."

Dar waited for a lull as she examined the bark on the tree near her, mottled with dark green moss that gave off a musky scent she could smell from where she was. Finally, she took a breath and turned. "All right." She let her voice lift in its trademark loud snarl. "Shut up!"

In pure reflex, they did, turning to stare at her warily. "I'm not standing out here all day waiting for you people to talk this to death," Dar stated flatly. "This is part of the program, so just get moving, and get this over with, or I'll get on the phone to Alastair and tell him who cooperated, and who didn't."

"You've got no right…" Eleanor burst out.

"Your choice," Dar overrode her easily, getting the words out in an intimidating bark.

They glared at her. She glared back. "Fine," Eleanor finally spat, "but believe you me, I'm going to have a talk of my own with him when I get back. I'm sick and tired of your overbearing BS." She turned and stalked towards the first obstacle. The rest of them stared uncomfortably at the ground for a moment.

"Well," Skippy murmured. "That certainly is a direct method, but you know, we sort of try to promote a more cooperative style here."

"Dar doesn't do cooperative," Steve informed her. "She's why we're here."

"That's not true," Mariana interjected immediately. "But let's not waste time arguing about it. C'mon." She led the way towards the obstacles with the others trailing after her.

Kerry walked beside her boss, watching the tension shift the thick cotton of Dar's sweatshirt over her shoulders. The pale blue eyes were cold and watchful, analyzing the first of the obstacles as they clustered around it warily.

It wasn't very difficult, really. A set of posts wound its way between the cement pad they were standing on over a pit filled with chilly-looking, but not very deep water. Atop the posts was a balance beam, roughly six inches wide, and the objective was, of course, to make their way over it to the other side.

At intervals on the way were dust-free patches, raised slightly.

"Everyone has to get to the other side without falling off," Skippy told them. "If you fall off, you have to come back to the start here, and do it again."

"And you get wet," Duks observed.

"Well, yes," Skippy agreed. "That's not good, so not falling is the whole idea." She folded her arms over her clipboard. "Okay, ready whenever you all are."

Steve promptly hopped up onto the beam and started across, moving slowly, but steadily, holding his arms out for balance. He got to the other side without much trouble, and jumped off, then turned, and held his hands out. "Next?"

Kerry stepped up onto the wood without hesitation. She paused a beat to find her balance, then ambled across as though she'd been strolling down the sidewalk, her adolescent years as a gymnast finally coming in handy. She stepped off the end and gained the security of the concrete, giving Steve a thin smile before she turned and looked back at the rest of the group. Dar remained in the back, watching the progress as Mark took his turn in getting over the water.

"You're pretty smooth on this," Steve purred. "Guess you're used to walking the old tightrope, huh? Working for Dar, I mean."

Kerry placed her hands behind her back, tangling her fingers to resist the urge to slap him. "I spent a few years in gymnastics," she stated. "I never feel like I walk a thin line with Dar. I'm really not sure what your problem is with her."

"Well…." He smiled at her. "Of course, I'm not in love with her."

Slowly, Kerry turned her head, and regarded him. "Are you insinuating that I am?" she asked carefully.

"Sure am, cupcake." His voice oozed with smug knowledge.

"Thank you," the blond woman told him, sincerely, "for the compliment to my good taste."

Steve's eyebrows lifted. "Hmm…maybe we can work out a deal then… you scratch my back, I keep my mouth shut. What about it, Kerry? You're a pretty smart cookie."

"Smart enough to file a sexual harassment complaint the next time you make a comment like that or discuss my personal life again." Kerry stared directly at him. "Dar may blow off your remarks, but I won't."

"Ooo, tough lady, huh?" Steve glanced up as Mark arrived.

"Hey." The MIS Chief stepped casually between Kerry and the much shorter Steve. "Nice going, Kerry, you're a natural."

"Thanks." Kerry managed to keep her voice even, swallowing the bitter taste in her mouth

🐾   🐾   🐾

"I can't do that." Eleanor backed away from the boards. "Forget it."

"Look, it's not so hard." Mariana demonstrated, balancing precariously on the wood. "Just go slow." She edged along the track, wobbling unsteadily.

"Mari, Mari." Dar held a hand up. "Stop trying so hard."

"Easy for you to say," the Personnel VP muttered. "You can probably do this on your hands."

"I'm sure she cannot," Duks rumbled. "Ah, look careful there…"

Mariana waved her arms in a windmilling motion, then lost her balance and toppled off the beam, landing in the water with a splash.

Eleanor chuckled. "Oh, that was almost worth going through this crap for."

"Very funny." Mari sloshed out of the water and gamely tried again, getting a little further this time before she slipped off again. "Shit."

"Tch." Duks gave her a hand out. The beam now was soaked with water, making the footing even more precarious. "Perhaps I should try." He stepped gingerly up and spent a moment trying to balance, then, with a look of serious concentration on his face, started across. "I will tell you that gymnastics is not a forte of mine."

"You're doing better than I did," Mari grumbled, shaking a leg out and scattering droplets of water everywhere. She watched in annoyance as Duks carefully negotiated the slippery area and reached the middle of the pond, where he hesitated.

"It is narrower here, I think."

"No it isn't," Steve called out. "You're imagining things."

"That is not possible. To earn your CPA, you must give up your imagination," Duks responded. "I tell you, it is narrower here." He edged forward, inch by inch, then finally got across. "Ah."

"All right, if you can do it, I can do it," Mari announced, getting up onto the beam. She got two or three feet, then slipped off. "Goddamn it."

Steve started laughing. Kerry gave him a look, then got onto the opposite side, and started recrossing over. "Maybe I can…"

"Hold it." Dar walked to the edge of the water and held up a hand.

"No, maybe I can help her, Dar…"

"Kerry, stop." Her boss's voice rose slightly. Reluctantly, Kerry obeyed, pausing where she was and eyeing Dar doubtfully. "Move forward a few steps." The blond woman hesitated, then stepped forward. "Okay, stop. Now get off on that block."

Kerry stepped off the beam and onto the concrete.

"Duks… c'mon." Dar motioned to him. "Get on that next one." She watched her friend move cautiously over and hop off. Then she got on at the beginning and ambled down the beam, stepping smoothly off it onto the closest square of concrete. "Okay, Mari, try now." She held both arms out, as though emulating a railing. "Grab on if you need to."

"Oh." Mari had been watching them curiously. Now she got up and sidestepped over, grasping lightly onto Dar's outstretched wrist as she moved past. "Good idea." She made it to Kerry, who had extended her hands also, then tapped Duks lightly on the head as she proceeded to the end of the beam and got off in triumph.

There was a momentary silence, then Dar merely turned her head. "C'mon, José. We don't have all afternoon."

They gathered at the other end after they all crossed and Skippy joined them. "Well… we usually like to see some kind of group trouble-solving discussion on this, and a joint resolution." The counselor said. "You should learn to depend on each other, not rely on one person to direct all the action."

"But isn't it true that sometimes you need someone to take the lead if they know what action to take?" Kerry spoke up, seeing the crease appear in Dar's brow. "Sometimes a committee approach just slows things down."

"Walk this way." Skippy directed them. "For the short term, sure, that works," she answered Kerry's question. "But in the long term, people get used to being told what to do, and they stop thinking for themselves."

"Hah," Steve snorted. "Not likely."

Dar laughed, stopping in mid-stride and leaning against a tree. "That's the only thing I've heard in two days that makes sense."

"I wasn't making a joke," Skippy replied stiffly.

Everyone glared at Dar except for Kerry, who rocked a bit on her hiking boots and regarded the leafy path with a studious expression.

"Dar," Mariana exhaled. "Please."

The Ops VP straightened and went quiet, her expression shifting from mild amusement to dour coldness with disturbing rapidity. "Fine. Then we should get moving and get this over with."

Skippy looked like she was going to reply, then thought better of it, and simply led the way on, making several notes on her clipboard as they followed her in silence.

Kerry caught up to Dar and fell in beside her, watching the jaw muscle twitch along one planed cheek. They unconsciously slowed their steps, dropping back behind the rest of the staff by a few paces until the wind gusting lightly against them could blow their words back, and give them a patch of privacy.

"That was a great idea with the beam," Kerry murmured. "No matter what she said."

Dar lifted a hand and rubbed her neck. "Thanks," she answered. "Glad you think so."

Kerry glanced ahead, then let her hand drop, circling Dar's wrist with her fingers and squeezing very gently. She was taking a big chance, she knew, but providing this tiny bit of comfort was abruptly more important to her than any consequences getting caught would bring. "Hang in there."

Dar exhaled in frustration. "I want ice cream."

"Ah." Kerry released her arm, but moved a step closer. "It just so happens I saw a Dairy Queen on the road just outside this place."

Slowly, the dark head turned, and pale eyes viewed her alertly. "Dairy Queen? You're sure?"

Kerry nodded. "Yup."

"Mm." Dar's outlook improved at once. "They've got brown bonnets."

"What?"

A crafty grin curled its way across the Operations VP's face. "C'mon."

🐄 🐄 🐄

"All right. This is the hardest thing you have to do," Skippy exhaled, looking a bit tired herself. "You have to go through this obstacle course, that's this climbing wall here, those tires, those tubes you need to crawl through, and then that pond with the ropes. Once you cross that, we'll have some lunch and relax before the trip home."

Mariana peered up at the climbing wall doubtfully. It was smaller than the ones you typically saw in a military type of camp, but it was high enough, with a net of hemp rope over it providing handholds and footholds. Suspiciously, she put her hand out and touched the rope, drawing it back and peering at it. "There's something on here."

"Mm hmm, grease," Skippy agreed. "Just a little, to make it harder." They stared at her.

"Well, I'll leave you to it." The counselor backed off, ducking under a rope fence and starting back towards the end of the course. "Remember, you all have to make it."

There was a moment of uncomfortable, angry silence. "All right, since you always have the answers, you go first." Eleanor pointed at Dar. "Go on."

Icy blue eyes glared back at her, but Dar stepped forward, examining the ropes warily, very conscious of the attention plastered to her. She lifted a hand and touched the hemp, feeling the unpleasantly cold slimeyness, then blew out a breath and started to climb. She wrapped her hands under the rope instead of over it, and gripped the slick surface tightly, keeping her balance over her slightly bent legs as she found footholds.

Nothing was secure. Dar paused, waiting for her equilibrium to settle.

"Not so easy, huh, big shot?" Steve taunted from below her. "C'mon, I wanna see you fall on your ass, Dar."

Grimly, she started moving again, going sideways to avoid the larger gaps in the webbing, and feeling her fingers start to cramp as she fought to keep a grip on the slippery rope. Suddenly, the surface under her jerked, and she lunged forward, losing her footing and dropping down, suspended only by her arms.

"Steve!" Mari's voice barked in outrage, followed by laughter.

Dar closed her eyes, willing her temper to settle as she concentrated on holding on. Then she carefully drew one leg up and found a purchase, pushing her body up and finding another foothold. Two more moves upward and she could grab the top of the wall, hauling herself up and pressing her body over the edge, then pausing, before she simply let go and allowed herself to drop to the ground, landing with a thump and a hop that jarred her joints unpleasantly.

Then she very deliberately walked over to a short, stunted tree nearby and seated herself under it, leaning her back against the trunk and wiping her hands off on her jeans with slow, disgusted movements. They wanted to make fun of her?

Fine. Let them find their own way over.

To hell with them.

"Why did you do that?" Kerry asked angrily.

"Aw, c'mon. Lighten up," Steve laughed in response. "G'wan, cupcake, you're next."

"Oh no." The blond woman shook her head. "You first." She pointed upward. "Go on…let's see how you feel if someone shakes the ropes while you're climbing."

"Yeah." Mark came up next to Kerry, putting his hands on his hips.

"Now…let's not escalate this," Mariana admonished softly. "I think we need to just back off, and everyone take it easy."

"I will go," Duks interrupted, nudging them out of the way and approaching the net. He was wearing a pair of dark khakis, sturdy walking shoes, and a plain green sweatshirt, and he paused for a few moments before he gingerly took hold of the ropes and started upwards. Halfway up, his feet slipped, and he slithered down the ropes, with Steve and José diving out of the way to avoid being hit. They both laughed as Duks landed on his behind in the mud.

Mari offered him a hand up. "C'mon folks. We need to work together."

Steve just pushed her out of the way. "Let me show you how." He nimbly scaled the ropes, his athletic frame clinging to the strands as he followed Dar's path up and over the top. Instead of jumping over, however, he settled on the top. "Okay, just follow me, right?"

Duks brushed his hands against his trousers and started his ascent again, this time gripping the ropes as Dar had, a hold that supported his heavier frame more efficiently.

"No, no, not there. Step over there." Steve pointed. "Not there!"

Duks looked up. "I would suggest that you continue your progress before my progress equals it," the accountant rumbled. "I do not need your instructions."

Mari sighed and rubbed her temples, giving Kerry a look. The blond woman was standing with her arms crossed, a dour look on her usually good-natured face. "Maybe I should suggest deep sea fishing the next time."

Steve hopped over the edge and disappeared, and Duks finished his climb soon after. Mark carefully followed, along with Elaine, and Peter, leaving Mari, Eleanor, and Kerry still on the other side.

"I don't think I can do that," Mari finally admitted.

Eleanor looked sharply at her, then exhaled. "I don't think I can either."

They both looked at Kerry. "I think we should try it together,"

Kerry said. "I do this a lot. I'll go in the middle, and we can help each other. How's that?"

It was doubtful for a moment, then they both nodded and joined her at the base of the wall.

🐃🐃 🐃🐃 🐃🐃

An hour later, they stood before the swinging ropes, their last obstacle before going home. A dour grumpiness had fallen over everyone, and there wasn't a hand or leg that wasn't covered in muck or mud. Mariana pushed her hair back from her eyes and left a dark smudge, then sighed. "All right. Now what?"

José picked up a rope. "We go over." He shook his head. "Stupidest thing I have ever seen." Wrapping his hands around the rope, he backed a step, then trundled for the edge, pushing himself out into space.

Theoretically, he should have hit the far shore, but it was longer than it looked, and he came up short, then swung back over towards the rest of them.

Up.

Back.

Up.

Back.

Finally he ended up in the center, and lost his grip, falling into the surprisingly deep pit of water beneath him. "Son of a puta." He stood up and simply sloshed through the pit, climbing out on the other side. "To the hell with it. I am leaving."

"He's right. I'm not going to do this." Eleanor walked carefully around the pit and joined José. The rest of them turned and looked at Dar, who simply grabbed a rope and shoved off, her lighter form clearing the pit easily as she dropped off on the other side.

Kerry followed, getting caught on the other end by her lover and not even bothering to look surprised when Dar landed her neatly on her feet. "Thanks." She tried to rub some of the grease off her hands. "I think I'm over this."

Mariana and Duks trooped around the edge of the pit as well. "I think I can chalk this up to an interesting experiment," the Personnel VP sighed.

Mark swung over, then Elaine joined them. Steve waited for the very end, then stylishly leaped onto the rope, and swung his way to the other side, jumping off with a little flourish.

"Come on." Eleanor said. "Let's get out of here."

"Oh no." Steve held a hand up. "You guys didn't follow the rules, and you know what Skippy said." He'd seen the woman approaching. "I'm going to have to tell her about it."

"No, you're not." Dar turned on him, her voice dropping.

"Don't give me the alpha bitch routine, Dar. If this is getting reported, I'm going to make sure our boss knows who cooperated, and who didn't, and I…"

Dar grabbed him, and swung him against the nearest tree, making the most of her height and weight advantage. "Shut up."

"You're in big trouble now," Steve warned. "Let go of me."

Dar leaned closer. "You listen here, mister. You. Are. Between. Me." She shoved Steve hard against the bark. "And Dairy Queen. So you better just keep your mouth shut."

Eleanor and José looked flummoxed, caught between agreeing with Dar and supporting their colleague. Exhaustion won out. "She is right," José finally said. "Keep your mouth shut, or I will have you scraping the floors at work tomorrow." He hesitated. "But Dar, get your hands off him, will you?"

"Gladly." Dar released her grip and stepped back. Marks from the grease on her hands smudged his shirt, and he glared at her, his body tensing.

She smiled back. "Go ahead, Steve. I can still kick your ass."

Skippy arrived, and absorbed the tense scene. "Well. I see we all finished, right?" she asked desperately. "We've got some fresh baked cookies up at the lodge. Why don't we all head up there and change, then we can recap our visit, okay?"

Silence.

"Okay?" Skippy asked again, hesitantly. "C'mon, ladies and gentlemen, we're all adults here, remember?"

"Some of us more than others." Eleanor wiped her hands together in disgust and headed off down the path. "Let's get out of here."

Dar held her position a moment more, then simply turned and followed, leaving Steve standing there with his hands balled up into fists in frustration.

🐾 🐾 🐾

It was a very quiet bus ride home. After Dar had commandeered the vehicle for a trip to Dairy Queen, ignoring the sarcastic comments and looks, she'd taken over the back seat of the bus and sprawled across it, nursing her ice cream cone in frosty silence. The rest of them separated, with Mark and Kerry wandering towards the back to settle near their boss, and the marketing and sales group going to the very front to put as much distance between them as possible. Mariana and Duks stayed in the middle, and not much was said for the first hour or so.

Then Eleanor walked back towards Mariana purposefully. "I want a meeting tomorrow," she said crisply. "In the morning, with Alastair on the phone. I have issues I want addressed, Mariana. I'm not putting up with this crap one minute longer."

"Sure," Mari sighed, leaning her head back against the window. "You want it catered?"

"Don't get smart with me. This is serious!" the Marketing VP snapped. "Mari, how long can we go on like this? It's ridiculous!" She glanced back to where Dar was. "I've had it. I want a conference with him, and I want changes made, and José feels the same way."

Mariana laid her forearm over her eyes. "Fine. I'll set up a meeting." She glanced past her wrist at the blond woman. "Anything else?"

Eleanor stared at her, then turned and walked back to her seat, shaking her head.

"This could be trouble," Duks murmured. "I do not think this ended up to be a very good idea."

Mari sighed. "No, really?" she muttered back. "I don't know what in the hell's gotten into Dar. She used to just laugh this stuff off. You'd think it was that time of the month with her, except that, with Dar, it's always that time of the month."

Duks exhaled. "Alastair is not going to be happy; our friend up there is foolish enough to start demanding things, and you know how he feels."

"Mm." The Personnel VP nodded. "I'm hoping they both threaten to leave if he doesn't get rid of Dar." She glanced over to see a startled look coming back at her. "Sorry. They're a pain in my ass, Dukky, and you know which option Alastair's gonna choose. He loves Dar."

"We cannot go on like this, however. She does have a point," he reminded her. "And you never know, Mari. He could decide against her this time."

Mariana peeked between the seat backs towards the rear of the bus, and sighed heavily. "She's not helping with that attitude."

Duks chuckled softly. "And when, my dear, have you ever known Dar not to have such a one?"

Mari simply grunted and shook her head.

🐾 🐾 🐾

"You know something?" Kerry prodded at her vanilla ice cream, a large scoop nestling in the root beer of her float. "Ice cream really does make you feel better." She looked up at Dar, who was neatly nibbling concentric circles of hardened chocolate off her cone. "Why is that? Because it's so bad for you or what?"

"Who cares?" Dar replied, catching a drop of melting cream with her tongue. "I just know when I was a kid, and bad stuff happened, ice cream fixed it." She bit off a chunk of chocolate and chewed it contentedly. "When my dad was home, Friday nights were movie and ice cream nights. We'd go watch something gory and violent, then go to Swenson's or Jaxson's and share a tub half the size of my car together." She took a lazy swipe of her tongue over the cone. "Even my mother gave up and joined in; she always stole the cherries."

"Mm...my parents would have had a heart attack if we'd done that," Kerry admitted. "I remember when I went off to college, the first night I spent in the dorms I went out to the local supermarket and got a whole pint of coffee chocolate chip ice cream and sat on my bed and ate it." She chuckled a little. "I got sick to my stomach, but boy, did I ever feel like I was quite the rebel that night."

Dar smiled briefly. "I can just picture that." And she could, right down to the look of intent glee on Kerry's very expressive face. "We'd have made good roommates."

Kerry smiled back and nodded, but kept her answer to that to herself, sparing an amused moment of imagination regarding Dar and her rather staid private college.

"Hey, boss?' Mark leaned over from the other seat, sucking on a milkshake. "Is this going to be one of those huge, 'let's have six million meetings and not decide a thing' kinda thing?"

Dar shrugged. "I don't care. I'm gonna go to work tomorrow and pretend it never happened." She set to work nibbling the sugar cone with a serious expression. "If José and his whipping boy want to make an issue of it, let them go to Alastair."

Mark and Kerry exchanged looks. "I thought this whole thing was his idea," Kerry ventured. "Won't he be pissed off it didn't work too well?"

"Too well?" Mark snorted. "Jesus, Kerry, it was a frigging disaster."

Dar shrugged again. "First big crisis, he'll forget about it." She crunched a mouthful of cone. "Besides, I told him it wouldn't work. Worst case is, there'll be a meeting where everybody screams at each other, and someone mentions the words 'improvement plan' and that'll be it."

Kerry settled back in her seat, and tried to ignore the resentment emanating from the front of the bus. Privately, she wasn't as sure as Dar about how much trouble the weekend would cause, and not only because of the failure of the retreat either. With a sigh, she closed her eyes and put the thoughts aside, resolving to leave the issue for another day.

Wasn't anything she could do about it now, at any rate, was there?

The conference room was frosty, even disregarding the chill of the early morning air conditioning that sent clouds of condensation over the windows and blurred the pale coral light of the recently past dawn. Mariana presided at the head of the table, her leather portfolio set neatly in front of her and a long, thin pencil moving edgily between her fingers. José and Eleanor perched side by side along one long axis of the table, and Steve Fabricini was seated across from them, his arms folded inside stone gray Armani sleeves.

José looked at his watch. "It is seven."

"Six, by his time," Mari reminded him. "Give him a minute to sit down at his desk."

"I want to make sure we take care of this early." Eleanor leaned forward, her rose-colored silk dress shifting with her. "First thing, before anyone complicates things."

"You mean, before Dar gets in to work and can defend herself," Mari responded coldly.

"That is not the point," José stated stiffly.

The phone rang, making them all jump. "Hmph." Eleanor straightened. "At least he's on time."

Mariana pressed the speakerphone button. "Alastair?"

"Good morning," the CEO's cheerful voice reverberated through the nearly empty room. "How is everyone?"

"Lousy," José blurted. "Alastair, this is the final straw. If you do not do something about this woman, it will be a disaster."

There was a pause. "Okay," Alastair replied, "suppose you start at the beginning, hmm? Who's 'this woman'?"

Mari leaned forward. "Alastair, it's Mariana. The weekend didn't go well."

"Ah."

"It...just wasn't the right venue, Alastair; too much at once, I think." Mari rotated her pencil. "Maybe a few shorter sessions, lunches or something, would have been better."

"It wouldn't have worked anyway," Steve interrupted. "Dar Roberts made sure of that. She was against the idea from the start, and sabotaged all efforts of the staff there to make any progress at all. A dismal failure."

José nodded. "Yes, Steve is right," he agreed. "Dar was very uncooperative, Alastair, despite that she knew you wanted this idea to work, yes?"

"Exactly," Eleanor added. "It's like always. Teamwork is impossible with her, and always will be. We went backwards instead of forwards." She paused. "Alastair, you need to make a change."

It was quiet for a bit. "So." The CEO didn't sound overly upset. "You're telling me that, despite my best wishes, Dar threw a spanner in the works out there, right?"

"Exactly," José and Eleanor stated together.

"She was obstructionist, and uncooperative, and generally, a bitch on wheels, right?"

"Yes." Steve lightly slapped the table, as the morning sun started penetrating, hitting highlights in the mahogany wood surface. "It's just like it is every day. Whatever we try, wherever we attempt to get ahead, there she is, one big roadblock."

"Well, I'm glad you all called me," Alastair told them. "It's a good thing when my staff feels they can relate their concerns to me, and expect me to resolve these larger issues for them."

José, Eleanor and Steve exchanged triumphant looks. "You will take care of things then, yes?" José asked hopefully. "It is for the best, Alastair, I believe that."

"Absolutely," the CEO assured him cheerfully. "You'll have to give me a few weeks, but I guarantee I can make some changes that'll just clear up those logjams in a jiff. All right?"

"Great." Eleanor sat back with a relieved smile. "I knew we could count on you, Alastair."

"Not at all. Go get some breakfast, you all; talk to you later."
Alastiar's voice faded on the last word, and they heard a click as he
hung up.

José stood. "Well, you win some, and you lose some, Ms. Mariana.
We won today." He gave her a big smile. "Come, let's go get some
cafecita and celebrate." The three filed out of the office, leaving a somber Mariana sitting there, the sun at her back, in a pool of shadows.

Chapter 9

"Oh God, is it Friday yet?" Kerry leaned her head on her hands, trying to block out the sight of her overflowing inbox. A glance at her calendar told her she was still one day short. "This week is lasting a month," she sighed, speaking to the empty space before her.

Her phone buzzed, and she hit the answer button. "Operations, Stuart."

A panicked voice answered. "Oh, great...uh, Ms. Stuart, this is Roger in Charlotte...uh, we've got a problem?"

"Okay." Kerry leaned forward, kicking her problem solving brain cells into gear. "What is it?"

A loud sound of splashing came through the phone. "Uh...ow!" Roger yelped. "Um, the sprinkler system went off over here, and umm—yeeow!" The phone fumbled and clattered, then was picked up. "Damn chair hit me in the—uh, well, anyway, we're flooded."

"Flooded," Kerry repeated carefully. "As in underwater?"

"Shit!" he yelped. "Uh, sorry…yeah, the control room's three feet deep, and it's not getting any…wow!" A loud popping and snapping was heard. "Yow…I think that was the main breaker panel going…"

"Roger?" Kerry spoke loudly into the phone.

"Yeah?" He answered. "Oh, wait, I gotta get up onto the desk…"

"Get out of there!" Kerry yelled, then put him on hold and dialed Dar's extension, waiting for her boss to pick up. "Help!" she barked into the phone, then switched back to the other line. "Roger?"

"Uh… I've got a problem, Ms. Stuart," the man answered nervously.

"More than one," Kerry told him. "What is it?"

"I can't swim," he answered, "and I think I just saw a 3270 float by." The phone suddenly disconnected.

"Shit." Kerry glanced up as she heard running steps, then half stood as her inner door burst open and Dar pounced inside, her pale blue eyes snapping, every inch of her bristling with unreleased energy.

"What's wrong?" she snapped.

The blond woman drew in a breath. "God, you look sexy when you do that."

Dar was obviously knocked off stride. "Wha… buh…" She blinked. "Kerry! You yelled for help; what in the hell's going on?"

"Oh, right…Charlotte's been flooded out," Kerry quickly explained. "Sorry about that…they're in big trouble." She walked over and put an arm around her lover. "Sorry, Dar, I didn't mean for you to think that I was, um…" She rooted around for a phrase.

"In mortal danger?" Dar relaxed a little. "I just knocked a Xerox repairman so far back onto his butt they're probably going to have to surgically remove the toner drum from his throat." She sighed and rubbed her face. "Okay, so we've got a potential disaster, right?"

"Mm…Roger from Netops just told me he thought he saw a 3270 terminal floating in the control room," Kerry advised her.

"Anyone check to see if they're burning hemp around there again?" Dar snorted. "3270s don't float." She tapped her foot. "Okay, let me go start working the problem. Try to get them back on the phone, or call the cells," she called back as she walked out shaking her head.

Kerry smiled a little as she heard the muted excitement in Dar's tone. *She loves this*, the blond woman realized. *She loves when things are really tough and hard, and she can go in and fix them.* With a soft chuckle, she turned back to her desk and called up a network schematic, wincing at the flashing red dots that indicated down sections. "Oh, that bites." She started dialing emergency numbers.

"Look, I don't give a damn about what you have to do to release that," Dar growled into the phone. "I need your damn president on this phone in five minutes or the next call is from our legal department. Your choice." She glanced up as Maria stuck her head in and waved a small cardboard tray. One hand lifted and waved her forward. "I'll hold."

Maria came over with the pastalitos and offered them to her. "I have three of those little queso ones," the secretary whispered. "I know you like them."

Dar's eyes twinkled gently as she nodded and put her hand over the receiver. She mouthed her thanks as she accepted the pastries and the steaming cup of creamy coffee, glancing up and meeting Maria's eyes. "Tough week."

"Sí," Maria agreed. "I will look forward to the weekend."

"Me too," her boss agreed wanly. "Maybe I'll take a ride down to the Keys."

"That is a good idea, Dar. Kerrisita will like that." She smiled and ducked out of the office, closing the door behind her.

Dar regarded the closed door in startled silence as a voice came back on the line. "Well?" she snapped.

"Ms. Roberts, we have a team of people heading out that way, I'm not sure…" the man hesitated.

"Look," Dar growled, sending her voice down to its lowest pitch. "I need to know what chemicals were in that sprinkler mixture and I need to know NOW!" She punched up the volume, feeling the sound reverberate in her chest. "Or you're going to take responsibility for the bill when I have to fly a chemical hazard team in there on a goddamned Learjet!" The insurance company was refusing to allow any employees to enter the networking office until the dangers were evaluated, and they had fully three quarters of the domestic network down, three hours after the accident had happened.

"Dar." Maria poked her head in. "Mariana on line numero dos." She called, in a low voice.

"Not now." Dar muted her current call. "I'm in the middle of a disaster." She watched as Maria disappeared, then propped her head up on one hand and released the mute button with the other. "Do I get that, or do I call my legal department? I'm done screwing around with you people."

Rustling papers, and low mutters. "Where do you need the information sent?" the voice stiffly answered. "We can pass along our usual information, but you have to understand that the composition will vary depending on local water quality, and the types of pipes, and…"

"Just send it," Dar interrupted him, and repeated the fax number at their insurance company's branch office in North Carolina. She looked up as Kerry entered and suppressed a smile. "And I'd like to know why that system discharged." An idea occurred to her, and she spent a moment analyzing it for loopholes. Then she smiled.

Kerry circled her and picked up a pastry, nibbling it as she perched on the corner of Dar's desk and listened to the agitated muttering coming from the phone. "Everyone's screaming," she mouthed.

Dar lifted her hands and let them drop. "Bite me," she mouthed back. "I didn't set off the goddamned sprinklers."

Kerry obligingly put her pastry down and captured Dar's fingers, lifting them and nibbling on a thumb instead. "Okay."

"Ms. Roberts, we just don't know what caused it yet," the hapless voice came through the phone. "It could have been a false heat reading, it could have been a mechanical error; there's no sense in speculating since we don't really have any data. My team is on their way there. As soon as they get there and figure out what happened, believe me, I'll call you."

Dar felt an enjoyable tickle as the neat white teeth scraped lightly across the sensitive skin on the side of her finger. "All right," she agreed. "But I have an entire data center down, and they can't even get in there to start cleaning up, so they'd better move their asses." She hung up.

The phone rang again, and she glanced at it. "Your line."

Both of their pagers went off simultaneously. "We can talk later." The blond woman gave her a grimace. "Wasn't anything big, really." She reached for the phone. "Operations, Stuart."

A harried voice answered her. "Kerry, this is John Collins. I've got the New York office breathing down my neck, and I can't get a hold of Dar…you gotta give me something to tell them."

Dar put the call on hold a moment. "John's a nice guy, but he's got the spine of a jellyfish. Whatever you tell him, he'll repeat as gospel," she warned with a smile.

Kerry smiled back. "All right." She spared a glance for the phone, still flashing. "So what in blazes do I tell him, Dar?"

"Huh?" Dar's brow creased as she followed Kerry's eyes. "Oh, right." She rubbed her temples. "Um...tell him we're sending an executive team to North Carolina to take charge and get the systems back up as soon as possible."

Kerry reached for the button, then hesitated. "We are?" she asked curiously.

A sneaky, seductive grin tugged at one side of Dar's mouth. "Yeah. I figure eight hours to get their asses in gear, and a couple days for us in a little cabin I happen to know about near there." She hesitated, both brows lifting hopefully. "Sound okay?"

Sea green eyes blinked. "You mean us?" She pointed at Dar's chest, then at her own. "You and me, we're going up there?"

Dar simply nodded, shunting aside the objections she knew would be raised. If she got it done...no one would remember how she did it anyway.

"Awesome," Kerry pronounced, then hit the button. "Hello, John?" She muted the mic for a moment. "They don't have any horseback riding up there, do they?" She released the mic. "John, we know it's really bad. You can tell them that Dar's going up there to take charge personally."

Pause. "No shit?" Collins replied, clearly impressed. "That'll get them off my ass. Thanks Kerry, you're the best."

"It's my pleasure," the blond woman assured him cheerfully, all thoughts of Steve dissolved. She disconnected the line and turned to Dar. "Now. We were discussing horses, right?"

A chuckle. "Yeah, they've got some trail riding, figured we could do a little hiking while we're up there," she offered. "If we leave tonight, we'll have tomorrow and Friday to get the network office back up, then the whole weekend to play. I'll get Maria to start making reservations."

Kerry smiled. "Want me to go home and pick up our bags?" she offered. "When's the flight?"

Dar rattled a few keys and looked up schedules. "Seven, and that would be a great idea," Dar praised her. "Make sure you pack some warm stuff; it's chilly up there." Her brows lifted seductively. "A little too much for any scanty lingerie, unfortunately."

Kerry stood and slid a fingertip down the buttoned closure of Dar's silk shirt. "I don't know, I think you look really sexy in just that old jersey of yours," she whispered.

A soft chuckle. "Oh, you do, do you?"

"Mm hmm." The blond woman lowered her voice even more. "But then, you're gorgeous, Dar. You'd look sexy in a burlap sack," she confided, brushing her lips against her lover's. "I'm going to go get our stuff. I need some fresh air anyway." She patted Dar's leg, then stepped around her desk, heading purposefully for the door.

Dar watched her go, then let out a long, slow breath. "Wow." She ran a hand through her hair. "I think I need a little fresh air myself." She knew she should be more worried about the problem, but she found herself unable to shift her attention far from the coming weekend, a stress relief she felt they both needed. "All work and no play makes Dar a bitch to live with... can't have that now, can we?"

The sunlight winked merrily at her feet in cheerful agreement.

🐾   🐾   🐾

"Yeah, that's right, Col." Kerry stretched her legs out and closed her eyes, sucking in a deep breath of the sun-warmed air coming in the window of the Mustang. "We're going to North Carolina...we've got a big mess there to take care of."

"Oh, right, yeah, I heard about that," Colleen informed her. "My boss was screaming because the interbank transfers won't go through." She cleared her throat. "No problem, Ker. Staying out there isn't any kinda hardship, you know? Breakfast on the ocean, little tuxedoed manikins puttering about...no problem at all."

"Great," the blond woman sighed. "I never thought I'd be glad of a disaster, but I can't say I regret this one." She stifled a yawn. "After we fix things, we're going up to a place Dar knows of near there for a little R and R."

"Oh?" Colleen sounded more interested. "Well now, me lassie, you didn't tell me that...so you and the tall dark one are finally taking some time off together. That's great."

"Yeah." Kerry smiled at the convertible's roof. "That'll be a first for us. Even over Christmas we had so much going on we hardly had time to breathe, much less relax. I'm really looking forward to a few days alone with her." And wasn't that the truth. Kerry found herself impatiently wishing the crisis was well over and solved, freeing them to leave the technical problems behind and concentrate on each other.

A weekend hiking up in the quiet of the wilderness was very, very appealing, and she knew they both could use the break. "You think they'll have a hot tub?" she mused.

Colleen laughed. "Well, if it's the kinda place I think Dar likes, I'm sure it will have...you can do some lovely skiing up in the mountains, y'know," she commented. "Get yourself a nice fireplace, and toast you up some marshmallows, girl."

"Mm." Kerry could almost taste the warm, slightly burned morsels. Then she imagined sharing them messily with Dar and grinned, feeling the skin around her eyes crinkling up in amusement. "Sounds good to me."

"Heh...your eating habits surely have changed," Colleen teased. "And then there's the food, as well."

Kerry almost swallowed her tongue. "Colleen!"

"Ah ah, don't you be Colleening me, little Miss Michigan snow-balls-wouldn't-melt-in-me-mouth," her friend chortled. "I'm just joshing, Kerry. Honestly, I think Dar's the best thing that ever happened to you."

"Oh yeah, she's turning me into a decadent little butterball, that's what," Kerry laughed. "But thanks," she added quietly. "I'm glad you ended up liking her." She put her car into gear as the ferry docked. "I'm going to get our stuff packed. Talk to you later, Col, and thanks again for staying over."

She hung up the phone, and steered carefully onto the island, pausing for the spraydown before she turned onto the perimeter road and headed to the condo. The sprinklers were on in the center of the island, making an interesting chatter and sending a whiff of mineral-laden moist air to Kerry's nose. She pulled into her parking spot, then paused, backing up a little. "Aww." She found herself grinning stupidly. The maintenance department had painted her name on the concrete bumper. "'K. Stuart'...check that out." She got out of the car and examined it, the neat black letters crisp against the white concrete, matching the "D. Roberts" right next to it half hidden behind Dar's tires.

It was such a tiny, insignificant thing, but it touched something deep inside Kerry, reinforcing her sense that this was, indeed, home. She gave the Lexus a little pat, then shouldered her briefcase and headed up the stairs, plucking the mail from the mailbox before unlocking the door. Chino started whining the minute it opened, and Kerry dropped her case on the loveseat as she headed towards the kitchen. "Okay, okay honey, I hear you." She ambled across the tile floor and opened the gate, letting the puppy out to attack her feet fiercely. "Hey, hey, careful." She put the mail down and crouched, petting Chino's soft fur. "Easy, I know, I'm glad to see you too."

Chino whined ecstatically, her whole body wriggling with joy as she chewed on Kerry's fingers. Then she cocked her head and looked past the blond woman expectantly. Kerry laughed. "Sorry, kiddo, she's not with me." She scratched the puppy's ears. "I know she's your buddy, huh?"

Chino blinked, then apparently gave up on Dar and concentrated on attacking Kerry's shoes. "Raowr." The puppy tugged on a lace, dropping it and barking in outrage when the thing persisted in remaining attached to Kerry and all the animal's pulling couldn't budge her.

"Why don't you go out while I get some stuff done, huh?" Kerry opened the back door, allowing the puppy to scamper down into the tiny, walled garden. It was safe for her there, since Dar had spent most of one weekend puppy-proofing it. She watched Chino sniff around for a minute, then she went inside and started getting together two bags, starting with Dar's.

Which was easy. Jeans, neatly pressed polos, two sweaters (which were all she owned), her one flannel shirt, the sweatshirt Kerry loved on her, and nice warm socks. And underwear, of course. Kerry had fun picking out her favorite ones of those, including the really cute ones with tiny pictures of Dogbert on them. Oh, and the baseball jersey and shorts, and her bathroom kit, including the small bottle of spicy talc powder Kerry loved to sprinkle over her. She sniffed it and closed her eyes, a tiny humming noise erupting from her throat that almost startled her.

"Jesus." She clapped a hand on her forehead. "I'm turning into such a hedonist," she muttered, putting the bag away and zipping up the carry on duffel Dar always used. But that's how Dar made her feel, she reflected, all sexy and sensual, like she was taking a bath in pheromones most of the time. Everything seemed more intense: the smell of her, the deep, rich color of her eyes...

"Oh boy." Kerry stopped and took several breaths. "I think I need a drink of water." She carried the bag to the couch and let it drop, then continued on into the kitchen and poured herself a glass of peach flavored iced tea, which slid down her throat in a cool, nicely sweetened wave. She leaned against the counter and sipped it, thinking about TCP/IP routing tables until her body had settled down again and she could head upstairs to her own room.

Her bag was a little tougher, mostly because she actually had winter clothes to choose from. She threw in a few pairs of jeans, though, since they were more comfortable than the heavy corduroy that were her other choice, Dar having informed her she really liked the way Kerry looked in jeans having nothing to do with the decision, of course.

Of course. Kerry smiled, as she flipped through her collection of soft wool sweaters, selecting two that were favorites of hers, and one whose color reminded her of Dar's eyes. That one was a gift from her brother, and it hugged her curves, bringing out an appreciative smile on Dar's face the last time she'd had the occasion to wear it. She tucked them inside her leather bag alongside a couple of long sleeved shirts she could wear under them. She also added a pair of mittens and her own warm socks and bath kit, glad she wasn't due for her period until late the week after.

Once she had everything packed, she started to go downstairs but stopped, setting the bag on her bed and going to the dresser where she tugged the drawer open and pulled out a small, velvet case. Pensively, she opened it, her eyes tracing the now familiar outlines of the beautifully sculpted ring inside. Was it time?

Kerry sighed, and closed the case, putting it back in the drawer. Part of her wanted to just push through the insecurities, and go ahead with the gift, but another part of her hesitated, caught between the fear that Dar wouldn't want that kind of commitment and the inner knowledge that she, Kerry, needed it in some deep, almost uncomfortable way.

Maybe... She chewed her lip. Maybe on Valentine's day? It was only two weeks... A nervous ball formed in her stomach. Maybe she could sort of feel Dar out this weekend, just to make sure she wasn't going to make a total fool out of herself when she did it.

Oh, come on, Kerry...you know she loves you, she chastised herself. *Jesus, she's not going to laugh or anything.*

Right? Kerry drummed her fingers on one thigh, then snatched the case up and tucked it into her bag, zipping it up and hitching the strap up onto her shoulder. Maybe she'd practice, she decided, going downstairs and putting her bag on the couch next to Dar's, then sitting down and leafing through the mail. She pulled out the three or four pieces that were hers, forwarded from the Kendall address. Two were bills, a third was an offer to beta test a new office applications suite, and the fourth... "Haven't heard from her in a while." Kerry turned the letter from her great aunt over in her fingers before she lifted the flap and pulled out the creamy, soft stationery, faintly scented with the smell of dust and memories. She opened it and spread the paper out on her knees, studying the thin, spidery script.

Dear Kerrison,

My dear, word has come to me that you are estranged from your parents - and this troubles me greatly. Not for their sake, as you know well that I never did get on with your father, but for your sake, as I know how much family means to you.

Your sister tells me you are well and living there in Miami, with a person she tells me you are quite fond of. With her usual feckless nattering, she managed to talk all around the subject, but I am going to assume this person is another woman, and while you may think my aged nerves can't take it, I will gladly inform you that this is not the case.

Splendid for you, my dear. I would love to meet this person, and I want to assure you that regardless of what your parents seem to think, your extended family is not cut off from you in any way. You are always welcome in my home, and I know Mitchell would love to see you. Please do call me when you get a chance, since I also would like to get the real story, as opposed to the bowdler-ized version your sister saw fit to grace my supposedly tender ears with.

With great affection,

Aunt Penny

Kerry grinned as she reread the letter. "Good old Aunt Penny." She shook her head, remembering the old but sharp woman whom she'd last seen before she'd moved to Miami—when she'd given her the old emerald ring, and laughed, making Kerry turn around in the light, watching her with twinkling eyes the same shade as Kerry's own.

Aunt Penny had been one of the only people in Kerry's life who had told her, point blank, that she was pretty, displacing years of her mother's continual harping on her looks. Kerry would have cherished her for that alone, but she'd always gotten a sense of warm affection from her aunt, and she was glad even this latest disaster hadn't broken that tie. She made a mental note to call her aunt after the weekend, and, on a whim, went back up to her room and got a small box of writing paper, tucking it inside her bag along with a couple of her favorite pens. "That's what I'll do, Chino, I'll write her a note…she'd like that," she told the puppy, who had curled up contentedly at her feet. "I bet she'd like you, too. She had a Scottish terror, I mean, terrier, who used to eat my shoes when I went over there."

Chino looked up, then settled her chin on Kerry's foot, and sighed. Kerry sighed too, and leaned back against the couch's soft leather, drinking in the peace of the place. She picked up Chino and cuddled her, smiling when the puppy sprawled across her chest, the warm breath sneaking between the buttons on her shirt.

She'd just relax here for a minute, then head on back to the office.

🐾 🐾 🐾

"Here you go, Dar." Maria bustled in, handing over two sets of airline ticket folders. "I have you both booked on the plane, and your hotel room is okay." The secretary gave her an impish smile. "They have only rooms with...how you say, a jaguar in them."

Dar stopped what she was doing and looked up, startled. "What?" She glanced at the tickets. "A jaguar?"

"Sí... with the bubbles." Maria made a circling motion with her hand. "In the water."

"Oh, oh, a Jacuzzi," Dar chuckled, and gave her a stern look. "It's strictly business, Maria."

"Sí, sí, but you know how important is it to stay very clean, Dar," Maria replied virtuously. "You know, it is bad if you come back with the germs."

Slowly, pale blue eyes lifted and regarded her, a mischievous grin tugging at Dar's lips. "Maria, if I didn't know better, I'd say you were encouraging me to do something against company policy."

Maria blinked at her. "Oh, sí," she nodded seriously. "I will see you Monday, Dar; have a good time." She trotted out, leaving a very bemused and somewhat taken aback boss sitting behind her desk. "A jaguar, huh?" She tucked the folders inside her jacket and glanced at her watch. "And speaking of which..." She picked up the phone and dialed Kerry's cellular number.

It took four rings before there was an answer, and the voice sounded a little dazed. "Oh shit."

Dar regarded the phone with some amusement. "And a good afternoon to you, too, Kerrison," she drawled. "What's up?"

"Shit, shit shit," Kerry fumed. "I'm so sorry, Dar. I got things packed, then sat I down and played with Chino for a minute and I fell asleep." Sounds of rustling came from the phone. "I'm on my way back. I don't know what in the heck came over me." She sounded disgusted. "God..."

"Hey, take it easy." Dar laughed. "We got up early, we didn't get too much sleep last night, and if you're tired, it makes sense to take a damn nap. You didn't miss anything." She reached over and took a sip of coffee from her cup. "The center's still down, they still need our help, I've got our tickets, and Maria booked us in a hotel room complete with a Jacuzzi."

Momentary silence. "Oh really?" Kerry had closed the car door, and the sound of the engine starting up was heard. "A Jacuzzi, huh? She's subtle. Sounds good, though; Colleen was tempting me with visions of you, me, a fire and some marshmallows."

"Ooo," Dar purred. "I could go for that…I love marshmallows." She stood up and started packing up her laptop. "I'll be waiting downstairs; we can pick up a quick snack at the airport before we get on the plane."

"Okay." Kerry stifled a yawn. "See you in a few minutes."

The half-full plane was quiet, and Dar took the opportunity to relax in her comfortable seat, a glass of white wine balanced on the console between herself and Kerry. The blond woman was curled up half on her side, a soft, blue blanket tucked around her as she idly watched Dar's profile. "We'll have to go out to the office as soon as we get there," Dar commented, laying a casual hand over Kerry's. "It's going to be a long night."

"Okay," Kerry mumbled, shifting over and curling her fingers around Dar's. "As long as I can spend it with you, I don't care how long it is." She closed her eyes and exhaled.

Dar gazed at her quietly, absorbing the unexpected compliment. "Thanks," she finally said, softly. A sea green orb appeared, and studied her. "That was a really sweet thing to say."

Kerry blushed gently and closed her eye again, giving the fingers held in hers a little squeeze. "You bring out the poet in me," she admitted softly. "It's the weirdest thing."

"Oh really?" Dar rolled half onto her side, facing the blond woman. "Got any handy?"

Alarmed green eyeball. "Any what handy?"

"Poems," her lover replied, a wicked twinkle in her eyes. "You said I brought that out in you. I know you're writing them; I'd love to hear one."

"B…" Kerry's brain ran around in circles for a minute. "I…b…"

"Well, that sort of rhymes, yeah," Dar mused. "Doesn't have much emotional impact, though." She took a sip of her wine. "Is that one of those haiku things?"

Kerry burst out giggling. "Dar!" she chastised her boss. "I, um…you know I…that kind of thing sort of embarrasses me." She looked up to see a look of veiled disappointment on Dar's face. "Well, maybe one," she relented, hesitantly. "But I'll have to drag my notebook out when we get there… I don't memorize them."

The blue eyes continued to regard her.

"Come on, Dar, I can't just make one up on command, you know." Kerry tried to avoid looking at the soulful expression. "It just doesn't work like that."

Dar sighed. "Okay." She let her head drop down onto the seat's surface and lowered her gaze.

Kerry chewed her lip, her brows knitting as she regarded the angular profile facing her.

In the darkness of the world we walk,
Unwilling pawns, and victims of the night,
With no guidance save that of false prophets.
But I walk the shadows and do not fear their dangers,
For my heart is shielded by the shining defense
That is the armor of your love.

She felt very awkward, and could hardly look at Dar's face as she finished, a solid, dark blush coloring her cheeks. "I know it's really kind of corny, and I have no idea what made me…oh."

Lips very gently brushed against hers, and she tasted their sweetness.

"It's not corny," Dar rumbled into her ear. "I think it's incredible." She kissed Kerry again, glad of the dimmed cabin lighting. "Just like you."

"Mm…" The blond woman found her hands moving irresistibly towards the warm body next to her. "Now which one of us is the poet?"

🦋   🦋   🦋

It was a dark and stormy night. Kerry rolled phrase around inside her head as she peered through the darkness surrounding them. They'd gotten to the airport safely and retrieved a rental car, then headed out to the networking office.

"Pretty remote out here," Dar commented, the small muscles on the sides of her face tensing as she tried to see through the rain. The road was a two lane blacktop, bordered by trees and rolling hills. Only the occasional street lamp appeared out of the gloom, and the rain was driving so hard it reflected Dar's headlights into a blurring glare.

"You said it," Kerry agreed. "Something like the area I'm from but more hilly." She hung onto the strap as Dar took an unexpected curve, then blinked as the road banked down and to the left. "Whoa."

"Yeah." Dar nibbled her lower lip. "I don't do hills very much, sorry." She consciously slowed down and ran a hand through her hair, wishing it was light out. "It's not that much further, though…whoa!" The car slid out from under her control and she instinctively steered with it, resisting the desire to slam on the breaks. They did a three hundred sixty degree turn and almost went off the road before the taller woman wrestled the car around straight and slowed down almost to a crawl. "What in the hell was that?"

Kerry put a gentle hand on her arm. "Ice," she exhaled. "Um, you want me to drive? I think I'm a lot more used to it than you are; they probably don't have icy roads much in Miami, either."

Dar considered that, then prudently pulled off the road and stopped, tugging her jacket up before she opened the door. "Okay… yeah, we get rain slicks, but nothing like this." She exited out into the frosty rain tinged with sleet to exchange places, settling into a cloth seat still warm from Kerry's body.

It was a surprisingly sensual moment, especially since she caught her lover's scent still clinging to the fabric. She sat back, a little bemused, and watched Kerry adjust the seat so her booted toes could reach the pedals. "Sorry, I should have moved that."

Sea green eyes suddenly glanced up, a hint of mischief in them. "Or you could have just stayed there and I could have sat in your lap."

A dark eyebrow crawled up Dar's face almost into her hairline. "Oh really?" Tempting. "Maybe after we get outta there. It'd be a little conspicuous pulling up to the site like that."

Kerry finished her adjustments, then put the car in drive and slowly pulled out. "Mm… yeah, I guess." She studied the road. "Straight ahead?"

Dar nodded. "Yeah…turn right onto the next major cross road, it has a state highway sign." She let her head rest against the seat back and stretched her legs out, giving Kerry a look as she reached down and adjusted the passenger seat all the way back. She decided she liked being a passenger because it gave her the opportunity to study her lover's profile at her leisure, admiring the slightly upturned nose and the smooth line of her jaw, the muscles shifting a little as she concentrated on the road.

Kerry was painfully aware of the eyes on her, and she fought the instinct to fuss with her hair nervously, which was a habit of hers. "Um…" She tried to think of something to distract Dar. "So, what are we going to do when we get there?"

"Get where?"

Kerry's forehead creased, her eyebrows rising. "The networking office? You know, the one that's down?"

"Oh. Right. That. Well." Dar folded her arms across her chest, pulling the leather of her jacket tight around her body. "It depends on what the situation is; probably we'll have to push a few people around, kick a little ass, get nasty… hey, Kerry?"

"Kick ass, take names, be nasty…huh?" Kerry flicked a glance her way. "What?"

"You're really cute." Dar grinned.

The car slid sideways, with Kerry hanging on and cursing for several seconds before she regained control of it. "Dar, don't do that," she pleaded, willing her blush to recede. "We're going to end up in a ditch."

Dar chuckled softly. "Sorry." She fell silent and let her companion concentrate on navigating the slick roads.

The dark countryside passed slowly, broken only by the occasional car or truck going in the other direction. It was another hour before Dar nodded towards a half hidden driveway. "In there…see where the arc lights are set up?"

Kerry nodded. "Yeah, I see the road, okay." She steered the car into the parking lot, seeing several trucks hazily in view through the rain. "Looks like a circus." Groups of people were milling around, and she parked near a large clump of them, putting on the parking break carefully and unbuckling her seat belt. "Well boss, now it's your turn." She glanced at Dar, who was watching the activity with sharp, shifting eyes.

"Right," Dar murmured, letting the warmer side of her personality slip away, and calling up the cool aggressiveness she knew she'd need to deal with the situation. "Okay…you got your cell and the laptop, right?"

Kerry nodded, watching her in uneasy fascination. "Yes."

"Right. Let's go." The dark-haired woman zipped up her jacket and opened the car door, slipping outside into the rain and closing it behind her.

"Okay then," Kerry murmured, tucking her phone into the pocket of her jacket and picking up her briefcase. She ducked out the driver side door and closed it, keying the lock and striding after her boss, who was already halfway to the building. "All right, so when can we get in there?" Dar asked, standing under a dripping tarp in the very center of the building's front lawn. Two men were opposite her, clearly uncomfortable.

"Ms. Roberts," one said, with a sigh, "look, the environmental people won't clear us because that chemical has been confirmed to be toxic." He gave her a look that indicated the last thing he'd expected was to have a VP Ops drop into his tent, where they'd been having a pizza.

Dar's face tensed. "How long?" she snapped.

He shook his head. "I don't know. The regulator told me an hour ago she wouldn't even have a team here until tomorrow noon."

Pale eyes almost silver in the glaring lights studied him thoughtfully. "Where is she?" Dar's voice dropped a bit, taking on a predatory burr.

The man glanced at her nervously. "Well, she's over there by that van of theirs, but let me tell you, ma'am, she doesn't take any bullshit. I've worked with her before."

"What's her name?" The burr deepened.

"Anne Simmonds," the man answered. "But…I mean, really ma'am, if she decides to get tough on us, we could be here for weeks."

Dar turned and stalked out without a word, letting the rain drive against her in freezing darts, conscious of Kerry's quiet form a pace behind her. She was met by a young man as she approached the van who was dressed in a white coverall. "I'd like to see whoever is in charge," she told him quietly.

He cleared his throat and pushed pair of glasses up the bridge of his nose. "Well, Dr. Simmonds is inside, but she's busy; can I help you?"

Dar stepped up closer and stared him down, her eyes inches above his own. She let the silence grow for a moment, watching him swallow a few times in reflex. "No," she finally told him. "I'd like to speak to Dr. Simmonds, please."

"Uh…." He looked past her to Kerry's damp head. She smiled

briefly at him. "Uh, well, I...I can ask her, but, um, okay, are you from this company or..."

Dar cocked her head and pinned him with a stare. "I'd appreciate that...my name's Dar Roberts, and I'm from our Miami office."

"Okay." He nodded. "Okay, um, wait here. I'll be right back." He turned and walked towards the van, startled to find Dar pacing next to him. "Oh...we...we're doing some experiments; I..."

"I'd like to get out of the rain," Dar overrode him. "I won't break anything, I promise."

He looked past her.

"Me either." Kerry smiled kindly at him. "Really. My mother used to take me into china shops when I was a child."

Dar hurriedly wiped a hand across her face to muffle a laugh, then cleared her throat as they approached the van, which had a tarp extending from its passenger side, shielding several worktables. The young man went over to a figure bent over a microscope and touched her arm.

"What?" the woman snapped, not looking up. "You just shook this whole slide. I'm trying to take pictures, Michael." She was very short, shorter than Kerry even, and slim, with dark auburn hair pulled tightly back under a close fitting cap. Her bearing was powerful though, and she exuded impatience.

"Um, yes, doctor, I know, but there are two people here from Miami. They wanted to talk to you, and I..."

"Tell 'em to go the hell back to Miami. I'm not having some stuffed suits smelling of Cuban cigars hanging around my neck asking stupid questions," the doctor snapped back. "Nothing doing, Michael, so you march your lily white butt back out there and..." She glanced past his shoulder, where two shadowy, strange forms were standing. "Get rid of them."

"Actually," Dar's low voice carried clearly as she strode forward, coming into the light with startling impact, "I don't think I'm going anywhere." She stopped precisely in the center of the tent, letting the garish light outline her in stark detail. "And I've never been partial to cigars."

The doctor was...surprised, Kerry decided, watching the smaller woman's eyes warily flick over her boss's truculent form.

An uncomfortable silence dropped over them, until Dar took a step forward and offered a hand. "Dr. Simmonds? My name is Dar

Roberts." She waited impassively as the doctor studied her for a long time before extending her own hand. "I need some answers."

It was the charisma. Kerry gave the doctor a brief smile as Dar released her hand and half turned. "This is my assistant, Kerry Stuart."

"I don't have answers." The smaller woman recovered her composure and scowled, giving Kerry a brisk nod. "I told you people that hours ago. That damn extinguisher company put so much toxin in that system, it's a damn good thing your folks evacuated, or they'd have been glowing like fireflies."

Dar exhaled. "What is it?"

"I have no goddamned clue and those people won't say," the doctor stated disgustedly. "So damn scared of a lawsuit they won't even admit to having first and last names."

Dar glanced at Kerry, who handed her the cell phone without a word. She dialed a number and waited. "Evening, Alastair."

"Jesus, Dar, it's…" A yawn. "Midnight. What in blue—are you in North Carolina?" He cleared his throat. "Listen, we've got twelve accounts set to cancel if we're not back up by tomorrow morning."

"Now you tell me?" Dar barked. "Good god, Alastair!"

"I wasn't worried after I heard you were on your way. In fact, I went to bed," the CEO told her cheerfully. "You know I've got all the confidence in the world in you, Dar."

The responsibility slammed down on her shoulders with an almost audible crunch. "How much business are we talking about?" Dar asked cautiously. "It doesn't look good here, Alastair."

"Well…" He paused. "It's not good, Dar." His cheerfulness vanished. "In fact, it's not very good at all. We can't lose them—not like this—and remain competitive."

Dar's eyes drifted out to the rainy ground. "I see." A dull throbbing started in the back of her skull. "Wish you'd told me that earlier."

"Didn't know until after six, you'd already left for the airport," Alastair told her. "And anyway, what more could I do? You're the best we have, Dar. If you can't solve it, no one can."

Dar rubbed her temples. "All right. I need someone from Legal to call whoever's in charge of that damn extinguisher company and threaten them with a full liability lawsuit naming the officers as personal respondents if they don't give the people here the name of the stuff they put in that goddamned system."

"Hell with Legal, I'll call him. I know him; he's my second wife's

third ex-husband's brother-in-law," Alastair advised her. "Call you right back."

"Right." Dar disconnected, studying the building thoughtfully. Then she dialed again, glancing over her shoulder "Call BellSouth. I'm going to need someone very high up in their provisioning department." Her voice had taken on a grim tone.

"Okay." Kerry got out her own phone and her palmtop and checked the number, then dialed, sensing the sudden change in her lover, and feeling a sick gnawing in her guts.

Dar listened for a minute, then heard Mark's voice. "Evening."

"Ah, Dar...hi." Mark's voice sounded blurry. "Um, I was just, uh..."

"Sleeping at your desk," Dar remarked dryly. "Listen, I need an inventory check; can we duplicate the setup in North Carolina?"

Momentary silence. "You're kidding, right?" Mark answered, faintly. "You know we can't do that."

"Thought so. Call up Cisco and find out what they have on hand," Dar sighed. "We're locked out of here." She hung up and faced the doctor. "I need to get in there and get equipment out."

"No way," the woman answered instantly.

"Look..." Dar started.

"Hey, I said no way." Anne put a hand up. "So don't try it, lady. I've said no to a lot worse than you."

Kerry put her hand over the mic on her phone and stepped artfully between the two women, seeing the sudden icy glare settle over her boss's face. "Here, Dar, it's some Executive VP of something or other...was that high enough?" She passed her the phone, watching the flare of Dar's nostrils as she took the instrument.

"Yeah. That's fine," she muttered, taking a breath before half turning away to talk.

"So." Kerry gave the doctor a grim smile. "Any coffee around here?"

"Well, that's it." Anne Simmonds closed up her cell phone. "All right, guys, pack it up," she yelled to her team, then turned to a waiting Dar. "Sorry. They're going to have to bring in a team to scrub the place. Thanks for getting me an answer, though."

Kerry shot a glance at her boss. "What does that mean?" she asked.

"Means the stuff is so toxic, we can't go in there without environmental suits," the doctor answered succinctly. "And I'll be glad to get out of this weather; you might as well do the same."

"How long?" Dar spoke for the first time, her voice sharp.

The doctor shrugged. "Who knows? Take the team a day, maybe two to get here, then probably a week or so." She packed up her kit.

"I can't keep this facility closed a week," Dar stated flatly.

"Well, that's just too bad," Simmonds replied, "because I'm leaving a trooper there to keep everyone out." She gave Dar a grim smile. "Have a nice day." She shouldered her bag. "Oh, and Ms. Roberts?"

Cold blue eyes watched her silently.

"My boss, Shari, says have a nice day too." She turned, and walked off, joining her group as they got into their van and closed the door, driving off and leaving them in the fitful, freezing weather.

Kerry watched them, then turned and studied her boss's face, which had gone dark and cold, with a glittering anger in the pale blue eyes that sent a chill down her back. "What was that all about?"

Dar felt the sour taste in the back of her mouth. "Old history," she replied shortly, then returned her attention to the building. "All right. C'mon, we're going to have to do this the hard way." She started towards the tarp the rest of their assembled group was huddled under.

"But…" Kerry caught up to her, tugging her collar up a little. "Dar, I don't…"

"Okay, folks," Dar stated, as she ducked under the blue plastic. "Bad news. We don't get in for a week, at the least." She pointed to the BellSouth regional service coordinator who had just arrived. "I need all the circuits in that building stripped and redropped and I need them tonight."

His jaw dropped. "You're joking, right?"

"No." Dar stared him down. "Just get started. I'll let you know where I need them dropped." She turned and faced the building manager. "I have seventy Cisco 7200s headed here on a charter. Find someone to go pick them up."

His jaw dropped too. "What in the hell are you doing, Dar? You make it sound like we're rebuilding the goddamn complex."

A dark brow lifted. "We are."

"That's impossible," he told her flatly. "There is no way this facility is going to be duplicated overnight."

"Have you ever tried it?" Dar countered, her temper building. "No? Then how do you know it can't be done?" She pointed. "Just get moving, and get me someone here with a truck who knows the area…and you…" She pointed at another woman who was muffled in a large mackinaw. "Start getting your people back in here." The staff had been sent home earlier.

"Look, Dar…" the regional manager objected.

She whirled on him and jabbed a finger into his chest. "You want a job tomorrow morning?"

Silence.

"Then start moving your ass," she snarled. "All of you!"

A low muttering sprang up as people started to move, more than one whisper of "crazy" leaking back to Dar's ears. She turned her back on them and walked to the edge of the tarp, staring out into the darkness and trying to calm the churning tension ion her guts.

Kerry took a breath, then stepped up next to her. "Hey, look, Dar, I think he's right; this is really crazy."

The back facing her stiffened, and it was a long moment before Dar turned her head and looked right at Kerry. Her face was an unreadable mask, but the turmoil in her eyes was unmistakable. "If you don't want to help out, just go back to the car and wait." The taller woman spoke with low intensity. "But don't stand here and tell me what I can't do. I don't need that from you."

Kerry felt her knees start to shake, and she sucked in a shocked breath, not expecting the fierce response. She tried to think of something to say, but before she could, Dar simply turned and walked away out into the darkness. Alone.

Chapter 10

The freezing rain now matched her mood completely. Dar stared into it, hardly even feeling the sting against her face as the last warm spot inside her dissolved, replaced by a damp bleakness that already regretted her words to Kerry.

Damn it. She tucked her hands under her arms, ignoring the pain the cold was inserting in her joints, and took a quick glance over her shoulder. Kerry had disappeared. The knowledge sank into Dar's guts, and she felt a long moment of just wishing she could scrap the entire night and go after her.

And say what? Sorry for being an asshole, it's just something you have to get used to? Wasn't it good old Shari who had told her she'd never have a successful relationship because she always put everything else ahead of it?

Dar swallowed slowly. *I knew I'd screw this up.* She blinked, a sudden warmth around her eyes that faded quickly. *I'm surprised it lasted as long as it did. Looks like Shari was right after all.* Funny she should turn up right at the moment to remind Dar all over again of just how unsuitable she was to be a part of someone else's life.

She took a breath. *Okay. Just hold on, Dar. A couple of nasty words doesn't mean you're breaking up with her. She's a lot smarter than the rest of them, remember?*

She let the freezing rain drive against her, numbing her face until heavy footsteps ran up and she turned to see the BellSouth supervisor pulling his yellow rain suit tight against him.

"All right, we've got the pairs pulled out," he told her, scrubbing his face. "Now what? I can't keep those guys up on those poles, Ms. Roberts. You need to give us some direction here. We're pulling all the stops out, but I'm not putting my guys in danger, and it's icing up."

More than you know. Dar rubbed her arms, then exhaled. "Okay, let's see where everyone else is." She led him back to the tarp, ignoring the angry looks she was getting by the rest of the team, channeling her focus only on the goal. "What's the status?"

"Plane just landed with the routers," one man grudgingly admitted, blowing on his hands. "I got a truck. We were about to leave to go pick them up."

"Good." Dar nodded. "Take off."

"Staff's headed back in, those I could reach," the older woman told her. "But I had to get pretty tough. No one's happy, and a few flat-out refused."

"Fine," the dark-haired woman told her. "Okay, now we just need a…"

"The warehouse next door is empty," Kerry's voice quietly interrupted her. "They have a telco punchdown, and the landlord's on his way with a key."

The flapping of the tarp was suddenly loud as everyone turned to look at her, and Dar felt an irrational jolt deep in her guts. She studied the set, serious face for a moment. "Thank you, Kerry…good work."

Kerry nodded, and stared down at the churned, half-frozen mud they were standing in.

"All right, let's move everything over there. We'll get inside as soon as they open it up. It'll be warmer and drier, at least," Dar stated quietly. "John, that's where we'll need the lines dropped; I think I spotted a block on the back end of that building."

"Right you are," the BellSouth manager nodded briskly, pulling out a walkie-talkie and speaking into it. "That's an easy swing—they might even be wired for it already; that used to be a telemarketing operation."

Kerry listened to the conversation until she was aware of footsteps leaving, and then silence. With a sigh, she lifted her head, almost jumping when pale blue eyes met hers. "Oh." She'd thought Dar had gone with them.

They studied each other for a long, pensive moment.

"Sorry about that, I…" Kerry started.

"Sorry I snapped at you, I…" Dar rumbled at the same time.

Silence fell again, then Dar released a breath and wiped a weary hand across her face. "You didn't deserve that."

Kerry stepped closer. "No, I shouldn't have questioned you, Dar." She put out a hesitant hand, and touched Dar's arm as though reassuring herself. "You needed my support right then, and I blew it."

Dar dropped her eyes to the ground. "I don't want you to think that," she said, after a moment's thought. "Sometimes you need to question me, Kerry. I don't know all the answers, and sometimes I push too hard and the result doesn't end up justifying the means." Her eye swept up in startling honesty. "You should know that." She sighed and looked around. "I don't know if this is the right thing to do, but I don't know what else to try, and I have to try something."

Kerry nodded, and moved another step closer. "I know. I went over to the truck there and sat down and I thought about it." She paused. "That's why I called about that warehouse. I knew that's where you had to go next."

Dar lifted a hand and gently laid it alongside her cheek. "Thank you," she murmured sincerely. "That really was well done…how'd you know about the punchdown?"

Kerry smiled, feeling her cold stiffened facial muscles protest. "Modern technology. I linked up to the local real estate page and did a search on available commercial property in this area, listed my specifications, and it popped right up." Her eyes twinkled gravely at the widening of Dar's eyes. "Even had the landlord's number there," she added. "He wasn't happy about me calling him at two a.m., but since I offered twenty percent more than what he was asking, he made an exception and said he'd get right over here. He lives about ten minutes away."

Dar gave a little shake of the head and impulsively pulled Kerry into a hug, reveling in the warmth as the smaller woman wound her arms around her and squeezed really hard. "You're the best."

Kerry smiled in pure relief, ignoring the dampness of Dar's jacket. Then she released her boss, and patted her gently on the side. "And hey, Dar?"

"Mm?" The now warm blue eyes regarded her.

Kerry lifted her chin. "If and when you want to talk about the old history, I'm here."

Dar's eyelids fluttered as she ducked her head for a moment. "Thanks," she replied quietly. "Maybe we'll have time this weekend." *For a lot of things*, she mused.

"Okay." Kerry exhaled. "Well, I think that's our landlord over there, I guess we'd better get started...but Dar, I have to ask you: we're replacing the routers, but what about the mainframes? We can't duplicate those, not even if you commandeer half the air force."

Dar slipped an arm over her shoulders and started to walk towards the now lit building behind the operations center. "No, but the mainframes are in a separate room. They connect over a fiber optic LAN bridge." She pointed. "And the access block is on the roof."

Kerry stared at the roof, then her eyes shifted to a new truck that had just pulled up, bearing the fiber optics division insignia of the telephone company. "Oh, you're just too good." She turned an admiring gaze on her boss. "That's slick, Dar, but do we know they have power and are turned on in there? I thought those environmental people turned everything off."

Dar let out a breath. "We'll find out, but we've got a lot to do before then, and it's going to be a race."

Kerry lifted her head and regarded the growing crowd they were heading towards. "I have a feeling I'm going to be present at yet another Dar Roberts legend in the making."

"Hmm. Let's just hope it's not my swan song," Dar muttered.

Kerry stood back and watched the group disperse inside the large, badly lit warehouse, scattering out from the door and trying to avoid the tumbleweed-sized dust bunnies that were rolling languidly across the stained carpet. It smelled like a cross between a dirty shed and a mildewed garage, and Kerry wrinkled her nose in pure reaction.

But at least it was warm, sort of, and not raining inside. Dar was standing in the center of the room, her hands on her hips and her eyes regarding the space they had to work with, and Kerry noticed the rain dripping off her jacket with a frown.

"All right," the dark-haired woman finally said. "Truck here yet?" She turned to the facility manager. "Thought I heard the engine outside."

He nodded. "Just got here. I'll have them stack the boxes over there and start unpacking things."

"Right...there should be racks with them, and a spool of Cat 5," Dar told him. "Better start having people make the jumper cables. I'll work with telco to get the lines dropped in."

"Okay." He rubbed his eyes. "Damn, wish we had an urn of coffee in here." He moved off towards a clump of grumpy technicians.

Coffee. Dar wished he hadn't said that. She could feel the day's exhaustion catching up with her, and she had to make a conscious effort to jumpstart her brain, turning it to the stuff still undone. The cold had stiffened up her muscles as well. With a sigh, she turned, almost slamming right into Kerry. "Wh...oh, sorry."

The blond woman pushed a bundle of cloth into her hands. "Here, go change—you're making my teeth chatter."

Dar put her hands up in reflex and found them filled with warm, dry clothes. "Whe...um...thanks." She gave Kerry a grateful smile. "Where's yours?"

Kerry showed her the bag slung over her shoulder. "I'm going to make a quick run out with Mary." She indicated the day manager who had called in the staff. "When I get back, I'll change...they're offloading the routers now."

Dar nodded. "I know. Okay, I'm going to start getting the T1s punched down."

"After you change," Kerry persisted, "right?"

A soft chuckle. "Right." Dar followed the hastily lettered signs that indicated the rest rooms and ducked inside the one marked "women," wincing at the smell of rotted grout. "Oh god." She debated holding her breath, then decided passing out would be a bad idea and simply turned her mind to more pleasant thoughts as she quickly stripped out of her soaked clothing. It was almost a sensual experience pulling on the clean, dry denim over her chilled legs, and she quickly tucked in the flannel shirt and tugged on her sweatshirt, thick socks, and dry sneakers as well. "Damn, that feels good," she commented to the empty room, draping her sodden clothing over a stall divider. She reveled in the simple pleasure of being warm and dry after so many hours of damp misery. She wondered briefly how long it would have taken her to do this on her own, feeling a little guilty about having Kerry have to nudge her into it. With a sigh, she stood and gazed at her damp reflection, flicking her fingers through her hair to order it somewhat. "Drowned rat. No wonder everyone thinks you're nuts."

She trudged back out into the open warehouse, wondering where Kerry had scooted off to.

🐄🐄   🐄🐄   🐄🐄

Kerry peered out of the windshield. "We need to find a place to get sandwiches or something for everyone; they must be hungry." Of course, she had a personal motive for asking, but it seemed much nobler to think of the group first. "Any 24-hour groceries around here?"

Mary looked at her. "You're joking, right?"

"Come on, we even had one in Saugatuck." Kerry eyed her. "Okay, a Seven Eleven, a Wal-Mart…anything?"

"How about a Big Fat Boy's Eat 'Em All?" Mary asked, with a perfectly serious face. "They've got some good pie."

Kerry held her breath to keep from giggling nervously. "Oh, okay, sure."

"And there's a Stop and Shop if you want," the woman added.

"Both." Kerry nodded firmly. "Um, the restaurant first; do they take credit cards?"

Mary just laughed.

"Okay then, the Stop and Shop first; maybe they have an ATM," Kerry sighed.

Mary put the car in gear and headed out, driving the dark back roads for twenty minutes before pulling into a lonely but fairly well-lit convenience store. Kerry wasn't surprised to find they were the only patrons. She went to the obviously brand new ATM, standing in a place of pride near the slurpee machine, and inserted her corporate card. Cash in hand, she prowled the aisles thoughtfully.

What a selection. She approached the cashier, who was watching her with sleepy eyes. "May I have a box, please?" The man gave her a puzzled look, but went into a back room to retrieve a cardboard carton, which he handed to her wordlessly. "Thank you." Kerry took it over to the shelf and scooped the meager choices of Twinkies and other goods into it. She stuck to recognizable items, leaving some dubiously packaged sweet rolls behind, and lugged the box up to the front. "Ring that up, please," she asked the man as she studied the freezer case. A brief grin crossed her lips, and she reached into the freezer. She paid the man, then claimed her box and followed Mary outside.

"I can't believe you're doing this," the woman commented, opening the trunk for her and watching as she put the box inside.

Kerry was about to answer when a shadowy figure wandered over.

"Hey there, cute stuff." His bearded face was slightly flushed, and he walked with a tiny stagger. "You look all wet, lemme dry you off." He put a hand out, but Kerry evaded him. "Hey…"

"No thanks, I'm fine, but thank you for offering." The blond woman backed off, moving around to the side of the car.

"Aw, c'mon." The man staggered after her, surrounded by a greasy cloud of alcoholic stench. "Nice little thing like you…c'mere, I won't hurtcha…"

"No, really, I'm fine." Kerry waited as Mary unlocked her side and reached inside to unlock Kerry's door.

He grabbed her jacket, and pulled her closer, bloodshot eyes eagerly looking at her face. "No, stop…"

Kerry sighed. "I'm just not in the mood for this." She wrenched her arm free, then grabbed his hand, swiveling around and pulling him over her shoulder in a well-practiced move that landed him on his butt in the freezing mud. Then she yanked the door to the car open and dropped into the seat, slamming the door shut and shaking her head. "Jerk."

Mary started the car without a word and pulled out.

"Did they send an Ethernet hub?" Dar leaned on the newly assembled racks and watched as yet another box was unpacked. The musty smell of the warehouse was almost completely overrun with the scent of newly opened electronics, and the worn and dirty carpet was covered with tired techs busily making cables and assembling wiring harnesses.

"Yeah, it's over there." The man she was addressing pointed without looking up, intent on his task and oblivious to the asker.

Dar didn't mind. She went over to the box he indicated and stuck her head inside, spotting the hub and hauling it out. She examined the device, then lifted it from its nest of packing and carried it over to the first rack, sliding it into place above the first of the routers and screwing it down. "There. If the patches are ready, we can start hooking these damn things up."

"Right," John Collins agreed wearily, plugging the hub into power. "At least they sent surge suppressors, but I'm glad we found those extension cords in the basement here."

"Mm," Dar agreed, flipping the switches on the installed routers. "Oh, shit." She rubbed her temples. "I need a damn straight through serial cable and 9 pin to program these damn things."

The facility manager cursed softly. "Christ. All right, let me see what we have; maybe I can have someone wire a piece of Cat 5 in serial."

Dar leaned against the rack for a moment, the straightened and moved over to where the telco technicians were screwing down two huge blocks and wiring. "How's it going?" she asked, examining the jacks. "Nice."

The nearer tech looked up. "Just about done. Ya got lucky, lady, this is the only multi jack in this part of the Carolinas. I got no idea how you got Inventory to give it up to us."

Dar's nostrils flared. "I'd tell you, but then I'd have to kill you," she joked faintly, recalling a twenty minute, top of her lungs, cursing in two languages conversation with a mid-level infrastructure manager at the phone company. "Can we start plugging in?"

He finished one last screw into the peeling paint on the punch down board. "Yeah, you got drop cables?" He looked up as Dar lifted a handful of the requested items. He started plugging them in while Dar connected the other end to the equipment. "What time is it, anyhow?"

Dar checked her watch. "Four thirty," she winced. "All right, is the fiber drop in?"

"Almost," the man remarked, moving towards the door.

Dar finished her task and stepped back and regarded the assembly of equipment. "What a mess." There were wires everywhere connecting the routers and the interconnecting hubs, not to mention the power cables running everywhere. Green and red LEDs were beginning to blink on the routers, and she ran a hand through her hair, trying to shove back the exhaustion as she figured out what needed to happen next. She pulled her cell phone out and dialed.

"MIS."

"Mark. We've got the…" Dar started.

"Circuits up, yeah, I see them, but they aren't terminated yet," Mark replied amidst a rattle of keys. "Shit, that was fast, Dar, what did you do, coerce the entire phone company?"

Dar sighed. "We got lucky; there were already terminator blocks in this damn warehouse, they just had to assign the pairs." She found a box to sit down on and took a deep breath. "That was the easy part. Now I have to configure the routers and get the fiber line in and hope to god those damn mainframes are still running off the generator, or we're doing this for shit."

"You sound beat," Mark commented quietly.

"Been a long day," Dar acknowledged, letting her elbows rest on her knees and allowing her eyes to close momentarily. "Wish I had some…" She stopped talking and looked up as the smell of fresh coffee hit her nose, and she found warm green eyes gazing back at her. "Oh, are you a sight for sore eyes," she murmured.

Mark chuckled in her ear. "Tell Kerry I said hi," he remarked cheerfully.

Kerry handed her the large cup of coffee and took the phone from her. "Hi Mark, can we call you back?" She waited for the answer, then hung up. "Sorry it took so long. You have no idea how hard it is to find open places up here at this time of day." She looked around. "Wow."

Dar sucked on her coffee without comment, feeling some life come back into her as the warm, sweet liquid hit her stomach. "I was about to send out a search party," she advised her lover. "We've got the circuits up, but…" Dar let a tendril of doubt in. "Damn, Kerry, I don't know if we can do this; there's just so much to get done." She cast a glance over her shoulder at the half assembled system. "Maybe you were right. I was crazy to try."

Kerry gazed at her in concern. Dar's face and her arms were covered with smudges of dust and dirt from the equipment and there were dark circles under her eyes, visible even in the dim light. "Dar, if you didn't believe this was going to work, you wouldn't have done it." She sat down next to her boss. "I brought back food for everyone, that should help, and I can program the routers if you give me a chance to change first."

The bloodshot blue eyes lifted and regarded her. "That's right, you are Cisco certified, aren't you?" Dar let a reluctant smile tug her lips. "Go change. I have them making up cables for the laptops. If we both work on it, we can get enough done so that the other techs can get in and start downloading the routing tables."

"You got it." Kerry slung her bag over her shoulders and headed for the rest room, changing quickly and hanging her wet clothing next to Dar's. She returned to find her boss hunched over a box, studying the screen on her laptop. The silvery reflection flickered over her tanned features, which shifted as Kerry put her own laptop down next to her. The blond woman smiled as a tech handed her a cable. "Thanks." She plugged it in, then ran the other end to one of the routers. "Oh. I'll be right back."

Dar nodded, absorbed in her screen. "Let's hope I remember how to do this," she muttered, shoving down her annoyance that they'd been unable to locate the hardware group for the facility, meaning that only she and Kerry really knew how to get in and program the complicated devices. "It's been a while." The scent of cooked food spread through the room and most of the techs had wandered over to where Kerry had left the boxes, leaving Dar in relative isolation as she puzzled through the software.

The screen started to fuzz out, and she stopped after what seemed like the twentieth screen, leaning back and rubbing her eyes as her back protested against her hunched posture. "I think that's it."" She commented to Kerry, who knelt at her side. "Wh…"

"Open wide," Kerry instructed, capturing her gaze.

Dar stared uncomprehendingly, then hesitantly opened her mouth, startled when a spoonful of chocolate ice cream was deposited into it. She blinked a few times. "Mm." She swallowed the rich cream. "Was that Häagen Daz?"

"Yes," Kerry informed her, offering up another spoonful. "And don't you ask me where I found chocolate Häagen Daz in the middle of backwoods North Carolina, okay?" She watched Dar's whole attitude perk up, and was convinced that if the dark-haired woman had possessed a tail, it would have wagged enthusiastically. "It's amazing what ice cream does to you, did you know that?"

Dar licked her lips. "Hey, it beats recreational drugs. What did you bring the rest of these guys?"

Kerry glanced over her shoulder. "The best of 'Big Fat Boy's All U Kin Eat' buffet," she told her boss, taking a spoon of ice cream for herself. "And a box of Twinkies, Snowballs, Ring Dings, and Mallomars."

The dark-haired woman covered her mouth quickly and stifled an almost hysterical laugh. "Did you get some buffet?" she managed to ask. "Damn, I thought it was more, uh…"

"You're joking, right?" Kerry fed her more ice cream. "I'd like to live to get back to Miami, thanks, and I got the lecture that yes, during the day, it's much more sophisticated around here, but those places roll up the sidewalks at night because all the workers go home."

Dar accepted another spoonful and chewed it contentedly. "It was a good idea, though. It might give everyone enough energy to get through the morning." She paused and regarded her lover. "So, no buffet for you?"

Kerry sucked on the spoon. "Um, no, actually, I..." She made a tiny face. "I have a weakness for Snowballs," she admitted, a touch embarrassed. "That was enough sugar to get me going."

Dar laughed. "Ah! I see...." she teased gently. "Those white ones with the chocolate insides?"

Green eyes batted their golden lashes at her. "Yeah," she confessed, a little shamefacedly.

"Wanna share a pack?" Dar inquired, one brow lifting.

Kerry cleared her throat. "Oh, no, I'm okay, I..." Then she glanced up. "Well, maybe one."

Dar grinned, finding the energy to stand up and stretch. She could feel her own determination returning, and she glanced out over the room, planning her next move.

🐾　🐾　🐾

Dawn broke, turning the darkness outside to a dull gray as the rain continued. Inside the warehouse, it was marked only by a break for coffee from the multitude of thermos bottles that littered the worktable.

"All right, Mark." Dar leaned against the wall, crossing her ankles and exhaling. "Can you see them?"

Clicking. "No...no...wait..." More clicking. "Ah, yep, there they are."

Dar closed her eyes in utter relief. "All of them?"

"Wait, I'm getting Unicenter booted," the MIS chief muttered. "Hang on, hang on, okay, yeah," he confirmed. "I'm seeing all the gateways, and both backbones." A beat. "Wow... tremendous work, boss. That kicks ass."

Dar let her head rest against the wall. "I had a lot of help," she muttered. "Okay, now I'm going to boot the fiber hub." She reached over and flipped a switch.

"I don't see it." Mark's voice cut through her exhaustion.

"Shit." Dar shoved her body off the wall and examined the piece of equipment. "I don't...it's connected...let me..."

"Did you set the IP?" Mark asked gently.

Dar thought about it. "I don't remember." She glanced up as Kerry came over. "Mark sees the backbones and the routers, but not this box. Did we program it?"

Kerry brought the laptop over, and connected it, then ran through a few screens. "Nope." She typed in a few commands, then reset the unit. "Try now."

Mark clicked a bit, then grunted. "Got it." He entered several commands rapidly. "Needs the secondary table, though, hang on. I'm in there… I can download it from here…okay." He sighed. "Got it. You're going to have to IPL the mainframes, though."

Dar and Kerry exchanged glances. "What?" Dar asked. "I thought they were up?"

"They are," Mark said. "But the ports shut down when you don't have activity after a certain point. It's a bug or something. You need to reset them."

Dar let out an explosive breath. "Son of a fucking bitch, Mark, we can't get in there!" she told him. "Can't you remote IPL?"

"Has to be a hardware reset," the MIS chief responded. "God, Dar, I'm sorry. I knew that, in the back of my head, I should have told you before. I didn't realize…"

No. Dar let her head smack against the wall, and she cursed softly under her breath.

Kerry chewed her lip in thought, watching her lover anxiously. "What if we cut the building generator off and on?" she asked suddenly. "It's outside."

Dar stared at her, then dropped the phone onto the fiber rack and took hold of the blond woman, kissing her soundly in full view of the room. "I love you." She patted Kerry's cheek as she headed past her towards the door.

Kerry stood rooted in place, stunned beyond speech. She had her back to everyone and could almost feel the eyes burning into the back of her head. Finally, she picked up the cell phone and cleared her throat. "Um, hi."

Mark also cleared his throat. "Hi," he responded. "Guess she liked that idea, huh?"

"Uh, yeah," Kerry winced as she slowly turned, relieved to see most of the techs still passed out and paying no attention to her. There were a handful of bemused faces, though, and she mustered a weak smile for them. "I just hope it works."

"Hey, that sure beats Q bucks," one tech laughed. "I think I'll move down to Miami; they got a better bonus plan." A round of tired laughter followed.

Kerry scrubbed a hand across her reddening face and sighed. "I'm gonna kill her for that," she muttered, then glanced up as Dar re-entered the building.

"All right folks, we've got fifteen minutes, and we'll know if this all has been worth it," the dark-haired woman announced. "And if it is or isn't, I'd like to say thanks to all of you who hung in there. I know we asked a lot."

A weary silence fell over them and everyone settled in to watch the routers, whose traffic LEDs were dark. Dar walked over to where Kerry was standing and slid down the wall, clasping her hands lightly in front of her.

Waiting.

Kerry sat down next to her and fiddled with the phone, sitting cross-legged and resting her elbows on her knees.

Fifteen minutes passed, and there was no change in the lights. Dar closed her eyes and let her head drop in defeat, hardly feeling Kerry's hand on her arm. Of all the times to fail, she had to pick this one. She refused to hear the disappointed murmur that echoed around the dimly lit room, as the tired waves finally crashed over her.

"It was a damn good try." Kerry rested her head against Dar's shoulder.

"Not good enough," came the whispered reply.

The blond woman moved closer, accidentally jerking the power plug of the fiber hub from the wall. "Oh, crap." She shoved it back in with an annoyed grimace. "For all the good that'll do," she muttered, turning her attention to her lover. "Hey, c'mon. No one could have done any more, Dar."

"Hey!" A tinny voice distracted her, and she lifted the phone.

"What is it, Mark? It didn't work," Kerry admitted.

"Bullshit! Yes it did!" the MIS chief yelled. "I'm getting packets!"

Dar's head jerked up on hearing that, and they both stared at the router racks, where LEDs were coming alive in an electronic dance. "Son of a bitch."

Yells were now coming from the techs, who were pointing at the routers.

"Wow!" Kerry let out a surprised, and delighted laugh. "I guess it just took a few minutes longer…"

"No." Dar looked up at the hub over her head. "You did it. You reset the optics hub." She grabbed Kerry and hugged her. "You did it!"

Dumbfounded, Kerry stared at her. "I did it?" She jerked around and looked at the plug. "It was an accident!"

"Waaahoo!" Mark yodeled through the phone. "Infriggingcredible, Dar! Give that woman a kiss for me."

Blue eyes now alive with mischief fastened on Kerry's face. "Oh, I think I can do that." She stood up and pulled Kerry up with her as a round of tired but enthusiastic cheers went up around the room.

"Uh, Dar?" Kerry whispered frantically. "Um, you know I love when you kiss me, I really, really do, but um, could we just kinda…" She jerked her head in the direction of the watching technicians. "I feel like a video game."

"All right," Dar chuckled and relented, draping an arm over Kerry's shoulder instead and walking towards the now excitedly talking group. She took the phone from Kerry. "So, everything coming online?"

"OH yes," Mark chuckled. "Oh wait, there's the hotline. Figures, sun just started coming up." He rustled around. "MIS Ops, Polenti." A pause. "Hmm? Oh yeah, we're up, no problem." Another pause. "Yep, that too, the whole network's online." A longer pause. "Yeah, I've got her on the other line, wh…ok, I'll relay that. Thanks." He hung up. "Hey, Dar?"

"Yeah?" Dar replied, accepting the cries of congratulations from the crowd.

"Alastair said to tell you he slept like a baby," the MIS chief related. "He said you'd understand."

She let a brief, humorless smile cross her face. "Yeah, I understand," she replied. "All right, let me get off this thing. I'm going to make sure this is stable, then go get some sleep." The thought of a warm bed and snuggling with Kerry was suddenly overwhelmingly attractive. "Later." She hung up and tucked the phone into her pocket.

Fresh staff was entering the building, cautiously peering around the doorframe until they spotted familiar faces. A supervisor was busy making a schedule, and two other new faces were pulling out monitoring consoles from boxes and setting them up. "We did it," Dar stated in wonder. "I don't believe it."

Kerry exhaled. "We sure did," she confirmed.

They both looked up as someone called Dar's name. A man trotted towards them "Ms. Roberts?" he asked as he reached them. "There's some people outside, I think it's the environmental people; they want to see you."

Dar went very still. "Same people as last night?" she asked cautiously.

He nodded. "Yeah, that same doctor, but she said her boss is here and wants to talk to you." He made a face. "They were kinda rude about it," he added, then turned and moved off as someone called him.

Kerry looked up at Dar's face, seeing the confusion and reluctance there. "You want me to take care of this?" she asked bluntly.

Pale blue eyes flicked to hers. "Thanks, but I'd better go," Dar told her heavily. "You wait here. It shouldn't take long since I don't really care when they clear the other building now as long as we keep the generators going."

Kerry didn't back off. "Sure you don't want company?" She had no idea what was spooking Dar so badly, but she was damned if she wasn't going to find out. "Two of them, only fair if there are two of us."

Dar hesitated. "Her boss and I have a past," she finally admitted. "Not a very pleasant one."

"I gathered," the blond woman answered quietly. "That was the old history, right?"

A nod. "Yes."

"Dar, it's been a really long night, you're tired, let me go take care of them for you," Kerry pleaded gently, seeing the stark indecision in Dar's eyes. "Or at least let me come, too."

She gave in. "All right." Dar ran a hand through her hair. "Let's get it over with. I want to get out of here." She picked up Kerry's duffel, and slung it over her shoulder. "We can just go after that."

They walked out, side by side, into a gray drizzle.

It was almost like her own stomach was twisting into knots. Kerry paced along side her boss, watching the jaw muscles bunch and relax on the side of her face as they moved around to where the networking office was. Two figures were standing under the overhang out of the rain, and Kerry felt Dar bristle as she spotted them.

This was potentially very ugly, she realized, studying the two people. One was Dr. Simmonds, she knew. The other, a taller, stockier woman with sun-streaked chestnut hair was standing quietly and watching Dar like a hawk as they approached. Kerry had an immediate, visceral desire to kick her in the shins, and had to wonder about her newly found physical nature. She moved a bit closer to her boss and only just barely kept from tucking a hand inside Dar's elbow.

"Hey, Dar!" A voice interrupted them, and they stopped, turning to let a jogging figure catch up. It was the BellSouth regional manager, who held a hand out to Dar as he came up to them. "Hear it worked; congratulations!"

Dar mustered a smile, and took his hand. "You made it happen," she told him. "You guys really came through for us; don't think I'll forget that."

They were close enough for the two women to overhear, Kerry realized, and she saw their faces fall. A grin worked its way onto her face. "It really was great working with you," she added, shaking his hand as well. "Your techs were wonderful, they got us back up with no problem." She made sure her voice was a little louder than necessary.

"Well, thanks," he grinned. "Can I treat you ladies to an old fashioned country breakfast?"

Dar regretfully declined. "We've got things to take care of, but thanks for the offer." She nodded towards the waiting women. "I think the scientists have something to tell us."

"Right; well, you take care." He waved, then trotted off, hailing one of the techs nearby.

"You know, Dar," Kerry fell into step beside her as they resumed their stroll. "If I didn't know better, I'd say those people were disappointed to hear things worked out." Her eyes flicked to their targets.

"Mm," Dar murmured, "you could be right." She swallowed to get the cotton out of her mouth and tried to ignore the pounding of her heartbeat, very aware of Shari's eyes on her. She summoned her coldest, fiercest outer persona, and wrestled it into place.

"Dar?" Kerry's voice dropped to a low murmur.

"Hmm?" She ducked her head a little, nervously clenching and unclenching her fists.

"I love you."

Dar blinked, then looked up as they came even with the two women. "You needed to speak with me?" she asked cordially, feeling the dread fall away, nudged aside by the living, breathing acknowledgement that Shari had been wrong all those years ago. Her eyes met her old lover's, and she gave her a small nod of acknowledgement. "Hello, Shari."

"Dar," the woman answered, in a low, melodic voice. Her eyes flicked to Kerry's face, then an eyebrow rose.

"Sorry." Dar felt a smile edging her lips. "This is my associate, Kerrison Stuart. Kerry, this is Shari Englewood."

"Pleased to meet you," Kerry responded politely, extending a hand and returning the firm grip with one of her own.

An awkward silence fell. "Would you two please excuse us?" Shari finally said. "I'd like to speak with Ms. Roberts in private."

Dr. Simmonds ducked away immediately, seemingly glad to get out of the situation, but Kerry paused for a long moment, gazing at the chestnut-haired woman steadily before she took the duffle from Dar and gave her boss a quick grin. "See you at the car."

Dar half turned her face, and winked at her. "Won't be long." She watched Kerry stride off towards the vehicle, ducking her head against the still falling rain. Then she turned back and folded her arms over her chest.

And waited. The cool gray eyes studied her, and she returned the look without flinching, keeping her expression noncommittal. Shari hadn't changed much, save that she'd gotten a bit heavier and her face had taken on a colder, more predatory expression. But she was, Dar acknowledged, still very attractive, and the look of those familiar eyes brought up old and painful memories she had to work at to shove back down.

"You haven't changed much," Shari finally said. "You still running around doing their dirty work?"

Dar refused to take offense. "Sure," she drawled. "Only now they pay me more to do it and I've got an office in the penthouse." It gave her quite a bit of satisfaction to say that, and a tiny smirk caught the edge of her lip as the jibe registered. "And incidentally, if the chemical team finds no trace of your dangerous substance, you'll find the bill for this sitting on your desk."

"Oh, they'll find it," she responded. "I wouldn't have bothered making that up. I was just so happy to hear it was going to screw you up that I had to come see for myself." Her eyes wandered over Dar's body. "But you pulled out the fucking rabbit out of your ass again, didn't you?" she snorted. "That sucks, Dar. I should have come over last night when Anne told me you were tearing your hair out."

"Sorry to disappoint you," Dar replied. "Now, unless you actually have something to say, I have a Jacuzzi and a nice warm bed waiting." She let a frank grin shape her lips, watching the minute reaction in Shari's pale eyes.

A tiny shake of her head followed. "I'd forgotten how different you look when you smile," the other woman mused. "You going to be in town long, Dar?"

Uh oh. "Just until tonight, then I'm heading up into the mountains for a few days," she replied, cautiously. "Why?"

A shrug. "Thought maybe we could just sit down and talk for a few minutes." She paused. "You seeing anyone?"

Dar could hardly believe what she was hearing, and she felt a cool anger start to brew. "Yes," she answered quietly, "not that it's any of your business."

Shari stuck her hands in her pockets, and rocked a bit, considering. "C'mon, Dar. We're both grown up now. You're a big girl, so am I."

"And you came out here to gloat just to prove your maturity?" Dar countered. "Nice."

The tawny-haired woman cocked her head to one side, acknowledging the strike. "Have dinner with me? Maybe we can bury the hatchet, after all this time." Shari moved a little closer, out of the wind, and pushed her bangs back with a damp hand. "I know a nice place near here, it's got steaks, just the way you like them."

"Sorry." Dar let a lazy smile cross her face. "I've got other plans." She turned the collar of her jacket up. "Excuse me."

A hand reached out and touched her arm, warm even through the leather she was wearing. "All right. Where are you staying? Maybe we can just have a drink later on. C'mon, Dar. I don't bite." Shari seemed slightly amused. "Haven't we fought long enough?"

Dar glanced over her shoulder, and saw a glowering pair of green eyes pinned on her, and more specifically, on the hand holdingy. A grin twitched at the corner of her mouth. "You'd better let me go before my girlfriend comes back here and clocks you," she drawled. "She doesn't like poachers."

Shari's nostrils flared visibly as she drew in breath, removing her hand and turning her head to see where Dar was looking. Kerry was leaning against the car door, arms crossed, head slightly lowered, her bristling attitude visible even from across the grass. "She's cute...but I didn't think you were into blonds."

Dar motioned just slightly with her head, and Kerry pushed off towards them, her strong, slightly rolling gait both sexy and sweetly intimidating. "Problems?" Kerry asked, as she came within range. "I didn't think the environmental problem mattered anymore."

A smile. "It doesn't." Dar draped an arm over her shoulders. "Shari and I were just talking over old times. You ready to go?" She felt Kerry's arm wind around her back and relaxed a little as she spared a glance for her old flame. "We're at the Hilton if you really want to drop by. "A pause. "Later. We've got some sleep to catch up on first."

Then she turned and headed for the car, Kerry keeping step next to her as the rain pelted them lightly from one side.

🐾　　🐾　　🐾

Kerry was glad it was light out, at least. She was tired, and she knew her reflexes were suffering, but the traffic was very light. "Right turn up there?"she asked softly, her eyes flicking to her companion.

Dar nodded.

Kerry was worried. Dar had been withdrawn since she'd gotten back into the car, allowing her head to rest against the glass of the window, her reflection bleakly evident to Kerry's watching eyes. A little hesitantly, she reached over and folded her hand over her lover's, encouraged when the long fingers tightened over hers immediately. "You okay?"

"Yeah," Dar sighed, "just tired." She turned her head and studied Kerry's profile. "I think I need a nap."

Kerry glanced at her. "Me too," she confessed. The blond woman waited a beat, then took a breath. "That woman still bothering you?"

The jaw muscles along Dar's face clenched, the relaxed. "It…she just brought up some old, bad memories, that's all."

"Mm." Kerry waited, but nothing else came. "Anything you want to share?'

Dar thought about that a long time, as rows of damp, gray shadowed trees went past them. "I…" She stopped, then cleared her throat. "I never…I've never really talked about any of that with anyone before. Maybe a pair of friendly ears would help." It was, she acknowledged privately, a huge chasm she'd just leapt over, but Kerry couldn't know that.

The corners of Kerry's mouth crinkled up as she guided the car carefully across the slick road and up a long driveway, where a sign announced the presence of the hotel they were staying at. "I think that could be arranged." She pulled the car up under the valet parking overhang and put it in park. "C'mon."

Dar willingly followed her up the stairs, shouldering her overnight bag and giving the valet a brief smile as Kerry turned the keys over to him. They approached the desk, where Dar gave her name to the desk clerk. "We were supposed to check in last night, but…"

"Yes, Ms. Roberts, your office called and told us." The woman smiled at her. "We held the room. It's no problem, and, uh…" She chuckled a little. "I think you have a little surprise waiting up there."

Dar and Kerry exchanged wary glances. "A surprise?" Dar asked. "What kind of surprise?"

The woman smiled cheerfully at her. "Now, if I told you, it wouldn't be a surprise, now would it? But don't worry, it's nothing bad." She handed over the room keys. "Here you go. We have room service available twenty-four hours, and you're on the concierge floor, so you can just ask as you get off the elevator if you need anything."

Dar sighed. "Thanks." She took the key and gave Kerry hers, then followed the smaller woman as they went to the elevator. "I hate surprises," she groused.

Kerry patted her belly tolerantly. "C'mon, Dar, it's probably a fruit basket," she scolded her boss. "Would you relax? All the hotels do that for VIPs nowadays."

"Mmph." Dar leaned back against the elevator wall and tried to stifle a yawn. "Yeah, I guess." She waited for the doors to open then pushed off the back wall and trudged through them, giving the wide-eyed concierge a nod before moving past his desk to their corner room.

The scent of chocolate hit them and stopped them both in their tracks. "Whoa," Dar squeaked as she flipped the lights on.

It was a large room, with a wide window and one big, comfortable-looking bed. A door to one side led to a bathroom, and one on the other to a tiled Jacuzzi. In front of them was a round table, which was currently covered with a huge, completely stuffed, overflowing basket of assorted specimens of the species chocolate. Dar found herself staring at it with a stupid grin. "Oo."

Kerry peeked past her. "Thought you didn't like surprises?" she commented, giving her boss a slap on the behind as she moved past her to put her bag down.

"Tell you what: anytime you want to surprise me with fifty pounds of chocolate, you go right ahead," Dar responded, plucking the card from the ornate holder and examining it. "It's from Alastair."

"Gee," Kerry grinned, "what a surprise." She came over and peeked at the card. "That's really sweet of him."

"Well." Dar poked into the basket's contents. "Considering we just saved his gray flannel butt, it's not unprecedented." She glanced at Kerry. "There were twelve major accounts on the line if we hadn't gotten that stuff working this morning."

Kerry stopped dead, and stared at her. "Why didn't you tell me that?" she asked, stung.

Dar glanced at the table top, and fiddled with the card. "No sense in both of us being worried sick, I guess; I don't know, I should have." She gave Kerry a contrite look. "Not that you could have done more than you were doing." She paused awkwardly. "I'm sorry."

Kerry gave her a vexed look. "No, but it would explain why you were so damned tense." She started to go on, then saw the almost imperceptible flinch in Dar's face. *Not now, Kerry.* Her mind warned her, *not now; she's tired, you're tired, and she apologized for not saying anything. Just drop it.* "Jesus, Dar, tell me next time, huh? So I can chew my nails along with you?" She gave her boss a lopsided grin.

Dar relaxed a little. "I will," she promised, stripping off her jacket and hanging it up in the small closet. "Wonder how long it'll take us to get through that basket." She turned a grin of her own on Kerry.

The blond woman gazed at the huge thing in trepidation. "I think we'll get sick to our stomachs if we try," she commented dryly, taking off her own jacket and tugging her shirt out from her jeans. "He must have worked pretty fast; it's not even nine o clock."

"Well…" Dar pulled off her sneakers and tossed them near her bag, then stripped off her shirts. "If I could get seventy T1 circuits and routers installed before dawn, I guess he could handle a basket of chocolate." She leaned back and stretched, wincing as both shoulders popped before she straightened and ran her fingers through her hair, rubbing the back of her neck. "God, I'm tired," she admitted. "I'm glad that's over. We can rest here until dinnertime, then drive up to the cabin. It's about an hour from here, and it looked like the weather's clearing a little."

"What about your friend?"

Dar was silent for a moment. "She was never my friend," she replied. "Maybe that was the problem." Her chest moved as she inhaled deeply and slowly let the air trickle out. "I don't think she'll be coming by, and I'm not going to worry about it." She circled Kerry's shoulders with both arms and touched foreheads with her. "Work time's over. The only things I'm concerned about right now are us, that bed, and some hedonistic chocolate consumption."

"Sounds good to me," Kerry murmured, already having shed her pants and half unbuttoned her shirt while she worked on unfastening Dar's jeans. Her fingers slid easily under the waistband, and she unhooked the first button, letting her thumbs trace the ripple of muscles just under the skin. She leaned forward and gently kissed the flat surface, feeling the ribs move under her lips in an uneven breath.

Then the room's air was cool against her skin as Dar peeled her shirt off, the taller woman's hands sliding slowly down her arms, then releasing them and moving across her ribcage, causing a jolt of pure sensation as the wandering fingers brushed over her breasts. "Thought you were tired," Kerry burred, nuzzling her face against a soft curve.

"The smell of all that chocolate must have woken me up," Dar replied, catching a thin fold of skin between her teeth and nibbling it gently. "Thought you were tired?"

Kerry undid the second button and moved lower, tracing the edge of her lover's navel, then working up to the tip of her breastbone. "I wish I could blame it on the chocolate," she murmured, inhaling greedily, "but it's not that smell that's giving me these goosebumps."

"Mm, yeah, lookit that." Dar's fingertip made a lazy trail across her shoulder, then her lips traced the same path as her body woke fully, forgetting about the long night and the frustrations of the day. Even the turmoil caused by Shari's appearance faded, replaced by the solid, comforting present now wrapped around her body. She stepped out of her jeans, finding herself being tugged towards the bed, and she gladly tumbled into it, her arms full of warm, bare skin.

Kerry rolled her over, and pounced on top of her, ending up with Dar's earlobe lightly caught between neat white teeth. " You let me know when I start squashing you, okay?"

Dar chuckled low in her throat, and gave her a pat on the butt. "Not a problem…I hardly feel it." Which wasn't quite true, but close enough. She stretched and wrapped her legs around Kerry's, and surrendered herself to a pleasant wave of passion.

🐾   🐾   🐾

The phone rang, dragging Kerry out of a sound sleep, and she fumbled the receiver off the hook, managing to get it somewhere near her ear. "Yeah?" She cleared her throat. "I'm sorry, I mean hello?"

"Hey." Mark's voice echoed weirdly. "Kerry?"

She pulled her wits around her, gently moving away from Dar's warm body. "Eyah. I'm here. Go on." She paused. "Mark?" A glance at the clock told her it was close to four p.m., and she rubbed her eyes, having been startled out of a weird, but interesting dream.

"Dar there?" Mark inquired.

Kerry glanced down at the long, powerful arm circling her stomach and grinned quirkily. "She's here. She's sleeping; what's up?"

"Oh, nothing really… um, she should probably, uh, check her e-mail when she gets a chance," Mark said innocently. "You know, nothing urgent."

"Actually, I was going to ship the laptops back to Miami; I was hoping for a few days without them," Kerry admitted. "Is it something important, Mark?"

He chuckled softly "Nah, Sunday night'll be fine; she'd just might want to check it before Monday morning, though. Alastair sent around a little congratulations note." A rattle of keystrokes. "By the way, you guys are furking big time no shit heroes around here today."

"I bet." Kerry let herself back down onto the pillow, and snuggled back against Dar, who immediately hugged her closer. "Mm."

"What was that?" Mark asked.

"Uh, I was just agreeing." Kerry mentally slapped herself. "Well, I'm glad everyone's happy about it. I guess there'll one huge meeting on Monday, though, huh?" She sighed. "That'll be a trip. I can just imagine the arguments."

Mark chuckled. "Uh, well, yeah, it's certainly going to be a Monday," he agreed. "Listen, you guys have a great time up there, okay? Relax, take it easy, unwind a little."

Kerry yawned. "Will do… I'll bring you back some maple syrup or pecans or whatever the heck they have up here." She listened to the laughter, then hung up and allowed her body to sink back down into the warm pit she'd been resting in while she sleepily regarded the quiet, peaceful room.

Dar was really out, she knew, glancing back over her shoulder. The taller woman had fallen asleep after they'd made love and had hardly moved an inch in the intervening hours. Kerry debated going back to sleep herself, then realized they'd have to start moving around shortly if they wanted to get up to the cabin.

"First things first," she decided, reaching for the phone. "The only thing we've both eaten in the last twenty four hours just about is a half dozen Snowballs and a gallon of coffee. Even Dar can't live on that."

"Sure I can." The soft mumble tickled her ear. "That's, what, two of the food groups, right?"

"Shh." Kerry dialed the phone after checking a card on the dresser. "Hi, this is…oh, you know what my room number is, great," she said as someone answered. "I see you've got pizzas? Okay, can I have two small…" She got a poke in the ribs. "Um, sorry, two medium pizzas, one a vegetable combo, the other with…" She gave Dar a look, "sausage and pepperoni on it." Another poke. Kerry sighed. "And extra cheese."

Dar grinned and nuzzled the back of her neck.

"Thanks, and a pitcher of iced tea, please…excuse me? Oh, yes; no, that'll be fine," Kerry finished ordering and hung up, then squirmed around in Dar's arms and regarded her fondly. "Mark says we're heroes."

"I bet," the dark-haired woman responded sleepily, her eyes still closed. "Guess we gotta get moving, huh?"

"Mm." Kerry idly traced a tiny scar on her lover's chin. "You said you wanted to get up there before dark." She watched as Dar's eyelids fluttered open, revealing her startlingly blue eyes, and allowing Kerry to gaze into them.

To drown in them. Slowly, she leaned forward and kissed Dar lightly on the forehead, then hugged her, unable to either define or explain the suddenly overwhelming sense of devotion and connection she felt.

This was just so precious, she wanted to cradle it gently in her hands and never let it go. Dar's hand smoothed the back of her hair in a familiar gesture, and she let herself sink into the embrace, feeling a resonance chime deep inside her.

"Hey," Dar whispered softly, a worried tone in her voice. "You all right?"

Kerry nodded mutely, breathing in the scent of Dar's skin. The feeling subsided, leaving her only conscious of a pervasive warmth that she could almost feel running between them, leaving her body and entering Dar's, and coming back again. "Yeah, I'm fine." She took a deep breath and let it out, aware of the beating heart under her ear. "Just felt like holding you, that's all."

The long fingers slid down the side of her neck and lifted her chin, and she had no choice but to look up at Dar, knowing she was wide open and helpless, tears edging wetly around her eyes.

"What's wrong?" her lover asked softly, capturing a tear with one thumb and gazing at her anxiously. "Did…something happen? Did…wha…"

She felt Dar's heartbeat pick up under the fingers she had pressed against her chest. "N…nothing, I…I don't know. I just…it got really intense there for a minute, I'm not really sure why, maybe I'm just overtired." She put her head back down and stroked Dar's side gently, needing the touch. "Felt so weird."

Blue eyes now alert flicked over her, as Dar took in a careful breath and released it. "Well…I mean, it felt kinda nice," she offered hesitantly. "Kinda…warm." She started stroking Kerry's hair again and felt the smaller woman relax against her completely, her body going totally limp. They stayed like that for almost a half an hour more until Dar glanced at the clock and stirred, regretfully. "Better put a shirt on…don't want to shock the room service person when they get here."

Kerry's eyes drifted open, pale green in the late afternoon light. "Hmm, you're right," she agreed peacefully, rolling onto her back and stretching her body out lazily, humming low in her throat as Dar took the opportunity to trace a gentle path from her neck to her groin. "Thought you said we have to get up," she drawled softly, giving Dar a look from half closed eyes.

The dark-haired woman smirked and inclined her head in agreement. "We'll have plenty of time later," she conceded, planting a hand on either side of Kerry and pressing her body over her lover's, landing neatly on the carpeted floor and straightening with a fluid motion. "Guess I get to open the door," she commented, as a soft knock was heard.

Kerry was too busy getting her eyeballs around her lover's sunset-lit body to hear. "Uh, what?" She blinked, then tugged the covers up as Dar slipped back into her shirt, managing to be decent by about two inches. "Uh, Dar? Don't bend over to pick anything up, okay?"

Pale blue eyes glanced over one tanned shoulder at her, and one of them winked. "Okay."

"Unless you're facing away from me, of course," Kerry added impishly, just as Dar opened the door.

That got her an over-the-shoulder look complete with an elegantly raised eyebrow. "Hi." Kerry smiled at the frazzled room service waiter. "You can just put that down next to the fifty pounds of chocolate we're going to have for dessert, thanks."

Muddy brown eyes went to her, then to the table, then back to her. The scraggly moustache drooped as he chewed it nervously. "Er, ma'am, I don't think I can put this tray down."

"Here." Dar slipped up behind him and lifted the basket out of the way, coming perilously close to breaking several county ordinances. "G'wan… put it down," she drawled.

He would have been all right if he hadn't tried to pull up his trousers and put down his tray at the same time. Dar managed to save the pizza by hastily dropping the basket and making a grab, but the iced tea evaded her, and it smacked the hapless waiter in the chest, sending ice cubes flying across the room. The waiter juggled the carafe, sending himself off balance until Dar braced a muscular thigh up against the chair and pinned him in place with her knee.

"You all right?" the executive demanded, setting the pizza trays down.

The man's eyes dropped slowly down her to where the long, sinewy length of her leg was braced against him, then they rolled peacefully back up into his head as he dropped like a rock.

Stunned silence fell for an instant. "What in the hell?" Dar complained.

Kerry pulled the covers up over her head and burst into laughter.

Chapter 11

It was just getting dark when they pulled up a long, sloping road to the quiet retreat Dar had chosen. It was up in the mountains, far away from city lights. Dar pulled the car up to the low-roofed main building, and turned the engine off. "Well, we made it."

Kerry was peering out the window, studying the peaceful scene with interest. Scattered up and down the hilly ground, tucked into alcoves and shrouded with trees were small cabins, neatly cedared paths leading the way towards each one. "Yep, we sure did, though I was wondering there for a minute after we had to revive your liveried friend at the hotel."

"Hey, it's not my fault he couldn't take the sight of a little skin," Dar objected mildly.

"A little?" Kerry giggled. "Your leg was longer than his whole body,

Dar. I'm glad we tipped him all right, though." She returned her attention to the outside. "Mm…"

In the distance, she could see larger buildings, and the lodge they were parked in front of, where yellow light poured from the windows and painted gilded stripes across the lightly frosted ground. "Wow, this is nice," she finally said, giving her companion a smile. "C'mon." She opened the car door, starting a little as the cold, pine-laden air hit her in the face. "Brr."

Dar smiled and popped the trunk. A warmly jacketed valet appeared as she was getting their bags and she tossed the keys to him, then shouldered the two bags and evaded Kerry's attempt to retrieve hers. "Ah ah…I got it." She waved Kerry on and chuckled as the blond woman swept the door open and bowed her inside. "Why thank you, ma'am."

They entered the lodge, a long building that doglegged to the right past the reception desk. Sounds from the other side of the building indicated some kind of restaurant, and Kerry could see a dimly lit bar just ahead, half filled with shadowy forms. They walked up to the desk, and Dar quietly gave her name to the clerk.

"Ah yes, Ms. Roberts…my goodness, we haven't seen you here in a long time." The clerk smiled and looked up, pushing a pair of half glasses up onto her nose. "I swear, you haven't changed a bit."

Dar smiled politely at the compliment. "Thanks, Milly; hard to believe you remembered me."

A salt and pepper eyebrow lifted at her. "You're pretty memorable, I'll have you know. We reserved the far cabin for you since you said you wanted some quiet space." She glanced up at Kerry. "And you've brought a guest this time, how wonderful. Welcome…Ms. Stuart, is it?"

"Kerry." The blond woman extended a hand across the counter. "Nice to meet you. This place looks fantastic."

Milly laughed. "Well, we like to think so. We've been here for over forty years." She folded a packet together, then handed Dar a pair of keys. "Here you go. Do you remember the way, or do you want me to have Charles take you over?"

Dar paused, then exhaled. "I remember the way. Thanks, Milly." She looked over towards the back of the room. "What's the special tonight?"

The gray-haired woman laughed. "Just your luck—it's roast beef."

Dar chuckled. "Just my luck," she repeated, then gently bumped

Kerry. "C'mon, let's go change, then I'll show you around. They've got a nice fireplace just inside."

"Lead on," Kerry said cheerfully as she followed, her eyes watching everything with interest. This was going to be great. Dar knew the place, and it held some good memories, Kerry decided, just from the childlike grin that kept trying to break through on her face. They'd have time to relax and just talk, something that had been rare since...Jesus. Kerry thought about it. They hadn't really had time away without any distractions since that business trip to Disney World. Even at home, there was always work, and the calls in the middle of the night, and complications. But not here. They'd left their laptops locked in the trunk, and after a bit of convincing on her part, both pagers as well. "Colleen has the number up here in an emergency," she'd argued, "and so does Mark, but they both know not to use it unless the world is coming to an end."

Dar had thought a moment, then shrugged and relinquished the device. "Okay."

Now, Kerry tugged up her collar as she followed Dar out the front door and down a path that sloped a little downward, her sneakers crunching softly on the cedar chips that lined it. "Mm." The air was sweet and rich with the scent of cold, and pine, and the wood she was walking on. "This is great."

In the semi-darkness, the sudden glitter of Dar's eyes was startling. "Glad you like it," she drawled. "I used to spend semester breaks up here. It's not an expensive place, but it's family-run...Milly's husband is ex-Navy."

Kerry nodded, looking around. "It looks like it's well cared for," she commented. "They seem to know you pretty well." She glanced up, seeing the quiet smile on Dar's face. "When was the last time you were here?"

The smile vanished. "Christmas, a few years back," came the quiet answer. "I'd...I'd just broken up with Elana...I guess I needed some...time out."

Kerry tucked a hand around her arm as the walked along. "Well, I hope you'll have better memories from this visit," she commented mildly. "We had a place out off the lake we used to go to in the summers, it was a little like this." She took a breath, aware of Dar's intent concentration on her words. "It was supposed to be a family vacation, but it was usually a circus, what with people coming and going, deals, the press...you know."

"Mm," Dar agreed, leading her down a fork in the path.

"Sailing was my favorite thing to do, but as we got older, my mother made sure there really wasn't much time for that. She had parties and whatever, kept us going from summer estate to summer estate talking to people I didn't have much in common with, even then," she sighed. "And dressing up...that was always a trial. Me and Angie paraded in front of her and usually my aunt to make sure we looked all right."

"Doesn't sound like much fun," Dar remarked as they came up to a small, tree-shrouded cabin with a wooden porch. "Closest I ever came to that was my mother making sure the rips in my jeans weren't going to get me arrested in some of the more rural counties down there." She put a hand on Kerry's back as they mounted the three low stairs, the wood echoing lightly under their steps. "I always liked this one." She turned and nodded. "Nice view."

Kerry also turned, and gasped a little, faced with a beautiful moon-lit lake, reflecting a canopy of brilliant stars. "Oh my god, yes." She let out a delighted laugh. "It's wonderful, Dar." She turned and poked her companion. "Very romantic...is this where you always bring special friends?"

Dar gazed at her, a little sadly. "No...you're the first." She turned and continued across the porch, opening the door and gesturing her inside. "I always used this as a very private retreat...I never considered bringing anyone else here before."

"Mm." Kerry ducked inside without further comment, flipping on the light just inside the door. "Oh." She blinked in surprise. "This is really nice." The cabin was mostly one large room, with a neatly made bed against the far wall under a window, covered in a thick comforter in shades of crimson and navy. There were Indian patterned throw rugs on the floor, and a thick sheepskin, stretched out in front of the small fireplace. A garment press stood against the wall, and a doorway led to a luxurious bathroom complete with a sunken hot tub surrounded by warmly weathered wood. "Oh, I think I like this."

Dar chuckled softly. "Oh yeah, that comes in handy after a day of horseback riding, especially if you're not used to it. Trust me." She put their bags down on the bed, and looked around. It hadn't changed, she mused, walking over to the window and peering out at the silent, gently murmuring lake.

Kerry was exploring the counter against the back wall. "I see we have the essentials... coffee, cookies, and hot chocolate." She investigated the supplies. "Cups and, let's see…tea bags…oh, and little muffins…this is really cute, Dar."

The dark-haired woman tossed a stuffed bag down next to her. "Well, we can add our little stash here," she grinned, her good humor restored. "Never thought we'd fit all that chocolate in there."

Kerry snorted, and lifted the bag up. "I can't believe we brought it all. We're going to get sick on it." She sniffed at the bag. "Mm. On the other hand…" The rich scent was alluring and she sighed. "Later. Dinner first?"

"Sounds good to me," Dar agreed. "Those pizzas were tiny."

"What pizzas…oh, those. Right." Kerry slipped out of her sweatshirt and pulled a heavier sweater over her head, settling the edge over her jeans. "Yeah, good thing I didn't order smalls or we could have used them as drink coasters."

"Could have used them as that anyway," Dar complained, changing into a thick sweater of her own, and rubbing her hands. "It's cold here, Kerry."

The blond woman turned, putting down the brush she'd been pulling through her hair, and walked over, taking Dar's hands into hers and pressing them against her body. "Aw, my poor little hothouse flower." She giggled at the blue eyes widened in outrage. "You southerners. Talk about thin blooded… we'll have to get you some mittens." She gently kissed Dar's fingers. "Thank you for inviting me up here, by the way."

Dar smiled at her, obviously charmed. "I'm glad you like it."

"Here, bend down." Kerry released one hand and recaptured her brush, running it through Dar's dark locks to bring some order to them. The silky strands crackled in the dry air and clung to the brush, winding themselves around her hands as well. "Ack…one nice thing about Miami… you don't get this much." She patiently untangled herself, meeting the watching blue eyes with a grin as she fluffed the usually disheveled bangs. "Your hair would look pretty in braids; want to try them tomorrow?"

Dar blinked at her, obviously surprised at the question. "Um, sure." She straightened as Kerry finished. "If I can do yours." She gently tucked the blond hair back into a tail, studying the effect.

Kerry smiled, loving the feel of Dar's fingers in her hair as they brushed against her sensitive scalp. "You're on," she agreed happily. "It's a vacation, right? We can do whatever we want."

"Yep." Dar put an arm over her shoulder, and nudged her towards the door. "C'mon, they've got some really good roast beef."

"Oh yeah?" Kerry obligingly slipped an arm around her waist. "With gravy?"

"Uh huh, and killer mashed potatoes," Dar promised. "And home-made ice cream for dessert."

Kerry let out a little moan. "Uh oh, I'm in trouble." She lamented. "I'm a sucker for homemade ice cream."

"Yeah, me too," Dar agreed sheepishly. "But it's vacation, remember?"

"Mm, good point. How much trouble can we get into in two days, anyway?"

🐾   🐾   🐾

"Dar?" Kerry's voice floated out of the darkness as they made their way back after dinner. It had gotten colder, and the sky seemed crystalline, the inky blackness drenched in pinpoints of light so numerous you could hardly see the constellations.

"Yeah?" The taller woman ambled along contentedly, sucking on a mint.

"If I explode, is that covered under workman's comp?" Kerry asked idly. "God, that was good; that chef is positively dangerous."

"Don't explode," Dar objected. "Do you have any idea the amount of paperwork I'd have to fill out if I had an employee explode on a business trip?" She and shifted her mint from one side of her mouth to the other. "Not to mention having to explain to Mari how I, a responsible corporate officer, allowed such a thing to happen."

"Allowed?" Kerry snorted. "You were feeding me maraschino cherries, you fink—you aided and abetted."

A soft chuckle. "Hmm, that's true... maybe I could claim I was performing research and development." She slipped an arm around Kerry and ducked her head, kissing her gently. "So we've got a couple of choices: we can take a run up the mountain for some skiing, or hike, or go out on the lake, or do a little riding...what's your poison?"

"Well." Kerry steered her up the steps to their cabin. "How about riding in the morning and then go out for a sail on the lake in the afternoon?"

Dar opened the door and exhaled. "Sounds good to me." She'd always mostly gone on solitary hikes to small caves just uprange for some pensive solitude. It would be strange to have Kerry along.

They went inside and Dar spent a few minutes in the bathroom before coming out to find Kerry efficiently stacking wood in the fireplace. "Whatcha doing?"

On one knee, Kerry turned and regarded her. "Making a fire." She put another log in place, then tucked some tinder inside it. "I know that's an alien concept for you, Dar, but it can be very cozy."

"It's not alien," the dark-haired woman protested. "I've been outside Miami, remember?" She studied what Kerry was doing. "I've just never had to actually, um…" She waved her hands a bit descriptively. "Make one." She knelt. "What's that?"

"Moss." Kerry packed it between the logs. "It makes the logs burn." She looked around. "Do you see any matches?"

"Um, no, but I think you use this." Dar took down a flint and striker from over the mantel, and offered it to her. "Right?"

Kerry giggled. "Not in this century, Dar." She stood, and put her hands on her hips. "I think I've got some…hey!"

Dar had studied the items, then cocked her head and positioned the striker, smacking the flint against it with devastating efficiency, and sending a shower of sparks down onto the neatly packed tinder. It obligingly caught fire and started to burn, little tendrils of smoke wafting up. Dar spread her hands out, and looked insufferably pleased with herself. "Like that?"

"Son of a bitch," Kerry marveled. "I've never seen a twentieth century human being actually do that before." She regarded her boss. "What other hidden skills do you have?"

Dar chuckled, returning the tools to their place and getting out of the way as Kerry gently blew on the flames, shepherding them into a crackling blaze. It was nice, she decided, regarding the flickering light and holding her hands out to the warmth as it grew. Behind her there was a low couch, covered in colorful throws, and she settled into one corner, wriggling into a comfortable spot and looking up as Kerry joined her. They both watched the fire grow in a friendly silence that was broken when Kerry shifted, taking a breath and studying her hands, before she looked up at Dar. "I think we're going to have fun this weekend," she started, tentatively, planning her words with care.

A smile pulled Dar's lips. "I hope so. It's been a long week, huh?"

"Yes, yes it has." Her lover agreed quietly. "A lot's happened."

"Mm." A very soft murmur.

"I want to have a fun weekend. I think we both need it…." Kerry felt the words getting out of her control a little. "I mean, well...I've got something I wanted to talk to you about before we...I..." She stopped, sensing something, and looked up, seeing an unguarded look of quickly veiled fear in Dar's eyes. Her train of thought derailed in reflex. "Why do you do that?" she asked instead.

"Do what?" the taller woman replied, with forced nonchalance.

"Expect the worst all the time?" Kerry asked.

A quick head shake. "I don't...what do you mean?"

"You do. I saw it in your face just then. You don't know what I'm going to tell you, but you think it's something bad. Why, Dar?" Kerry asked, very gently. "Have I done something that makes you worry about that?"

Dar looked trapped. She turned her head, and knitted her fingers, long digits twisting around each other in upset. She hadn't expected Kerry to ask. Not like this, not...

Not so soon. "I... you didn't do anything, Kerry," she finally muttered. "It's my hangup... it has nothing to do with you."

"Of course it does." Kerry felt her way gingerly, putting a casual hand on Dar's knee. "If it's part of you, it has everything to do with me." She could sense Dar withdrawing, and the dark-haired woman exhaled unhappily and folded her arms, tucking her hands against her sides. "Please talk to me," she asked, simply. "I want to understand. I don't want to hurt you."

It took a long moment, as Dar stared into the flames, their flickering light outlining her sharply planed features in exotic detail. Then she apparently made a decision as she nodded slightly. Her head turned, and the ambered blue eyes regarded Kerry seriously. "There's no really simple answer to that, I guess," she sighed. "I'm not very good at discussing myself. I try not to think about why I do what I do most of the time; it just gets too strange."

"Mm," Kerry murmured encouragingly, hoping by the time Dar finished telling her whatever it was, she'd have the guts to go ahead with her own issue.

"I guess you know I...haven't been really successful in relationships," Dar continued, awkwardly. "I don't know, it's probably my fault. I get so driven...I get so caught up in work, and..." She shrugged a little. "Anyway, I...I guess I was in my senior year at college. I'd just figured out my orientation, that was a shock." She exchanged grim little smiles with Kerry. "At any rate, I don't know, I guess I must have been a dreamer when I was a kid, always expecting things to be like the books, I guess I…" She stopped, trying to find words.

Kerry just stroked her leg, gently.

"I, um, I guess I fell in love." Dar said it as thought she wasn't sure. "And I was this idealistic kid, and I'd read about…fairy tales, mostly…I guess I thought that's what it was going to be like. I threw everything I had into it. I figured I'd found my future." She thought back to that golden fall wistfully. "It was…I remember being deliriously happy." A pause. "Stupid. I know."

Kerry's eyes closed in empathetic understanding.

"Anyway, it went along great for a while; she was older than I was, really pretty, successful in school. I couldn't believe it; I felt like I belonged to something, to someone, for the first time ever." Dar's voice was gentle, almost abstract. "I figured she felt the same way I did, so one day, I remember it was a Saturday, we were supposed to go to the movies…"

Kerry picked up a walnut from the dish and fingered it, her body tensing against what she knew was coming. "Yeah?"

Dar shrugged. "I told her how I felt, how I wanted to spend my life with her."

Kerry looked up, reading a long ago pain in her lover's face. "And?"

The answer was almost spoken casually. "She laughed at me."

The sharp crack startled them both, making Dar jump a little. She stared at Kerry, who blinked and looked at her hand, where shards of walnut were tumbling down. She opened her clenched fist to reveal the cracked nut and sighed. "Sorry."

A tense little smile caught Dar's lips. "Anyway, she proceeded to tell me just how deficient I was in all aspects and how she wouldn't have been caught dead with me at any place other than one of our local pool halls." Dar looked down at her hands. "She said I was unsophisticated, which I was, and uncultured, which was also true, and that I'd never have a relationship based on anything other than mutual bed sports because I just wasn't emotionally capable of it." This last with a pained grimace. "And she was right."

"She was not!" Kerry shot back angrily. "She was stuck up piece of horse's ass without the sense that god gave a dead hedgehog, Dar."

The taller woman laughed gently. "I know that, now," Dar stated softly. "But the kid I was then didn't, and I believed her…I think some parts of me still do," she admitted lowly. "So that's where that reaction comes from, Kerry; there is a part of me that remembers what she said and what she told me about nothing being permanent and how people really just use each other until they're ready to move on." A pause. "I guess intellectually I know better, but emotionally, I'm still waiting for the other shoe to fall," she finished, regarding the flames quietly. She decided she wouldn't tell Kerry about the little prayer she said every night as they were falling asleep. "So, what's bugging you?" she asked quietly, knowing something had been, and for some time now. *At least she talks about it,* Dar mused. *At least she'll give me a chance to try and fix things if that's what's wrong.* She watched Kerry pluck at her sleeve, and noticed the slight tremor in her hands. *If it's that simple.*

"Dar." Kerry picked up her hand, feeling the chill in it, and kissed it gently. "I guess that brings me to my…little problem." She cleared her throat nervously. "I, um…I've been really thinking about things, and about what I…about what I need in order for me to live…my life, I guess."

Dar gazed at her, with an open, haunted expression. "Yeah?" her voice cracked, and she wondered what was coming.

"And see, I've got this…I'm not really sure what you would call it, maybe it was the way I was brought up, I don't really know…" she stammered. "God, I'm having such a problem with this. I don't know what's wrong with me; you'd think I could just spit it out." She stood, and paced back and forth, visibly trying to relax. "Okay." She turned and saw blue eyes round with apprehension. "Oh, Dar, don't look at me like that; you'd think I was going to tell you I was a cross-dresser or something."

It broke the tension, and Dar muffled a relieved laugh. "Sorry, but the way you're pacing…. Jesus, Kerry, you're putting me all in knots just watching you. What is it?" She swallowed once. "I thought maybe…I thought you were maybe still mad about last night, or…"

"Last night? Oh." Kerry exhaled, thinking about that. "Um, next time, you might want to let me in on what your plan is, just so I understand what's going on first."

Dar nodded and exhaled. "Yeah, I'll try." A pause. "So…was that what was bothering you?" She felt a little proud of herself for figuring it out, communication never having been one of her strong points, and she knew that.

"Um, no." Kerry stopped, and turned, facing her. *Now or never; just suck it up, Kerry, and do it!* She hesitated, then took two steps forward and knelt at Dar's feet, resting one hand on the taller woman's knee for balance. "I have this thing about commitment."

A double thump of the heart. *Jesus…she knows I've never been in a long term relationship, maybe she…god.* Dar's eyes scanned her face alertly, then a brow edged up a little. "You do?" she murmured softly. "Um…I mean, well…yeah, I know you're a very, um…you seem to be a very loyal, and committed kind of p…Kerry, what exactly is this about?" If her lover was having a problem with her, she wanted to know right now. "Just level with me."

The blond woman scratched her jaw. "Um." Now that she was right down to it, the whole thing started to seem really silly to her, and she hesitated, torn between continuing and just…. "This is going to sound maybe a little crazy to you," she temporized, "and I just want you to know it's… it's just something that I…" She stopped, and dug in her pocket, pulling something out and focusing her attention on the tiny, embroidered fir trees that were dancing across Dar's chest. "Okay, look…" She put her closed fist against Dar's stomach, still staring intently at her sweater. "I tried to find a way just to let you know…how important you are to me…and how important our relationship is to me."

"Okay," Dar responded, obviously deeply at sea. "Kerry, it's very important to me, too. I hope you know that…it's changed my whole life."

Kerry regarded the sweater. "Is it a good change?" she whispered.

Long fingers gently grasped her chin and tilted her head back, so that she had no choice but to meet Dar's now very serious eyes. "Is that an honest question?" Dar replied. "I hope not; I hope you know the answer to that already." She paused. "Yes, you've been the best thing that's ever happened to me."

Kerry managed a nod. "Good," she whispered, folding Dar's fingers around the small box she'd taken from her pocket. "Because for me…it's this all my life thing…and I want you to know that…I want you to understand that even if we can't go into a clerk's office and say this, I want this to be forever, Dar, that whole…in sickness and in heath, for richer and for poorer, in good times, and bad…and have death never part us…" Her words fell into a shocked silence. "…kind of thing." A long pause. "Okay?" *Well. That was the stupidest proposal in the history of the lesbian world, wasn't it? Maybe I should have downloaded those practice scripts from the internet….* She eyed her lover unhappily.

There was a soft, almost incoherent sound as Dar started breathing again. "K—" Her voice disappeared into a soundless squeak, and she self-consciously cleared her throat and tried again. "K—Kerry, did…did you just…p—propose to me?" Dar stuttered.

Kerry chewed her lip, trying desperately to gauge the response. "Um, yeah…I did." She glanced down. "On bended knee, no less." *At least she realized that's what it was; there's a plus.* She watched her lover's face trying to process several different emotions at once. "I…what I really wanted you to know, Dar, is that you're not going to roll over one morning and find me not there."

Dar very slowly lifted a hand, and slid it across Kerry's cheek, cupping the back of her head in an almost hesitant gentleness. "I'm not sure what in the hell I ever did to deserve this, but I can't think of any single thing in the world that would make me happier than to accept it." She pulled Kerry towards her as her eyes misted. "C'mere." She wrapped her arms around the utterly relieved woman, who practically climbed up into her lap and threw a bear hug around her. "You know you didn't have to do that…"

"Yes, I did." Kerry mumbled into the wool of her sweater. "Yes, I did, because I want you to understand you're stuck with me, Dar. You're not going to be able to get rid of me, okay? Not unless you…I don't know, toss me off a cliff or something."

Dar let out a strangled laugh, trying to ignore the tear that tracked its way down her face. "There aren't any cliffs in Miami, Kerry," she replied softly. "But if there were, and you fell…I'd jump right off after you." She cradled the younger woman's head, stroking her hair and pressing her cheek against its softness. "Thank god you had the guts to do this; it would have taken me either half a lifetime or half a bottle to have done it."

Kerry peeked up at her, seeing the dampness glinting in the firelight. "Really?"

A hesitant nod. "I made myself a promise that I'd never let myself risk what I felt when I was that poor, stupid kid back then ever again." Another tear spilled out. "I never realized that when it happened…I wouldn't have a choice." Dar regarded her wistfully. "I've never been so scared in my life."

Kerry gently wiped away the tears, feeling a sense of overwhelming relief go through her. It was what she'd been scared of: that Dar wouldn't, or couldn't, allow herself to accept the commitment Kerry was offering. But maybe she was right, maybe she didn't even have a choice.

Maybe Kerry didn't either.

She wasn't sure she wanted one. "Are you going to even look at it?" she asked, shyly. "It took me forever to pick out. I kinda wanted one like that old one I have, but they don't make those anymore."

Dar slipped her hand around in front of her, and offered it. "Open?"

Kerry leaned against her, her legs sprawled over Dar's as she sat quietly in her lap. "Okay." She took the box and opened it, watching Dar's eyes pick up the glints of the fire off the ring. "It was kinda...I mean, you're sort of tough to pick a ring out for, you know that?"

Dar gazed at the item, her eyes following the Celtic interlace that surrounded a square cut, understated diamond. "It's beautiful," she managed to get out. "Dear god, Kerry. You didn't have to...that must have cost a..."

"I have no idea," Kerry replied, simply. "I didn't look at the prices, and it hasn't hit my credit card statement yet."

Dar stared at her, her jaw dropping a little.

"Well, it was less than the card's limit, Dar," she replied, putting a finger on her lover's chin and closing her mouth. "Stop looking like I bought Pro Player Stadium."

"W...what was the limit on that card?" Dar spluttered. "Good grief!"

"Um...." Kerry was enjoying herself, now that she knew Dar's feelings. "Well. I don't really know. It might have been the platinum; I'll have to check." She almost giggled when the blue eyes widened even further. "Oh, calm down." She leaned over and gave Dar a light kiss on the lips. "It wasn't that bad." A pause, while a hesitant smile claimed the dark-haired woman's mouth. "I think. Besides, I'm only going to do this once."

"Kerry." Dar realized she was being tweaked. "Well," she drawled softly, "at least you won't have anything to say when I give you yours, then." A slow, sexy smile appeared. "Because I didn't look at price tags either, but I know I got a bouquet of twenty-four red roses from the guy who sold it to me at the office the next day."

Kerry's mouth dropped open. "Uh." She glanced up guiltily. "So that's where those came from."

"Yeah, I guess he..." Dar stopped, and stared closely at her lover, who was showing a slow flush up along her neck. "Were you wondering?"

Kerry didn't know where to look, so she just dropped her head and didn't answer.

"Kerrison." The gentle voice recalled her, and she peeked up, reluctantly. "You could have asked me."

The blond woman sighed. "Jealousy is a very embarrassing, not to mention generally icky emotion," she admitted. "I wasn't very proud of how I felt."

Dar lifted their linked hands and brushed her lips across Kerry's knuckles. "No, I know, but it's…" She rubbed the unresisting hand against her cheek. "It's very flattering," she offered. "From my perspective, I mean."

Kerry's eyes softened and misted over. "So you were thinking of making this more formal, huh?"

Dar dropped her gaze, her fingers tracing a light, idle pattern "I have this thing about commitment, too," she finally answered, her throat working. "I discovered I really like being a part of someone else's life." She paused, then indicated her carry sack. "Hand me that?"

Kerry handed it over, watching her as she dug inside and pulled out a small, velvet bag. "You carry it w—with you?"

Dar stared at the bag, then looked up and nodded. "Yeah, so if I ever found the courage to do it, I wanted to be ready." She held out her hand. "Go on. I'm not very good at picking things out for other people; shopping for this was…an interesting experience." Her mind remembered the conversation. *"Is this for you, ma'am?" "No, this is for someone as opposite from me as you can get and still be the same species."*

Kerry took the bag, startled a little at its weight, and opened the velvet cord, shaking the bag gently over her hand until a ring tumbled out.

The room went very still. "Oh," Kerry sighed, softly, finding it hard to catch her breath. It was so pretty. It sat in her hand, winking at her, a sturdy, yet elegant band that cupped up into a rose, whose delicate petals framed a brilliant, round-cut diamond. She tipped it up a little and looked at the inner band, where she spotted some engraving. "Dar, wh…" She looked up as the skin under her arm grew very warm, and she was shocked to see the profound blush on her lover's face. The blue eyes were fixed firmly on the fire, and Dar's nostrils were flared slightly. She looked back down at the ring, then bent her head closer.

Forever Yours.

With the words, something clicked home in Kerry's awareness, with a certainty that made her lightheaded. "Dar," she managed to whisper.

"Yes." The response was clearly, and precisely, enunciated.

"I think I'm going to pass out." Kerry felt a strong grip take hold of her, and she let herself go limp, one hand closing loosely over the ring. She floated in a pleasant haze for a moment, hearing in the back of her mind a soft, affectionate chuckle. "That is so beautiful."

"The ring?" Dar murmured, into her nearby ear.

"The words," Kerry corrected her.

"Oh."

"The ring's gorgeous too."

"So…you like it?"

Soft lips were the answer.

It was too quiet. Dar cocked her head as a tree branch brushed against the window, making a soft scraping noise. She'd forgotten how quiet it really was out here without the ever-present sounds of traffic or airplanes.

Or air conditioning. She glanced at the ceiling in mild amusement. The AC provided a white noise that most Floridians were subliminally used to. Its absence was almost uncomfortable as the silence beat down on her ears, broken only by Kerry's soft breathing.

Her soft, adorable breathing, which was warming the skin right above Dar's heart, since the blond woman was nestled against her right side with her head pillowed on Dar's shoulder, one arm wrapped securely around her stomach.

It was nice and cozy, and she'd discovered, much to her own personal amazement, that she really, really enjoyed all this cuddling stuff.

A revelation. Her parents had been anything but physically affectionate, even with each other; Dar had only seen the occasional hug. A pat on the back, sure. A gentle slap on the leg, her father's favorite attention getter, yes. But hugs?

Hell no. In fact, she honestly couldn't remember the last time her mother had touched her…oh, no, maybe she could, Dar reflected quietly. Yeah…the first, no, second time she'd broken her arm, the bad one, when the bones had been sticking out of her arm and had left the thin, straight scars Kerry always liked to trace.

Mom had held her then, while she tried so hard not to scream.

But then her father had come in, and she'd bitten her lip almost through to keep the crying inside, her efforts rewarded by a brief pat on her cheek, and his approving "That's my tough girl."

Dar chewed her bottom lip reflectively. It had been an ever-present argument between them, she knew, until her mother had just given up and allowed her to follow in his footsteps as far as she was able.

It couldn't have been easy to watch, she realized. She hadn't been a pleasant child, and her adolescence had been one long string of fights, a series of trips to the principal's office, and threats of reform school. She'd had one principal who wanted her out in the worst way, with only one thing blocking his case.

She'd been a straight A student.

Musta driven them all nuts. Honors everything, advanced placement, the whole nine yards. She'd gotten into college on an academic scholarship and frustrated her friends, what few there were, by her ability to breeze through classes with little studying and less preparation.

She'd graduated in the top two percent of her class, with honors, but at that point in her life, she hadn't cared. She'd tossed her rolled up diploma into a basket in her room at her parent's house and spent an entire weekend so drunk she still had no recollection of it.

She'd gone out and found the first job that would pay her enough to cover the monthly payments on a car, rather than just her junk food budget, and spent her free hours under water, away from everything.

Alone.

Kerry stirred, shifting a little, then lifting her head and looking up. "Hey?"

Dar exhaled, and gave her a fond look. "Hmm?"

"Why are you still up?" The blond woman rested her chin on Dar's breastbone. "Do you want some hot milk?" Her dreams had nudged her uneasily awake.

A quiet smile, as Dar rubbed her arm lightly. "No, I was just thinking, that's all."

"Mm...'bout what?"

Dar hesitated, then shrugged, pursing her lips a bit. "Nothing really concrete...my folks, a little bit about school..." She moved a stray lock of hair out of Kerry's eyes. "Go on back to sleep; you looked so peaceful."

Kerry considered her words. "I wasn't really fond of school," she commented. "I wasn't that good at it, except stuff like English," she admitted. "I belonged to a lot of clubs, Key Club, Young Republicans, that kind of thing."

Dar smiled. "You were a Young Republican?" she queried. "I think the only club I ever joined was…." She stopped to think. "Some jock club or other. I was on a lot of sports teams in high school."

"Oh, gee, there's a surprise," Kerry grinned at her, then her expression faltered. "Not me. I wanted to play softball, but…" She paused in memory of her mother's horror at the very thought, then sighed. "I probably would have sucked at it anyway. I got stuck with golf."

"I'm sure you wouldn't have," Dar objected, mildly. "You've got good eye-hand coordination and a nice running form; you'd have been fine," she analyzed. "I never had the damn patience for golf; how in the hell did you stand it?"

Kerry peered at her in silence, then let out a quiet breath. "Do you know something, Dar?" she asked softly. "Do you want to know when the very first time was that I was told I was capable and intelligent?" She had no idea why she was going into this, save that it had been a night of open truths and this had been weighing on her.

The blue eyes peered at her in puzzlement. "Sure."

"You should know," the blond woman told her. "You wrote it in an e-mail."

Dar stared at her in shocked silence.

"And you hardly knew me. You'd met me for what, half an hour?" Kerry shifted, propping her head up on her fist. "Even the bosses at Associated…I mean, sure, I was always spoken of as a hard worker, a nice girl, always on time, but despite what Robert said, the only reason I got that job was because the guy in there before me left with the accountant's wife in the middle of the night and they needed someone real fast, and real accessible."

"That's not true, Kerry; you were an excellent director. Your personnel record carried the highest recommendations in it," Dar argued. "You're highly skilled, highly motivated, very intelligent, and…and…."

Kerry gazed at her wistfully.

"And adorable," Dar finished, having run out of professional adjectives. "Don't tell me that's why you decided to come work for me—because I stated the obvious?"

A soft sigh. "It might have been obvious to you, but it sure wasn't obvious to me," Kerry admitted. "I had a mental note somewhere to say thank you for that, by the way...I think you were the first person in my life who just took me at face value and didn't assume I was some fluffball muffinhead who got the job because of my father. Even Robert, who liked me, when he put me in as manager, he told me he didn't expect much, just that I should try to keep things going until he could find a real director."

Dar watched her, stunned. "You're kidding," she muttered.

A slow nod. "What did you see in me, Dar, that no one else did?" Kerry wondered aloud.

Dar slapped her own head. "Okay, for starters, you had guts," she spluttered. "And you held yourself together in a very stressful situation, and you came up with some very good, and very intelligent plans for the takeover, and...and you told me to go hell, for chrissake—do you know how many people have done that and gotten away with it?"

"Not many, huh?" Kerry was guiltily soaking up the praise like a sponge.

"Try one." Dar hitched herself up and regarded her lover. "Listen, I know talent when I see it; it's part of my job, Kerry, and believe me, my talent meter went off the scale when I saw you." She sighed, perplexed. "Good grief, Ker; you'd think I hired you because I had the hots for you or something."

An awkward silence fell as Kerry's eyes dropped to the comforter, the sudden strike at her own hidden insecurities going home with a vengeance. "I..."

Dar felt her heart drop. "You didn't think that," she questioned softly. "Kerry? Look at me."

Fearful green eyes slowly lifted to hers.

"Kerry, I hired you because I thought you would be a tremendous asset to me and an excellent assistant," Dar told her gently. "And I was very, very right. What would make you think otherwise?" She felt a little bewildered.

Kerry's eyes dropped again. "I...I don't know," she confessed softly. "Maybe because I've been told all my life that's how things work." Her eyes crept up Dar's still body. "You don't get things because you work hard, or because you deserve them, you get them because someone pays for them, or because someone wants something from you."

Dar looked stricken. "Kerry..."

"I know." Kerry let her head fall and rest against Dar's skin. "I know...my head knows, and god, my heart knows differently, Dar, but sometimes...sometimes I look in the mirror, and I can't help thinking...why me?" She lifted her head. "It's like I'm in a fairy tale and one day a wicked witch is going to wave her wand, and I'll be back home, or you'll get t—tired of me, or..." She blinked her eyes, and tears hit Dar's shoulder. "I can't help it."

Dar exhaled in dismay, understanding a little more about her lover. "Kerry...." She cupped the smaller woman's cheek, seeing the glittering tears. "I meant those words, and I promise you—I promise you, I'll always be here for you...no matter what," she reassured her. "I will never leave you."

"What if I screw up at work?" Kerry asked. "What if I can't do this?"

"Sweetheart, I don't give a damn," her lover told her. "If you want to quit and do nothing but sell seashell futures over the internet from the condo, that's more than okay by me. Are you really worried about it? You do a fantastic job."

"I don't want to ever disappoint you," Kerry whispered.

Dar tucked the blond head against her chest and hugged her. "You won't."

Kerry rested there for a moment. "Sorry," she finally muttered. "I'm not sure where that little bout of insecurity came from." She played with the edge of Dar's sleep shirt. "In the middle of the damn night, too."

"Shh, it's all right." Dar rubbed gentle circles against her back, willing her pounding heart to slow. "We've both been through some rough times."

Kerry nodded. "I know...it makes it very hard to trust this, doesn't it?" She gently returned to her position, curling an arm back around Dar's belly.

"Yes, it does," Dar admitted, circling her with both arms and pulling her closer, "but we'll get through it."

Kerry relaxed against her. "Together," she added quietly.

"Always," Dar confirmed.

"Brr." Dar snuggled further down into the covers, giving the early morning light an evil look. "It's cold out there." She glanced at the thermostat, then back at her trying-not-to-giggle bedmate. "We forgot to turn the heater on."

"You are such a wuss." Kerry butted her head into Dar's chest, then rolled onto her back. "All right, I guess I have to prove my northern roots and get up to turn the heat on." She ducked out from under the covers and winced as her feet hit the cold floor. "Yow!" She scampered across the surface and got to the thermostat, turning it up into the broil range, then bounded back and hopped into bed like a large blonde kangaroo. "Yikes, that is cold."

"Hah hah," Dar grinned. Then she relented and tossed the covers around Kerry, pulling her back into a pocket of wonderfully Dar-smelling warmth. "Thanks."

"Ungh." Kerry ducked her head under the blanket and deliberately snuck her chilled hands under Dar's shirt, grinning as she heard the taller woman gasp. "Heh. You're nice and warm." She gently tweaked the skin under her fingertips.

"Yeah, except for these blocks of ice up against my stomach." Dar gave her a mock glare, now very wide awake. "How did you get so cold in that short a time?"

Kerry shrugged, snuggling closer. "Heat all rushed to my brain, I guess, to keep me from plowing into the window." She yawned, making a soft, squeaking noise. "So…a little riding, then some sailing, right?" She found herself really looking forward to the day.

"Breakfast first," Dar corrected. "Milly makes the best cheese grits I've ever had."

"Cheese grits," Kerry sighed. "That ranks where on the health meter? Between munching on a solid stick of butter and swallowing chocolate syrup?" Sometimes she seriously wondered how Dar had actually lived as long as she had and was in the physical condition she obviously was. Maybe her chemistry burned things differently or something. "Jesus."

Dar chuckled softly, used to the woebegone protests by now. "I think they serve a sprig of parsley with them if it makes you feel better," she told her innocently. "Besides, you like them." Green eyes peeked warily up from the dark recesses of the comforter. "You are a bad influence," Kerry informed her. "You tricked me into liking them."

"You're the one who brought home Snowballs for dinner the other night," Dar teased the blonde woman, who tickled her in revenge. "Hey!"

"Like I had a choice?" Kerry persisted, finding a good spot just under Dar's ribcage that was making her squirm. "It was either that or eat The Eggs from the Black Lagoon and Son of Maybe it Once was

Bacon, but now, who knows?" She shuddered. "Believe me, the mystery crème in the snowballs was much safer."

Dar was laughing helplessly. "Okay, okay, I give up...you win." She draped her arms over Kerry's body and exhaled, watching the rising sun inch its way into the window. The gentle pink beams were broken by the leaves outside, laying an intricate pattern over the blankets. "Nice day out."

Kerry burrowed up a little and peeked at the window. "Mm...yeah, this is going to be fun." She looked up at Dar with a frank, happy grin. "I haven't been riding in years. I hope I remember how."

Dar gave her a squeeze. "Don't worry, it comes back to you," she promised. "They've got a nice string of horses here, only one or two meanies."

"One or two, huh?" Kerry eyed her speculatively. "Let's see..." She raised a hand to her head and pressed her fingers to her temple, then closed her eyes. "My psychic ability is telling me...those are the ones you pick." One green orb opened, and its brow tilted up. "Yes?"

Dar let out a low, throaty chuckle and rewarded her with a sexy grin. "Very good, Madame Poo Poo." She inclined her head in agreement. "Hey, I can get you a 900 number for the office, make you a profit center. How about it?"

Kerry laughed. "Oh yeah. I can see that: 'Operations and Prognostication, Stuart speaking,'" she mimicked herself, rolling her eyes when Dar started laughing too. "I'd be a real hit in sales meetings."

"Nah," Dar disagreed. "What would they do with their Ouiji board and the 8 ball José keeps stuffed up his butt?"

"Oh god, that's bad. What a visual." Kerry winced, covering her eyes.

"Here." The dark-haired woman fished her out of the covers and pulled her up, kissing her soundly. The contact continued past where she'd intended, and after a long moment they broke off and looked at each other, panting a little. "Better?" Dar asked, on an irregular breath.

"Than what?" Kerry wondered, gazing at her in goofy adoration. "Is it just my opinion that you're such an awesome kisser?" She reached up and traced Dar's lower lip with a finger, shaking her head a little. "Or is it that everything you do takes on such a deeper meaning for me?"

Dar cocked her head and thought about that. "I don't know," she finally answered, honestly. "I've never had anyone tell me that before…but I've noticed that just about everything I do with you is, um…" She pursed her lips and rocked her head from side to side. "Right, if you know what I mean."

"Mm." Kerry waggled her eyebrows. "I know what you mean," she stated, then blushed a little and tucked her head into Dar's shoulder. *God, Kerry, you are turning into a wanton little hussy, aren't you?* "Shall we go and find you some cheese grits, boss?" She gave Dar a squeeze. "Maybe you'll humor me and have a nice chicken sandwich for lunch, hmm?"

"Sure," Dar agreed amiably, remembering Milly's chicken sandwiches, which consisted of a deep fried breast covered in gravy on a toasted buttery roll. "No problem."

Kerry eyed her suspiciously, but the blue eyes peered back with devastating innocence. "You know I'm just doing this for your own good, right?" she queried. "Not just to be a pain in the neck."

Dar touched her forehead to the blond woman's. "Yes, I know that. It's actually kind of nice to have someone be worried about me; my parents gave up on that a long, long time ago."

"Really?" Kerry murmured.

"Yeah," her lover admitted. "Mom told me when I was…I guess sixteen or so, that if I did whatever I wanted, and had my body fall apart at age thirty, don't come back and complain about her being right all those years."

Kerry peeked under the blanket, then gazed at her. "Dar?"

"Hmm?"

"She was wrong."

"I know. My father always said his genes could beat the pants off of a diet that would kill just about anyone else." The dark-haired woman laughed a little self-consciously. "I guess I'm just lucky I take after him."

"Hey Dar, I was just wondering…" Kerry wrapped a thick lock if dark hair around one finger and gave her a wistful smile. "Do you think we're best friends?"

The silence of the cabin lengthened as Dar regarded the covers pensively. "I have no idea what that means," she finally admitted, looking up at Kerry. "I have nothing to judge it against."

"Mm." Kerry let out a small breath.

"I do know I feel closer to you than I have to anyone else in my life before," Dar offered, a touch hesitantly. "I've told you things about myself that I've never said to anybody else. Or wanted to." She searched Kerry's face. "Does that count?"

"It's hard to remember." The blonde woman rolled out of bed and paced across the floor, running her hands through her hair. "It's been a long time for me." She walked over to the hot water dispenser and picked up two cups, dropping a fragrant peach-scented teabag into one and a blackberry bag into another for Dar and steeped them. "Angie and I were always pretty close, but it was a sister thing. I had friends in grade school, but they kinda got fewer as I got older."

Dar had gotten out of bed and came up behind her, putting her hands on Kerry's shoulders and gently squeezing them. "That happens." *How would you know, Dar? You've had what, six friends in all? Including dad?* "People grow apart."

Kerry nodded, stirring sugar into the cups. "I know. I had a…a best friend in high school," she answered. "Peggy. Her parents and my parents were friends, so we saw each other a lot." She turned, and handed Dar her cup. "We had sleepovers, went to movies, shared our crushes, you know."

Dar studied her. "Yeah."

Kerry took a sip of her tea. "You don't know, do you?"

Surprisingly, the taller woman chuckled. "Kerry, I was the girl your mother told you to stay away from," she admitted. "The one who ran with the guys, got into trouble, picked fights, and raised hell." She sighed. "No, there weren't many sleepovers in my checkered youth…the movies were mostly R- and X-rateds we snuck into, and crushes…" A faint shake of her head. "I didn't have time for those." She glanced up. "You still talk to Peggy?"

A quiet, sad look crossed Kerry's face. "No." Her gaze dropped to the floor. "In our senior year, she got into trouble; a guy she'd been dating got a little frisky, and she didn't know enough to say no…she got pregnant." A quiet pause. "They sent her away somewhere. I got two letters from her…the second time she told me she'd had her baby, a little girl."

A silence fell. "And?" Dar gently prodded. "What happened?"

Kerry looked up. "I don't know. I never heard from her again. When my folks found out about the letters, they were furious. They told me if they caught me with any more, I'd be punished." She exhaled slowly. "I never got close to anyone again after that; it was just…too complicated."

"You're friends with Colleen, though." Dar objected, a little concerned at her lover's pensive air. "Kerry, everyone loves you. I haven't met a person yet who doesn't, unless it was a total asshole who even his own mother would hate." She spread a hand out. "You could have hundreds of friends, you know that."

"Too many people to worry about," Kerry responded seriously. "I've tried to keep my life simple since then."

"Until now," Dar stated quietly. *Until me. Which one of us took the bigger risk, I wonder?*

"Mm," her companion softly agreed.

"Kerry?"

"Yeah?"

Dar put a hand on her cheek. "I think we are best friends." She leaned over and kissed her forehead. "C'mon, let's go get some breakfast."

Kerry smiled, then raised herself on her toes and claimed a proper kiss. She could taste the blackberry on Dar's lips, and decided it went well with her peach. It felt so good, after all these years, to be unloading a little of this stuff. She wondered if Dar felt the same about it. "Okay, you're on."

They washed and dressed quickly, but not so quickly that a sponge fight was missed, then headed across the dewy ground in the brisk early morning air.

"So." Kerry linked an arm through her companion's. "You were a hell raiser, huh?"

"Oh yeah," Dar confirmed. "First class. I even had a switchblade."

"Did you really?" Kerry gazed at her, in bemused surprise.

"Yeah. Of course, the one time I almost had to use it I opened it backwards and nearly cut my own finger off, but…"

They both started laughing as their steps scattered the rising mist.

It was a very…tall…horse, Kerry thought as she collected her reins and gently nudged her chestnut mare in the ribs with hesitant knees. *Wow, has it ever been a long time*, she sighed, watching Dar enviously as the taller woman vaulted up on just the snazziest looking gray stallion with neat black hooves and a beautiful black mane and tail. The horse was restive, but Dar settled into her seat as though she was used to doing this on a daily basis, her calves pressing against the sleek gray sides and calming the agitated horse.

It figures she's good at this too. The blond woman sighed, trying to remember exactly how she was supposed to direct the horse, recalling memories from her early high school days when her mother had grudgingly allowed her English riding lessons from a local stable.

She'd loved the horses themselves, really, more than riding them, the feel of the sleek, hard bodies under her hands as she learned how to clean them, and the soft feel of the tiny hairs on their muzzles as they lipped corn from her palm. They were simple and undemanding, wanting only good grass and clean water, and from her, nothing but corn and the odd apple if she felt so inclined.

Kerry smiled in memory and patted her mare's neck, comforted when the sedate animal craned her head around and snorted a little at her. "Hey there, girl...we're gonna be good friends, right?"

The mare tossed her head, then looked up suspiciously as the gray stallion closed in, picking up his feet meticulously. "Hey, you ready to move out?" Dar asked, reaching around to adjust the pack she carried behind her, which was full of a neatly wrapped picnic lunch. "We can go up a nice trail just north of here. It ends up on a little plateau overlooking a little spring. It's a nice place, about a two hour ride."

"Sounds great to me," Kerry agreed, tipping her head back and drinking in the sunlight. The weather had cleared nicely, and it was cold with a light breeze. She was wearing a thick sweater and her heaviest jeans, complemented by a pair of boots Dar had insisted on buying for her, saying she couldn't ride all that way in sneakers.

Sure I could, Kerry reasoned, glancing down at the soft, creamy tan leather that snugly covered her calves. *But they're killer boots, and I've wanted a pair like this, so...* She settled her heels contentedly and glanced over at Dar, who was resplendent in the very cheerful, heavy red sweater Kerry had insisted on reciprocating with. It contrasted nicely with her dark hair and tanned skin, and Kerry decided she very much liked Dar in that color. The taller woman's hair was pulled back into a neat braid, and her eyes sparkled in the sunlight, delighting the watching Kerry.

Her own hair was also neatly braided and tucked into a knot at the back of her neck, and she enjoyed the warmth of the sun on her skin, and the cool touch of the wind. She nudged her horse into a walk, following Dar's stallion towards the start of a secluded path going upward.

It was a wonderful day for a ride, and she nudged her horse a little faster until she was side by side with Dar as they ambled up the path together. The trees, pines mostly, rustled overhead, and she became aware of the small sounds of the forest around her.

Dead leaves rattling softly down.

The wind moving branches.

The soft, rhythmic footfalls of the horses.

Her breathing, and the rustle of wool as Dar turned and glanced at her.

"It's beautiful," she murmured, glancing back. "God, it's been so long since I've done this."

Dar adjusted her hold on the reins, settling into her saddle with a feeling of quiet contentment. She'd managed to keep up her riding skills mostly due to a friend in the Redlands, who had a stable full of retired racers and half broken mustangs he'd let her rope and ride on during the odd weekend she could escape from the city. It had been a while for her, though; the last time she'd gotten down there had been in early September, and she suspected her legs were going to remind her of that when the day was over. She watched Kerry out of the corner of her eye, and speculated they might be spending the evening giving each other massages.

A grin took over Dar's face. "Good boy." She patted her stallion's neck enthusiastically, finding nothing wrong with that prospective thought. "Yeah, it is nice up here. I've been up here when the leaves are changing colors; that's a sight."

"I know." The blond woman laughed. "I've seen them… that was one of the weirdest things to get used to about living in Miami—no seasons."

"There are too seasons." Dar gave her a mock scowl. "Summer's different than winter."

"Oh, right, 88 degrees and 100 percent humidity, versus 88 degrees and 70 percent humidity." Kerry grinned at her. She straightened a little, then relaxed into her mare's walk. "This type of saddle's more comfortable than the one I learned on."

"English?" Dar inquired, receiving a nod in response. "I learned bareback."

"Figures." Kerry laughed. "I bet you open cans with your teeth, too."

Dar laughed with her. "Not these pearly whites, thanks," she disagreed cheerfully, then pressed her knees into her mount's sides and urged him into a faster pace. "C'mon, let's see if these guys can move."

"Oh...um...er..." Kerry frantically tried to remember how to balance as her mare followed the now cantering stallion. "I think I...oh..." She leaned forward a little and caught her balance over the horse's stride. "Okay, that's better." The mare was apparently encouraged, and she sped up to match her stablemate's pace. "Good girl...yeah, that's it." She gripped hard with her knees, and leaned forward as the mare caught up to Dar's horse, and she came even with her lover, who was grinning happily. "Very nice, Dar, very nice. I like this!" she shouted.

"You do?" The blue eyes twinkled merrily. "Great!" With that, Dar leaned forward and gave the stallion a nudge, pushing him from a canter into a full gallop as the path opened up into a long, narrow grassy area. "C'mon!"

"Oh boy." Kerry settled down and hung on as her mare sped up doggedly to match the gray horse, her pace moving into a gallop that whipped the wind past Kerry's ears, and made her eyes tear up. It was a very shaky moment before she relaxed a little and began to enjoy it. "Yeah!" She urged the mare forward. "Go get 'im."

The two horses raced alongside each other, the grass whipping against their legs, the wind tearing across their laughing riders.

Dar let the race continue until she knew they were coming to a narrowing in the path. She gently pulled the stallion up and allowed Kerry to thunder past her as the blond woman quickly pulled back on the reins to slow when she saw Dar do so. They cantered down the narrowing path, and up into a steepening slope for the next part of the ride. "Wow, that was fun." Kerry grinned. "Brings back a lot of good memories." She exhaled and caught her breath.

Dar gazed at her, smiling at the way the activity had brought a healthy flush to her face. "Yeah? For me too." She slowed her mount to a walk, patting the warm neck with an idle hand. "Here." She handed over a water bottle.

"Thanks." Kerry gratefully accepted it, and sucked down a mouthful, tasting the mineral tang of the local water as she swallowed. "Oo, did you see that squirrel, Dar?" She pointed with the bottle at a bushy brownish red animal, who was clutching to the far side of a tree near the path, peering at them suspiciously.

"Sure do." Dar slowed her horse and stopped him, then carefully fished a handful of nuts from her pouch and tossed one at the ground under the squirrel's tree.

Then she waited, sitting in perfect silence, the wind blowing stray tendrils of dark hair about her face.

The squirrel peered at her, then slowly inched down the tree and scampered across the leaves, sniffing at her offering warily.

Kerry watched her lover, the angular face quietly intent, pale blue eyes flicking minutely as she watched the squirrel pick up the nut and nibble it. A smile pulled at the dark-haired woman's lips as she tossed another nut down, and the squirrel scampered right over to snatch it, apparently assured of her harmlessness.

Too bad I didn't bring my camera, she mused. *Dar Roberts feeding squirrels…no one would believe it. I'd put it on my desktop as a wallpaper.* "He's cute," she commented softly, getting a suspicious glance from their tiny friend. "Yeah, you," she told him.

Dar shifted her eyes to Kerry and held a nut up at about shoulder level near the tree the squirrel had been perching on. Obligingly, the animal scuttled up the bark, edging around until his head was level with hers, and they could see his earnest brown eyes.

"Here you go," Dar murmured softly, holding it closer.

"Dar…" Kerry held her breath, watching the creature's sharp teeth get closer to her lover's hand.

One clawed foot worked itself loose and made a grab for the nut, brushing Dar's fingers as she released it. The squirrel darted around the back of the tree, and onto a branch, where he sat, nibbling the nut and chittering at her impudently.

One long finger pointed at him. "Watch it, buddy; there are Fortune 500 CEOs who've gotten less from me with a whole lot more trouble," she warned the animal, then pressed her knees into her horse's side and moved away from the tree.

Kerry joined her, glancing back at the squirrel, who was watching her with a vaguely disappointed air. "That was pretty amazing."

Dar glanced at her. "What, that he ate nuts?" She raised an eyebrow. "No it wasn't."

A gentle laugh. "Okay, if you say so," Kerry agreed amiably. "But I know you wouldn't have caught me getting my hands that close to something with teeth that sharp."

Dar just laughed and led the way upward.

It was a pleasant ride, mostly in the shade, passing quiet trees and mossy rocks, the scent of the forest strong around them, cold air brushing over their skin. Finally, the climb let out onto a small plateau, which sloped to a rocky spring. It was sunny, and Kerry found a smile cross-ing her face as they pulled the horses to a halt and she leaned back in the saddle. "Wow, this is nice."

"Thanks; glad you like it." Dar shook her boots free of her stir-rups and swung her leg over her stallion's neck, dropping down off his back and landing with a little thump. "Whoo." She stretched cautiously, moderately pleased at the relative lack of stiffness. "You up for some lunch?" She laid a hand on the mare's neck. "There's a nice spot over there. I used to come up here and just spend some time, listening to the water and mostly just thinking."

"Sure." Kerry got off her mare in a more conventional manner, getting her boots on the ground and easing her knees straight. "Oh brother." She rubbed her thigh. "I'm going to feel this, that's for sure."

Dar took the mare's reins. "Come over here. I'll get the lunch and try to work the kinks out of you, okay?" She felt a little guilty about dragging Kerry out on a ride this long. "You could have said you wanted to do something shorter."

"No, no, I'm fine." Kerry tensed and relaxed her quadriceps. "Really." She walked gingerly after her lover, feeling the cramping diminish as she kept moving. "It was great. It was definitely worth it, Dar."

"Uh huh." Dar tied the horses under a tree where there was a patch of edible grass and removed the lunch pack, carrying it with her as she guided Kerry up to a sunny spot near the spring. She set the pack down and dropped to the ground next to it, patting the earth. "Siddown."

Kerry did so, cautiously stretching her legs out in front of her and leaning back on her hands. "I feel bowlegged. That horse is a lot bigger than the ones I used to ride." She studied her mare. "A lot chunkier, too."

Dar chuckled and eased down with one knee between her lover's calves. "Okay, just relax." She began to work on the tense muscles under the snug denim.

"Ungh." Kerry closed her eyes in pleasure and exhaled. "You are sooo good at that." She relaxed as the long fingers worked their magic, easing the tight cramping.

"Better?" Dar finished, patting her leg lightly.

"Uh huh," Kerry agreed, gazing at her through half closed eyes. "Do I get a repeat when we get back?"

Dar settled on the ground cross-legged and pulled the pack over. "Sure. That hot Jacuzzi sounds good, doesn't it?"

"Mmmmm…" Kerry sat up and gingerly crossed her legs. "You bet. Whatcha got?"

Dar pulled out packages containing sandwiches. "Chicken sandwiches," she told her companion innocently, handing Kerry hers, "just like you asked for."

Kerry peeked under the wrapping and burst into laughter. "Dar, you are just a…a…." She slapped the taller woman on the leg. "You're so bad." She smoothed the paper out and sighed. "Smells good, though," she admitted, as the scent of the crispy fried chicken sandwich rose to her. "What else?"

Dar pulled out two padded cases out and handed one to Kerry. "Newest gadget. Keeps things warm for over three hours." She opened up a large cloth onto the ground and set her case on it, then pulled out small dispensers of salt, pepper, and three small jars.

"What in the…" Kerry unzipped the container and was surprised when steam escaped, bathing her face in a gentle, familiar scent. "You brought Mr. Potato Head on a wilderness picnic?"

Dar peered inside. "Yep. I have salt, butter, pepper, chives, sour cream, and bacon bits for them, too," she announced in a satisfied tone as she speared a mini carrot with a toothpick and stuck it in Kerry's potato. "There. I even brought you a carrot. Look, Mr. Potato Head has a nose."

Kerry removed it and stuck it in her mouth. "Not anymore."

The taller woman chuckled, then broke open her own potato and applied everything she could get her hands on to it. "Steve sort of reminds me of a Mr. Potato Head," she commented wryly. "Must be those ears."

Kerry laughed as she neatly sliced up her lunch. "Yeah. Maybe I'll get you one of those to keep in your office."

A dark brow cocked. "So when I say 'off with his head' I can demonstrate?" she inquired. She finished up her sandwich and scooted back a little, leaning against a sun-warmed rock and stretching her legs out. Kerry tucked her wrappers away as well and crawled over to her, snuggling up against her chest and relaxing as Dar wound an arm around her waist and she leaned back.

Dar felt the warmth of the rock at her back and the warmth of her lover against her and decided it was about the most pleasant feeling she'd ever had. She gazed over Kerry's shoulder, watching the running spring with a peaceful sense of contentment.

And familiarity. Her brow creased. No, she and Kerry had never done this before, that she was pretty sure of, and yet…

She gave the blond woman a little squeeze, and Kerry reciprocated by pressing a hand against hers, and laying her other hand on Dar's leg, stroking it gently.

She could smell the clean scent of Kerry's shampoo, where the blond woman's head was resting just under her chin, and she let her cheek drop a little to rest against it, feeling a sudden wash of strong familiarity that brought a faint smile to her face.

It was her dream, one of them. One of those strange ones, where she clearly remembered resting in a quiet glade not too different from this one, with the soft sound of water, and the smell of the forest around them. She'd been leaning on a rock, her arm wrapped around a warm, somnolent body, whose fingers had gently traced across her thigh just…

Exactly…

As they were now.

Dar shivered in pure reflex, her eyes opening as a silver hued image of the dream flashed through her mind.

"Hey?" Kerry turned to look up at her. "What's wrong?"

A soft exhale. "Just a bit of…I don't know, déjà vu, I guess." She forced a laugh. "Or something from a dream…I…"

Kerry's eyebrows knit. "You know, I get that a lot around you," she commented casually. "Or I have these weird dreams where you and I are doing really strange stuff."

Dar gazed at her. "Me too," she admitted softly. "Like just now." Her eyes shifted. "I think I had a dream a lot like this: trees, water, you and I lying like this. I was holding onto you…. Weird."

Kerry shrugged. "It happens. I used to have dreams like that when I was in school about stuff going on there; it's just your brain cleaning house."

"Yeah," the taller woman agreed, feeling a sense of relief, "you're right. Hey…" She picked up a flat stone and flipped it towards the spring. "Can you do that?"

"I've always wanted to; figures you can." Kerry dug into the ground next to them and came up with a couple more relatively flat stones. "Here, teach me."

With a tender smile, Dar reached and arm around her and guided her arm, feeling a sweet echo in her words. "Okay, like this, sideways."

They spent a very pleasant hour just tossing rocks and snuggling in the sun as the horses contentedly cropped grass and the sun rose overhead. Finally Dar patted her leg. "You ready to head back?"

"Mm." Kerry had her head pillowed in Dar's lap, and was stretching her legs out in lazy bliss. "At least we get to sit down this afternoon. Are you going to let me teach you to sail?"

"Sure." Dar agreed readily. "I've never been on one of those small boats. On the big ones you just keep out of the way of the crew. I'm looking forward to it." She tickled Kerry's ear. "C'mon… let's get going."

They stood and gathered their things, with Dar packing everything neatly back inside the lunch pack while Kerry wandered over to the spring and tasted its water. "Hey, that's not bad." She grinned at Dar. "It's sweet."

Dar glanced over. "Yeah. Watch it; looks like there's a beehive over there. Be careful."

Kerry blinked. "Oh, thanks." She carefully skirted the spot and walked over to her mare and gathered up the reins.

Kerry put a foot in the stirrup, hoisted herself up, and slid forward a little in the saddle and tried to find a comfortable place for her knees to grip. They were still a little sore, and she shifted, then half turned. "Do you—whoa!"

The mare had stepped sideways, and one hoof caught on a root. With a snort, the horse bucked a little and almost threw Kerry off. "Whoa!" The blond woman hung on, though, and pulled the mare's head around, grabbing tight as she jumped up out of the little hollow she'd moved into and bolted towards the stream for a few steps.

Enough to bring her right up against the bush with the beehive, her hindquarters brushing its outer leaves and disturbing the sluggish insects.

"Kerry, uh…" Dar's eyes widened a little. "Be careful there, I…"

"I'm being careful," the blond complained, trying to get the mare straightened out. "C'mon, you a—holy—whoa, whoa—shit!"

The mare squealed as several bees stung her and she bolted, jerking the reins out of Kerry's hands as she headed out and down the long sloping path. "Hey! Hey! Slow down!"

"Son of a bitch!" Dar slapped her stallion on the side, kicking him into a run as she gave chase. "Kerry!"

I'm in trouble. Kerry hung on to the front of the saddle, watching the reins fly uselessly near the ground. *Shit.* "Hey! C'mon, c'mon, slow down!" she called to the snorting mare. Both back heels kicked up, almost tossing Kerry over the horse's head, and she gripped the saddle frantically. "Okay, okay…"

The mare whinnied and bucked, then chose a cedared path down the hillside, shaking her head as the reins irritated her. Kerry heard hoofbeats and she half turned to see the gray stallion bearing down on her, Dar's body pressed to his back, one hand free, the other clenching leather reins.

Cursing, she turned around and leaned forward, trying to grab one of the flapping pieces of leather, which flicked annoyingly just out of her reach.

"Hang on, Kerry," Dar yelled as she closed, her horse snorting as his nose neared the mare's flying tail.

Unfortunately, this only spooked the already terrified mare, who redoubled her pace and slipped a little in the cedar chips. "Whoa, whoa," Kerry yelled, her eyes widening as she saw a bend coming up. "Whoa, take it easy, wh…" The horse spun and kicked and she lost her grip, her body going the opposite direction and flying gracefully through the air. The mare got around the bend and took off running as her former rider slammed unceremoniously against a tree trunk and dropped to the ground with a leaf-scattering thump.

Oh my god. Kerry just lay there for a long moment trying to get air back into her lungs, almost not hearing the rapidly slowing hoofbeats and the thump as something large hit the ground running, scattering cedar chips all over her as the steps came skidding to a halt at her side.

Hands touched her, and Dar's urgent voice reached her ears. "Don't move."

"Couldn't if I wanted to," she murmured, counting the stars circling her head. "Ow. Damn, that hurt."

"Where did you hit?" the low voice asked. "You got any shooting pain anywhere? How about your neck?"

Kerry had to think about it. "My shoulder." She flexed her hands a little. "Fortunately it was my butt that hit the ground. I'm sure I didn't take any damage there." The numbness was wearing off, replaced by aching. "Whoo."

"Can you feel everything?" Dar asked nervously. "Your hands, feet—no numbness?"

Fingers, toes, eyelashes… "Yeah," Kerry sighed, moving her head a little. "It's all there, it just hurts. I think I just got the wind knocked out of me," she told her companion. "We weren't going that fast."

Dar sat down heavily next to her. "Jesus." She gently eased Kerry back from her curled up position, examining her carefully. Her sweater and heavy jeans had protected her from the tree bark, and she appeared relatively unharmed. "You scared the hell out of me."

Kerry managed a grin. "Me too. What on earth happened?" She moved her arms and legs, shifting her feet to a more comfortable position, and took a deep breath. "Did that horse go nuts, or what?"

"I think she got stung." Dar explained, slipping an arm over Kerry's shoulders and supporting her solicitously. "You sure you're okay?"

Kerry leaned her head against the convenient shoulder, and sighed. "I'm shaking like a leaf, but yeah." She glanced off down the path. "Looks like I'm walking home, though." She exhaled as the throbbing receded.

"You most certainly are not," Dar snapped, her adrenaline still surging, making her hands shake almost uncontrollably. She took a few deep breaths, willing her heart to calm.

Surprised green eyes glanced at her, reading the ghosts of recent terror there. "Hey, it's okay," she said gently. "I'm all right. I'm not the first person who ever fell off a horse." She laid a hand on Dar's chest in comfort and inhaled sharply as she felt the racing heartbeat under her fingers. "Take it easy there, tiger."

"I'm fine," Dar replied, a little shortly. "You can ride my horse. I'll lead him."

Kerry put a hand on her lover's thigh. "No, Dar, you're not going to walk five miles back to the cabin. Just relax, I'm fine. I just got shook up a little."

Stubborn blue eyes glared at her. "We'll both ride then; he's a big horse," she replied. "We'll take it real slow."

Kerry considered arguing, but she saw the set jaw and the tensed muscles and relented. "Poor horsie. You better get him some apples when we get back."

"He'll survive." Dar relaxed a little. "We're still under the weight limit," she added, letting a slight grin cross her lips, referring to the three hundred pound sign prominently displayed on the stable wall.

Kerry poked her. "Not by that much," she teased. "You still owe him apples." She allowed Dar to lift her up to her feet and stood gingerly, testing her body out before she nodded. "Okay, I'm all right. Let's go."

Smokey stood, watching them suspiciously as Dar collected his reins and studied him. "I'll drive," she decided, putting a foot in the stirrup and pulling herself up, then neatly sidestepping the horse over to where Kerry was standing. "Grab on. I'll pull you up."

Kerry felt herself smiling for no apparent reason, and as she reached up, her hand slid past Dar's to grip the taller woman's arm above the elbow, giving her a handle as she also reached for the back of the saddle.

The sensation of being lifted was so familiar she almost laughed as she threw her leg over the horse's hindquarters, and settled in behind Dar in the large saddle. "I'm going to squish you," she warned.

"No problem," Dar replied, feeling the warm pressure as Kerry's body melded into hers. "Just hang on."

A gentle laugh bubbled its way up through her lips as Kerry wrapped her arms around Dar's body, squeezing her a little. "Absolutely no problem there," she assured her lover. "Where you go, I go, buddy."

Dar stopped, and half turned, gazing back at her with one eyebrow lifted. "Buddy?"

Kerry grinned charmingly at her. "Aren't you my buddy?"

With a shake of her dark head, Dar turned back around and nudged her mount down the trail. "Okay, Smokey, nice and easy. I don't want any bumps."

🐃   🐃   🐃

They got in an hour later than they had expected, since Dar insisted on keeping poor Smokey to a pace somewhere between a snail and a turtle. The stable man had ridden out to find them after Kerry's mare had returned alone, and he took Smokey's reins as Dar jumped down and solicitously caught Kerry as she tried to follow.

"Thanks. You can let me go now, I think." She straightened her legs with a wince, but they held.

"Oh. Sorry." Dar gave her a little pat on the back and cleared her throat. "Listen, let's save the sailing for tomorrow, okay? Give you time to recover." Her eyes flicked to the stable man's. "Anything going on here tonight?"

He considered. "We've got a hay ride scheduled," he offered. "Out to the big firepit after dinner."

"That sounds wonderful," Kerry spoke up with a grin. "I love hayrides. C'mon, Dar, I bet they'll have marshmallows."

"Yes, ma'am, we do. The riders make s'mores, in fact." The man smiled back at her. "And we've got a couple folks who play guitar and some that tell stories, too."

Kerry gave Dar a wishing look and was rewarded with a tolerantly knowing grin. "Sure." Dar agreed. "C'mon, let's go change into something that smells less like horses and relax before dinner."

🐃   🐃   🐃

The warm water felt absolutely wonderful, Kerry decided, as she squirmed around to let the jets rush against her ribs and watched Dar approach bearing a couple of nicely chilled glasses.

Not that she noticed the glasses, especially, since her eyes were mostly fully engaged by her hormones due to the fact that her lover was jaunting around the cabin buck naked.

"Here." The dark-haired woman sighed and handing her a glass as she seated herself, stretching her long legs out and letting her head rest against the edge of the tub. "Boy, that feels great." She paused, expecting an answer, then glanced over when all she got was silence. "Kerry?"

"Sorry." The blond woman took a sip of the chilled champagne and swallowed it. "Just thinking." She wiggled her toes contentedly and exhaled. "I suppose it could have been worse; we could have gone skiing."

"Probably would have been me that slammed into a tree then," Dar remarked. "How's your shoulder?" She peered worriedly at the smoothly muscled body part in question, examining the bruise that covered Kerry's arm. "You sure nothing else hurts?"

"Dar, can I ask you a question?" Kerry peered at her. "How can a person so oblivious of her own physical well being be so damned solicitous of mine?"

The taller woman stopped, and drew back in silence. "Sorry," she muttered. "Didn't realize I was bothering you."

Kerry studied her, a little bewildered. "No, it…it didn't…doesn't bother me, I just didn't expect that…of you."

Dar gave a little nod, and took a sip of her drink. Truth be told, she hardly knew why she was so damned concerned herself. The woman was obviously all right, so she should just back off, and let her be. After all, that's exactly what she'd want in Kerry's place, right?

Right. She hated when people fussed over her, and here she was, being the biggest fusspot this side of an old-fashioned nursery nanny.

No wonder Kerry was annoyed. With an effort, she relaxed, and closed her eyes, trying to recapture the good mood she'd been in at lunch.

She was surprised when a warm body fit itself around hers unexpectedly, and her eyes popped open in startlement to see two pale green ones peering back at her from a very close distance. "Uh, hi."

"Hi," Kerry answered, with a quietly apologetic look. "Sorry, I assumed that because you hate people pawing over you, that you naturally would just expect everyone else to buck up and pretend gaping head wounds are nothing."

"No," Dar said, shocked. "I don't expect that at all."

"Good. Then could you give me a hug, please? I really feel like crap; my legs are killing me, and my entire back feels like an accordion." Kerry sighed. "And what kind of good drugs did you bring that might help?"

Dar felt a curious smile crossing her face as she put her glass down and folded her arms around her lover, then lifted her, gently cradling her in the frothy water. "Let me take some tension off your back, then," she replied, as the blond woman nestled her head against one of Dar's shoulders. "Just put your arms around my…yeah." She gently stretched Kerry's body out, working the stiffened muscles with one hand while supporting her with the other. "I've got some Percogesic; it's pain killer and a muscle relaxant. How does that sound?"

"It sounds great," Kerry mumbled. "But I feel much better already. I think you're one kickass drug yourself, Dar." She snuggled closer, absorbing the chlorinated warmth of the water and the even warmer silkiness of the skin she was nestled against.

Dar felt a sincere and thorough sense of relief. "Well, I doubt it," she joked. "The AMA would never approve me, that's for sure, but let's get you out of here and comfortable, okay?"

"Sure," Kerry agreed amiably. "Wha—Dar!" She grabbed a tighter hold as she was lifted out of the Jacuzzi. "Stop that! You'll hurt yourself."

"Nah." Dar stepped carefully out of the tub. "Grab that towel," she instructed, then carried Kerry out into the nicely warmed cabin, and set her on the bed. Taking the towel, she knelt. "Hold still. This won't hurt."

"Bu…" Kerry spluttered, then subsided, slowly relaxing as Dar gently dried her.

It was remarkably erotic, and she had a hard time keeping her hands still as the soft, fabric of the towel brushed against suddenly sensitized skin. She had to force herself not to react, force herself to let Dar take complete control.

To trust completely.

Her breathing slowed, and let herself become aware of Dar's close presence, to feel the warmth as her still-damp skin brushed by Kerry's hand. She could hear the soft breaths, and the whispery sounds of Dar's hair as it slipped over her bare shoulders. She could smell her, that inimitable faintly spicy musk that clung to her lover's skin, along with the chlorine scent of the water. Her world stilled for a perfect instant.

And then lips touched hers, and the towel's rough warmth was replaced by knowing fingertips that traced a path across her skin, leaving a shiver of anticipation in their wake. She let her eyes slide open, to see Dar's looking back at her, a teasing grin moving her lips. One long finger came up and balanced itself on her nose. "Don't go away." Dar told her softly, as she stood and went to their baggage, coming back with a bottle and a cup of water. She knelt down again and shook out two pills, handing them to Kerry. "Here."

Kerry gazed at her, mesmerized. "Do I need these?" she asked softly. "It doesn't hurt anymore." She reached out and bypassed the pills, resting her hand on Dar's cheek. "I just need you."

Dar put the bottle down without breaking eye contact, and eased down on the bed, stretching her body out next to Kerry's and laying a hand on her stomach. She felt the muscles contract under her fingers, and watched as the pale green eyes darkened at no more than that light touch. "All right." She leaned over and brushed her lips against the soft curve of a breast. "I can't guarantee it's going to be relaxing, though." She moved up, feeling the sudden intake of breath as Kerry felt the teasing pressure. "You sure you're up to it?"

She finally let her hands loose, and they greedily reached for Dar's close presence, tugging her closer as her body growled with desire.

"Guess that answered that." Dar chuckled low in her throat and succumbed to the insistent tug, feeling a warmth of connection between them that was pulling her closer, and closer, until she could swear...

That they were simply two halves of a whole.

Of course you are, her mind whispered at her, as she let go and allowed the passion to take her, hearing a faint, knowing chuckle somewhere deep in the back of her mind.

🐏   🐏   🐏

"You're being awfully quiet," Kerry commented, glancing over at Dar as they mounted the steps to the lodge. Her hands were tucked firmly in her pockets against the chill air, and her breath escaped as puffy clouds of vapor.

Dar also had her hands hidden, and she sniffled a little against the cold. "I'm not generally speaking a noisy person," she responded mildly. "I was just thinking, that's all." She reached out and pulled the heavy door open, then inclined her head for Kerry to precede her.

"You always do that," Kerry commented. "Open doors."

"Well, you need to, Kerry, or you crash into them and get a lot of splinters in your face," the taller woman responded dryly. "How's your shoulder doing?"

"It's a little stiff, but okay," Kerry replied. "Actually…" She blushed a little, and moved closer. "My butt hurts more."

The blue eyes twinkled a little. "You probably bruised your tail-bone." She patted the spot gently. "I'll have to get you a pillow for the office for a week or so."

They went into the dining room, already half full with guests at the scattering of tables. A table near the window was made available, and they settled into it, gazing out at the view of the last rays of sunset over the lake. The room was fairly dim; wall sconces made to look like candelabra and torches were the motif, and they spread a warm, reddish glow rather than a harsh brilliance. A fireplace in the rear crackled merrily and leant to the rustic atmosphere.

"It smells great in here," Kerry commented as their server arrived, bearing a basket of warm, fresh biscuits and a bowl of sweet butter. "Is it the wood they're using in the fire?"

Dar glanced over at it, as she snagged a yeast biscuit and broke it open. "Um… that might be hickory, so yeah." A tiny hint of a smile appeared. "You know, this winter stuff isn't all bad." She tugged on her collar. "Except that this wool's driving me nuts."

Kerry laughed. "Well, you look really nice in that sweater, even if it's tickling your chin." The turtleneck, a rich, solid electric blue, brought out the color of her eyes like nobody's business, and framed her angular face wonderfully.

Dar looked pleased at the compliment. "You look very nice, your-self," she returned, eyeing the blond woman's layered flannel and sweatshirt combination. Kerry's face had a gentle tinge of color from the wind they'd ridden through, and her pale hair was pulled back into a ponytail, with a few wisps escaping around her pink ears.

Which grew a touch pinker at the words, something Dar found eminently adorable. "I'm glad our flight's not until eight tomorrow, gives us the whole day," she remarked. "You're going to teach me to sail in the morning, right?"

"Teach you? Dar you've been on the ocean all your life; what do you mean teach you?" Kerry protested, smiling a thank you at the server as he set cups of frothy local ale in front of them.

Dar took a sip, and raised her brows. "Not bad. I can drive about anything on the water that uses petroleum products, and I even got to sit at the controls of something that uses..." She paused, and waggled her head. "A more esoteric form of fuel, shall we say, but I've never sailed."

"Really?" Kerry thought about that. "Esoteric? I don't..." She remembered what branch of the service Dar's father had been in. "Oh, oh, I get it, right." Pause. "They didn't let you drive a submarine, did they?"

Dar held up a finger to her lips. "Shh. I didn't even have a driver's license at the time."

Kerry covered her eyes. "Oh. I suddenly feel so...soo...safe," she sighed.

"I didn't hit anything," Dar objected mildly. "And I'm a safe driver, you know that."

Their conversation was interrupted by the entrance of a large family who took a table not far from them. The father was an older man, gray-haired and stocky, dressed in a flannel shirt and corduroys, and he directed the three assorted children to sit down while his wife pulled the waiter aside. The children were all slimly built and meticulously dressed, and the mother had, incongruously enough, a mink stole around her shoulders.

Dar snorted as she took a sip of her ale, then glanced over and saw the pensive look on Kerry's face. She reached over and covered the blond woman's hand with her own, chafing the fingers of it lightly. "Hey."

Green eyes flicked her way, then held.

"Memories?" Dar guessed.

"Something like that," Kerry acknowledged softly. "When we were younger, we used to go up to a Christian retreat up in the north lake area. It was a little like this, except that the focus was bible teaching and family building." She let out a faint, bitter laugh. "Family building; what a joke. It was just one big excuse to get us all together in one place so we could be preached at for week and told our faults."

Dar winced. "Not all families are like that," she told her friend, giving the nervously moving fingers a squeeze.

Kerry dropped her gaze to their hands. "I know." She looked up. "But I see kids like that…" She jerked her head towards the family. "And I always wonder."

Dar studied the children quietly, noting the almost furtive glances as they looked around. The eldest girl was probably about sixteen, and the youngest about ten, she reckoned. As she pondered, the oldest happened to look her way, and their eyes met briefly. The girl immediately dropped her eyes, and a blush made itself evident on her face.

A dark brow lifted as Dar wondered what had garnered that reaction before she realized she and Kerry were still holding hands. Ah. She drummed the fingers of her free hand on the table. Well, well. "So." She casually pulled Kerry's knuckles over and brushed them with her lips, then released them. "What were we talking about? Sailing, wasn't it?"

"Um…" Kerry looked a little flustered. "Dar…you know, we are in North Carolina."

Dar blinked at her. "I know that."

Green eyes flicked around the room, then back to her face. "Don't they still lynch adulterers here?"

The dark brows knit for a long moment. "Wha…oh." Dar sat back, nonplused. "I…" She looked around in a startled manner. "B…"

Kerry hid a smile behind one hand. "Dar… Dar… relax… I…didn't mean…" She covered her eyes, and felt her skin warm. "I just…I sort of had you pegged, I thought, as someone who didn't do PDAs." She peeked at her lover hesitantly. The angular face was very still, as Dar processed her words, then an indescribable look took it over. "Dar?"

"I…" Dar released a breath. "I didn't think I did either." She folded her hands and studied them. "I'm sorry; I didn't realize it was bothering you." Her voice was steady and casual.

But Kerry had learned something about her companion over the months. Sometimes she said what she thought the person she was talking to wanted to hear rather than what she was feeling in her heart, and it usually showed in subtle shifts in her body language.

Like when her neck muscles relaxed and it dropped her shoulders a little. It wasn't quite slumping, but Kerry could see it nonetheless. "N—no, it doesn't bother me..." She hesitated, choosing her words carefully. "I love when you touch me; you have no idea how special that makes me feel." She watched the dark head lift, and wary blue eyes peeked out at her. "I guess I'm just not used to being conspicuous."

"Conspicuous?" Dar repeated.

"Yeah. I, um..." Kerry twiddled her thumbs. "I made it a practice to attract as little attention to myself as possible; it was sort of a survival reflex."

"Oh," the dark-haired woman murmured. "I never thought of that." She played with her roll. "I never really cared if I attracted attention or not."

Kerry rested her chin in her hand and gazed at her magnetically attractive companion. "No, I bet you didn't," she remarked wryly. "But it's going to take me a little while to get over that."

Dar bit her lip, looking for all the world like a scolded child being denied dessert. "Sorry. I...I wasn't doing it on purpose, I just..." *Damn it, I should have realized—what in the hell is wrong with me?* "I'll try to keep my hands to myself from now on."

Kerry felt a definite pang hit her in the chest just hearing that self-disgust in Dar's otherwise even tone.

It was a quiet dinner, and Kerry noticed neither of them ate much. She zipped up her jacket and followed Dar as she made her way out the front of the lodge towards where the hayride was forming up, a soft round of laughter coming from the people who were waiting. A large wagon full with hay was standing there with two large workhorses hitched to it, their placid, gentle eyes regarding the crowd with little or no interest.

The family had decided to go, and so did six or seven other couples, two of them with children. Kerry bounced on her feet a little in the chill, as she watched them all mill around, waiting for the lodge worker to allow them to climb up onto the wagon.

Dar stood quietly nearby, her hands tucked into her pockets, a look of polite interest on her face. Her breath showed as a gentle stream of vapor, and as Kerry kept an unobtrusive eye on her, the stream doubled as she let out a long sigh.

"All right, folks, let's get aboard. We want to get over to that campfire real soon, 'cause this weather ain't getting any warmer," the cheerful driver told them, as he unhooked the chain and let the back gate down, the put a set of stairs in place. "Up you go."

Dar and Kerry were the fourth set of people to get into the haywagon, and they settled themselves in one of the front corners out of the way of the giggling children who were burrowing in the hay, tossing bits of it around. Dar drew her knees up and put her arm against them, resting her chin on one forearm.

She thought about what Kerry had said, and found herself resenting the other couples, who were free to hug and kiss each other, with no fear of any adverse reaction. In fact, the two older couples were watching one pair of lovebirds with an indulgent look on their faces.

She felt, in that moment, as though something very important had been taken away from her, and it was making her mad. So was Kerry's assumption that she wouldn't like public displays. So was the annoying cold that was drying out her throat and giving her a headache.

She crossed her arms over her chest and leaned back, letting herself slide into a full-fledged, self-aware, grade A, really bad mood. Part of it was at herself, since she really should have guessed that Kerry wouldn't be comfortable announcing their sexual partnership to the world, especially here in what she assumed was a bastion of conservatism. Another part of it was because she hadn't even realized she was doing it, which made her kick herself for being so damned self-absorbed.

The cold pressed in on her, and she dropped her head a little and let it in, remembering the last time she'd been here.

Living through the hurt, and rebuilding her defenses, determined to go back out there, and never, never let anyone get close enough to make her feel that lousy ever again.

So what the hell was she doing here now?

Then the other half of her slapped her upside the head. *Get a grip, Dar; she didn't blow you off, she just asked for some time to adjust. So just chill out.*

Well, at least that was easy enough. She glared morosely at her visible breath, bracing her feet as the wagon started and the other occupants laughed in delight. The horses started to pull them down the road, their hoofbeats making a regular pattern in the still, cold air. *Stop behaving like a spoiled brat, already. Jesus, Dar. What would dad say? He'd kick your ass for acting like this.* "Pretty night out, huh?" She forced her bad mood down and turned to Kerry, shocked at the effort it took not to reach out and gently move aside the soft blond hair obscuring her face.

Kerry's jaw was working, and her brow was knit. She turned her head towards her lover in almost slow motion. "Yes, it is," she responded thoughtfully. "It's cold, though."

"Yeah," Dar agreed softly, as she rubbed her arms with her hands.

The blond woman studied the wagon's occupants, noting the huddled duos with a speculative eye. Then she took in a breath, and expelled it. "Dar?"

"Hmm?"

Kerry chewed her lower lip a minute. "I'm over it," she announced. "I guess the world'll just have to expand its horizons."

Startled blue eyes regarded her. "What exactly do you mean?"

The smaller woman shifted across the short distance between them and wrapped herself around Dar's body, tucking her head into the hollow of her lover's shoulder and exhaling. "Is this explicit enough, or do I need to suck your tongue?"

Dar felt a surge of heat erupt as a flush colored her skin, warming her rapidly. "Uh, no…no, this is fine; I get the idea," she blurted, knocked off balance by Kerry's sudden change of heart. She put her arms around the blond woman and settled back, letting their conjoined body heat chase away the chill of the air. "What made you change your mind?"

Amazing, how fast a bad mood could vanish, whisked away on the cold wind.

Kerry thought about the question for a while, as she regarded the people around them. After a few initial, startled glances, they were mostly ignored, which was fine with her. "Well." She picked up a stalk of hay and chewed it. "I thought about how uncomfortable I felt about everyone staring at me, and then I weighed that against how comfortable I knew I'd feel if I was snuggling with you, and snuggling won."

"Just like that?" Dar asked, in mild disbelief.

"Essentially, yeah," Kerry replied. "Oh, there was more to it, and I'm still wrestling with stuff, but I realized when I thought about it that you've been doing all that stuff ever since we, um…"

"Yeah."

"So…just because we're in a strange place, why should that matter? I know I joked about them lynching people, but then I figured out if anyone's got a problem here, you could probably kick their ass, so…" Kerry shrugged. "What the hell? I never rebelled as a teenager. Maybe it's time."

"Oh."

"Maybe I'll get a tattoo."

"Uh…" Dar peered at her. "Don't get all drastic on me, okay? How about we start with a rainbow sticker for your bumper."

"I don't know, Dar," Kerry mused. "A nice knotwork design around your name right on my, um…" She glanced down.

"Uh, Kerry?" Blue eyes glanced at their neighbors, one of the older couples who were watching them with interest.

"Shoulderblade," the blond woman finished, with a twinkle in her eyes. "I bet that guy at the desk knows where I could get one around here."

"All right." Dar gave her a look. "Now you listen here, Kerrison Stuart. I am not going to stand by while you get my name tattooed on any part of your body in some hack shop in the backwoods, you hear me?"

Kerry's nose wrinkled up as she grinned. "Would you do it?"

"Get your name tattooed on me?" Dar countered.

Kerry nodded but said nothing.

The angular face went serious, suddenly intense as Dar met Kerry's eyes and held them. "I already have that," she whispered, touching her chest above her heart with a finger. "Written so deep there, nothing could ever remove it."

Kerry just looked at her, forgetting their watchers, her eyes softening and carrying the sudden glitter of unshed tears. She started to speak, then shook her head, and buried her face in Dar's shoulder.

Hmm. The dark-haired woman rested her cheek against Kerry's pale hair. Not bad, from a hard-bitten, cold and ruthless bitch from hell, huh?

Up ahead she could see the brightening glow of the campfire, sending crackling sparks up towards the bright stars winking over them.

Chapter 12

The sun poured down on ruffled blue waters, un-
obstructed by a single cloud and warm enough to
offset the chill of the wind that coasted over the
lake. Kerry expertly turned the small boat and filled
the sails, sending it over the waves and causing a
cold spray to dust their skin.

Dar was seated in the bow, her long body sprawled over a padded
seat and her face turned into the breeze as they plowed through the
waves. "This is great," she sighed.

Kerry smiled, as she moved the tiller, and checked the tension on
the sail. "It sure is," she agreed, her body dredging up old memories of
many hours spent out on Lake Michigan in boats not much larger than
this one. "The best day of my young life was the day I got qualified in
a sunfish and I didn't have to have anyone with me when I went out."

Dar reached out and touched the canvas sail as she watched Kerry's smooth and precise motions. "You're good at this," she commented, enjoying the sight of her lover's wind-whipped figure. "And you look really cute."

"Oh sure. I probably look like an afghan hound with his head out the window of a car going down US 1," Kerry laughed. "Glad the sun's pretty strong, though, or it'd be really cold out here." She tied down the sail, then balanced herself and pulled off her heavy sweatshirt, leaving herself only her collared rugby top over her jeans. "Whoo, that's better."

Dar followed suit, taking off her tan sweater and tucking it under the seat, and pushing the sleeves up on the bright red shirt she was wearing underneath. "You ready for some breakfast?" she inquired.

"You bet. I'm starving." Kerry informed her, as she edged the boat towards one of the small islands that dotted the lake's wide surface. "I figure we can shelter on the lee of that land there, until we're ready to go back." She studied the wind. "I'll have to tack back, but that's okay. We've got all the time in the world, right?"

The words brought a smile to Dar's face. "Right." She edged closer to where Kerry was sitting and broke a freshly baked blueberry muffin in half, offering a portion to the blond woman. "Here, take a nibble of this."

"Mmm…." Kerry captured it in her teeth and chewed contentedly. "Oo, you have more of those?"

"I have more of those." Dar informed her. "And I have those ones with all the nuts in them you liked and some cornbread."

She moved down the padded seat while Kerry skillfully moved around one of the small islands, blocking the wind. She took down the sail and tossed over the small anchor, then squirmed over to where Dar was, leaning against her as they rocked gently in the waves.

She let her eyes roam the skies over head, watching a hawk circle lazily. Dar reclined next to her, breaking off mouthfuls of her assorted goodies and popping them in Kerry's mouth as they shared companionably. "Jesus, this has been such a long week," the blond woman commented.

"Uh huh." Dar fed her a bit of cornbread. "I'm glad we had a few days up here just to relax. Well, sort of," she chuckled, "barring a fall from a horse or two." She brought out a large thermos and uncapped it, releasing the intoxicating scent of chocolate into the air.

Kerry accepted the cup of hot chocolate and gave Dar a gentle kiss. "It's been wonderful—despite the horse." She gazed into the blue eyes. "We'll have to come up here again when we can spend more time." They were sitting in the bottom of the boat, with their heads resting against the padded back seat, and Dar shifted, slipping an arm behind Kerry and drawing her closer.

Kerry put the cup down and slid her hands over Dar's shirt, tangling her fingers in the fabric as she willingly met the lips searching for hers. They tasted each other for a breathless moment as Dar reached up and stroked Kerry's face. "I wish we didn't have to go back."

Kerry studied her face, evaluating the statement. "You mean that."

The blue eyes dropped. "Yes." Dar exhaled as she regarded the rippling water. "I keep trying to dredge up interest in going back into that office on Monday, and I just can't," she confessed. "I don't know if I can just go back to business as usual."

Kerry's blond head cocked to one side. "Dar, I don't understand; I thought you'd worked things out. Did something else happen?" She put a hand on her lover's arm in concern.

A soft laugh. "Sort of." Dar's lips twisted into a wry smile. "We happened. I don't think I can put that aside when I have to be the company bastard anymore, and it's starting to get to me. Maybe it has been for a while, but lately I know I've been losing it."

Kerry felt a little shocked. She hadn't expected that, hadn't even considered it, really. "Dar, you don't know that. I mean, we've hardly had a chance to…"

"I do know it," the dark-haired woman interrupted gently. "I knew it that afternoon up at Vista." She picked up Kerry's hand. "When I wouldn't trade a roll in the sack for a contract just because you were there."

A slow intake of breath, an exhale. "Oh."

"Yeah," Dar murmured. "What you think of me matters, Kerry. I've never had to worry about that before." She tangled her fingers with her lover's. "I can't do things the old way and I don't know how to do it otherwise."

Kerry tried to jump start her brain into action. "Find another way, then," she offered, faintly. "We can do it…you and I."

A long pause. The hawk called overhead, lonely and regal.

Finally, Dar blinked. "Maybe," she murmured. "I guess we'll find out." She smiled. "Just another challenge, right?"

Kerry nodded, profoundly relieved. "Right." She rubbed Dar's hand against her face. "Speaking of challenges, you ready to learn to sail?"

The smile widened. "Yeah." She cupped Kerry's cheek affectionately. "Teach me."

🐄 🐄 🐄

"Morning." Kerry smiled as she entered the small cafeteria, and nodded as the waitress behind the counter held up two fingers.

"Morning, Kerry. That was sooommmme freaking day on Friday, huh?" Mark was seated with two of his cronies, devouring Cuban egg sandwiches. "Good job!"

Kerry chuckled, leaning against the counter as she waited for her and Dar's breakfasts. "Don't thank me, I didn't do that much. Dar was incredible," she told him, peripherally aware of the listening audience. "She got there and just started making things happen. About all I did was find a new place for her to put the stuff."

"And rebooted the optics hub," Mark reminded her. "That was like, so cool. I was on the phone to Alastair, and I was like, 'we're up,' and he was like, 'of course we are,' but you could hear the 'holy crap' in his voice when he said it."

"When did you get back, Kerry?" one of the marketing admins asked from across the floor.

"Sunday night," Kerry replied. "Dar wanted to make sure everything was going to stay stable. You know how she is."

A round of laughter followed, but Kerry detected an odd tinge to it.

"Rumors flying again," Mark muttered. "Every damn time you two go on a trip together, they start up."

Kerry rolled her eyes. "What is it this time, that we used the weekend to run off to a secluded mountain retreat?"

"Nah," Mark shrugged. "Just that three days in Carolina must have been so boring, you guys had to have found something else to do."

"Oh." Kerry took the bag from the waitress, and smiled. "Well, spread the rumor that we used the time to run off to a secluded mountain resort where we spent our time toasting marshmallows, horseback riding, and sailing on the lake."

"Uh, sure." Mark glanced around, then lowered his voice again. "How true is that?"

Kerry smiled at him, wrinkling her nose and showing her neat, white teeth. "Gotta go." She patted him on the shoulder. "See you in the Ops meeting at ten."

She took her brown bags and exited the café, headed toward the nearest elevator.

Unfortunately, it was occupied. "Well, what do we have here?" Steve asked, hitting the door close button. "Dar's lackey. Bringing the old witch her breakfast, sweetie?"

Kerry's better sense neurons went on strike. "I sure am." She gave Steve a big old smile. "If I do it, she doesn't need to use the food taster."

That made him pause for a moment. "Very funny," he complimented her. "She does act like she thinks she's the Queen." He changed the subject. "We were trying to contact both of you late on Friday."

"I saw the page." Kerry shrugged. "We had to sleep sometime; we were up all night at the facility." She shifted, glancing at the climbing lights and willing the elevator faster. "We figured anything after that could wait until we got back."

"Sleeping? Oh, I'm sure you were doing that." Steve looked at her. "I bet you two just lit up North Carolina."

Kerry turned and looked at him. "Mind explaining what you're talking about?"

The doors opened, and he half bowed, gesturing her to go ahead of him. Kerry felt vaguely uneasy at the smug look on his face, but she complied, moving purposefully down the hall towards Dar's office with her bags.

🐄 🐄 🐄

Something was up, and Dar was already in a bad mood. Fallout from the previous week had been dumped into her inbox, and she'd realized very quickly that no one had tried to handle the customers who had been screaming for answers—they'd merely deferred them to her and kept their hands clean of the situation.

Dar stalked into the executive committee meeting after lunch with a pile of the stuff, and she dumped it on the table before she claimed her usual chair, steepling her fingers and glaring at the rest of the committee from behind them.

"Well, I guess we're all here," Duks started, being the facilitator for the week. "We might as well get started. I'm sure the chief topic of conversation will be the systems failure from last week."

"I have an issue," Dar interrupted him sharply.

Eyes went her way.

"I wanna know why not one goddamn person in this room was willing to step up and be a spokesman for the company while I was freezing my ass off in North Carolina trying to solve a problem."

"Nobody had any goddamn answers!" José shot back. "What in the hell were we supposed to tell them, Dar? It's not like you were letting us know what was going on!"

"Lie." Dar came right back. "You do it all the time anyway, what's the problem?"

"Dar." Mariana gave her a warning look.

Dar rolled her eyes. "How hard would it have been to tell the damn customers we had a facilities failure and that it was being worked on?" She gave the stack of papers a push. "If you think I'm having someone from my staff go and write up all these situational recaps, you're deluded."

Duks cleared his throat. "For those of us who use computers as footwarmers, Dar, what did happen?"

The Ops VP sighed and picked up a pencil. "The halon and regular fire systems discharged in the center."

"Why?" Eleanor asked.

"I have no idea. The engineers are going in there as soon as the environmental people clear it," Dar answered with tolerable politeness. "The EPA shut the door on us, we could not gain access."

"Jesú."

"The only option even remotely feasible was to duplicate the facility."

There was a momentary silence. "What?" Duks asked, obviously surprised.

Dar shrugged. "Seventy routers counter-to-countered from Cisco, ditto an Etherhub, ditto several miles of Cat 5, ditto twelve integrated racks, and one fiber hub with interconnects."

"You...had them do that in one night?" Duks was having problems visualizing the concept.

Another shrug. "It cost us a million dollars, but yes, I did." She watched the shock roll down the table. "That, and having the entire telecom endpoint rerouted...we got lucky. Kerry located an old telemarketing warehouse right next door and got us access to that. Telco just had to swing the circuits over."

"Son of a puta." José cradled his head.

"Yeah. It was a long night," Dar acknowledged softly. "We didn't get a positive resolution until sunrise. I didn't think anyone would appreciate a phone call at that point. MIS and Ops were notified, and Alastair was told. Whoever else found out wasn't my problem."

"What do you mean, it wasn't your problem?" José snapped back. "We had customers to answer to, damn, it Dar! You owed us a report!"

"Go to hell."

"Dar." Mariana rubbed her eyes.

"You were too busy screwing your little friend to care, I bet." José stood up. "It's disgusting!"

Dar felt a cold anger take her, and she stood, facing off against him. "That's out of line, José," she warned softly.

"It is most certainly not!" the Cuban man stated. "It is no secret. The whole damn company knows about the way the two of you are...what do you think we are, idiots?" He threw his minutes down on the table. "It's not bad enough you waltz around in here, you have to go and do disgusting things in front of half of North Carolina?"

There was a frozen silence.

"I've always thought you were an idiot, yes," Dar finally replied coldly. "You just confirmed it."

"Well, I'm sorry, but I have a problem with the two of you taking a weekend on company expense, leaving us here to hang out to dry," Eleanor chimed in. "Let's not even get into the legal issues of this, or the moral ones, for God's sake. How could you be that stupid, Dar!"

Dar felt a sort of sad calm settle over her. "Well, if what Kerry and I did over the weekend is more important to you jerks than the fact we saved a dozen high profile accounts, fine." She pulled her ID badge off and tossed it gently on the table. "Find another VP Ops. I've got better things to do with my life than spend it saving your sorry asses."

"Where in the hell do you think you're going?" José demanded. "We're not finished here, damn it!"

Dar turned and stared right at him. "Since you're too stupid to understand what I just said, let me repeat it to you in one syllable words, José: I quit."

And then, she simply walked out, unhindered by even a squeak as the room sat in absolute shock.

🌀　　🌀　　🌀

"You what?" Kerry barely got the words out, standing next to her lover behind Dar's desk as she watched the taller woman lay keys on the table. "Dar...wait...wait...hold on. You can't just do this."

"Sure I can." Dar mentally counted, then pulled out her two pagers and the cell phone. "Oh, wait. No, this cell's mine, the company just picks up the bill." She clipped it back on her belt. "I'll call BellSouth and have them transfer the account over."

"Dar."

Blue eyes looked up at her. "I know. I'm being an asshole. I'm leaving you in the lurch. I'm a jerk, I'm being irresponsible, I'm being totally selfish. Anything else?"

"So you're just letting them win?" Kerry took a step back.

Dar just looked at her.

"I can't believe it." Kerry gave a half shake of her head, then turned and left without another word, slamming the door behind her.

Dar stared at the empty spot in shock. Hesitantly, she took a step to follow Kerry when her outer door opened and Mariana came in, closing it behind her. "Dar, let's talk."

"I'm over talking." Dar turned, and gave her a direct look. "I've had enough, Mari, enough sniping, enough potshots. They hate my guts so much? Fine. Let 'em find someone else."

"Come on now." The Personnel VP held up a hand. "Dar, this isn't worth your job. Since when do you care what José says?"

"Since you let him hire someone specifically to nail me," Dar shot back. "Since everyone in the damn company, including you, stands back and lets me take every piece of abuse those two-bit assholes lay down on me, and when I say something back, I'm the one who gets the warning."

Mariana stared at her. "You give as good as you get, Dar, and we both know that."

"Go to hell." Dar turned and walked towards the door. "I have to defend myself—no one else will." She turned the knob and stepped through, then slammed it behind her.

Mariana stared after her in shock, then turned as the inner door opened, and Kerry re-entered the room. "Oh." Kerry murmured. "I... um. Sorry." After an awkward moment, Mari and Kerry looked at each other, and the younger woman sighed, tucking her hands under her arms to hide their shaking.

"What in the hell is going on with her?" Mari asked bluntly. "Since when does she fly off the handle at some bit of stupid gossip?"

Kerry exhaled. "Since it was true," she admitted shakily. "Maria told me what they were saying about someone seeing us in North Carolina. Well, it happened."

Mariana's jaw dropped. "You're shitting me."

A head shake. "No. It was very late, and very, very stressed, and Dar knew what kinds of consequences were laying on her shoulders. We thought we'd failed, and I did something, and it worked, and…" Kerry lifted a hand. "Jesus, if I'd have been a guy, no one would have thought twice about it, Mari."

The Personnel VP sank down on the edge of the desk. "I can't believe this…and she knew after it came out it would either be her, or you, and she…"

Kerry hadn't even thought about that. "Her or me?"

Mari stared at her. "Surely you knew what going public would mean?"

"I wasn't thinking about that at all." Kerry covered her eyes. "Jesus… I'd have left in a heartbeat. How could she have thought…" She took a breath. "God, what a mess."

🐾 🐾 🐾

The ferry terminal was awash in warm, golden light, the deckhands gathering in small clusters chatting during this slow part of the day. Dar drove into the resident's lane and parked, waiting for the ferry to arrive, its low rumble audible through the open window she opened.

Across the dock, several men sat on the seawall, idling the day away with watching the gulls circle, and the large ships go through the cut, occasionally shifting to eye the cars parked waiting for the island shuttle. Dar cocked her head, regarding them curiously, wondering if they were just drifters or free spirits who could spend their hours any way they liked.

One was fishing, a long line suspended from a short, plain pole gripped in a tanned fist propped against one denim-covered knee. Something about the outline was vaguely familiar, but just as Dar was searching her memory, the ferry arrived and she was forced to pay attention to the deckhands loading the vessel up.

She missed the eyes that turned to watch her speculatively from within a dark windbreaker hood before they went back to studying the ruffled surface of the water.

It was weird getting on the ferry in broad daylight. Dar slid back in her seat and rested her head against the doorjamb, thinking about what she'd just done.

Quit.

The word made her a little queasy, remembering her father's highest praise of her, that if nothing else, Dar wasn't any kind of a quitter. But this was different, right? She couldn't have gone on after that—after they'd dragged her and Kerry out in the public like that, and…

Dar sighed. *C'mon, Dar…you always knew this was a possibility. Hell, you knew it was a probability. Nothing stays secret forever, and once it was out…better you leave than have to fire Kerry, or move her under someone else and have her have to deal with all that political bullshit.*

It sounded sensible. If Dar left, attention would focus on her, and Kerry would more than likely be allowed to stay in her position, or…Dar recalled her latest evaluation sent to personnel. Maybe they'd even offer Kerry her job.

Would Kerry take it? After the way she'd left the office, Dar was suddenly not sure. She felt a quiet thread of fear start to eat its way across her heart, doubt suddenly filling her.

Dar put the car into gear and drove up the ramp and through the spray, and parking under her condo. She got out and paused, gazing at the empty spot marked "K Stuart" for a very long moment. It brought a tiny, sad little smile to her face before she trudged up the stairs and keyed the lock, opening the door to a chorus of frantic yipping from the kitchen.

🐾   🐾   🐾

Kerry got back to her office and sat down, staring at her desk for a long time without moving. "I can't believe she did that," she finally sighed. "I can't believe she did it without even talking to me about it, like I was some kind of kid that needed protection or something." She stood and began pacing back and forth.

"I can't let her do that."

Pace pace pace.

"I know she thinks she's doing it for the right reasons. I know she wants to protect me from all that legal crap. But what she doesn't realize is that I'm a lot more politically savvy than she thinks I am; she forgets who my father is."

Green eyes regarded the window. "Right. So what in the hell am I going to do?" She drummed her fingers on her desk. "The first thing I need is allies." She regarded the phone, then dialed a number. It rang several times before dumping her into voice mail. "Damn it, Mark! Where are you?"

She was answered in unexpected fashion when her door opened and Polenti slipped in, an angry look on his face. "Oh, you heard."

"What the hell is going on?" Mark asked, putting his hands on his hips. "Did she just quit?"

Kerry sat on her desk. "It's complicated, but essentially, yes, she did." She crossed her arms. "The question is, what are we going to do about it?"

"Hold on. Can we start with why?" Mark held up a hand. "Not that I'm not with you in doing something, but I'd kinda like to know what book I'm reading, much less what page we're on."

Kerry pursed her lips. "Bottom line? She did it because they accused her of dereliction of duty because we didn't answer our pagers this weekend."

"What? After what you guys did!?" Mark was incredulous.

"They were more interested in how we spent our time together." Kerry shook her head. "Dar just had it, and to tell you the truth, after what she's been through the last few weeks, I can't really blame her."

Mark looked at her curiously. "I bet that asshole Fabricini's behind this. He came in this morning spreading trash around all over the place, said he's got a cousin in BellSouth field services up in North Carolina that saw Dar...um..."

"Kissing me?" Kerry inquired, wincing.

"Um..."

"Well, she did," the blonde admitted. "You heard her, as a matter of fact."

"Shit. Yeah, I did." Mark sighed. "So he was telling the truth. Wow, that sucks."

Kerry shrugged. "It...probably wasn't the smartest thing we've ever done, but it was late, we were both exhausted, overstressed..."

"She a good kisser?" Mark came back with a knowing smile.

"Yeah." Kerry felt the word escape before she could censor it, and she blushed.

"She should have just stood her ground." Mark shook his head. "They need her more than they need that asshole. Wish she'd have just slugged him."

"I know, but I'm not going to let her get away with it," Kerry acknowledged. "So, first off, how much trouble can you cause him?"

Mark sat down and put his hands between his knees. "Trouble? Well, I can boot him off the network, or reroute his mapping so he can't find his files."

Kerry leaned forward and caught his gaze, green eyes glinting. "No, Mark, not that kind of trouble. The real kind. The kind I know you're really good at."

He cleared his throat, blinking at her in surprise. "I didn't think you…. Well, okay, I can cause him a lot of trouble, why?"

Kerry smiled. "I would like you to cause him as much trouble as you humanly can, okay?" She ticked off points on her fingers. "I'm talking credit cards, taxes, driver's license, legal, utilities…everything."

Mark's jaw dropped. "You're serious."

She nodded. "I'm serious."

"Wow." He rubbed his nose. "You're nasty." He glanced up with a rakish grin. "I like that." He got up. "What are you going to do?"

Kerry's face hardened, and her eyes went cool and calculating. "I'm going to make them understand just how indispensable she really is," the blond woman told him, as she circled her desk and looked something up on her screen. "Let's see, where was…oh, okay…yeah, there it is." She dialed a number on the phone, which was answered on two rings. "Yes, this is Kerry Stuart in Miami Ops. I need to speak with Alastair McLean, please." She paused. "It's urgent." She put the call on mute. "Start with turning off his electricity, Mark; I like the idea of him walking into sentient mildew."

Mark grinned. "Yes, ma'am." He trotted out the door, closing it behind him.

Kerry nodded at the door grimly. "Mess with me, will you? You pitiful little excuse for half-baked dog poo…"

"Excuse me?" A male voice asked, from the phone. "Didn't quite catch that…is this Ms. Stuart?"

"Sorry, I was talking to someone else." Kerry bit off an embarrassed grin. "Yes, it is. Mr. McLean? I think we need to talk."

Chapter 13

A lone seagull circled over the beach, riding the warm air drafts. The soft hush and whisper of the waves was the only sound that came to Dar's ears as she sat quietly on the porch with her bare feet propped up against the stone porch railing. Her head was resting against the glass as she gazed, eyes half lidded, at the gull.

On the table, a half finished bottle of sweet wine rested, a glass next to it. Dar lifted an arm and filled the glass again and took a sip, rolling it around in her mouth before she swallowed it. Chino was sleeping on the tile near her feet, the puppy exhausted from her delighted antics at Dar's unexpected arrival.

The phone had rung several times inside, but Dar had decided to ignore it, preferring instead to gaze across the horizon and evaluate her options.

It felt strange not to be working. It felt even stranger not to be sure that the decision she'd made had been a good one. The incredulous disgust in Kerry's tone echoed in memory, sliding right down into Dar's guts and churning them uneasily.

"Think I screwed that up too, Chino?" Dar let her head drop back. Twice, she'd picked up her cell phone to call Kerry's office, and twice she'd put it back down, unable to stomach what she might find on the other end. "You're getting chickenshit in your old age, Dar. " She accused herself softly. "What would daddy say about that, huh?"

A dragonfly meandered past, impudently landing on Dar's bare knee. Chino cocked her head at it, then sniffed, sitting up and scrabbling her paws against Dar's thigh as she tried to get a better look. The insect lurched, then bolted in outrage, making its way off the porch and into a patch of hibiscus on the other side.

"See?" Dar took another sip of her wine, aware of the faint sense of dislocation from that much alcohol in her mostly empty stomach. "Knows what's good for him, Chino. Doesn't stick around when things get tough." She paused. "Like me."

For a long moment, she stared out across the horizon, then a faint laugh forced it's way out of her. "Well, Paladar Katherine. Are you done being a self pitying son of a bitch now?" she asked the sky. "Suck it up, and make the damn call." With that, she picked up her cell phone and opened it.

It rang just as she did, and she almost dropped the instrument onto the stone tile floor. "Shit." She made a grab for it in mid-air and got it to her ear. "Hello?"

"Hi."

Dar felt a gentle wave of relief pass over her. "Hi."

"You at home?" Kerry asked.

"Yeah." Dar listened intently. Kerry didn't sound particularly pissed off. Maybe it was okay after all.

"You're not answering the phone there."

"I know. I'm outside on the porch with Chino," the dark-haired woman replied. "So, they give you my office yet?"

A soft laugh answered her. "Well, since I just got out of a meeting where I told two senior VPs to kiss my ass, that's probably not in my cards today."

"Mm." Obscurely, that pleased Dar. "Which two?"

"José and Eleanor. Mariana went home," Kerry replied. "And I'm out of here, too. Since the entire division's on strike, there's no real need for me to be here."

"Mm…that's nice. Wait." Dar sat up. "What?"

"Must have been something in the cafeteria. Fifty-two people in operations, coincidentally, all got sick and had to go home," Kerry told her blithely.

Dar sighed. "Kerry, it's a nice gesture, but that's just going to get everyone in trouble."

"Dar, I didn't ask them to do that," Kerry's voice came back. "I don't think you quite realize just how much these people respect you. Maria tendered her resignation, there are ten more of those pending, including Mark's, and Personnel's been bombarded with official letters of protest. You know it was Fabricini who started all the rumors this morning."

"Was it?"

"He's got a cousin in telco up there who was at the facility when we managed to get it working."

"Oh." Dar murmured. "And he saw us…"

"Yeah."

"Ah." Dar exhaled. "Well, can't really refute that, can I?"

"No, not that I'd want to," Kerry told her. "It feels kind of nice not to have to pretend anymore." She shifted a little. "So Fabricini's got a bunch of people pretty pissed off at him. He was waltzing around the hallways earlier before he found out his network access somehow vanished."

"Oh?"

"And his car got keyed."

"Oh." A different emphasis.

"And his tires got slashed."

"Ah, Kerry…"

"And his electricity, phones, gas, and water got turned off."

"Kerry…." Alarm now.

"And his credit cards got canceled."

"Hey!"

"His auto deposit got rerouted into the Women's and Children's fund."

"KERRY!"

"Just kidding about that one," Kerry chuckled.

"Come on now, you're going to get yourself in a lot of trouble," Dar told her in an aggravated tone.

"Yes, and I'm perfectly capable of getting myself in and out of that, Dar; I don't need you throwing yourself in front of situations for me," Kerry responded, just as seriously. "I'm really pissed off that you quit over something that involved me and didn't even have the courtesy to talk to me about it first."

She had no answer for that. What was worse, she realized bleakly that it had never occurred to her to talk to Kerry first. She felt the silence lengthen awkwardly, and she swallowed, tasting the iron tang of the wine suddenly in the back of her throat.

"Dar?" Kerry's voice altered subtly. "Listen.. I... "

"You're right to be pissed off." Dar replied quietly. "I'm sorry. I guess I managed to screw this up pretty badly." She regarded the gull glumly. "Maybe I should have just stayed home today."

"Hold on a minute," Kerry replied.

"I should have talked to you first. I'm just not used to that," Dar muttered. "I just reacted without thinking; you know, the crap I'm always telling you not to do? Great example."

"Dar?"

"Yeah?"

"I love you." Kerry said. "So don't worry about it. We can talk later."

A little wave of warm relief flowed over her unexpectedly. "Oh." A faint smile twitched at Dar's lips. "I love you too." She paused. "Sorry if I overreacted."

"Apology accepted, if you forgive me in advance for trying to get you to change your mind."

Dar smiled a little sadly. "Out of my hands now," she admitted. "Maybe it's better that way."

Kerry chuckled.

"What was that for?" Dar inquired, curiously.

"I'll see you in a little while," her lover replied mysteriously. "Bye."

Dar regarded the phone. "Now, what's she up to?" she asked a sleepy Chino, who wagged her tail. With a sigh, Dar pushed herself to her feet and caught the edge of the door for balance, surprised at her lightheadedness. "Damn, Chino, that was only a lousy half bottle of wine," she complained. "Guess that's why I don't drink much, huh?"

The condo phone rang as she trudged into the kitchen, and she stared at it, debating. Then she shrugged and picked it up. "Hello?"

It was quiet on the other end, though Dar thought she could hear the surf and a clanging that meant ships. "Hello?" she asked again, a little impatiently.

"Hello, Dar," a low, raspy voice answered, hesitantly.

Dar slowly turned and leaned against the counter, unable to believe her ears. Her heart went double time, and she felt her legs shake in pure reaction.

"Dar?" The voice again, uncertainly.

"D... Daddy?" she whispered. "Is that you?" Her knees unlocked suddenly, and she grabbed onto the counter.

"Yeah, it is, Dardar."

The childhood nickname almost wrecked her. Dar sank to the tile floor and just sat there for a minute, pressing the phone to her ear. Chino huddled between her legs, brown eyes anxiously watching her. "D...d...I...I thought..."

"Long story." The low voice sounded tired, and a little lost. "Just wanted to see how you were."

"Daddy." Dar stared at the tile. "Where are you? Can I...can I come see you? Are you here? In Miami?"

Her father didn't answer for a bit. "I ain't much to look at," he finally said. "Don't want t'scare you too much...maybe..."

"Where are you?" Dar asked again. "Please. I'll catch a plane, or whatever, I don't care."

"Well." The voice took on just a hint of warmth. "Ain't no need for that. I'm over here t'other side of the cut, watchin' them ferryboats take off."

"H..." Dar fought the impulse to drop the phone and run. "Don't you move. Don't you move. I'll be right over there."

"All right."

Dar hung up and pulled herself to her feet and caught her breath, several emotions warring to gain control of her. She put the phone down and walked in a dream state to the living room, where she picked up her keys and continued on to the door. "Be right back, Chino," she murmured to the whining puppy following her. "Be right back."

Outside, she went to the Lexus, then looked at her shaking hands and decided driving wasn't a good idea. She took a deep breath, and changed directions, lurching into a run down the tarmac road towards the far off sound of the ferry.

Kerry walked into the condo, immediately aware there was something wrong. She found Chino out and the floor covered with toilet paper, the puppy's contribution to the décor. It was too quiet, though, and she went to Dar's bedroom, glancing in to see the bed empty and the room very quiet, only Dar's work clothes folded neatly on the dresser, everything else in perfect order.

"What's going on, Chino?" she asked the puppy now cradled in her arms. "Where's mommy Dar?"

Chino whined.

Kerry searched the rest of the condo, seeing that her partner hadn't even gone in her study. She spotted the wine bottle on the table outside, however, and wandered out there, picking it up and peering at the level. "Half a bottle…mm." Dar rarely drank; finding this wasn't a good sign. She'd known from Dar's tone of voice that the stress had been getting to her. This just confirmed it.

Kerry went back inside and checked the kitchen, finding the phone on the counter, but little else. She checked the caller ID and found her own two unanswered calls, one from Houston she'd bet was Alastair, and another one, a pay phone that looked like it had come in shortly after she'd spoken to Dar on the cell.

"Pay phone?" Curiously, Kerry dialed the number, but it wasn't answered. She put the phone down and sighed, wondering what to do next. "Ah." She dialed Dar's cell phone, and heard a buzz nearby. "Damn. She doesn't have it with her."

Where could Dar have gone? Kerry searched for a note, but found nothing. With a frustrated sigh, she trotted upstairs and went to her office, putting down her briefcase and pausing as she spotted something on her desk. She sat down in the chair and picked up the small but nicely formed rose that had been nestled between two of her favorite chocolates.

She breathed a sigh of relief. "Okay, so she's not mad at me." She unwrapped a chocolate and bit into it, enjoying the dark chocolate truffle. "Maybe she went to the store, so just chill out, Kerry, and give her a while to get back." She glanced at the computer, then picked up the other chocolate and wandered into her bedroom to change. "What do you think, burgers for dinner, Chino? Nothing fancy?"

"Yawp." Chino nuzzled her.   🦋🦋   🦋🦋   🦋🦋

Dar stood the entire trip over the channel, her face plastered against the glass window in the passenger's lounge of the car ferry. If she'd been allowed, she'd have just stayed on deck, but rules were rules, and she'd been banished to the indoor room, which had molded fiberglass seats for those people who chose to ride back and forth and not bring their cars.

She watched the dock, her eyes searching the darkness intently, finding the bank of payphones empty, but surrounded by dark corners that could easily hide a man in them.

An ordinary man, that is. Dar found one corner that seemed less empty than the others and fastened her eyes on it. She went through the door as the ramp was coming down, ignoring the deckhand's instructions and hopping on it before it finished moving, heading up the sloping metal surface and onto the mainland, oblivious of the curious stares around her.

It was cool, and slightly cloudy. The moonlight lit half the ferry base in silver and she passed through bars of it as she walked directly towards her chosen corner, hoping her legs wouldn't collapse from shaking before she got there. Her eyes were already trying to resolve the shadowy form, and as she passed through a wide patch of street lamp enhanced moonlight, she saw motion there, a shifting....

Then a body was outlined dimly against the wall, and she felt a smile start to move her lips. It was tall, topping her by several inches, and broad, the head covered in a hood that obscured any visible features, but she felt no fear, and as she came closer, a hand lifted towards her, and the very motion struck chords of familiarity that launched her into a run, covering the remaining distance between them in mere seconds.

"Easy there, Dardar."

She halted mere feet from him and reached out a hand. "Dad?"

Her hand was taken, in a warm, callused grasp and she walked forward in a dreamy daze, finding herself being enclosed in a pair of strong arms she'd last felt what seemed like half a lifetime ago. She let out an audible gasp and felt hot tears rolling down her face in heartfelt reaction.

"Hey, Dar." Her father's voice sounded hoarse, and raspy, but the familiar tone was there.

"Oh god, I can't believe it," she murmured into his shoulder. "It's really you."

"Yeap." A hand patted her back comfortingly. "Been a long time, I know."

Dar pulled back reluctantly, just enough so she could look at him. He had his back to the streetlamp, so she could only see vague shadows, but the moonlight reflected off his eyes, which met hers for a long, wonderful moment.

She had to tilt her head back to do that, something she had to do so very infrequently.

He put his hands on her shoulders and turned her towards the light a little. "Lemme see ya."

Dar obliged, blinking as the light hit her face and revealed the tears. "H…how long…um, wh…"

"Hang on." Her father thumbed the moisture off. "I ain't been round too long, Dardar, just had t'pick the right time, I guess…I been through a bunch, an it's kinda scary lookin'."

"Have you called mom?"

"No. And you will not do that."

"But—"

"Paladar, promise me." Her father's voice was very serious. "I got my reasons. Don't make me regret callin' you."

Dar started crying, unable to prevent herself, unable to control the reaction. She clamped her jaw shut and held her answer, swallowing hard and trying to stifle the almost overwhelming emotion.

"Hey, now…" Her father's voice changed, and become much gentler. He reached out and pulled her close again in wordless comfort, holding her as sobs jerked her body. "Honey. I'm sorry…easy, now."

Dar got herself back under control, taking deep breaths to steady her nerves. "I'm sorry; it's just so much to take in," she mumbled. "And it's been a…really long day; first I quit my job, now this." Her voice was shaking though, and she could feel the erratic jumping of her heart.

He released her, then took her hand, chafing it gently. "It's good t'see you, Dardar. Sorry it knocked you all to hell and all."

"No, I'm all right." The moon flickered out from behind a cloud, and she got a very brief glimpse under the hood at twisted skin and angry scars before the shadows returned. "Will you come over to the island with me?"

Her father hesitated. "Maybe we should wait 'nother night; you seem kinda shook up."

"Please." Dar's voice cracked a little. "You can't just leave again. At least let me talk to you for a while," she pleaded softly. "I'd like you to see where I live… just for a little while?" She didn't want to release him, afraid he'd disappear again, and be gone forever. "Please, daddy?"

"All right," he agreed finally.

Dar felt a sense of relief flow over her. She held a hand out to him, and closed her fingers around his when he took it. "C'mon, we can catch this ferry back."

They walked together across the dock, and down the ramp onto the ferry. Dar lifted a hand towards the deck hands, who nodded back to her as she led her father into the dimly lit passenger lounge. The ramp lifted, and the ferry's engines rumbled as it backed off from the dock, then changed pitch as they started driving the ship forwards across the lightly choppy channel.

❦❦   ❦❦   ❦❦

Kerry checked her watch for the sixth time, then ran a nervous hand through her hair. "All right, that's it, Chino. I'm taking the golf cart and going hunting for her. It's a small island; she's got to be somewhere." She grabbed the key to the cart and headed for the door, pausing as she heard footsteps outside. "Ah. Of course. I should have tried that earlier."

Chino heard them too and started hopping up and down in her cage, yipping excitedly and confirming the identity of the visitor, as if Kerry had any doubts. She dropped the key back down and headed for the door as it opened, taking in Dar's tall form with a relieved sigh, then stopping in surprise when she realized her partner wasn't alone. "Hey."

Dar gave her a quick, almost nervous smile, and stood back, allowing her companion to enter. "Hey… sorry I didn't leave a note but, um…"

Kerry walked forward curiously, cocking her head at the tall, broad-shouldered figure who paused inside the door, a thick cotton hood covering his head, and hiding his features. "It's okay… um…" She got closer, and now as he turned slightly, she could see his face.

Horrible scars crossed it, twisting one side into a painful knot and raking the other side, as though a huge cat had clawed him.

But Kerry's eyes went right past that to the pale, ice blue eyes that flicked to hers, framed in an angular bone structure she immediately recognized despite the disfiguring marks. "Oh…" she breathed in shock. "You're Dar's father, aren't you!" she blurted in surprise, the picture in Dar's study flashing vividly into her memory.

One of his eyebrows lifted, visible even through the scarring. "That's right," he rasped softly.

Dar recovered herself from her own surprise. "Uh… yeah. Kerry, this is my father, Andrew Roberts." She took a breath. 'Dad, this is Kerry Stuart, my, um…partner."

"Wow." Kerry trotted forward and paused before him, reaching a hand out tentatively, and finding it grasped by one much larger than her own. "This is so fantastic." A smile creased her face in genuine delight as she shifted her eyes to Dar's face, and saw the almost heartbreaking, shy wonder there. "I was about to go searching for you. I just put Chino in her cage."

The puppy was whining piteously, and Dar cleared her throat. "C'mon in. Ker, let the puppy out…um, I'll give you a tour, and maybe we can have some dinner?"

"All right," he agreed quietly. "Nice t'meet you, young lady." He released Kerry's hand and exhaled. "Lord, May never did do this by half, did she?" He seemed to relax a little.

"Nope," Dar agreed, leading him through the living room. "That's my room…my office." She watched her father examine everything with characteristic curiosity. "Three more rooms upstairs. Kerry has a bedroom up there, and her office, and a spare room."

"My gosh." Andrew paused by the television and picked up a picture of Dar in her younger years. "I remember that outfit." He murmured, then glanced down as his foot was engulfed by a frantic ball of cream-colored fur. "Well, well. What have we here."

"That's Cappuccino," Kerry answered, coming back in the room and crossing over to Dar. "Um…I was going to order some dinner…can I get something for you, Mr. Roberts?"

Andrew looked up from examining the puppy, who was on her back under his petting hand and wriggling happily. "I'm not much fer fancy stuff, thanks."

"I was thinking maybe burgers, actually." Kerry smiled at him. "And French fries." She glanced sideways at Dar, who was watching her father with a wide-eyed wonder. "Sound okay to you?"

"Sure," Dar agreed absently.

"All right." Andrew nodded. "That'd be fine, thanks." He paused, and stood up. "Don't suppose they got any ice cream?"

Kerry burst into laughter, clapping her hand over the receiver she'd just started to speak into.

"Was that funny?" the tall man asked uncertainly, giving his daughter a quick look. Dar was gazing at the tile floor, a smile on her face. "You still fond of ice cream, Dardar?"

"You could say that, yes," Dar replied with a faint chuckle. "That's what Kerry is laughing about. Now she knows where I get it from."

"Ah." Andrew stuck his hands in his pockets. "Wanna show me the rest of this place?" He followed Dar as she led the way.

🐃　🐃　🐃

"I think Chino has a new friend," Kerry commented, chewing on a French fry as she watched the puppy tap Andrew's leg with an imperious paw. "She loves fries."

Dar's father eyed the little animal. "She does, huh?" He tested the theory, and found it sound. "Cute little sucker."

"She likes you."

"I'm feeding her; 'course she likes me," Andrew replied, with a rakish grin in Kerry's direction. "So you work with Dar?"

Kerry studied him, noting his almost embarrassed shift as he pulled his hood a little closer to hide the horrible scarring. It was pretty scary to look at, but she'd found her eyes getting used to it after a while, watching his eyes for reactions more than facial expressions that seemed painful for him to make. "Yes, I do. I've learned a lot from her."

"Mph." Andrew chewed a fry reflectively. "She's a sharp kid."

"Very." Kerry's eyes twinkled. "I think that's what impressed me the most when we started working together; she has an uncanny instinct for finding what the problem really is. When she first hired me, I'd sit there and listen and just shake my head."

"She picked you then? You must be pretty sharp too; my kid don't suffer fools none."

Kerry blushed. "I like to think so." She glanced up, noting that Dar had been gone for a few minutes. "Um, I'll be right back." She got up and trotted into the kitchen, spotting her lover leaning on the counter staring out at the waves. "Dar?"

The dark head turned towards her, as Dar quickly wiped her sleeve across her eyes. "Sorry, I just…"

"Hey." Kerry came closer, and put her arms around the taller woman. "Are you okay?"

Dar shook her head. "No." She sniffled. "I can't believe this is happening." Her eyes wandered over the kitchen in an almost bewildered way. "Just too much."

"Easy." Kerry murmured. "I know it's been a long day." She heard another sniffle. "But what an awesome ending to it."

Dar laughed faintly. "Yeah." She agreed. "I just can't believe it."

Kerry hugged her tightly. "Dar, it's so wonderful. I can't believe it either." She felt her lover suck in a breath and release it, and she rubbed Dar's back comfortingly. "And your dad is such a sweetheart. I knew he would be but…. I really like him."

"Yeah?" Dar whispered in her ear, as they swayed a little, together. "He's not like me at all huh?"

Kerry snorted. "I know you're joking; you are so his image," she marveled. "You both even do that eyebrow thing the same way." Dar didn't answer, she just held onto Kerry, burying her face in Kerry's hair and warming her scalp with soft breaths. "Two of a kind, right?"

A pensive sigh. "We used to be," Dar murmured. "I don't know what he'd think of who I've become now."

Kerry was puzzledly silent for a moment. "What part of you being a successful, intelligent, beautiful woman is he going to object to?" she asked in confusion. "Or is it us you mean?"

Dar didn't answer for a few seconds, then she snorted a little, and released one hand, rubbing her face with it. "No, it's not us; my brain just went south for a minute on me. Thanks for mailing it a map." She circled Kerry's shoulders and nudged her. "C'mon. My burger's probably an ice cube by now."

They reentered the room, and Andrew glanced up from his steadfast new friend, the edges of his mouth quirking up as he watched them enter together. "Found her, I guess."

"It's a big kitchen," Kerry replied, keeping her arm around Dar as they sat down. "She was hiding behind the cookies."

Dar managed a startled smile, glancing sideways at her. "You're the one who can't reach the cabinet they're in."

"Hey, no short jokes!" Kerry warned, shaking a finger at her. "Or I'll start keeping the milk on the bottom shelf of the refrigerator." She earned a faint laugh and felt some of the tension in Dar's back relax as the taller woman sat back in the loveseat and pulled her burger over. Kerry stole a fry and ate it, then winked at Andrew, who chuckled silently.

"What parts you from, Kerry?" he asked.

"Michigan," Kerry answered. "Saugatuck, as a matter of fact."

"Uh huh. Been up there a few times," Andrew acknowledged. "Big change from this place."

"Oh yeah," she agreed. "A nice change. I like the weather and a lot of other things down here much better." Her eyes went unconsciously to Dar, then back to him.

"Got family back there?"

Sigh. "Yes, my, um…my parents, and a brother and sister."

Andrew must have sensed her mood change, because he looked up and studied her, then flicked a glance at his daughter before resuming his assault on the medium rare burger she'd ordered for him. "Bad question?"

Dar was glad of something to distract her from her own nervousness. She put an arm across Kerry's shoulders and felt her cuddle instinctively. "Kerry's family is not exactly enthusiastic about us," she told her father dryly. "At least her parents aren't. I think Michael and Angela are okay, though, aren't they?"

Kerry nodded, concentrating on chewing her French fries, reluctant to talk about her family.

"Yeap, well, been there done that myself," Andrew told her. "It's rough, ain't it?"

Their eyes met, and Kerry saw the gentle understanding there. She nodded again and pressed her lips into a little smile. "It was worth it, though." She looked up at Dar. "I have no regrets."

Andrew smiled, as though at a private memory, then looked down and offered a French fry to Chino. "Naw. I always figgered Dar for a good catch."

"Dad!" His daughter protested mildly. "That's not what you told my senior prom date."

The atmosphere eased considerably as Andrew lifted an eyebrow at her. "That was not a date, young lady. That was a person with a damn tattoo bigger than an aircraft carrier's anchor."

Kerry snickered. "Got any pictures?"

"No," Dar stated.

"I just might." Andrew gave Kerry a sideways look. "Longside of the ones I got of Dardar in her nappies."

"Oh God." Dar hid her eyes.

Kerry beat the clock awake, and she carefully reached over and turned the alarm off before she half turned to gaze at her lover. Dar was normally a very light sleeper, but this morning she was still deeply asleep, her face totally relaxed and unresponsive. She'd been very quiet, almost withdrawn the night before as they'd gone to bed, but it wasn't an unhappy kind of quiet, just a stunned one.

The three of them had talked far into the night about the company, and their jobs, skirting around painful subjects, like what had happened to Andrew, but getting a sense that he'd been somewhere he couldn't talk much about and had only recently returned to Miami.

It had been so late when they'd finally wound down, that Andrew had hesitantly allowed himself to be persuaded to stay over, bunking down in the spare room upstairs after they promised him a ride to wherever he wanted to go the next day.

Andrew was, Kerry discovered, a genuinely nice guy with a dry, humorous wit, and a sweetly obvious love for Dar that made clear to her the reason for the equally obvious adoration she had for him.

The father-daughter resemblance was startling. Dar shared her father's height and sturdy build, dark hair and pale eyes, and the planed facial structure that was rugged in Andy, and strikingly angular in his daughter. They had the same way of moving, and even some of the same expressions. Kerry had found herself smiling every time she looked at Andrew, knowing how incredibly happy having him return had made Dar.

Unfortunately, the entire thing had thrown her partner very much off balance, and she also sensed that Dar was in a very vulnerable state at the moment, not a good thing given what was going on with work.

What am I thinking? To hell with work, Kerry reminded herself. *This is so much more important to her than that stupid company. My God, she lost him for all those years, and now...wow. I can't imagine what that must be like,* Kerry marveled. *To have someone come back into her life like that...everything else is just so irrelevant.*

Kerry had a few minutes, so she indulged herself in watching Dar doze peacefully, her face outlined faintly in the early morning gloom, only a faint, irregular twitching moving the soft, tanned skin. Kerry twirled a lock of dark hair idly around her fingers and brushed it against her lips, absorbing the peace of the moment. It was hard to pull herself away, and she found herself fighting against the urge to remain here at Dar's side, to hell with the company.

Finally she sighed and edged carefully out of bed, tucking the comforter back around Dar's body before she padded out into the living room, heading for her bedroom upstairs. She stopped short when she almost collided with a seated form on the floor. "Oh."

"Morning," Andrew Roberts uttered in a low voice. He had Chino between his knees, and was playing with her, the delighted puppy rolling around on her back as he rubbed her belly. "Thought I'd catch a ride out early with ya."

Kerry knew Dar wanted to ask him to stay for a while. She could read it in her lover's face and in the wistful looks as she regarded her father, but she'd kept silent, as though she were afraid if she pushed him, he'd just vanish again. *Well.* Kerry regarded the dim form before her. *Maybe I can help that.*

She settled herself cross-legged on the cold tiles next to him, and pushed her hair behind one ear absently. "Um, I don't suppose I could convince you to stick around here today, huh?"

He glanced up and scowled at her. "Naw, c'mon now, Kerry. Last night was nice, but I've got to get going, and I…" He paused, pinned by the soft green eyes. "Why?" he asked, warily.

The blond woman exhaled. "Well, I have to go into work," she stated quietly. "I don't want to; it's going to be a mess, and I'm not sure I can deal with all of it, but I have to."

"Uh huh."

"And if I leave Dar here all alone, she's going to go crazy between being bored and wondering what's going on," Kerry continued. "I think she could use some company, and I know she'd love to spend some time with you."

"Mm."

"And I'll be a nervous wreck all day, wondering what's going on with her. But if you're here, she won't be bored, and I won't have to worry," Kerry finished, her eyes settling on him in silent appeal. "Please?"

"Y'ever think of going into diplomacy, young lady?" Andrew Roberts queried wryly.

"It's the truth. I mean, you know Dar better than I do; isn't it?" Kerry replied reasonably.

He looked down at his hands, the edges of the hood obscuring his ruined face. "All right," he finally responded, reluctantly. "I'll stay for a bit…can't say I don't want to see my kid, neither."

Kerry squeezed his hand. "Thank you. I won't be all day, I promise."

He nodded, and tickled the puppy. "She's a cute little thing," he commented.

"Mm, yes, she is," Kerry replied. "I think she really likes you." She laughed softly as the puppy squirmed happily against his foot. "I think you know her grandpa...General Easton?"

Andrew's eyes lit up. "Gerry? This is one of Alabaster's get?" He glanced down at the animal. "How d'you like that," he murmured.

"Jack brought her down for Dar's birthday, only she turned out to be my Christmas present." Kerry scratched her ear. "I'm not really sure how that happened."

"You want one?"

Kerry fingered Chino's soft paw. "Yes. I had a puppy when I was younger, but...anyhow, Dar knew that, so..." She shrugged a tiny bit and looked up.

"Kid's got a good heart," Andrew acknowledged.

"I bet I know where it comes from," Kerry replied with a smile. "I'm really glad I got a chance to meet you, sir."

He scowled at her. "Don't you have to get dressed to go on into that place, or do you work in your jammies?"

Kerry stood up and grinned at him. "I get the hint." She trotted towards the stairs, trying to psych herself up for the day to come. Then she paused, and walked a step or two back. "Thank you, Mr. Roberts."

The darkness hid his face, but she had the feeling he smiled. "You're welcome, Kerry."

◆◆　◆◆　◆◆

Andrew paused in the doorway for a bit, leaning there and just watching his daughter sleep. Dar was curled half on her side with one arm wrapped around her pillow, the firm, toned muscles obvious even in the faint light coming in the blinds.

Eight years. The tall man shook his head sadly. He'd left Dar a somewhat gawky young woman unsure of where she wanted to go in life, and come back to find her grown up, into a confident, beautiful person he wondered if he even knew anymore.

He glanced around the room, finding a familiar neatness and order, and he smiled to himself, shaking his head a little before he entered, walking over and dropping to a knee beside the bed, regarding one of the two faces that had kept him company in his dreams for seven long years. "Dardar?"

There was no response. Andrew hesitated, then put a hand on the bare shoulder nearest him and shook it a little. "Dar?"

The tanned face slowly took on tension, then Dar's eyelashes fluttered open, revealing pale blue eyes that tracked immediately to his face and held there. First utter wonder, then a look of sleepy surprise appeared. "Hi." Dar cleared her throat of its hoarseness. "Wh…" She looked at the clock. "Wow… I um… I didn't expect you to still be here. I…"

"Yep, me neither," her father drawled. "But your little green-eyed friend had other ideas."

Dar rubbed her face. "I feel like I'm in a dream," she admitted, rolling over and stretching her body out as she recalled the events of the previous day. "Guess I'd better get my lazy ass out of bed, huh?" She was a little embarrassed at having been caught sleeping in. "I don't usually sleep this late."

Andrew poked the mattress. "Good lord, what is this?"

"A waterbed," Dar remarked wryly. "Appropriate for a navy brat, I thought."

Experimentally, her father pressed down on it. "Damn thing's warm."

"It's heated," Dar muttered, feeling direly decadent. She eyed her father's face in apprehension, wondering what he was thinking.

Andrew whistled under his breath. "Y'know, I like that idea."

"Really?" Dar smiled in relief and rolled over, clearing a spot and patting it. "Wanna try it?" She watched as he cautiously slid over the railing and onto the water mattress, making her rock slightly as his weight was cradled. Then he lay down flat and peered up at her ceiling in sober speculation. "Well?"

"I do like this." Andrew nodded, flexing his body a little. "Feels real nice on these old bones."

"Mmm." Dar rested her chin on her wrist and studied him, wondering if the scars hurt as much as they looked like they did. "Tell me where you're staying and I'll get you one," she coaxed slyly.

A blue eye pinned her. "I do not think the Navy would appreciate that, Paladar." His voice softened. "But thank you for the offer."

They both looked away, a little embarrassed, then Andrew rolled carefully up and out of the bed. He stood and extended a hand to his daughter. Dar took his hand and let him haul her up. "All right, let me splash some water on my face, put some shorts on. I can give you a tour around the island if you want."

"Later, maybe." Andrew picked up a piece of bright orange cloth. "You call them shorts?" He viewed the skimpy cut skeptically.

Dar looked, then cleared her throat. "Um, those are Kerry's." She felt her skin warm.

"Oh." Her father seemed equally embarrassed, then they both chuckled, and Dar swiped the shorts from his hands and folded them, placing them on the dresser. "Cute color."

🐃   🐃   🐃

Kerry felt like she had a huge red white and black target painted right on her chest as she walked into the building. She already had a stomachache, and she hadn't even hit the elevator yet. She nodded nervously at the guard as she moved past him.

"Ms. Stuart?" the man said, leaning towards her a little.

"Yes?" She paused, wondering if he had orders to stop her or something.

He walked around the desk and came closer. "Is Ms. Roberts doing okay?" He shuffled his feet nervously, and looked around. "I know you guys usually come in together, so…"

Kerry smiled warmly at him. "She's fine; thanks for asking," she reassured him. "Did anyone else from my floor come through here yet?"

He knew what she was asking. "No, ma'am. You're the very first."

Kerry nodded. "Okay, thanks. I'll tell Dar you were asking for her." Her green eyes twinkled. "Wish me luck today."

He licked his lips. "Are you…" He left the statement unfinished.

Taking over? "Oh no." Kerry shook her head firmly. "But someone has to hold the paper bag up while everyone else jumps through it, you know?" She knew the word would spread within minutes. "Dar asked me to."

He nodded. "Gotcha." He sketched a salute at her. "Good luck, ma'am."

Kerry continued on, riding in solitary splendor up to her floor and exiting into a very empty corridor. Her steps took her to Dar's office first, and she used her key for the first time, letting herself in to where Maria would usually already be working. The outer office was somberly silent; the secretary's desk was neat as a pin, but missing the usual personal items Maria had kept there. Her cube of pictures, for instance, and the intriguing prism that scattered light over the room, a gift from Dar.

Kerry felt irrationally sad at the sight, and she ran a hand over the wood of the desk, swallowing down a surge of frustration. "This is so senseless." She picked up the contents of the inbox, then moved into the inner office, feeling her lover's absence like a physical blow. She noticed that Dar had left everything the way it was; even the fish were sitting forlornly on the clean surface of the desk, the light from the window catching them in flashes of blue and crimson. The only thing she'd taken, Kerry realized, were the crystal dolphins she'd given her.

"Oh, Dar." Kerry exhaled, feeling sick. The laptop sat in silence, giving mute testimony of its owner's abandonment. She wondered what had gone through Dar's mind as she'd given that up? It was the tangible badge of her office, really, giving her access into the heart of the company. Giving her the authority, which now, albeit briefly, rested in Kerry's hands. With a sigh, she collected what was in Dar's inbox as well, and then stepped around the desk and headed for the back entrance to her own office.

She could, she knew, boot up the computer in Dar's office and work from there, but she had no intention of sending that particular message. She even had Dar's passwords, the ultimate expression of her lover's trust in her, and if she'd wanted to, she could have brought down mainframes all across the world with Dar's top clearance and access, which she knew Mark hadn't touched before he'd left yesterday. But she had no intention of sending that message either.

She entered her office and put the papers down, reaching over and booting up her computer, then grabbing her coffee cup and trudging across the hallway to get some coffee.

Her back was to the door, and she didn't see who entered, but it also gave her a moment to decide on her response when the newcomer greeted her.

"Kerry." Mariana's voice sounded very tired.

The blond woman turned, and took a breath. "Hi."

"I didn't expect to see you here," the Personnel VP told her honestly. "How's Dar?"

Kerry took a sip of her coffee. "She's all right...taking it easy at home." She paused. "She tried to call you last night."

The other woman sighed, and leaned back against the wall. "I went out and got drunk," Mariana admitted. "I saw her number on the caller ID; I was going to call her back today." She looked at Kerry. "You know Alastair has put a hold on her resignation."

"Yes, I know," Kerry answered quietly. "I spoke to him." She exhaled. "Let's go into my office a minute." She followed Mari into the room and closed the door. "Look, I don't know what's going to happen," she began.

"He's on his way here, Kerry," Mariana told her wearily. "And he is royally pissed off."

"I know. I talked to him for about an hour yesterday. I told him everything—about José, about Eleanor, and about that pig bastard."

"Fabricini?"

"Yeah, although…" Kerry wiped her face. "It's not like it wasn't our fault. We both knew the risks; neither of us was thinking straight that night."

Mariana slowly sat down in one of the visitor's chairs. "No," she disagreed quietly. "Oh, yes, I mean sure, you're right, but he never should have gotten that far, Kerry." She leaned on her elbows. "Dar was right…I should have stopped it."

The woman looked like a truck had driven over her. Kerry sighed. "Well, no sense crying over spilt milk, they always say." She turned and regarded her mail, wincing at the pages and pages of urgent marked messages. "Let's see what happens when Alastair gets here. I know he considers Dar a very valuable employee."

"That he does," Mariana agreed. "She's really come through for him on a number of occasions. She's really come through for all of us, and that's why this whole thing is so…disgusting."

Kerry regarded her hands, folded on the desk. "You said you should have stopped it. Why didn't you?"

The older woman glanced at the carpet. "I spent half the night thinking about that," she admitted. "And the conclusion I came to was that we're all so used to Dar doing the dirty work, taking the hits and drawing the fire to herself that we've all gotten to be…" She paused. "It was easier just to stand back and let her go."

Kerry nodded, accepting that. "I was hoping that was the case," she said softly. "I was hoping it wasn't just that everyone was standing back and letting her take a fall." She glanced up at Mariana's startled expression. "She once told me that everyone she'd ever trusted in business had turned on her, and last night, before we went to sleep, she told me if I…if it turned out that I saw everyone here celebrating her leaving, that I shouldn't feel bad about it."

A soft exhale. "Kerry, I think you know that's not true." Mari spread her hand out. "You've got a dozen empty offices to prove it. You've got a division in pieces, the CEO headed out on the first flight…. Duks wouldn't even come in today. Hell, I only came in because I can't avoid it; all the stuff that's going to hit the fan is going to hit **my** fan. For god's sake, most people don't hate her."

"I know," the blond woman acknowledged softly. "But, I guess the few that do are so much more vocal, it seems that way sometimes." She turned a pencil over in her hands. "When I started that's all I heard for the first few weeks, was what a horrible bitch she was."

Mariana sucked on her lower lip.

"I had to find out for myself how wrong they were," Kerry sighed. "But most people don't get that chance."

"She doesn't make it easy," Mari stated quietly. "She keeps everyone at arm's length, Kerry, even Duks and I, and we've been friends for years." She sighed. "Even Mark, whom everyone knows is hopelessly in love with her."

Kerry's lips tensed into a faint smile. "You know, I never saw her like that, so...I mean, I knew she had a tough side, because I saw that right off, but there was always something.... I don't know. I could always just see there was more to her than the alpha bitch."

"Well." Mariana gave her a wry look. "You had a mitigating circumstance, as the lawyers like to say." She pondered that. "But I see your point. If this does work out all right, I think we need to change the way some things are handled, do some workgroup things to try and reduce some of the stress and the infighting."

Kerry accepted that.

"Things will change, though," Mariana told her gently. "For both of you, I mean."

Kerry studied her twined fingers. "It's so stupid. We both like what we do, we're both pretty good at it..."

"That's not the issue, Kerry. You're not just pretty good, you're excellent, and you have months of solid performance to back that up. I don't think anyone's questioning that," Mari stated flatly. "You are, and I want to say this, without doubt, more than qualified to do what you do."

"But."

"Mm," Mari agreed, with a sigh. "It stinks, Kerry. Do you know how long we searched to try to find someone who could work with Dar, handle her antics, and not go insane in less than a week?"

Kerry made a face. "Sorry."

"Professionally, I hate you. Personally, I was very glad the two of you found each other. Dar's been alone too long." She inhaled. "Well, let's see what the day holds. Who knows? Maybe Alastair will come in and fire the lot of us." She shook her head and walked out, leaving Kerry to stare after her thoughtfully.

"Who knows?" Kerry's phone rang, and she watched the keypad indicating it was a forwarded call from Dar's office. "Here we go." She punched the button. "Operations, Stuart."

"This is John Bucknell in Providence. We've had an order pending for a new circuit for a week. What the hell's going on down there!"

Kerry sighed inwardly, giving Mariana a look. "Just a moment. What's your account ID?" She typed in a number and started to work.

🐃🐃   🐃🐃   🐃🐃

They were both still a little nervous, and a little tongue-tied, Dar realized, as they sat quietly, her stretched out on the couch with Chino on her stomach and him on the love seat, his back to the window and his face thrown into shadows.

Well, neither of them were real conversationalists, but someone had to start things. "So…have a place to stay?" she asked, quietly, nursing a tall glass of chocolate milk.

"Couple of 'em," her father answered. "This place, that place, you know." He regarded her in silence for a moment. "I do a few little things here and there. They give me this card." He pulled a small folder from his waist pocket and displayed an innocuous silver plate that looked like a credit card. "I just put everything on that, and they take care of it."

Dar nodded slowly. "Because of mom?" she hazarded a guess, remembering the sometimes obscure, unfathomable ways of the government.

"Yeap." He tucked the folder away. "She's got my pension, the benefits…that's how I want it. They take care of me." His voice seemed to end that line of questioning.

All right, round two. Ding ding. Dar nodded again, playing with one of Chino's soft ears. Then she looked up and studied his face, regarding the scars that twisted the flesh into an almost unrecognizable mask thoughtfully. "What happened? If you can say." Then she just waited.

He thought for a long time. "Just a gig that went bad," he finally said, almost emotionlessly. "We went in to check out some stuff we'd heard about a chemical weapon. It was a setup. Three guys died, and I ended up wishing I'd been one of 'em." He reached up and touched one of the scars, wincing a little.

Dar considered that. "I'm only going to say this one time," she stated, softly. "Mom wouldn't give a damn about what you look like."

He studied his hands in the silence. "I know that," he admitted, falling silent for a bit. "But she didn't want me to go this time."

"I remember." Dar quietly exhaled. "But I thought...." That they'd worked things out; at least, that was how it had appeared to Dar: her mother upset, yes, but supportive as always. "Dad, how can you not call her? Losing you..." Dar paused. "Look, I know how I felt seeing you again. I can't imagine how she'd react."

"Yeap, well...she done told me if I went, she wouldn't be there when I got back this time," Andrew replied flatly. "Said that was my choice." He blinked a few times, his eyes moving restlessly in his scarred face. "Going, or her."

Dar was truly shocked. "She wouldn't have left you."

Pained blue orbs lifted to hers. "Wasn't her leaving. It was me, the way she looked at it." He swallowed. "She was right, Dar; it was my choice—and I chose to go." He took a breath. "Thought I could work things out when I got back." He stared at the table. "Except I didn't."

Dar absorbed it. "She was just trying to get you to stay," she finally said. "She was afraid for you. She was afraid of losing you," she protested. "She would have been there when you got back, and you know it."

His eyes closed. "I like to think that." His voice was quiet and sad. "It's this little game I play with my head, keeps me from going nuts and just takin' a dive off a bridge somewhere." His voice was lightly ragged. "Tried calling the numbers I remembered when I got back here, but she'd moved on."

"Dad, why don't you call her?" Dar leaned forward, willing him to listen. "You can go home; she'd understand, I know it." She held out a hand. "I've got her new number; Richard gave it to me."

He looked at her. "Rich Edgerton?" A pause. "You use it much?"

Dar felt trapped, but there was no escaping those eyes. "No." She found a spot on the tile to stare at. "Mom hasn't talked to me since the funeral."

The silence lengthened. Finally Andrew sighed. "Paladar."

"It was her choice," Dar bit off. "Not mine."

There was a creak of leather, then hands covered the ones she had resting on her knees, and she had to look up. "She tell you she didn't want you calling her?" Andrew asked, gently.

Dar nodded. "Said I reminded her too much of you."

He flinched, and his eyes dropped for a long moment, before lifting again. "Honey, I'm sorry. I know you two never got along too good, but I never wanted that to happen."

"I know." She managed a halfhearted smile. "You were always the peacemaker." She met his eyes, so close to hers now. "So I guess now it's my turn. Call her, daddy. I know she waited for you."

A very tired sigh. "I can't," he answered softly. "'Cause then I'd know, y'see? And if she didn't, if she meant that, or if she...." An agonizing pause. "I can't face it, Dar. I can't live with that. You understand me?" he pleaded softly. "I can't face knowing that she doesn't..." He just stopped, his throat working audibly.

Dar let out her held breath in a pained trickle. "Oh, daddy," she whispered.

He sighed. "Doesn't make much sense to you, I reckon." He rubbed an impatient hand over his eyes. "Damn."

She gazed at him in bleak understanding. "Yes, it does." Dar shook her head in long remembered pain. "I went after what you and mom had, and I thought I'd found it. And I was wrong. I...I kinda gave up on it after that."

Her father grunted. "Till now." He glanced up shrewdly at her. "'Cause I don't know how you feel about her, but that little green eyed gal's lost her mind gone for you, Paladar."

Dar smiled, wistfully. "Until now," she acknowledged. "When I met Kerry, I realized I finally had found the real thing." Her eyes found her father's. "So I do understand, daddy. That's why I think you should call."

He got up and sat down next to her, and they regarded each other in silence. "You stuck on her?" Andrew finally asked, watching her face.

"Yeah," Dar answered without hesitation. "Like a superglue factory."

Andrew put a hand on her knee. "Don't you ever let go."

🐾　🐾　🐾

The phone buzzed for what seemed the thousandth time, and Kerry glared at it balefully as she rested her head on one hand. "No, no, I don't know, no, it's not ready yet, I have no idea, no, she didn't tell me, no, and no," she muttered before hitting the speaker button. "Operations, Stuart."

"Hi."

It was like a mouthful of ambrosia. Kerry found a smile working its way onto her face before the syllables even faded and she let out a soft sigh. "You have no idea how good it feels to hear a friendly voice."

"Mm, rough, huh?" Dar rumbled softly through the speaker. "How's it going?"

"Sucks." Kerry rubbed her eyes. "I feel like I've been dragged behind a dump truck hauling chicken poop all day," she replied. "Alastair is here. He's been in meetings with Mari and the others for a couple of hours. How's it going there?"

"Eh," Dar answered. "I slept late, felt washed out all day. Dad and I talked for a while, then we had some lunch; now we're watching Crocodile Hunter." She hesitated. "Thanks, by the way, for asking him to stick around."

Kerry smiled and tapped a pencil against her upper lip. "Thought you might like the company," she replied quietly, then glanced down as her phone buzzed. "Hold on a minute." She picked up her other line. "Operations."

"Ms. Stuart." Alastair's voice sounded quiet, and rather grim.

"Yes, sir," Kerry answered, feeling her stomach drop. "What can I do for you?"

"We're having a meeting in the executive conference room. Could you come over, please?"

"Certainly," Kerry replied evenly. "I'll be right there." She took a breath before she picked up the other line. "Hi."

"Bad news?" Dar inquired.

"Don't know. That was Alastair; they want me up in the big conference room. Look, the worst they could do is fire me, Dar, and like, whoop, you know?" She shook her head a little. "After today, I'd probably thank him," she added grimly. "My respect for you has jumped even higher."

"Mm." Dar considered that. "Relax, be honest, don't let him rattle you," she instructed gently. "Keep your head up; you've only ever done good for the company, Kerry." She hesitated. "He's not a bad guy; he's always found a way to be in my corner, even when it probably wasn't a good idea for him to."

"I got the feeling he likes you," Kerry agreed. "All right, I can do that. But if he or anyone else starts trashing you, they're toast."

A soft chuckle answered her. "That's my Kerry."

The blond woman grinned. "You bet your boots I am." She stood up and straightened her collar, then donned her jacket. "Wish me luck. I'll call you one way or the other when I get out of there."

"Good luck," Dar answered obediently. "I'm with you."

"I know," she replied softly. "Talk to you later." She hung up and ran a hand through her hair. "All right, let's go."

It was a short walk to the conference room, and she gathered her wits along with the knowledge of Dar's confidence in her as she reached the door and knocked lightly on it.

"Come," the voice inside sounded, and she pulled the door open and walked into a room where the hostility was so thick it was almost like a smoke pall. José, Eleanor, and Steve were there, as was Mariana, and, of course, Alastair. Kerry lifted her chin a bit, then walked across the carpet to the end chair directly across from the CEO, resting her hands on the back of it and regarding them coolly.

"Sit down, Ms. Stuart," Alastair said courteously, his eyes regarding her with interest.

Kerry took the end chair—the one Dar usually sat in—and settled into it, folding her hands on the table and cocking her head in a listening stance.

She waited, patiently. Make them talk first, Dar had advised her. Let them lay their end on the line before you do.

Alastair cleared his throat. "Well. We've got quite a mess here."

"Yes, we do," Kerry agreed mildly. "I've done pretty much all I can, considering the circumstances."

"That's bullshit!" Steve stood up. "You haven't done squat except for screw things—"

"Shut up," Kerry snapped at him, "you clueless, spineless, worthless piece of wannabe macho pissant." She caught the motion of Alastair's gray eyebrow rising across the table, and she stood up, feeling the blood pump through her. "Ten thousand things are going wrong, and all you people can do is sit around and bitch about it. I haven't seen a more useless collection of idiots in my life—no wonder Dar is always cursing at you."

"Hey, you can't—" José stood and challenged her.

"Sure I can," Kerry responded hotly. "You people couldn't find your way out of a paper bag unless Dar wrote directions on the inside of it, and you've got the balls to be in here criticizing a situation that's your DAMN FAULT." Her voice rose to a yell, all the anger she'd been holding in for two days boiling out.

"We didn't ask her to quit!" José responded.

"Oh, but isn't that what you were after?" Kerry countered, leaning forward on her hands. "Or else why hire someone with the specific intent to go against her?" She pointed at Steve, who was seething at his side. "Someone who had written instructions from YOU—" She pointed at Jose—"To 'find that bitch's weak spot and put a knife into it.' Wasn't that the quote?"

Silence.

"Well. You got what you wanted," Kerry continued. "And now the problem is everyone knows the only thing that kept the damn company running was her. You sure can't." A long pause. "I know I can't. After one day, I can't imagine how in the hell she managed to put up with all this for so long."

José stared at Mariana, who was chewing on a pencil. "You're going to let her get away with that?"

The Personnel VP shrugged. "Ms. Stuart is speaking her mind. We claim to value that, as a company." She paused delicately. "In theory."

"That's just because you and Dar are thick as thieves," Eleanor cried. "No wonder we can't get anything done. God knows the four of you probably…"

"Excuse me," Alastair barked, an impressive volume of noise that set the glasses rattling.

Everyone looked at him in silence. "Thank you." He adjusted his tie. "I would like everyone to excuse themselves with the exception of Ms. Stuart." He paused. "Now."

In silence they filed out, avoiding Kerry's gaze with the exception of Mariana, who patted her shoulder as she passed.

The sound of the door closing behind them sounded unbelievably loud to Kerry, but she didn't react to it, instead sitting down and folding her hands on the table.

Alastair regarded her across the entire length of the conference table, then he stood up, and walked around to where she was, perching on the edge of the wooden surface and crossing his arms over his chest. "That was gross insubordination, Ms. Stuart," he remarked coolly.

"I know," Kerry replied, looking up at him. "I hear that runs in my department."

Alastair McLean had grayish blue eyes almost as striking as Dar's. Right now, they were regarding her with the faintest hint of…something. "Your former boss was not known for a being a team player."

Former. Kerry felt a little sad. "No, it's just that she refuses to play on a losing team," she replied. "I was given to understand you approved of that."

He nodded a little. "I have her position to fill, Ms. Stuart. You're smart, you're sharp; I think you'd do well in it."

Kerry gazed at him. "Respectfully, sir, I wouldn't work for someone who allowed someone like her leave without just cause. Regardless of the incentive."

He cocked his head. "I believe that's the most politely put 'kiss my ass' I've ever heard, Ms. Stuart," Alastair remarked. "So you don't want the job? It comes with a nice raise, good perks—a big advancement for someone your age and experience level."

The green eyes glinted dangerously. "I guess I didn't explain myself clearly." Kerry cleared her throat. "Kiss my ass. Sir."

The CEO rubbed his jaw, then got up off the desk and pulled the chair next to her out, sitting down in it so they were knee to knee. "You know, Ms. Stuart, when you first got brought on board, I thought Dar was nuts." He twiddled his fingers together. "I had no idea what she was up to, but I let her go ahead with it because I trust her judgment." He paused reflectively. "She's earned that trust."

Kerry remained quiet, merely watching his face intently.

"I've had to put up with her since she was twenty years old, and she's been a thorn the size of Texas in my side most of the time since then, but you know what, Ms. Stuart?"

"What?"

"When my balls are in a vise, she comes through every single time," Alastair informed her. "She's never let me down. Do you understand just how valuable that is for someone in my position?"

"I think so."

"Do you understand that I can't put a price on what that's worth to me personally, and to the company?"

Kerry gazed at him, chancing a hint of a smile. "Yes."

"You think you can get me an audience with her?" Now the blue-gray eyes took on the faintest hint of a twinkle.

The blond woman glanced down at the table, hiding a smile, then looked up. "Yes, I can do that," she answered softly. "She's at home."

Alastair smiled at her. "Good."

Kerry took a breath. "That was a test, wasn't it?" she hazarded warily. "Offering me her job?"

The eyes twinkled visibly now.

"Did I pass?"

"Like a champ," he replied, with a chuckle. "You've proven a true disciple of Dar, Ms. Stuart, so take it easy."

Kerry exhaled. "Sorry, it's been a really long day," she admitted as she got up and walked across to where a phone rested on a wall side credenza. "Hang on." She dialed a number, not surprised when it was picked up before it even rang once. "Hi."

"Hey." Dar's voice was worried. "Everything okay?"

"I think so," Kerry told her in a low voice. "Alastair wants to come see you."

"Ah." Her lover mulled this over. "Yeah, sure, why not?" she consented. "If you can bring him over then run dad back over to the mainland, give us a few minutes to duke it out."

"Gotcha." Kerry felt a quiet sense of relief flood over her. "See you in a few." She hung up and returned to the conference table. "I'll give you a ride over there if you want," she told the CEO.

"Best offer I've had all day," Alastair replied, cheerfully. "Let's go."

🐾 🐾 🐾

Dar put the phone down and glanced at her father. "Well. I guess I'd better go take a shower and put some clothes on; my boss is coming over."

Andrew put his hands behind his head and stretched out his body, stiff from a long afternoon of crocodile watching. "He all right?"

"More or less, yeah." Dar hoisted herself to her feet and moved towards her bedroom. "Be right back."

Her father scratched Chino's head and crossed his ankles. "Be careful, now, Dardar, don't be slipping up in there."

The dark-haired woman stopped, unseen, at the doorway and gazed at him with quiet affection. Then she shook her head and moved into the bathroom, stripped off her pajamas, and stepped into the shower. It felt great. She scrubbed her body and washed her hair, letting the water pressure ease some of the tension out of her.

Then she reluctantly shut the water off, and stepped out of the shower, grabbing one of the long, fluffy beach towels she kept in the bathroom for drying off. She wrapped it around her, then took a second and roughly dried her hair before she exited the bathroom.

What to wear. She considered, then shrugged and pulled on a polo shirt and a pair of jeans. "Gonna have to do."

"Hey, Dardar?" Her father called from the other room.

"Yeah?" She headed back to the living room, finding him near the sliding glass doors. "What's up?"

He turned. "You have a nice birthday last month?"

Dar walked over to him. "Yeah…." She nodded, hesitantly. "I did… Kerry made me a party here, and I…. It was nice."

Her father carefully examined the horizon. "Almost called you that night." He met her eyes briefly. "Sorry I didn't."

What a birthday present that would have been. "It's okay," Dar reassured him. "I'm just glad you did now."

Andrew seemed nervous all of a sudden. "Yeap, well…" He cleared his throat. "You still go out there?" He jerked his head toward the sea.

Dar nodded. "I stopped for a while," she admitted quietly. "But Kerry loves it; she got certified and we go out almost every weekend."

"Good fer her. She's a nice kid."

A soft chuckle. "She's got me back involved in a lot of things." The dark-haired woman sighed. "I was…considering getting back into competition."

Her father's eyes lit up. "Were ya?" He studied her seriously. "Looks like you could." He poked her experimentally. "Better than some of the pups they sent out with me the last time, I tell ya that."

Dar laughed, a touch embarrassed. "Yeah, I kept that up. You're responsible for that; I always thought you'd be disappointed if I hadn't."

Andrew remained silent for a moment, then he put a gentle hand on her arm. "Honey, I could never be disappointed with you." His voice was sincere. "Doesn't matter what you ended up doing, who you ended up being. You're my kid, and ain't nothing gonna ever change that."

Dar found herself unable to answer, and she swallowed a lump in her throat.

"'Nuff of that mush." Andrew cleared his throat. "You go back into that stuff, you let me know, hear?" He fumbled a white card from his pocket and handed it to her. "That'll get me."

A pager number. Dar smiled and tucked it into her shirt pocket. Then she walked over to her briefcase and removed one of her own cards. She scribbled the home phone at the condo on the back and handed it to him. "Fair's fair," she told him. "Give us a call sometimes."

He stared at the card, turning it over in his fingers. "Paladar, you did not exactly ever get around to telling me what you did for that company now." He gave Dar a look. "You are the Vice President of that thing?"

"I was." The past tense sounded strange. "I even had an office with a nice, big window."

Her father laughed softly. "They get you to dress up fancy?"

Dar laughed with him, a little sheepishly. "Yeah; I even wear heels," she admitted. "I kick them off under my desk, though." Self consciously, she stuck her hands in her pockets, remembering teenage arguments over torn jeans she knew her father was also recalling. "Wanna see pictures?" she asked hopefully, wanting to distract those twinkling eyes.

"Hell yes," Andrew responded immediately.

Dar went to the cabinet nearby and drew out the manila folder of pictures Kerry had gotten back from the New Year's Eve party. She pulled out the one Mark had taken of both of them and handed it over. "Proof."

Andrew took it and dipped his head to examine the image. A low, melodic whistle emerged from his lips. "Son of a gun. Wouldja look at that pair of gorgeous young ladies."

Dar scratched her ear, caught somewhere between extreme pleasure and extreme embarrassment.

"Would you mind if I took this and had a copy done?" Andrew asked. "They got a photo lab on the base now."

"You can have that one. We've got the negatives," Dar told him, happy he asked. She gave him an extra envelope that had come with the picture. "Kinda big, though."

Andrew very carefully put the image inside, and closed the top. "I appreciate that, squirt."

They both heard the sound of a car outside. "Guess that's them," Dar said regretfully. "Thanks for sticking around today."

"You can thank Kerry for that, was her idea," Andrew mumbled. "Well, I'll go round back and wait for her. You take care of yourself, you hear?"

Dar hugged him tightly. "I love you, daddy," she whispered. "I missed you."

He took a shaky breath, and patted her side. "Same here." He broke off and cleared his throat. "Be good." He gave her arm another pat, then slipped out the back door and into the darkness.

Dar watched until his shadow blended into the foliage, not turning until she heard footsteps outside the front door.

Kerry parked the Mustang and glanced at her passenger. Alastair had been looking around with great interest, and it gave her a chance to study him in return. He was in his sixties, of medium height and stocky build, with gray hair and intelligent eyes. He had a round face with a snub nose and thick eyebrows that moved her way as he turned to address her.

"Nice place." He'd chatted amiably about the area as they drove, avoiding any mention of work.

Kerry nodded. "Well, that's the condo, so…" She opened the door and got out, waiting for him to join her before she led the way down the walk and up the stairs. As she approached the door, she lifted her hand to knock, then hesitated and made the decision to let her fingers drop to the keypad instead, keying in her code and unlocking the door.

Alastair made no comment.

"After you." The blond woman opened the door and held it, gesturing with the other hand. A quick peek inside showed her Dar leaning casually against the back of the love seat, regarding them. There was no sign of Andrew, but she hadn't expected there to be. "Hi."

Dar's eyes flicked to hers, and she gave her a tiny wink. "Hi." Then her attention turned to Alastair. "Hello, Alastair; c'mon in."

Kerry lifted a hand and moved a step back. "Later."

Dar lifted a hand in response and watched the door close behind her lover before she turned her gaze on her boss.

They regarded each other in silence for a moment, then Dar exhaled and stood up. "Siddown. You want a drink?"

"I think I need one," Alastair replied dryly, as he took the invitation and settled on the couch, leaning back and glancing around. "Nice place, Dar."

The dark-haired woman nodded. "Thanks." She went over to the cabinet against the wall and took out a bottle, pulling the top off and pouring a portion of honey golden liquor into two glasses. She handed Alastair his before settling in the easy chair across from him.

He took a sip, eyebrows raising at the taste. "Very nice."

"Thought I remembered you liked scotch," Dar responded, taking a sip from her own glass. The smooth, twenty year-old single malt burned warmly on the way down, and she was glad she'd had a healthy sized lunch not long ago to buffer it.

"That I do," Alastair agreed, "that I do." He looked around. "You know, Dar, not that I spent a whole lot of time thinking about it, but I never pictured you in a place like this." His eyes fell on the spacescape. "High tech apartment in a high rise off Brickell, sure, but..."

Dar smiled briefly. "An aunt of mine willed it to me."

An awkward silence fell.

"So," Alastair said. "Where do we go from here, Dar?" He sipped his scotch and watched her over the rim of his glass. "I think you probably realize I've got someone real hefty sitting on that resignation request of yours."

"How flattering."

"Let's not bullshit each other." Alastair straightened. "We both know I consider you an essential part of my management team, and it would kill me to lose you. Especially over something as ridiculous as this." He waited, but she didn't comment. "So what really happened here, Dar? I've heard Mari's side, and José's side, and Eleanor's side, and I just don't get it. I thought you had a thicker skin than that."

Dar regarded him in silence for a moment, then she exhaled. "Good question." She shook her head. "It's gotten to the point where I've been attacked more by my own company than any of our competitors, and maybe I started to wonder what in the hell I was doing here."

Alastair thought about that, sipping his drink slowly. "You're a high profile kinda gal, Dar; you've always attracted slings and arrows, you know that. Was this guy really that much of a needle in your shorts?"

A shrug. "Maybe because it was personal, not professional, maybe because I knew a colleague had brought him in deliberately to attack me..." She shifted the glass in her hands. "But I think I could have dealt with that."

Alastair nodded twice. "But?"

"But he went after my people," Dar concluded. "And I'd just had enough." She looked up at Alastair. "I'd had enough of being the whore bitch from hell until you needed something."

Alastair leaned forward. "Dar, the fact that most of the operation is at a complete standstill and I have over fifty empty desks should tell you not everyone feels that way," he replied gravely. "And I think you know that I don't feel that way either, or I wouldn't be sitting here right now. I'd be at home in Houston watching a ball game considering who I was going to promote to VP Ops."

Dar cleared her throat a little. "I should have called you first," she conceded. "I owed you that."

A tiny smile crossed Alastair's face. "An apology from Dar Roberts? Thank god I'm sitting down," he kidded her. "I think that's a first."

"Probably," Dar acknowledged. "I don't know, Alastair. It's just been building and building lately, or maybe I've just become more sensitive to it."

Shrewd eyes studied her. "Could be that once you open up part of your life to something new, it's hard to keep everything around you from being affected."

A faint shrug. "Maybe."

Alastair leaned forward. "Do you really want out, Paladar?" he asked her seriously. "If you do, I'll slit my wrists, but you'll get the best parachute I can staple together for you."

Dar pondered that. Finally, she exhaled. "I can't keep doing business the way I have been," she told him. "I'm not going to fight an uphill battle for everything up to and including the toilet paper changing frequency anymore. I can't do it."

"I'm not sure you should have to," Alastair replied. "We believe in a peer system, Dar, but when you have a group of very strong minded peers, like we do here, sometimes that gets out of hand and creates more gridlock than it solves problems."

A tilt of her head. "Interesting perspective."

"From my perspective right now, I'd say you've been holding this end of the operation together with a bucket of guts and your own willpower. True?"

Dar shrugged. "What choice did I have? Someone had to force things to happen, and I yell the loudest."

"Right, except that if you have to divert that willpower to some other object, say, a significant other, you start resenting that need to yell, don't you?"

A sigh. "Yeah."

"And you start resenting having to spend twenty hours a day at the office, and working Saturdays, and pulling everyone's cojones out of the fire eight days out of seven. Right?"

Dar gave him a look. "Yeah."

"So, that's why you got in that room, got hit with a boatload of BS, and decided to chuck it all."

"Could be." A wry smile tugged at Dar's lips. "I guess that's why they pay you the big bucks, huh?"

"Honey, I've been there, and done that. I've got thirty years on you, remember?" Alastair reminded her. "What I had to do was find some-one who I could trust, and let them take half the load." A smile. "And that's what you did, too, which was great idea, except…"

"Except the solution was the cause of the problem," Dar finished, meeting his eyes.

Her boss nodded slowly, then inhaled. "Dar, I'm going to ask you a question, just between you and I, and I want you to tell me the truth. I don't care what it is, all right?"

She nodded.

"When you hired Kerrison Stuart, was it because you two were romantically involved?"

"No." Dar answered easily and immediately. "And on a conscious level, I have to tell you it was strictly a matter of acquiring someone who my gut instinct was telling me would be good for the company."

Alastair looked relieved. "That's what I thought. And you two just clicked, and it went on from there."

"Yes."

"She's a sharp cookie," her boss admitted. "Based on what I've heard from other people, and what I saw today, I think you made the right decision."

Dar smiled.

"As usual," Alastair complimented her graciously.

They were both quiet for a moment. "Dar." The older man paused to collect his thoughts. "For a lot of totally selfish reasons, I don't want to lose you." He studied her. "If I can fix it so that the gridlock gets better, are you willing to remain my employee?"

Dar considered the request. "Will you leave Kerry where she is?"

A sly twinkle. "She'll either remain at, or exceed, the position she's in currently, yes. I don't generally go around breaking things that work—there are enough broken things for me to worry about."

"Okay."

A hiked eyebrow. "That's your only condition?"

Dar nodded. "Oh…well, there's one other small thing." A faint smile appeared. "José's little bastard."

Alastair laughed. "Saw that coming." He leaned back, obviously relieved. "My problem is, I need a way to bounce him legitimately. Otherwise, the little bastard is going to sue for wrongful dismissal, and I don't want the publicity."

A slow, sexy smile crossed Dar's face. "I'll give that to you…if you let me be the one to ax him." Her eyes glinted dangerously. "Absolutely legit."

Alastair nibbled his lip. "It's going to be a rocky few weeks; there's a lot of hard feelings in there. But I have a lot of confidence in you. I'm not worried." He finished off his scotch. "Now, onto more pleasant subjects. You free for dinner? I hate to waste an opportunity. I hardly ever get to see you."

Dar's lips twitched. "Actually, I had plans, but you're welcome to join us," she said blandly. "There's a great little Italian place over on the other side of the island, and it's casual."

His eyes twinkled a little. "Well, I did enjoy my conversation with the enigmatic Ms. Stuart…sure she won't mind?"

Dar was outraged to find herself blushing, and she was glad the fading twilight hid it. "I'm sure she'll be fine." She got up and went towards the kitchen. "In fact, let me page her."

"She could have stayed…I wouldn't have cared," Alastair remarked. "After all, she lives here, doesn't she?"

Dar chuckled as she put the phone to her ear.

🐃🐃   🐃🐃   🐃🐃

"Hope things go okay." Kerry put her Mustang in park as the ferry got under way. "I don't want to repeat the day I had today."

Andrew grunted. "Feller flew all the way here from Texas, I'd guess he's got something on his mind he wants to say."

They exchanged shy glances. "Whatcha got there?" Kerry nodded at the envelope curiously.

"Picture of two real pretty ladies at a party," Andrew drawled.

Kerry thought, then blushed slightly. "From New Year's?"

"Yes, ma'am," he assured her cheerfully.

"Eek." Kerry grinned wearily, and let her head rest against the seat back. "My scary green dress? God, the trouble that caused."

Andrew cocked his head at her. "You catch a chill in it?"

She laughed. "No; Dar really likes it, and w…" Kerry cleared her throat. "Um, I mean, it um, kinda started people talking—again." A pause. "I don't know why, it's not like we even talked to each other all night. I really wanted to dance with her, too." A sigh.

"Kumquat, you don't have to chit chat with my kid; your eyes tell the whole tale just fine," Andrew informed her.

Kerry turned her head. "What did you call me?" she asked, incredulously. "Is that one of those Navy things?"

"Naw," Andrew chuckled. "It's a…well, it's a bitty orange, grows wild round here; real pretty color, smells nice, but it's tart inside. Shocks the daylights out of you."

Kerry's nostrils flared, as she sorted through the explanation, trying to figure out if it was a compliment or an insult. "Um, okay…"

"Favorites of mine," he amended.

"Phew." Kerry muffled a nervous giggle. "I was hoping you weren't calling me a little tart fruit."

"Tch."

They exchanged glances, then started laughing.

The ferry docked, and Kerry put the Mustang into gear. "Where to?" She steered up the ramp and across the salmon cobblestones.

Andrew considered the question. "There's a spot near the beach, 'bout ten minutes north. You can leave me off there."

Kerry simply looked at him. "You're not going to tell me you sleep on the beach, are you?"

"Sometimes," Dar's father muttered. "Depends. I like the stars at night over me." He glanced at Kerry. "I got a bed to sleep in, don't get yer feathers all ruffled." He shifted. "Just got a lot to think about tonight. Rather do that without a bunch of noise."

Kerry put the car into gear and turned onto the causeway, heading out towards the beach. "I understand. When I want to think, I go out to the beach too," she told him. "So does Dar."

Andrew nodded. "I know that; it's where I first caught sight of her couple months back, just sitting out there, looking at the stars." He plucked at the seam running down the leg of his denims. "Knew her right off."

"You didn't go over to her, though." There was no judgement in Kerry's tone, only curiosity.

"No, I…" His lips tightened. "I was still pretty messed up, thought it was better just to…" He never finished the statement, just looked outside the window at the passing lights.

"Why now?"

For a long time, she got no answer, and they drove in silence through the night. Kerry didn't push the issue, she just navigated the busy streets through Miami Beach, heading down to the spot he'd mentioned. It was a nice night out, only one or two fluffy clouds obscuring the stars, and a cool breeze was coming in from the northwest.

She pulled into the small parking lot next to the public access beach and stopped the car, opening the windows and turning the engine off. Immediately, the sound of rustling palm fronds drifted in, with muted traffic noises and the rhythmic hiss and rush of the surf. The air was tinged with salt and the smokey scent of a barbeque in progress, that made Kerry's stomach growl as she remembered forgetting lunch.

Her cell phone rang, making her jump. "Hello?"

"Where are you?" Dar's voice answered, a warm note evident in its tone.

"Off Southpointe park… is everything okay?" She caught Andrew's head turn as he listened.

"Yep."

Kerry gave her passenger a thumbs up. "Great…are you still working for us?"

"Yep."

Kerry's nose wrinkled into a grin. "Still my boss?"

"Yep."

She did a little dance in her seat. "I knew you'd work it out. Boy, am I ever glad." She winked at Andrew, who smiled back at her. "I told your dad, too."

"C'mon back; Alastair's going to have dinner with us." Dar told her. "Give dad a hug for me."

"If I can get away with it, sure," Kerry told her. "Be over in a minute." She hung up and folded the phone into her pocket. "Everything's fine."

"Good to hear." Andrew looked relieved. He opened the door and started to get out, then hesitated. "Thanks for the ride, Kerry."

She got out on her side and circled around the car, meeting him as he stood up uncertainly. "Please don't be a stranger." Their eyes met. "Whatever your reasons were, I'm really glad you decided to call. That was a pretty big hole in Dar's life you just filled back in."

He gazed at her. "Didn't have a choice." The words seemed to come out only reluctantly. "I just couldn't go another day without seeing my kid." He studied his sneakers, as a hand lifted and touched his chest. "She's a pretty big piece of me."

Kerry thought about asking permission, then just decided to go for it. She stepped forward and put her arms around Dar's father, who at first stiffened in wary surprise, then relaxed and somewhat awkwardly returned the embrace. He was much bigger than Dar was, but, she found, he had the same solid feel to him, and she gave him an extra squeeze before she released her hold and stepped back. "Thanks, Mr. Roberts."

"Hey." A blue eye cocked at her in the dim light. "Ain't no such person."

"Excuse me?" Kerry replied, uncertainly.

"There's a Commander Roberts, Andy, or shithead, take yer pick, but there ain't no Mister Roberts," Andrew informed her.

Kerry gazed at him in the dim streetlight. "Would you mind very much if I called you dad?"

Dar's father regarded her in surprise. "Why would you want t'do something like that?"

Good question. Kerry gazed at the sidewalk, then lifted her head. "'Cause I think you're a really good one."

The shadowed face shifted, visible even inside the hood. "Decided that already, have ya?"

"No." Kerry shook her head. "I decided that a long time ago, just listening to Dar talk about you." She took a breath. "I'm a little jealous of her over that."

Somehow, she got the impression that Andrew was blushing, even though she had no way to confirm it. He made a small sound, perhaps clearing his throat before he answered. "You go ahead and call me that if you want, Kerry."

She smiled warmly at him. "Thanks, Dad." Impulsively, she reached over and squeezed his hand, then backed off.

He closed the car door and tucked his picture under one arm. "You take care, all right kumquat?" A hand reached out and patted her shoulder as he started off towards the waiting sand.

"All right," Kerry whispered, watching him for a moment. "You too."

Dar looked at her watch as they entered the condo. "Jesus, it's past midnight," she remarked in surprise. "Didn't think it was that late."

"Uh huh." Kerry yawned, trudging inside and collapsing on the couch. "That was a nice dinner, though. He's sort of an interesting person." She picked up Chino, who had bolted out of the utility room when Dar opened the door. "Hey honey. Whoa, whoa! Don't chew up mommy's fingers, okay?"

Dar came back in with two tall glasses of chocolate milk, one of which she set down on the table. "Here." She eased down on the couch next to her lover and slid back, extending her legs out and groaning. "Too much pasta."

"I don't think so. I told you not to have that second gelato," Kerry reminded her, with a poke. "How about a few minutes in the hot tub?"

Blue eyes turned to her and brightened. "Now that's a great idea. It's a beautiful night out... c'mon." She allowed Kerry to support her as they wandered into the bedroom to exchange jeans for bathing suits.

"I like that one on you." Dar snuck up behind Kerry and slid both arms around her middle, hugging her gently. "It's the color of your eyes." Kerry's suit, a shimmering, almost translucent teal, glittered in the low light, accented her toned body.

Kerry leaned back against her and folded her arms over Dar's. "Thanks."

They went outside, taking their glasses with them, and Kerry held them both as Dar eased into the water.

"Ungh." The dark-haired woman stretched her arms out and took the milk. "This feels great." She watched as Kerry joined her, nestling up against her immediately. "I'll put these down."

For a few minutes they just sat there, absorbing the sensation of the water, a mist of warm, chlorinated water wafting across their faces. The ocean was at high tide and beating against the seawall, and off in the distance they could hear the buoy bells ringing on the inshore wind.

"It's beautiful out here," Kerry murmured, tipping her head back and regarding the starry sky, scattered with the odd, occasionally puffy cloud.

Dar turned her head and regarded the moonlit profile next to her. "It sure is."

Kerry caught the glance and smiled a little, blushing lightly. "So." She cleared her throat. "Everything worked out okay, huh?"

"Mmm." Dar wiggled her toes contentedly. "Alastair asked me to reconsider, I told him I had two conditions, he met them, presto. That was it." She stifled a yawn. "You were one condition, Steve was the other."

Kerry mulled that over. "So, did he know about us, or…"

"He knew," Dar chuckled softly. "He said he knew when he saw those first sets of pictures from Orlando, but he was content to let that fall in the background."

"Isn't that a problem?" Kerry queried. "I mean, we've been doing this cat and mouse thing for months because it was this big rule, so…?"

Dar shrugged. "It comes down to what's more important—company rules, or profits? He can make exceptions, and yes, it's a problem, but it's not like it's never happened before, Kerry, and what the rule is for is mostly to protect the junior of the two employees."

"Protect?" Kerry cocked her head. "Oh, from harassment, that kind of thing?"

A nod. "Exactly. It's so bosses don't take advantage of their subordinates, and it's a good rule." She reached over and brushed a droplet of water off Kerry's cheek. "But I told him I needed you, and he's satisfied you're not being pressured or coerced in any way, so he's going to just work around it."

"Oh." Kerry thought about that. "Awesome." She kissed Dar's shoulder. "So I can bring you lunch and not feel guilty, right?"

Pale blue eyes shifted her way. "So I can wander down the back corridor a couple times a day and not feel conspicuous," Dar replied dryly. "I mean, it's just like anything else: we treat each other professionally at the office, we just don't have to worry about people finding out what we do outside of it."

"Hmm." Kerry nodded a little. "So can I call the rest of the staff and tell them to come back in tomorrow?" she asked, wistfully. "Because I don't think I can handle any more days like today was."

Dar smiled. "I'll call 'em in the morning." She rested her head against the blond woman's. "They're a loyal bunch."

"With good reason." Kerry smiled back. "We love our boss."

The taller woman exhaled gently, and let her head rest back against the tub's wall. "What a day." Her mind lingered over the earlier part of it, absorbing the wonder. "Did Dad say anything to you when you let him off?" She tasted the words with uncommon pleasure.

"A few things," Kerry murmured. "He's such a sweetie. I can see why you're so crazy about him."

Dar tilted her head. "My daddy," she breathed in amazement. "I'm glad you like him. I hope he's not going to just…vanish again. I mean, just knowing he's out there is great, but…"

"I don't think so, Dar," Kerry answered slowly. "He said the reason he contacted you is because he couldn't stand not seeing you for one more minute."

A smile tugged at Dar's lips. "He told you that? Really?"

'Yes, he did," Kerry assured her. "I don't think he's going to disappear again, and besides, he said I could call him Dad." She grinned. "That is so cool."

Dar hugged her. "I knew he would if you asked him that. He's always loved kids." She told her partner. "I think he'd have liked more, but I guess after me, they figured one was more than enough." She exhaled. "I wish he'd call my mother, though."

Kerry stroked her. "Give it a little time, Dar. It took him time to contact you, remember?" She smiled. "I have a feeling it'll all work out."

"Good." Dar ducked her head again and found Kerry's wandering lips, and she pulled her over onto her lap, sliding an arm around the blond woman's waist securely. She felt Kerry's hands glide down her shoulders, and her eyes closed in reflex as their bodies pressed against each other in knowing familiarity.

They'd deal with all that trouble tomorrow. That was another day. Right now, all that mattered was the rich, night breeze, and the stars, and each other.

🐾   🐾   🐾

Kerry stifled a yawn as she trudged across the kitchen, headed for the coffee machine. She mechanically portioned the Irish cream grounds into the basket and started the coffee going, blinking drowsily as she leaned against the counter.

She could hear Dar's voice as a low murmur coming from her office, and she guessed her lover was making the promised phone calls to their stubbornly missing staff. "Any luck?" she called in, as she heard the phone disconnect.

"Oh yeah." Dar moved to the doorway of the office, stretching and catching the edges of the sill with her fingers as she rocked her head back and forth to loosen her neck muscles. "I got Mark; he cursed me out because he was planning on working over one of his bikes, but he said he'd be in and that he'd call the rest of his staff so I didn't have to do it." The dark-haired women released the door and walked across to where Kerry was standing. "Now I have to do the tough one: Maria."

"Ouch." Kerry slid a hand up Dar's belly, feeling the warmth of her skin under the fabric. "She was sooo pissed off, Dar. You should have heard what she called José."

"That Latin temper," Dar acknowledged, laughing. "I bet she could kick his butt, too." She moved past the blond-haired woman and into the kitchen, retrieving a bowl and her Frosted Flakes from the cabinet. "Want some?"

A sigh. "Dar, do you think you could make me feel better by at least putting a little banana in that?" Kerry asked, mournfully. "And no thanks. They crunch too loud and hurt my ears this early in the morning." She bumped Dar out of the way and opened the refrigerator, snagging a fruit and cheese danish from a neatly packed box. "I prefer a quieter, gentler breakfast. I'm going to go grab a shower, okay?"

Dar grinned, munching away noisily, and pressed a key on the kitchen console.

"Dar Roberts, 656 new messages, 234 Urgent," the computer responded promptly.

"Oh, Jesus." Dar almost inhaled a flake. "Delete all unmarked," she instructed the computer. "Forget it. They can resend the damn things."

"Deleted. Dar Roberts, 234 new messages, 234 Urgent."

"Delete all messages, duplicate subjects that also have same sender." She glanced at Kerry, who was chewing her Danish filling two large mugs. "That should get rid of half of those."

"Deleted. Dar Roberts 155 new messages, 155 Urgent."

"I'll read them when I get in," Dar decided, closing the program and wandering over to the window.

She had, she realized, mixed feelings about going back to work. Part of her was glad, needing the excitement and the challenge, but there was another part, a guilty, hidden part that had been secretly hoping the resignation would stick so that she and Kerry could then take a few weeks off and just....

Dar's eyes found the horizon. She'd found herself wanting very much to take time out and spend it getting to know her lover better, take her places Dar liked—maybe even out skiing, down to Key West— all the things they didn't have time to do now.

She sighed and nibbled her lip. Well, one good thing: if Alastair knew about them, and they decided to take off the same week, it would be all right. *In fact*, she decided, *that's exactly what we're going to do.* She straightened and went back inside. *Pick a week, and take off. To hell with the company.* She sighed heavily and headed for her own shower.

Where she heard the sound of water running as she entered her bedroom, and spotted the naked, patiently waiting figure leaning against the door, arms crossed, darkened green eyes watching her with seductive intent.

Oh yeah. Dar sucked in a breath as a sensual jolt hit her right in the groin. *Absolutely to hell with the company.* "Well, well. What do we have here?" she inquired playfully, moving closer and sweeping her eyes across the lithe body in front of her. Kerry's appearance had changed quite a bit since she'd met her five months earlier. Her indoor pallor had deepened into a golden tan, and the painful thinness had disappeared. Dar had always found her attractive, but the changes had also brought Kerry a new self-confidence that seemed to glow inside her, rendering her almost mesmerizing in Dar's appreciative eyes.

"Gotta make sure you don't slip and fall in the shower, Dar," Kerry informed her cheerfully, reaching up and unbuttoning the top button on her shirt. "I just got my boss back. I don't want to lose her again." She unbuttoned the second button. "Do you mind sharing a shower?"

"Heh." Dar slid both hands down her sides, and traced the now barely visible ribs with gentle thumbs. "Oh, I think I could suffer through that all right." She ducked her head and kissed her. "Somehow."

Kerry unbuttoned the third and fourth button, sliding the shirt up and over Dar's shoulders and letting it fall to the ground. Then she traced a gentle pattern down the tall body and got to the shorts, sliding those down as well. "I bet you could." She nibbled the soft skin over Dar's jugular and stepped forward, brushing their bodies together. "You taste so good," she murmured.

Dar felt her heart jerk, and start pounding. "Do I?" She moved closer and slipped her arms around Kerry, feeling her shoulderblades move as she reciprocated and the warmth of the contact between them surged. She ducked her head and captured an ear, tracing its curve with the tip of her tongue. "So do you," she purred, hearing the sharp intake of air as Kerry's breathing caught.

Slowly, they moved into the shower, trading the chill air for warm mist, and the spicy scent of Dar's favorite soap flowed around them.

Dar squeezed a little of the gel onto her hands and began to lather Kerry's back, moving her fingers over the strong shoulders and down across her hips.

A soft sound escaped the blond woman, who had started spreading soap down Dar's sides. She pushed away a little, allowing the taller woman's hands to continue their motion up her belly as she let her fingers trail down along Dar's thighs. "My pastor always taught me that cleanliness is next to godliness," she murmured, moving back against Dar's soapy body.

"Oh yeah?" Dar inclined her head and nipped the skin on Kerry's shoulder.

"Mm…I gotta send him a card sometime and let him know how right he was," Kerry uttered, starting a slow, tantalizing progression right down the center of Dar's body, with a few east and west detours.

Dar just chuckled.

Chapter 14

Kerry unfolded the paper that had been resting on their porch and set it on her knees to study it as Dar drove onto the ferry. "Cajun Festival's next weekend; you interested?"

"Why yes, my spicy little mud bug," Dar drawled, giving her a tickle along her ribs. "Let's see if Mari and Duks want to go."

"Okay," Kerry agreed amiably, ignoring the sports section and checking the business headlines. She blinked, then looked closer at one. "Hey, Dar? What's a CIO?"

"Chief Information Officer," Dar replied promptly. "A member of a company's board of directors who's responsible for IS direction and implementation, that sort of thing. Why?"

"ILS doesn't have one?"

"No. Alastair's been waffling on that since his last one left four years ago," Dar replied. "I didn't care because it removed a layer of management I had to deal with."

"Oh. Well, we have one now," Kerry informed her. "Named this morning."

"No kidding?" Dar was shocked. "You'd have thought he'd… guess he's hedging his bets. Who'd he name?"

"You."

Dead silence.

"Excuse me?" Dar turned all the way around in the seat and stared at her.

Kerry held up the business section, which featured a large picture with very familiar blue eyes staring right back at her. "Way to go!" She muffled a laugh at the look of utter shock on Dar's face. "Nice picture, too."

"I'm…" Dar cleared her throat, as the word came out in a squeak. "I'm gonna kill him." She scrambled for her cell phone. "Oh, I'm gonna kill him. I'm gonna book the first goddamned flight to Houston and beat him to death with his own necktie…"

"Dar, Dar, Dar." Kerry grabbed the phone. "It's six a.m. in Houston. He's probably still sleeping. Besides, I thought the reaction to a promotion is supposed to be 'thank you,' not 'I'm going to kill you.'"

"That son of a bitch." Dar fumed. "How in the hell can he have done that without goddamned telling me!?" She was ridiculously indignant. "He said nothing would ch…" A pause. "Wait a minute…. So that's what he meant."

Kerry lifted her brows in question.

"I asked him if you were going to be left in your position, and he said you'd maintain or exceed it, at the very least. Damn him. He knows he can do it because he's finally got someone who can take my position in Ops."

"Who's that?" Kerry inquired.

Dar looked at her.

"Oh, no. No no no." Kerry waved a hand. "No no. Oh, no, Dar. I can't do your job. No, no. I tried that the last few days. No no. Not me. Uh uh."

"You could do it," Dar disagreed, folding her arms.

"Dar, no, I can't." Kerry shook her head.

They studied each other as the ferry's engines shifted for the turn to the mainland. "Guess I'll have to turn him down then," Dar remarked. "Because there's no one else I'd trust to replace me."

"That's not fair."

A shrug. "Life isn't, sometimes." Dar watched her a moment more, then dropped her eyes. "Would you at least think about it?"

"Dar." Kerry knew what would happen next, and sure enough, before she could turn away, the gently entreating blue eyes had captured her, tugging at her heartstrings irresistibly. "Dar, I've been fighting for years to get out from under my father's shadow."

"And? Won't this achieve that, Kerry? This is all by your own efforts," Dar protested.

Kerry sighed unhappily. "If you promote me, there's not going to be anyone who won't believe it's because we're lovers."

"Bullshit," Dar snapped immediately, starting the SUV's engine. "You've been here long enough for everyone to know how good you are."

Had she? Kerry folded her hands. "Well. Let me think about it," she answered softly. "No promises."

Dar reached over and patted her knee. "I'm still going to kill him."

Kerry poked her lip out and scowled. "Me too."

Dar smiled. "Well, let me give Maria a call, see what's going on." She dialed the office number.

"Good Morning, Operations, Maria is speaking," the voice came back, a tad more official than usual, given that it was eight o' clock in the morning.

"Morning, Maria," Dar drawled.

"AEEEIIII!" the secretary squealed, startling Kerry, who jumped. "Dar! Dios Mío! You are higher than el presidente now!"

"Well, yeah, sort of," Dar laughed. "Take it easy, Maria; I haven't accepted the damn job yet."

"Oye, Dar, have you seen the paper this morning?" Maria inquired.

"What paper?" Dar asked, innocently.

"You mean the one with her picture in it?" Kerry interrupted helpfully.

Maria laughed. "Sí, si. Mark has put the picture into the computer, and we all have it as our screens."

"What!?" Dar barked.

"Oh, that's wild." Kerry chortled. "Did he get it on mine?"

"Don't you start in," Dar warned her, shaking a finger. "Maria, you tell him I want that off the desktops by the time I get in there, or he'll be wearing one of those monitors."

"Aww, c'mon, Dar," Kerry objected. "I think it's great."

"It's not your picture, is it now?" her boss shot back. "Maria, get Mark on the phone."

"Dar…" Kerry turned gently pleading eyes on her. "I wanna see it. I bet he did a great job; it was a fantastic picture of you."

"Absolu…" Dar felt herself melting at the sight of those beseeching orbs, and sighed. "All right, just until we get there. But then, OFF IT GOES!"

🐾　🐾　🐾

It was a very weird experience. Kerry paced quietly alongside Dar. Usually they split up when they entered the building, but today…no. Today she kept her head up and regarded the people around them, knowing they were without a doubt the center of attention.

"Morning, Ms. Roberts, Ms. Stuart," the guard greeted them, giving Kerry a wink.

They got on the elevator, and the conversation cut off as though the other riders had suddenly contracted acute, spontaneous laryngitis.

It was deafening. "So." Dar finally said, making everyone jump. "How's the weather been here?"

"Fine"

"Great"

"Warm"

"Raining"

"Lousy"

Dar nodded. "I see." She leaned back against the wall as the elevator seemed to take forever in its upward motion. "Good to hear."

Fortunately, the doors slid open, allowing them to escape. "Thanks," Dar commented wryly, as they scooted out, leaving her and Kerry to continue up another two floors. "Think I was the topic of conversation before we got on?"

"Gee, you think?" Kerry cracked as the doors opened and they got out. "Wait. I'll go down to the cafeteria for coffee and see how fast a hush falls over that room, despite the fact that most of the conversation is in Spanish, and I know about six words of it," she remarked wryly. "You want some?"

"Oh, god yes," Dar murmured pathetically, as they reached the outer door to her office. "And all the cheese pastalitos they have." She pushed the door open and smiled at Maria. "Morning."

The secretary beamed at her. "Buenos Dios, jefa." She waggled her fingers at Kerry. "Buenos Dias, Kerrisita."

"Any mail?" Dar crossed to the desk, shifting the strap on her briefcase a little. "I was expecting the new batch of contracts in." She reached down to pick up the stack in the inbox when her hand was captured.

"Mi Madre." Maria's eyes widened. "Dar, that is so beautiful."

The executive found herself suddenly speechless as her brain frantically rooted around for some kind of coherent response. She'd forgotten she was wearing the damn thing, and on "that" finger, and that surely someone would eventually notice.

"Um…thanks," she finally replied, taking her hand back and flexing the fingers a touch nervously. "Listen, I'll be inside trying to catch up." She clutched her papers and headed for her office, ducking inside the door and closing it behind her with a sigh.

Then she looked up, stopping short as she caught sight of her desk. "Holy shit."

Kerry felt herself blushing as Maria gave her a knowing smile. "Um. I think I'd better go get some work done." She cleared her throat. "I'm going to, uh, get some coffee; you want any?" she asked, rubbing the side of her face and feeling the heat against her fingertips.

Maria walked over, and took her hands. "Kerrisita."

Sea green eyes peeked at her uncertainly. "Yes?"

"You have been such a gift to her," Maria told her softly. "God bless you."

Kerry dropped her eyes and felt her blush intensify, almost making her lightheaded. She sucked in a few breaths and finally looked back up. "Thanks," she choked out. "I think this feeling is God's greatest gift to anyone," she managed. "I'm glad I was in the right place at the right time."

"Sí." Maria smiled at her. "It is a wonderful thing."

Kerry kept that warmth with her as she ducked outside and got in to the elevator. She put her hands behind her back as she leaned on the wall, gazing with total lack of interest at the buff weave on the inside of the elevator. It would be weird day, she knew, and as if to confirm that, the elevator stopped on the ninth floor and two of the marketing secretaries got on. Their chatter stopped the minute they saw her, and they lapsed into silence.

I could get tired of this real quick, Kerry decided. "Hi."

They exchanged glances. "Oh, hi, Kerry," the older one said, a fake smile plastered across her face. "So how's things?"

"Great," the blond woman replied. "How about you?"

"Oh, great, great." She turned to her companion. "Right?"

The shorter of the two women nodded. "Yep, everything's terrific."

An awkward silence fell. Fortunately, the elevator reached the bottom floor, and they could all escape. Kerry headed off towards the cafeteria, shaking her head a little. At the entrance, she almost collided with Mark, who was just coming out. "Oh, hey."

"Hey!" Mark gave her a big grin. "Great, that means the big kahuna's here too, right?"

Kerry muffled a smile. "If you mean Dar, yes, she's upstairs; we just got here." It was so nice just to have someone be normal, she reflected. "Just trying to get things settled down. It's a little wild today."

"Uh huh." Mark sipped his coffee, regarding her. "Word's out about you guys," he added, lowering his voice quite a bit.

Kerry picked up a napkin, looking around and seeing the eyes dart off of her. "I figured," she replied. "After that whole thing with Steve, I knew he'd spread that around." She exhaled. "We'd pretty much decided to just be open about it anyway... after all, Alastair doesn't care."

"Mm," Mark grunted. "Kinda rough on you, though, isn't it?" He gave her a sympathetic look. "People assume shit."

"They can bite me," Kerry responded. "They assumed all kinds of things anyway, Mark. The hell with them." She glanced up as her order arrived. "Thank you." She reached out and took the bag. "Let me get back upstairs. I know it's going to be a zoo today."

Mark touched her hand, giving her a hesitant grin. "Nice ring ya got there."

Kerry paused, flexing her fingers a little. "Thanks. Yeah, um..." She felt herself blush. "Dar gave it to me."

"She's got good taste." The MIS chief admired it a moment longer. "But then, we kinda knew that." He winked at her, chuckling as her blush deepened. "Listen, don't let all the crap bother you, Kerry. You do a great job, and most everyone knows that. A lot of the shit's just jealousy. There're people that have wanted to get inside that office and, you'll excuse the disgusting comment, inside Dar's skirt for years." He shrugged. "It drives 'em nuts that you just walked in here, and shazam—" He snapped his fingers. "You got the job, the perks, and the hottest VP this company ever had all in one bigass fell swoop."

Kerry took the cover off her coffee and took a swallow. "Thanks, Mark. I know it's kinda hard to believe; in fact, sometimes I find it kinda hard to believe myself. It's like magic, you know?" She glanced up at him. "I feel like a little kid at the circus."

He gazed at her, a little disconcerted. "I don't know; that's kinda beyond me, Kerry. I don't know about a lot of that stuff, but I do know Dar's been through a lot of shit, and if she finally found someone she really likes, fuck the company, you know?"

That got a smile from the blond woman. "Yeah, I do know," she agreed quietly. "We'll work it out; it's just going to take some time for everything to settle down again." She leaned forward, changing the subject firmly. "Did you really put her picture up on everyone's desktop?"

He grinned. "You friggin' betcha." He stood and motioned for her to precede him. "C'mon. I've been hiding 'cause I know she's gonna kick my ass when she sees it, but it was too good a shot to pass up."

Kerry laughed, and held the door for him. "Oh yeah, she was having a fit, but I convinced her to leave it until we got in because I wanted to see it."

They walked outside and almost crashed into Eleanor and José, who were entering. Both executives backed up and gave them dirty looks. "Good morning." Kerry smiled at them.

"Good morning," José replied gruffly, circling her as though she were some kind of dangerous animal. Eleanor followed him without a word.

Kerry and Mark exchanged looks. "Ooo." The MIS manager winced. "Gonna be some meeting this morning."

Yeah. Kerry watched the reactions as they got back into the elevator, and noticed a subtle, but distinct edging away from her. *Is there such thing as a scarlet L? Or do they think it's contagious?* She leaned back, trying to wash the thought out of her mind.

"Hey, Kerry."

She looked up, to see Elaine, one of the data entry supervisors actually coming closer to her. "Morning."

"I hear you guys did a kick ass job up in NC; way cool," Elaine enthused with a grin. "You going to meet with the climbing group Wednesday?"

Kerry smiled, relaxing a little. "Yes, I think so." She gave Elaine a grateful look. "I missed going this past week. Be nice to get back to it." Her eyes moved to where they were getting a disgusted look from one of the administrative assistants. "Do you have a problem?" she asked the woman directly.

Only the squeak of the elevator was heard for a long moment.

Kerry held the woman's gaze, her own unamused and stony. "You can say 'yes, ma'am' or 'no ma'am,' take your pick," she added icily.

The woman sucked in a breath. "No, ma'am, I have no problem."

The doors slid open on the eight floor and the two younger women escaped hastily. Kerry settled back against the wall and sighed. "Jerks."

Elaine rolled her eyes. "'Phobes." She shook her head, then glanced at Kerry. "Don't let them get to you."

Them. Kerry considered, as the elevator went to the fifteenth floor. "So it's us and them," she ruminated. "Are there a lot of us?" she asked Elaine curiously.

An enigmatic smile crossed the tall blond's face. "I'll send you an e-mail," she promised as the doors slid open. "You'd be surprised."

Kerry watched Elaine and Mark saunter off down the hall. "Would I?" She shook her head and trotted towards Dar's office, opening the outer door and slipping in. "Hi Maria, I'm back." The secretary glanced over and smiled at her. "I got you some coffee."

"Muchas gracias, Kerrisita." She pointed at the door. "I think la jefa is still in the shock; you better go see."

Puzzled, Kerry set down Maria's little cup of cafecito, then took her bag and entered Dar's office.

The scent of roses almost bowled her over. "Jesus." She blinked, trying to find her lover behind a huge arrangement of three colors of the flowers, which dwarfed her desktop. "Hello? Dar? Do I need to go get a machete?"

Blue eyes peeked out from behind a creamy, peach-colored rose. "Hi." It was Dar, at her most sheepish. "It's a little big, huh?"

Kerry edged around the desk, to find her lover slouched in her chair, regarding her flowers with some treipidation. "Dar, it's gorgeous! Who sent it?" There must have been three dozen blooms in red, peach, and yellow. The scent was almost overwhelming.

Wordlessly, Dar handed her the card she'd found on it.

That's my girl. "Awww…" Kerry bit her lip, giving her companion a delighted look. "That is sooo sweet, Dar. I told you he was proud of you."

Dar leaned back in her chair, bracing one foot against her desk and fiddling with her pencil, looking oddly adolescent. "Guess so," she replied gruffly, almost but not quite masking the little grin that trembled around her lips.

Kerry leaned over and kissed her on the head. "You're daddy's little girl, all right." She watched as Dar struggled with what was evidently an overload of emotion, then finally sighed and gave into a broad grin. "Here you go." She handed over the coffee, then gently cupped a rose in her hand and sniffed it. "Oh god, these are incredible. I love that smell."

"Mm." Dar buried her muzzle in the cup and regained her composure. "Guess we can take them home and put them on the dining room table for a few days, hmm?"

Kerry giggled. "Thank god you're driving and not me. I can't imagine trying to get us and these flowers into the Mustang." She looked past Dar to the monitor, and laughed. "Oh wow, he did a great job with that!"

Dar sighed, peeking at the screen. Mark had taken the shot from the newspaper and scanned it in, then composed a scroll background with little dancing Dogberts all over it. "I'm gonna kill him for this," she groused, then sighed. "I have thirty-two pages of mail to get through, six inches of inbox, three meetings, and I can't even get to my desk because there's a jungle on it." She paused. "Can I just go home?"

Kerry divided her inbox stack. "I'll take half." She carefully moved the floral arrangement, carrying it over to the side credenza, where she set it down and arranged the flowers. "There. Forward me any stuff you don't want to deal with. I'm going to get started on my own avalanche." She headed towards the door to her office and looked back over her shoulder, regarding a happily munching Dar. "Dar, at least save a few for after lunch or you're going to get sick if you eat all of those."

Dar licked a flake of pastry off her lips and took a sip of coffee, then poked her tongue out at her lover.

Kerry sighed, and shook her head. "Stubborn, let me tell you what," she sighed as she left.

🐾　🐾　🐾

First things first. Dar dusted her fingers off, and dialed a number on her speakerphone. A pleasant voice answered.

"ILS Corporate Executive Offices, Beatrice speaking."

"Beatrice," Dar purred, "Alastair there?"

"Hm," Alastair's longtime admin replied, "you mean the Alastair whom, on hearing your voice, just tried to hide himself behind my office plant? That Alastair?"

"That'd be him."

"Hang on. He's putting on his plate armor." Bea put her on hold and she listened to the annoying music for a few minutes before the line clicked open.

"Why, hello there, Dar." Alastair sounded desperately cheerful. "Great morning, huh?"

"It was. I had a wonderful morning, right up until the moment I unfolded the Miami Herald and saw my picture on the front page of the business section," Dar replied. "You must have had that in motion before you saw me last night."

"Well…"

"What in the hell were you going to do if I hadn't agreed to come back?"

"Let's just say I considered it an acceptable risk." Alastair sounded smug now. "Besides, you wanted me to fix the logjam; well, lady, I fixed it for you." He paused. "And, in all seriousness, Paladar, it's something I've been thinking about for quite a while."

Dar sighed.

"You said you wanted the chance to do things your way. Now you have it," her boss said. "You've got a protégé I respect, also."

"Kerry's not sure she wants to step into that role right now," Dar told him. "And I'm not going to push her. We'll see how it goes."

"I'll leave that entirely to you," the CEO replied. "Still mad at me?"

Dar sighed again. "Alastair, it would have been nice to have been asked. That's a lot of responsibility."

"Well, I did give you a raise with it, not that I thought you'd really need that as a deciding factor, and you get all the usual perks, ditto. Besides, it really helps our EEOC profile on the board, which I don't need to tell you is full of stuffy old white men like me."

"You're not stuffy," Dar finally relented, "you hired me, remember?"

Alastair chuckled. "I must be getting a wild streak in my old age. Maybe I should go get a tattoo. That'd shock the missus."

Dar had to laugh. "Y'know, Alastair, I always figured you for an anchor tat on your backside."

"Ahem. Well, talk to you later, Dar; gotta go," her boss signed off with a chortle, leaving Dar to regard the phone bemusedly.

It obliged her by buzzing.

"Dar, I have Mariana on line one for you," Maria said quietly.

"Ah. Okay." Dar pressed the button. "Morning."

"Hi." The Personnel VP sounded hesitant. "Could I ask you to come over here for a few minutes? I want to talk to you, and there's a matter Alastair said you'd take care of."

"Sure." Dar hung up and stood, picking up her coffee cup before she left her office.

"Think you won, huh?"

Kerry continued to mix her tea. "I think ILS won," she replied quietly, not looking up at Fabricini. "I was glad to see that Alastair McLean makes decisions based on the good of the company, not on bullshit personal crap."

"Sure wrecked your little innocent image though, didn't it?" Steve leaned on the counter next to her. "I didn't figure you for a dyke, though. You surprised me."

"I did figure you for an asshole." Kerry now looked at him. "You didn't surprise me at all."

Fabricini lifted a brow. "Showing your true colors?"

"You should talk," Kerry snapped back.

"Honey, I wasn't the one locking lips with my boss all over North Carolina."

"Damn right we were." Kerry turned and straightened, her eyes flashing. "After Dar pulled off a goddamned miracle to keep all those customers for this company, in a damn ice storm, with uncooperative assholes running around all over the place, she moves heaven and earth to get the job done, and what do you do? Do you care about that? No. All you care about is getting one up on Dar." She pushed him backwards. "Well, it backfired, didn't it?"

"Hey, watch it," he warned.

"You watch it," Kerry growled. "And while you're at it, take your snarky remarks and get your ass back to the sales department and out of my sight."

A throat clearing made them both look up. José was in the doorway to the break room, a look of grim irritation on his face. "Steven, come with me please."

Fabricini looked at Kerry, then at his boss. "Fine," he spat as he followed José from the room.

Kerry let out a breath and leaned on the counter, closing her eyes as Duks got up from the table he'd been sitting quietly at and came up behind her. "Ugh," she murmured, very surprised when he put a hand on her shoulder and squeezed it.

"Kerrison," the Finance VP rumbled. "Your fierceness inspires me."

"My what?" Kerry exhaled. "I don't feel very fierce right now. I mostly feel sick to my stomach."

Duks gazed solemnly at her. "You actively practice the art of friendship. That is very rare." He patted her arm. "Come, let's take a walk outside."

Kerry picked up her cup and followed him through the hall and out the back door to the fifteenth floor balcony, which was drenched in morning sun. They leaned against the railing and gazed out over the water, its peaceful blue green surface only lightly ruffled with fluffy white breakers.

"It was unfortunate that someone in the Carolinas knew our friend in there," Duks offered, conversationally. "Nothing would have come of it otherwise."

Kerry shook her head. "It was just...I feel so stupid when I think about it, and I know Dar does too." She glanced at Duks. "We were both just so exhausted, and there was so much riding on what we were doing. Dar was so stressed. She knew more about the consequences than I did, even, and there was a scientist there, someone she'd known a long time ago stirring up some ugly memories."

Duks blinked. "Not Shari, surely."

Kerry nodded. "Yes."

The accountant exhaled. "How unkind," he murmured. "When I first met Dar, and we started working together on various projects, the teams used to go out after work and socialize." He sipped his coffee. "Occasionally, it would get quite rowdy, but I noticed that no matter how wild things had gotten, Dar would never indulge."

Kerry watched him.

"I asked her once, since I am a curious sort of person, why she never drank to excess." Duks pondered. "She told me the last time she'd gotten drunk, she'd almost killed herself." He looked up at Kerry. "It was quite matter of fact, you understand, so very much like Dar is."

"Yes."

"I was on the account where we acquired the company this Shari was working for, and Dar terminated her. She told me, very briefly, of course, that it was in repayment for…how did she put it? The situation that last caused her to become drunk."

Kerry remembered those hauntedly fearful eyes looking back at her, and now tiny things fit into place, and made sense. "She told me a little about it."

Duks was quiet for a bit. "I am glad you were there with her, no matter what the consequences."

"Me too," Kerry agreed softly. "Me too."

Dar stood near the window, gazing out over the city spread before her. Mariana's office was on the opposite side of the building from hers, and traded a water view for one of the city and the daily colorful sunsets.

The door opened, and Mariana came in, walking quickly to her desk and taking her chair, swiveling it so she could watch Dar. "So."

Dar turned. "So."

"Sit down." Mari leaned back in her chair, as Dar took a seat in one of her visitor's chairs. She sighed before she started talking. "I'm sorry, Dar." A pause. "I wish I'd realized things were getting so out of hand."

"Wasn't your fault, Mari." Dar crossed her arms. "I'd acted a certain way for so long, you'd all developed a way of dealing with me. Then I up and changed and didn't send a memo first…yeah, it was getting a bit much, but I should have come to you before now."

Mari relaxed a little. "How are you feeling today?"

A dark eyebrow lifted. "Now that I've been promoted to CIO, you mean?" Dar answered wryly. "Well, it was a uniquely Alastair way of resolving what he considered to be a major issue. We'll see how it goes."

"Fair enough." Mariana pulled a folder across her desk and opened it. "Now, about Mr. Fabricini."

"We're going to fire him," Dar said. "More specifically, I'm going to fire him."

Mari looked warily at her. "Could be trouble. He's an asshole, Dar. We don't need a lawsuit." She stood up and paced behind her desk, fingering her gold pen. "Can't you find a way to work with him? He's got a good skill set. Now that you're…"

Dar was shaking her head. Mari sighed. "Don't cross Dar Roberts, wasn't that always the rule?"

"For good reason," Dar replied, unrepentant. "But you don't have to stick around, Mari." She smiled. "And don't worry about a lawsuit."

The Personnel VP hesitated, then nodded once in acquiesence. "All right." She picked up her coffee cup and examined it. "I'll be back in a little while."

Dar watched her leave, then settled on the edge of Mari's desk to wait. It didn't take long. After about five minutes, a firm knock came at the door. "C'mon in."

The door opened and Steve entered, paused when he saw her there, and closed the door behind him with a grim look. He took a very visible breath before he walked forward and took a seat, crossing one ankle over his knee and regarding her. "Go ahead," he smiled. "Make my day."

"You're fired," Dar complied pleasantly. "Get your ugly ass out of my office building."

Steve smiled back at her. "It's going to look great in the papers. Wonder how your board is going to feel about my lawyer explaining just how screwed up this company really is," he shot back. "Can't you see the headlines in the Journal? Glad I don't own stock."

Dar's eyes narrowed. "You're not going to talk to the press, Steve."

"Oh, yes I am," Fabricini laughed. "I'm going to tell them all about the stinking dyke and her whore girlfriend and how Alastair McLean is the most pussy-whipped old white man in Texas." He got up and moved closer. "So unless you want to be the shortest lived board member in ILS history, you'd better rethink firing me and start talking about how much it's going to cost you to keep me happy." He pressed the tip of one long finger against Dar's shoulder. "Or I call my lawyer."

Dar forced herself to remain still, her arms folded over her chest and her expression calm and neutral. Then, slowly, she freed one arm and reached over to the phone, lifting the reciever and holding it out to him. "Go ahead."

He stared at her for a moment. "You're not that stupid."

Dar smiled, without the slightest trace of warmth. "No, I'm not," she said. "But you are. So go on." She pushed the phone closer. "Cross me."

His eyes flicked over her with a touch of nervousness. "I've done my job. You've got no reason to fire me."

A sexy chuckle of triumph tried to work its way out of her guts, but Dar held it in. "Sure I do," she purred. "You should read the fine print more often, Stevie." One hand reached back and lifted something up, showing it to him. It was an employment application. "Tch. Saying you were a vice president of sales at Intercom when you were only an account manager...that's falsifying data."

"Everyone enhances their resume," Steve snorted, but he backed off a pace. "Nobody gets fired for that."

"No," Dar agreed, letting the chuckle emerge. "Not unless we need a reason." She wafted the copy at him. "Thanks. You made my day. Now, get out." She let the phone drop back in its cradle. "Or I'll have security carry you out."

His eyes held a look of bleak hatred. "So you think you won, huh?"

"No." Dar stood and faced him. "I know I did." Now it was her turn to advance. "You want trouble, Stevie? I could always give you more than you could handle. You want to talk to the press? Go on. I'll have a field day exposing your sordid little background and how you managed to be driving around in that Mercedes these days."

He stared at her. "You don't know shit."

"Then go ahead and talk. You've got nothing to worry about," Dar answered. "You've got ten minutes to be out of the building."

Their eyes locked for a long, tense moment, then Fabricini's lip curled, and he turned and walked out of the office without saying a word more.

Dar let out a breath of relief and ran a hand through her hair uncertainly. She'd expected to enjoy doing that, but she was surprised to find herself shaking and slightly sick to her stomach.

She walked over to the window and peered out, resting her hands flat on the glass and absorbing the warmth of the sun through it. Her reflection shimmered in the glass, and she hesitantly met her own eyes in its glare.

"What in the hell's wrong with you, Dar?" she murmured, fogging the glass a bit with a sigh. "Losing your edge?" She leaned her head against the warm surface. "Or are you getting a conscience after all these years?"

Dar considered that for a moment, then chuckled, pushing herself away from the glass. "Nah. Nothing a little coffee won't fix." With a shake of her head, she dismissed her worries and headed for the door.

"I'll be right in." Dar gave Mariana a wave as she ducked into the bathroom. Fortunately, it was empty, so she spent a moment just twitching at her clothes and giving herself dire looks in the mirror. She was wearing the gunmetal gray suit today with a black silk shirt, the only splash of color the pin Kerry had gotten her down on the boardwalk.

Okay, Paladar. Her jaw muscle twitched. *They're all in there, waiting on you. This isn't an executive committee meeting anymore. This is a staff meeting. They're your staff now.*

You are their leader.

Dar winced and grimaced. *Ugh.* The slightly widened blue eyes gazed back at her mournfully. *I'm too young for this.* With a sigh, she reached up and ran her fingers through her dark hair, arranging it in some kind of order, then took a deep breath and let it out, settling the neatly pressed fabric over her broad shoulders. *Okay. How do we do the 'tude…*

Grumpy? Casual? Bitchy? Annoyed? *Hey…I could say I was PMSing.* She considered that for a moment, then discarded the idea. *Nah. They'd never be able to tell the difference.*

She lifted a brow experimentally. How about…. She let a sardonic grin edge across her face to join the brow. *Okay, I can do amused. I'll just think of them all in their underwear.*

The grin widened. *And I've seen some of them like that, too.* With one last look, she left the bathroom and headed into the executive conference center, where the rest of the upper management staff was waiting.

"Whereinthehell is she?" Duks whispered, nudging Mariana with one knee.

The Personnel VP glanced at him. "She'll be here in a minute; would you calm down?" she whispered back, eyeing the restless group. José and Eleanor were seated next to each other with frosty looks on their faces, and the rest of the staff was a mixture of excited, annoyed, scared, or just plain bored.

The door opened, and everyone stopped talking as Dar let herself in. All eyes fastened on their new CIO, who strode across the room with a smooth, powerful stride, and took her end chair in a blizzard of self-confidence that simply rolled down the table at them.

In silence, Dar let her icy blue gaze go from face to face before a slow, lazy, amused grin pulled her lips upward just slightly. "Morning." Her low, richly toned voice echoed slightly in the silence. "Let's get started, shall we?"

Everyone swallowed, Mariana noted, astounded at the amount and quality of sheer presence Dar could produce when she was in the mood to.

"For...obvious...reasons, we didn't have a meeting last week." Dar put her fingerips on the table, and leaned on them slightly, the fabric of her jacket tensing across her shoulders. "And since I've got crap piled up on my desk six feet tall, this is going to be a short one."

Silence.

"First item on the agenda." The tall, dark-haired woman gazed down the table at them. "Every department gets a fifteen percent operating budget cut. Effective today."

Jaws dropped. Dar waited.

"Hold on a goddamned minute." José stood up. "What in the hell, Dar?"

A chorus of protest rose after him, belatedly courageous once the Sales VP had broken ice, so to speak.

Dar waited. Silently. Blue eyes roving from face, to face, her attitude one of quiet menace.

The voices trailed off, until they were left again in uneasy silence.

"I'm going to take that budget, and I'm going to duplicate the networking hub," Dar continued, as if nothing had been said, "because, let me tell you, ladies and gentlemen, I am not spending another night out freezing my ass off in North Carolina jury-rigging some goddamned patch panel to run this company off of."

Duks chewed on his pencil. "Budgets are already figured for the quarter, Dar," he commented neutrally.

"Rework them," she shot back inflexibly. "Or sell your damn desk chairs, I don't care, but I'm going to go ahead with the facilities regardless."

José was still standing. He put his hands on his hips. "I think we should consider the options, here, Dar, and I..."

She pointed at him. "This. Is. Not. A. Committee." Her eyes smoldered. "There are no options."

Silence. Dar watched them. "All right, we're going to go around the table, you bring up what you think you need to, but be quick about it. I've got a ton of things to do." She finally sat down and took a sip of water from the glass in front of her, then leaned back and gazed at Duks, who was closest to her. A brow lifted at him.

Impudently, he poked the very tip of his tongue out, where only she could see it. "Congratulations, my friend."

Her eyes twinkled soberly at him, the faintest hint of a grin pulling at the corners of her mouth. "Thank you."

"I have some good news," Duks went on. "The retirement fund had an investment in a group of technicals, and we made a killing last week. We're thirty percent over expectations in the fund."

Murmurs went around the room.

"Nice," Dar complimented. "Who picked those?"

Duks named one of his assistants. "Damn good job of analyzing. I put a commendation in his file."

"Put a little commendation in his paycheck," Dar suggested, "before Merrill Lynch steals him."

A faint, nervous chuckle skittled across the table. "That it for you?" Dar inquired.

Duks nodded, then turned, to where Mariana was seated next to him. "Next?"

They went around the room, receiving clipped replies from José and nothing from Eleanor, and everyone left when she closed the meeting, save Duks and Mari. Dar waited for the door to close, then glanced at them. "So."

Duks leaned on his elbows. "That was different. Giving notice that your reign is not going to be business as usual, my friend?"

"Give me a break," Dar snorted, leaning back and allowing herself to relax from the almost painful tension of the meeting. Her entire body ached from it, and she exhaled in relief. "You know it won't last—next week they'll all be in here bitching again."

Mariana laughed softly. "I don't know about that, Dar; you made quite an impression. You have a very powerful presence, you know."

Dar grimaced. "Well, I don't hold out a lot of hope, but at least we didn't spend five hours going over crap we've been through for the last two years." She sighed and studied her pen, which she turned over and over in her fingers. "I'm going to need to pull a project team on that new facility."

Mariana nodded. "I gathered. You want to put in a new orgid for you? We can slot them in there and charge them off against the operating budget."

"Sounds good," Dar concurred. "Well, I've got two phone conferences, four client briefings, and a major proposal to review, so I'd better get to it. You two going to be around later? Maybe we can all have dinner or something."

Duks and Mari exchanged looks. "I hear you know a good Thai restaurant down on Biscayne; sound good?" Mari asked. "We can save all our chitchat for there. Will you be able to unbury Kerry from her desk by then?"

Dar chuckled. "Yeah, I think so." She caught their eyes and realized where they were looking. Just barely keeping herself from sticking her hands in her pockets, she merely flexed her fingers instead. "I'm not going to fill my position right away."

Silence, as they digested that. "Good idea." Mariana nodded approvingly. "You slowly going to shift responsibilities to Kerry?"

"Yes."

"Smart." Duks nodded also. "Give everyone a chance to see what she can do."

Silence again. Mariana cleared her throat gently. "Are you going to um…" She considered, fishing for a way to ask delicately. "…change your beneficiary information in CAS?"

Dar almost laughed, as she kept her eyes on her pen. "Yeeahh, it looks like it," she admitted, glancing up to see a twinkle in Mari's eyes. "Subtle."

Duks chuckled. "C'mon, Mari, we've got things to do, and so does the grand poobah, here; let's be getting a move on." He stood, then leaned over and clapped Dar on the shoulder. "Good job, Dar."

"Likewise," Mari added, as they pushed their chairs into place. "I think it's going to turn out for the best for everyone. "

Dar felt her pager go off as she watched them leave, then she sighed, looking around the empty conference room. "I sure hope so." She stood and went to the phone nearby and rang the office. "Maria, what's up?"

🐾 🐾 🐾

So much for dinner. Dar leaned back in her chair and closed her eyes, letting the argument over the speakerphone travel past her. The moon shone in her window, and she half turned to contemplate it as she lifted a hand and rubbed the back of her neck.

Board meetings, when your board was international, were a pain in the ass. But Dar hadn't been able to wriggle out of this one, since Alastair was using the opportunity to introduce her to the rest of the board members.

She sighed. Kerry had gone home hours ago, dropped off by a cooperative Mark, and she wished she could just hang up on the group and go join her lover.

"Don't worry about it," Kerry had said. "We've got all week, and besides, it's been a really long day."

Yeah, yeah, yeah, Dar grumbled silently, closing her eyes and wishing she had some aspirin. She tried to put the headache out of her mind and think about something more pleasant instead. Hot tubs, for instance. Kerry had definitely mentioned hot tubs for tonight, and a spicy chicken stir-fry with noodles that was very, very tasty....

"Dar? What do you think about that?" Alastair's voice interrupted her daydreaming.

Oh shit. "What I think about that is that it's ten o clock here in Miami, and we're going rapidly nowhere. Why not schedule a meeting when everyone has their acts together?" There. Throw a few insults, see if that gets things moving. "That's what I think," Dar added, for good measure.

She took a contented sip of chocolate milk as the soft hiss from the phone indicated a shocked, worldwide silence. *Another Dar Roberts legend in the making, I bet.* She rolled her eyes, regarding her bare feet resting on her desk, crossed neatly at the ankles. *Regretting your decision already, Alastair? Next time, you'll ask first, huh?*

A gentle clearing of the throat. "Well," Alastair responded. "That would be a novel idea. Okay, so the week after a disaster was a bad choice of times. Let's reschedule for next Friday, same time?"

Fine. She'd call in from her cell phone while floating on the Atlantic. "Sounds good to me," she agreed, stifling a grin. "I'll have the proposal for the new networking center by then."

"Good, good. All right then, good night, ladies and gentlemen." He paused. "And Dar."

It hit her unexpectedly, and she burst out laughing, hearing a rustle of sound as the rest of the group belatedly joined in. "Good night." She hit the release button, and shook her head. *So much for my first board meeting.* But at least it was more productive and less antagonistic than their usual staff gatherings, so maybe that was a good sign.

It was very quiet in the office, with only the soft hum of the air conditioning and the gentle, sporadic clatter of her hard drive to break the silence. With a sigh, she slipped her shoes back on and stood up, pulling her jacket over her arms and shouldering her briefcase.

The elevator ride was quiet also, and she was conscious of her own footsteps as she crossed the long, empty lobby and headed for the door. The security guard met her and opened it, touching his brow in a military fashion.

"G'night, Ms. Roberts," he remarked, politely. "Late night, eh?"

"Night, Pete." Dar gave him a smile. "Same old, same old. You know how it is."

"Yes, ma'am, but we haven't seen you here at night for a while. I was wondering if you'd changed offices."

No, just priorities. "I've been here... just not late. Take care."

She walked across the parking lot and unlocked the Lexus, dumping her briefcase inside and getting in, exhaling as the cool, soft leather surrounded her. She closed the door and sat for a moment, resting her hands on the wheel before she started the car and pulled out of the parking lot.

🐾　🐾　🐾

Kerry was curled up contentedly on the couch, her head resting on the arm, and Chino tucked up in a ball against her belly. She let her eyes follow the action on the television screen, though she found herself watching the clock almost as much. *Darn it, Dar... what kind of stupid meeting can you have this late at night?*

C'mon, Kerry, it's her job, remember? Don't make her feel bad for doing it. There are going to be times when you're stuck at work, too, so there.

Oh well. She snuggled down further into the couch and watched the crocodile man try to trap a crocodile. He was just stringing his net when the phone rang. She picked it up immediately. "Hello?"

"Hey." Dar's voice sounded over the dull roar of boat engines. "I'm on the ferry."

"So I hear. How'd the meeting go?"

"Bullshit," the executive replied bluntly. "It was mostly Alastair just blowing hot air across three continents. I finally called him on it and he rescheduled for next Friday."

"Ew," Kerry replied. "That's no fair."

"Nah, we'll be out on the boat. That's why god made cell phones," Dar chuckled. "How'd your night go?"

Kerry rolled over, and let her head rest on the sofa arm. "Well, I got home and put together a little dinner for us, then I stuck that in the fridge and took Chino for a nice long walk."

"I could live on Frosted Flakes, you didn't have to do that," Dar protested gently.

"You cannot live on Frosted Flakes, Dar Roberts, so hush," Kerry shot back. "So then I went over to the gym and worked out for a couple of hours."

"I haven't seen much of it lately," her lover responded ruefully. "But it's pretty well stocked. They've got a circuit there I really like; the gym by work doesn't have it."

"Mm, yeah. So then I got home and took a shower, and now I'm just watching Steve Irwin and waiting for you," Kerry concluded.

Dar couldn't help the silly little grin that crossed her face at Kerry's words. "Waiting for me?"

"Yep," Kerry confirmed. "Chino and I are right here, watching the door."

A soft laugh. "Well, I'm pulling into the parking space right now, so I guess I'll see you in a minute." She hung up and got out of the car, closing and locking it and heading for the condo entrance. At the door she paused, reflecting.

How many times had she come home, just like this, to a quiet emptiness? How many years had it been? The idea that someone was in there...god.

Thoughtfully, she keyed in the lock and opened the door, stepping inside as a scrambling puppy and a smiling blond greeted her. "Hey guys." Dar dropped her briefcase and knelt, playing with Chino for a moment before she stood and faced Kerry.

"Hey. Here, let me take your jacket. You look wiped." Kerry reached for it, only to have her hands caught and held, as Dar stepped closer to her. "Wh..."

Dar released her hands and let her arms rest on Kerry's shoulders, gently interlacing her fingers behind the smaller woman's neck. She gazed into the puzzled green eyes, and wished she had the words to fit the emotion she could feel roiling up inside her. She tried, but nothing would come out, so she merely drew Kerry's head forward, and gently kissed it. "Thank you."

"Dar?" Kerry inquired softly, pulling back and little and giving her a worried look. "Are you okay?"

There was really no way she could explain. "Yeah." She managed a smile. "Just been a long day, that's all." Awkwardly, she dropped her hands, then backed off a step. "I'm going to go change. I think I need some coffee." She rubbed the back of her neck wearily. "Haven't had a headache like this in a while."

Kerry cocked her head to one side. "Mm, let me help." She gently drew Dar into their bedroom and peeled off her jacket, draping it neatly over the back of the chair near the dresser.

"I am capable of taking my own clothes off," Dar protested mildly, finding herself intrigued by the absorbed look of concentration on her lover's face.

"Well, sure, I know—but it's a lot more fun for me if I do it," Kerry replied, working the buckle loose on the thin, ornate belt, then reaching around to unbutton Dar's skirt. "Because if you do it, it's just like…well, you know, changing. But if I do it…" She slid the zipper down, and removed the skirt, leaving Dar in her silk blouse.

"If you do it," Dar repeated softly, tracing the line of her jaw. "It becomes a lot more interesting."

"Right." Kerry slowly unbuttoned the shirt and letting it fall open, releasing a scent that was mostly Dar, with a touch of perfume. She slid her hands under the fabric and let her fingers slide up the smooth, powerful back, clucking softly at the tension she felt there. "C'mon, lie down." She gently peeled the shirt back, and Dar let it fall down her arms to the floor, feeling the slight chill as the conditioned air brushed her skin.

It felt like a dream, really, but Dar couldn't find it in her to protest. She allowed herself to be led over to the waterbed and gently pushed down onto it, feeling the surface give under her weight. She rolled over and spread her arms out a little, feeling the cool air suddenly warm on her back as Kerry settled over her, straddling her hips.

Fingers slipped under the hooks of her bra and released it, then smoothly rubbed the area. Kerry's hands were warm and strong, and Dar felt the stiffness relax almost immediately as her companion started to work, kneading her shoulders and wringing tiny murmurs of appreciation from her. "Ungh."

"God, you really are tense." Kerry slid her hands up Dar's back to her neck and shoulders, which eased grudgingly under her touch. "We've got to get you a recliner for your office or something." She felt Dar chuckle through her fingertips as they eased around the taller woman's ribs.

"Hey," Dar chuckled again.

"Whoops, sorry. Forgot you were ticklish there," Kerry teased, hitting the spot again on purpose, just to hear the laugh. She reached over and got a small bottle of oil from the nightstand and uncapped it, putting a little on her fingertips and rubbing them together before she started back to work. "How does that feel?"

The oil left warm traces across her skin, and Dar let out a long, satisfied breath. "You're the best."

Kerry regarded the smooth, tanned back with a distinct feeling of pleasure. "I am? The best what?"

"Everything," Dar mumbled. "The best assistant, the best cook, you give the best massages…"

The blond woman chuckled delightedly. "That's really cool. I've never been the best at something before, except debating. But that doesn't really count; all it means is I can win arguments."

Dar folded her arms, and rested her chin on them, glancing back quietly. "You're my best friend," she added, with a touch of wistfulness. "I never thought about having one of those until I met you."

Kerry gazed down at her, then she leaned over and placed a gentle kiss on the center of Dar's back. "I'm glad you feel that way." She moved up and put another kiss a little higher. "Because you're my best friend…and the best thing that's ever happened to me in my life," she decreed softly, right into Dar's ear.

She got a gentle smile in return. She rubbed Dar's shoulders lightly. "Turn over so I can get the front."

That got her a saucily raised eyebrow as Dar twisted under her, and she was suddenly face to face with those amazing blue eyes, and a bare, powerful body trapped neatly under her own.

Whoa. Kerry put her hands down lightly on the flat belly, spreading her fingers out and starting a gentle, rhythmic massage. God, Dar was so strong. She could feel it as she moved up across her collarbone to her shoulders, feel the thick, powerful muscles just under the skin that flowed into her upper arms. Kerry leaned forward to get enough pressure and found herself looking almost straight down at those twinkling, amused blue eyes. "You know…" She paused, holding Dar down and feeling the faint motion under her fingertips. It was almost scary. Almost intimidating.

"What?" Dar asked, watching her face.

"I think I know how Steve Irwin feels when he's on top of a crocodile," Kerry told her.

Both dark brows shot up. "Gee, thanks," Dar drawled.

"No no no, I don't mean you look like a crocodile, Dar," Kerry laughed. "It's just that they're always so much stronger than he is, and you get the feeling that at any moment, the croc might—yeow!"

Kerry felt the room whirl and a heavy, warm weight settled over her. She cracked one eye open to see a blue orb inches from her. "Uh oh."

"Might turn the tables?" Dar asked with a seductive grin as she leaned forward and pinned her lover down, taking a gentle nibble at her neck. "Like that?"

Kerry felt her breathing go ragged. "I'm pretty sure a croc nibbling his neck doesn't make old Steve feel like this," she breathed, swallowing a few times. "But yeah."

Dar rolled back over and allowed the blond woman to resume her place. "I kinda liked it this way." She reached a hand down and stroked Kerry's calf. "Where were we?"

Kerry slid up and found her lips. "Right here." She felt Dar's hands start to roam, lifting up the light t-shirt she was wearing and letting the cool air brush against her skin. "I was just about to say…" She tasted Dar's lips again, then slowly lowered herself down, feeling the instant heat as their skin touched. "…that I love you."

Dar soaked the feeling up in quiet wonder. "I love you too," she responded, on an irregular breath. "And I always will."

Chapter 15

Dar woke abruptly, disoriented for a minute as she caught her bearings and shook the sleep out of her eyes. The bed next to her was empty, though she could still faintly catch Kerry's scent on the sheets, and she put her head back down, wondering what had awakened her so violently.

The fragments of a dream faded out of her consciousness, something dark and vaguely frightening, and she thought she remembered walking down a long, dusty road at night, all alone, in tears.

Ugh. What was that? Dar shook her head to clear it, then put the thought aside. *Can't blame it on dinner, since we skipped it…just one of those weird ones, I guess.* Then she cocked her head, and listened, expecting to hear Kerry moving around in the bathroom, or maybe coming back from the kitchen. She heard neither, and her brows contracted. *She's a big girl, Dar. She can probably handle getting milk by herself,* she sternly told the niggling anxiety.

It didn't help. An uneasy tension in her guts sent the covers flying back, and Dar rolled out of the waterbed and padded off in search. The bathroom was empty, and so was the quiet, dark living room. She stuck her head in the kitchen, then made her way up the stairs to the second floor. Kerry's door was partially ajar, and she poked her head in, spotting her lover curled up in the large bed, her arms wrapped around her pillow.

For a long moment, Dar froze, unsure of what to do. Surely Kerry had the right to sleep wherever she wanted to without being questioned on it, right? Dar nibbled a fingernail, running her mind over the evening's course, and trying to figure out if she'd done something wrong.

No. Not unless her understanding of 'right' and 'wrong' when it came to Kerry was way the hell off base. Kerry had been in a very good mood when they'd dropped off to sleep, so…

Just then, the figure on the bed shifted, and Dar heard a sharp intake of breath, and a tiny sound of pain. Without further thought, she bolted across the floor and knelt at the bedside, putting a hand on Kerry's tense arm. "Hey."

Green eyes gone silver in the moonlight blinked at her. "Wh…oh, Dar. God, you startled me."

"What's wrong?" the taller woman asked, softly. "Are you okay?"

Kerry sighed. "Yeah, it's…I've got cramps, really, really bad." She gave Dar a rueful look. "I was expecting it this week, but it just got me a lot worse than usual." She curled her fingers around Dar's hand. "I didn't want to wake you up."

"Mm." Dar gazed at her. "Sorry about that. Did you take something?"

"Yeah, a handful of Advil," the blond woman muttered. "They'll work, eventually." She reached over and pushed a lock of dark hair out of Dar's eyes. "Go back to sleep, I'll be fine."

Dar hesitated, finding herself unwilling to leave Kerry, but not having any good reason to stay. "Um, all right, I guess." She paused. "Can I get you something? Hot tea, maybe?"

"No, I'm fine, really. Go on, you need to get some sleep," Kerry told her.

Reluctantly, Dar stood up. "All right," she agreed unhappily. "Call me if you need anything, okay? I've got some muscle relaxants left if those Advils don't help after a while." She stroked Kerry's upper arm in attempted comfort. "Or maybe a hot water bottle…that usually helps me."

The blond woman smiled at her. "All right, Dr. Roberts," she teased her companion gently, feeling a little better just to have her nearby. She wished she could just ask Dar to stay with her, but that would be totally irresponsible, since the poor woman had to work tomorrow, and there was no sense in both of them being zombies. Right? "I'll call you if I…" She stopped, seeing the worried look in Dar's eyes. "Boy, that's so stupid."

"What is?" Her lover knelt again, and rested a forearm on the bed.

"Like I ever stop needing you," Kerry admitted, with a smile.

Dar's face, though thrown into shadows, appeared quite pleased with that. "Actually…" She cleared her throat a little, embarrassed. "Waking up downstairs was um…" She paused, searching for the proper word. "Strange."

"Alone, you mean," Kerry clarified.

The dark head nodded.

Kerry considered that. "Big bed." She indicated the surface she was resting on. "It's kinda empty and cold up here," she added. "I'd go back downstairs, but I sort of have to move around a little, because of the pain, and I didn't want to bother you." She sighed. "Which is kind of pointless, I realize, because here you are, right?"

"Right," Dar agreed. "Mind some company?"

"No." Kerry curled up a little tighter as a spasm hit her. "Ugh."

A solid weight settled behind her. "Here, let me try something."

Kerry felt fingers touch her back and start a slow kneading rhythm down her spine. Maybe it was the warmth, or just Dar's presence distracting her, but the cramps seemed to lessen a little, and she stretched her body out to allow her partner better access. "Ooooo…you have magic fingers."

A dark brow lifted saucily, unseen in the murky darkness. "Oh really?"

"Oh yeah, your hands are poetry in motion," Kerry murmured. "Spreading little bolts of wonderful all over me."

Dar's eyes widened at the phrase. "Little bolts of what?" She leaned over and nibbled Kerry's ear. "You're the poetic one, kiddo." She rubbed her thumbs in little circles above Kerry's kidneys, then slid an arm around her waist, and began a slow massage of her belly.

"Ohhh…" Kerry felt the tension slowly relaxing, and she leaned back against Dar's warm body in utter relief. She wasn't sure if it was the ibuprofen finally kicking in or her lover's attentions, but she frankly didn't care, since she'd been tied up in knots for over an hour and a half, and it was just nice to not be in agony for a while. She felt guilty about bothering Dar, but not guilty enough to make her leave, especially since the taller woman didn't seem to be minding too much. "Sorry I wo...wait, I didn't wake you up, Dar. What are you doing up, anyway?"

Dar put aside the memory of the nightmare. "I dunno, I just woke up. Maybe the AC clanked or something," she temporized. "You weren't there, so I figured you went to get a drink or whatever, but I couldn't hear you, so I decided to go see what was going on." She glanced at the bedside clock. "It's almost four; how long have you been up?"

Kerry sighed. "Since two; I was having trouble sleeping anyway." She exhaled, blinking a little as the gentle massage continued. "So I thought it would be better if I just came up here. I usually don't get it this bad."

"I know." Dar pulled her a little closer, and felt Kerry's body relax against hers. "You're one of the luckier ones; doesn't last long for you, either."

"Mm, we're both lucky that way," Kerry remarked, biting her lip to stifle a yawn. "Though I was contemplating the other day how choosing an alternative lifestyle ought to bring a magic pill to eliminate this stuff at the same time."

"Heh. If we advertised that, the one in ten would be two out of three," Dar snickered. "Besides, lots of gay women want and have kids, Kerry."

The blond woman sighed. "Yeah, I know, but they can be selectively fertile, if you know what I mean. They don't have to worry about accidents." She couldn't stifle the yawn this time, and gave into it. "Mm, think those pills are getting to me now."

Dar rocked her gently, and watched the pale green eyes flutter closed. "Good, get some sleep." She settled her arms around Kerry's body, feeling the breathing deepen as she did so. "Atta girl."

"Mm." Kerry mumbled sleepily. "You're the best."

Dar sighed happily and put her head down, gazing out over her now sleeping companion through the window. The stars winked solemnly at her, and the trees outside swayed in a silent wind as she reflected on a simple change in her viewpoint.

She'd never wanted to be responsible for anyone. That's why she'd never considered kids, never gotten a pet; she'd been very, very damn sure she didn't want the hassle or the headaches of all that.

So how come taking care of Kerry felt so damn good?

She rested her cheek against the soft, pale hair and peered out at the lapping waves. *Tell me it's a long suppressed, deeply skewed maternal instinct surfacing. Right?* She glanced down as Kerry stirred a bit, then snuggled closer to her, with a contented little sigh. *God, what in the hell is happening to me?* Dar felt a surge of protectiveness wash over her. *I don't even recognize myself anymore.*

Another sigh. *But is that good, or bad?* Dar considered thoughtfully. She finally decided. *Something that feels this good can't be bad and not be illegal. So I guess it's good.* She yawned and closed her eyes, letting a peaceful sleep take her.

Kerry pulled her pale blue terrycloth bathrobe around herself and sipped at her tea, trying to muster up the energy to go and take a shower. The drugs had worn off after she'd woken, and even taking more wasn't really helping at the moment. The ache was making her cranky and tired, and she wished she could just crawl back into bed. "Well, no time for that, Chino. I'd better get moving."

Bare footsteps made her look up to see Dar ambling into the kitchen, a towel tucked neatly around her damp body. "Hey." The taller woman glanced at her, then put the cup down she'd been reaching for and stepped closer. "You still feeling lousy?" she inquired.

Kerry shrugged. "I'm okay, just a little sore. Give me a minute and I'll get going." She eased off the stool in the kitchen, then paused, biting back a grimace. "Jesus."

Dar took her cup out of her hand and grasped her by the shoulders. "I think you better stay home," she decided, speaking in a firm voice.

The blond woman straightened, and shook her head. "C'mon, Dar, don't be goofy. I'm not calling in sick for a dumb stomachache, that's crazy." A cramp hit her, and she leaned on the counter. "I'll be fine."

Dar put her hands on her terrycloth covered hips and gave her a look. "You listen here, Kerrison Stuart. You are not going to develop all of my damn bad habits just because we live together, got me?"

Kerry peeked up at her, speechless.

"You are staying right here, in that cute little bathrobe, and watching Oprah all day," Dar proclaimed. "That's an order."

"But…"

"Ah ah!" Dar put a hand over her mouth. "You can logon from here if you have to. That's why I have a damn ISDN in the house."

Kerry kissed the palm of her hand and smiled as it was withdrawn. "Okay." She felt a huge wave of relief, knowing she didn't have to wrestle into her business clothes and put up with how that would feel all day. "Thanks, boss," she added gratefully.

That got a frank, open grin from Dar. "That's better." She leaned over and kissed Kerry's forehead. "Play with Chino, munch on ice cream, and relax, all right?"

"Nice prescription." She stuck her hands in the pockets of her robe. "And I do have some things I need to take care of, so maybe it's a good idea anyway." She butted Dar's arm with her head. "G'wan, you're going to be late."

With a satisfied chuckle, Dar turned and walked out, humming lightly under her breath.

🐾 🐾 🐾

"Computers are great things, Chino," Kerry enlightened the dog as she reviewed her screen. She was curled up in her leather office chair, her robe tucked around her and soft, fluffy pink booties on her feet. "Online banking really does make life a lot easier." She clicked on a screen, then typed in an amount. "Okay, that's the last of the bills to pay. I got my car, the credit cards...all set." She made a tick mark on a piece of paper sitting next to her keyboard. "Let's not let mommy Dar see that one, hmm?"

The puppy glanced up at her and licked her chops.

"Yeah, that's the bill for the ring, and she'd have my head on a platter, I think." Kerry laughed gently, picking it up and looking at it. "But it was worth it, and they said you should budget two month's salary for that kinda thing, right?"

"Yawp." Chino yawned.

"Well, it's just our secret." She tucked the bill away. "Okay, let's see where we are." She reviewed her bank balance, pleased with the result. "Hey, that's not bad, Chino." She glanced at her payments. "Okay, I think it's time to reduce one part of this." She picked up the phone and hesitated, then took a deep breath and dialed. She waited through three rings. "Hi, Mr. Mahoney?"

A low, pleasant voice answered her.

"It's Kerry Stuart...yeah, I know, the lease is up next month. I won't be renewing it." The words felt so strange, and had taken her so long to decide to say. "No, no, it's great, I just... well, I'm living with someone, and I wanted to make sure it worked out...you know."

The landlord was very understanding. "You've been a great tenant, Ms. Stuart. Anytime you need a referral, you let me know, okay?"

"Thanks," Kerry responded. "I'll be by to pick up the few things I've got there, but there's nothing valuable, so you can show the apartment if you want to."

"Right you are, and I know it's in great condition. Thanks for letting me know, Ms. Stuart. I really appreciate it." He paused. "And best of luck to you. I hope things go really smooth."

"Me too," the blond woman responded. "Talk to you later." She hung up and regarded the phone. "Well, Chino, that's that." She glanced at the puppy. "I mean, it's not like I haven't been really living here before, but..." It was a line crossed, and she knew it. "She's stuck with me now."

"Grrrr...yawp." Chino rolled over, and put her head down, peering up at Kerry sleepily.

Kerry returned her attention to the screen. "Now let's order some groceries." She switched over to the internal Island site that allowed her to pick and choose what she wanted from an extensive list and have it delivered. "Let me check...oooo, Dar, you little piggy wonk, I'm gonna hurt you." She shook a finger at the screen as she clicked into the personal options and changed the credit card the groceries were billed to back to her own. "Damn it, I can afford this, Dar; how many times do I have to tell you that?"

Irritated, she clicked over to her e-mail and whipped off a short, scolding note to her lover. "Bad girl."

Chino lifted her head and whined.

"Not you," Kerry reassured the puppy, scratching her ears. "Let's see..." She selected a variety of fresh produce and some staples, then drummed her fingers and went over to the goodies section and clicked on a number of Dar's favorites. "By all rights, I should restrict you to brussels sprouts for that trick, but..." A mental image of the little puppy dog eyes Dar was capable of when the mood struck her surfaced, and caused a grin to appear on Kerry's face. "I can't resist that pout and you know it."

She finished her shopping, which she'd discovered one night while roaming around the Island website, and which Dar had no idea existed.

"Not surprising," Kerry snorted softly. "Coming from Ms. I Can Live on Frosted Flakes." She reached over and took a sip of her ginger peach tea, breathing in the fragrant steam with a sense of quiet pleasure. The drugs had kicked in again, reducing the pain to a gentle ache, which was better than the spasms of the morning. Still, she was glad she was curled up here in her robe with a heating pad nearby if she needed it.

Not that the pad could equal the comfort provided by a living, breathing Dar, but…Kerry smiled quietly, recalling her lover's solicitous attentions. She'd cope.

She set about balancing her checkbook and putting things in order. "Hmm…we've got a little extra here this month, Chino; let's see if we can find a treat or two." She surfed over to an online computer store. "Ooo, digital camera. What do you say, hmm? Does that sound good? Is that a treat?"

The puppy heard the word "treat" and immediately got up and trotted over, standing up on her hind legs and putting her small paws up on Kerry's thigh. "Rgrro?"

"Oh, you want a treat?" Kerry laughed and fished a puppy biscuit from her pocket for the animal. "Here you go." She watched Chino crunch for a minute, then returned her attention to her browser. "Yeah, that would be cool; gimme." She glanced down as her mail icon flashed. She clicked it and smiled as she noted the sender.

> *Roberts, Dar - Sent 11:22 AM*
>
> *All right - consider me chastised. I switched it so I could take care of the boat charges, and forgot to switch it back. We could just get a joint card or something.*
>
> *Dar*
>
> *PS. how are you feeling? I didn't want to call in case I woke you up.*

Kerry studied the note, feeling a little prickle of recklessness. She hit reply, typed in a few words, and hit send. "Let's see what your answer is to that, Paladar." She grinned and resumed her surfing.

Dar paused outside the conference room, running her fingers through her hair before she put a hand on the latch and pushed it down. She entered the long room and let the door close behind her, aware of the several pairs of eyes that fastened themselves on her. "Good afternoon." She moved around to the head of the table and sat down. The rest of the room contained representatives from two companies they'd just signed alliances with, along with representatives from sales and marketing and one of Duks's people.

"All right, we're here to discuss the potential acquisition of the statewide benefits contract in Idaho." Dar pulled out a folder, and flipped it open. "Suppose you people fill me in on what progress you've made with the state government so far?" She flicked a cool glance at the company representatives from that state. "You want to start?"

They glanced at each other, then the older man cleared his throat. "Well, all right…"

It was a long meeting, and Dar was slightly frustrated by the time it ended, sensing a communication problem but unable to pinpoint exactly what it was. She kept trying to get information from the newcomers, but she could tell the older man, at least, was being evasive, and they all seemed to want to keep their strategies under their hats and keep her company around just to pump cash into things.

That wasn't going to happen. Dar fiddled with a pen as they filed out and scowled a little. "Elle, hang on." The marketing representative paused, then walked back across the now empty conference room and stood, visibly uneasy. "Relax, sit down a minute."

The woman did, folding her hands on the table and waiting.

"What did you think about them?" Dar inquired.

"Me?" Elle's brows lifted. "Um, I don't know. They were okay, I guess, a little on the quiet side." She sniffed and pushed her thin, wire-framed glasses up on her nose. "I took them on a tour before the meeting. They were kind of prickly, if you know what I mean."

Dar nodded, pursing her lips. "Yeah, I got that feeling myself. Well, okay. Thanks."

Elle blinked at her. "Um, you're welcome." She stood and ducked her head a little awkwardly, then turned and left.

Dar sighed, then stood and gathered her things, walking back to her office in time to see Maria returning with a large white bag. "Hello, Maria."

"Is your meeting over, Dar?" The secretary held the door for her and followed her inside. "I brought you back some arroz con pollo from my trip outside."

Dar smiled at her. "Thanks. Yeah, it just ended. I've got another one after lunch, then a conference call after that."

Maria bustled over to her desk, and put her bag down. "And how is

Kerrisita doing?" she asked, pulling out a Styrofoam container and handing it to Dar. "I stopped at the farmaceria, and you take this home to her, yes?" She handed Dar a bag. "Is to make tea, is good for her."

Dar held the bag. "Um, I…I don't know, I haven't spoken to her since I left the house. I'm sure she's fine, and thanks, she likes tea."

Maria gave her a severe look. "Poor Kerrisita is home so sick, and you don't call her?" she scolded her boss.

"Uh." Dar was caught flat-footed. "It's just some cramps, Maria. She's not a baby, you know."

"That is not the point, jefa," Maria stated. "Is good she knows you are concerned, no?"

"Uh…" Dar gave up. "Yep. You're right. I'll go call her." She fled the outer office and escaped into her own, putting her lunch down and circling her desk. "Jesus, you'd think she was an infant or something. I bet she's napping, doesn't want me calling every five minutes…" With a sigh, she sat down and dialed her home number. It rang several times, and she was about to hang up when it was answered. "Hey."

"Hey!" Kerry's voice perked up audibly as she recognized the caller. "Wow, I was just thinking about you."

Dar settled her chin on her fist. "I was just thinking about you too. I just got out of a meeting I wish you'd been at; maybe you could have given me some insight into a few new associates." She sighed. "How're you feeling?"

"I answered that in the e-mail I guess you haven't seen yet."

Dar sat down and rolled her trackball to check her mail. "Ah, no, I just got back. Let's see… oh." She started laughing. "Well, I'm glad you liked the service last night." She felt a blush coming on.

Kerry chuckled as well. "It's on and off. I take drugs, it gets better, then they wear off, and I feel like a manure pile. I don't know what's with me this time." She sighed in disgust. "Chino's keeping me company, though, and I've been surfing."

"Uh oh. That could be dangerous."

"Mm, yes, it certainly could. Did you know Victoria's Secret has a great website?" Kerry asked innocently.

Dar's blue eyes widened. "Any particular reason you're letting me in on this little tidbit of news?" she inquired hesitantly.

"You like blue, right?" Kerry asked, ignoring the question.

"Um, yes…why?" Dar felt her curiosity crawl up her spine and perch on her shoulders, almost making her lean forward towards the phone. "Kerry?"

"Yes?" the blond woman purred. "Something wrong?"

Dar chewed her lip. "Um...no." She felt a little thrill of excitement, almost of danger. "Nothing."

Her intercom buzzed. "Hang on." She pressed a button. "Yes, Maria?"

"Dar, I have a Mr. Evans, from Interlock; he is wanting to talk to you?"

Ah. Her reluctant associate. "All right. Give me a minute, Maria, then show him in." Dar pressed her other line. "If you're done teasing me, I've got a potato farmer that wants in here."

"Teasing? I'm not teasing you, Dar," Kerry objected, with a chuckle. "Can I interest you in a couple of burgers with the works for dinner? The beach club just updated their menu, and they've got some new ones."

Dar smiled at the phone affectionately. "Sounds great to me. See you in a bit."

"Right, have fun." Kerry hung up, and Dar smiled, glad she'd taken Maria's advice. She glanced up as the door opened, and the tall, gray-haired man entered. "Come in, Mr. Evans. Maria, thank you for reminding me of that pending issue."

The secretary looked blank for a moment, then she smiled and shook a finger at her boss, but said nothing as she closed the door behind her.

Dar motioned to her visitor chair. "Sit down, Mr. Evans. I hope you won't mind if I catch up on my lunch while we talk." She didn't give him a chance to answer as she pulled her Styrofoam container over and popped it open, releasing the scent of saffron and garlic into the air. "What can I do for you?" she asked, pulling out the fork that came with the lunch.

He seated himself and crossed his legs, resting his hands on his knee and studying her. Dar maintained the eye contact while she speared a piece of chicken and munched it. One brow lifted in question at him.

"Ms. Roberts, I'm not quite sure how to broach this." He spoke the words carefully. "I've spoken with my colleagues, and they feel as I do, and I'm afraid we have a difficulty with you—ah...your corporate culture."

Dar took a mouthful of rice and chewed it while she considered the words. "Our corporate culture?" she repeated, then waved her fork at the walls. "You don't like oak paneling and maroon carpet?" she

queried, honestly puzzled. "What corporate culture are you referring to?"

He hesitated. "It seems to us that your company has a
very...open...policy on personal behavior," he stated. "As well as a
great deal of diversity in your employee base."

One of Dar's brows rose. "Most people consider that a corporate
asset," she informed him. "But what exactly are you getting at?" She
chewed another piece of chicken. "Whose personal behavior are you
getting offended by?"

He cleared his throat, obviously discomfited. "Yours, actually."

Dar stopped chewing and just stared at him. Then she swallowed
and took a sip of water from the glass on her desk. "Excuse me?" She
almost laughed. "What is it you find offensive: my tendency to doodle
in meetings, or my eating lunch in front of you without offering you
any?"

He looked at her. "We spent some time in your cafeteria this morning, and heard of a situation between you and your assistant."

It stopped being funny. Dar felt a cold wave of fury sweep over
her, and she knew it must have showed in her face, because she saw his
reaction. She put her fork down slowly and precisely, then folded her
hands on her desk. "And your problem with that is what?" She heard
the drop in her voice, and felt the dark anger stir in her guts.

Dead silence for a dozen heartbeats. "We come from a god-fearing
part of the country, Ms. Roberts, and I, personally, find that kind of
behavior disgusting." He looked right at her, lifting his chin a little.
"And my colleagues feel the same."

A dozen nasty retorts crossed Dar's mind, and she discarded them.
"Well, Mr. Evans, our company's official policy is one of non-discrimi-
nation, and I'm pretty damn proud of that. I'm sorry you don't feel the
same." She paused. "Let me make sure I understand, though: you've
got a problem with me because I'm gay, right?"

His face twitched at the word. "I accept God's word on his views
about that, so yes."

"Let's not get into a debate on religion," Dar retorted. "You won't
like my views on that, either, I'm sure." She took several deep breaths
to bleed off the angry tension. "All right, well, Mr. Evans, in the first
place, my personal life is no business of yours."

"I don't think we'll be comfortable dealing with you," he interrupted. "And even if that were not so, your bowing to foreign culture

here is something we find very upsetting. Ms. Roberts, do you realize a good portion of your employees do not speak English in the workplace?"

Dar felt her nostrils flare. "Mr. Evans, fifty percent of our employees have something other than English as their native language, based on the fact that they are citizens of another country," she reminded him. "We are an international organization, in case that slipped your mind."

"We find that…" He never got to finish. Dar stood up, and came around the desk, cold sparks flashing in her pale eyes.

"Do you know what I find offensive?" she growled, leaning on her desk. "I find your small-mindedness offensive, Mr. Evans. So I'll tell you what. I'll call down to our marketing group, and we'll just call this little arrangement off, all right?"

"That was my objective, yes." He stood stiffly. "I'm sorry you cannot understand our feelings in the matter."

"I'm not." Dar let out a short laugh. "But let me tell you, I'm going to have the publicity group release a statement saying we cut you loose because you were too prejudiced for us to deal with."

He drew himself up. "It's not prejudice, Ms. Roberts. It has nothing to do with that. It's just how we see ourselves, and who we prefer to deal with."

Dar just shook her head. "Then you'll find yourself on the inside of a circle growing smaller day by day, mister, and you know what?" She leaned closer, watching him edge back. "We'll go in there and take all the business away from you anyway."

"Not after we talk to those clients, and let them know what kind of people you are," he told her, smugly. "The rest of the country isn't like this place, Ms. Roberts."

Dar smiled at him. One of her nastiest ones. "Mr. Evans, when I'm done cutting a deal for them, they won't care if I'm a cross-dressing transgendered muskrat." She dropped her voice to a low growl. "Now get out of here before I have you thrown out."

He walked to the door, and looked back at her, his hand on the latch. "You are an abomination in the eyes of God, Ms. Roberts."

"Any god I believe in doesn't know what the word hate is, Mr. Evans," Dar replied mildly. "I pity you." She watched the door close after him, and let her held breath out. "Shit."

Damn it all to hell. Stupid piece of shit righteousness stuffed up his butt son of a... Dar walked around her desk and dropped into her chair, shaking her head in disgust, as she considered what to tell José.

What a way to start out her new job.

🐾   🐾   🐾

The afternoon sun poured into Dar's office, painting the carpeted floor and warming her back. She took the paper she'd been reviewing and marked on it, then tossed it into her outbox and flipped the pen she'd used in her hands. "I may almost be a quarter of the way through this crap," she commented to her fish, who wiggled their fins at her. "Oh, that's right; I have to feed you today, huh? Your best buddy's not here."

Her phone buzzed. "Yes?"

"Dar, I have Richard Edgerton for you on numero dos."

Dar glanced at the phone in surprise. "Really? Okay, I'll take it." She hesitated before picking up the line, wondering what her family's lawyer wanted. "Richard?"

"Hello Dar... long time no talk to." The cheerful voice echoed slightly. "Haven't seen you in quite some time... how are you?"

Ten thousand answers to **that** question. "Fine, thanks, and you?" Dar replied, recalling a mental image of the forty-something lawyer, a former college football tackle who still retained his bulldog physique and almost military crew cut. "Yeah, it's been a while." Her father's funeral, to be exact.

"Oh, doing all right. Listen, it's a small thing, but it seems your aunt May had a lock box over at People's First National that nobody knew about."

"Yeah?" Dar leaned back in her chair and nibbled her pen. "And?"

"There's a box of stuff in there, and by the terms of her will, it goes to you," Richard advised her. "The bank's closing down, and they called us to tell us since we were her executors of record."

"Oh." The dark brows knitted. "All right, have it sent down, I guess. I'll sort through it. If it's stuff that can be donated somewhere, I'll do that in her name."

"Great, great. So, how've you been, Dar? I saw your mother last week, she's doing okay; her stuff's being shown at a gallery up here in a little bit."

Dar exhaled, feeling the usual stab of pain thoughts of her mother brought. "I'm doing just fine, glad she is too," she got out civilly. Then an idea struck her. "Listen, Rich, I'm glad you called. I need to ask a question."

"Shoot," the lawyer responded briskly.

"First off, I, um, I need to modify my will." Dar interlaced her fingers and regarded them. "And second, I need to know what kind of...I'm not sure what you call it, but something that would legally give someone the right to make certain decisions for me if I wasn't able to, for instance."

"Uh." Richard stuttered. "Is everything all right Dar? I mean, with you? You're not sick or..."

The executive chuckled. "No, no, I'm fine; never felt better, in fact." How true that was. "Just send me over the draft of the will, and I'll amend it. I need to leave everything to someone other than the Humane Society."

"Oh." He sounded relieved. "Well, sure. And as for power of attorney, there's a couple ways you can go with that, depending on how much authority you want the person to have, how much you want to trust them, that sort of thing."

"All the way," Dar replied softly. "What do you need from me?"

"Just the name," Richard answered. "Dar, are you sure about this?"

A slow smile appeared. "If I've ever been sure of anything in my life, it's this," she confirmed, giving him Kerry's name. "Make sure you spell it right."

"Okay, but, listen, Dar, it's awful sudden, and you've got quite an estate here—are you really sure about this? You're sure it's not some treasure hunter, or anything like that?"

Dar regarded the mantel for a long moment, considering his words. "I'm sure," she finally said. "She has no idea of the size, or even that I'm doing this."

"Okay," Richard surrendered amiably. "Just keeping your best interests in mind, Dar." He cleared his throat. "I'll draw up the papers and send them down to you end of the week, okay?"

"Perfect." Dar smiled. "Thanks, Richard."

"Anytime, Dar...and watch for that case," the lawyer added. "Knowing May, it could be anything."

Dar acknowledged that and hung up, feeling a quiet satisfaction. Yeah. It was time. She turned to her computer and called up a session, then entered into the employee files, and called up her own records.

A few keystrokes, and the contact information was changed for emergencies, and then a few more, and her insurance beneficiary was likewise edited. She paused, watching the blinking cursor for a moment, then hit send.

Update Complete. Dar retrieved a cashew from her trail mix, munching it contentedly. Yeah.

🐃   🐃   🐃

"Two of these divisions aren't showing much profit." Duks pointed to a line on the page. "I think some changes need to be made there. Perhaps you could take a look."

Dar regarded the paper and nodded. "They're not writing good contracts." She shook her head. "They're just putting in new business, and not really adding to the bottom line." The late afternoon sunlight reflected into the office and warmed her back. "I'll have their new stuff put under technical review."

"Good, good." Duks stretched. "So, how's it feel?"

Blue eyes regarded him in puzzlement. "How does what feel?"

"Being the master of all you survey?" the Finance VP replied with a twinkle. "Did I hear a rumor you were going to cancel the Interlock agreement? What happened?"

Dar regarded her desktop. "Mr. Evans didn't think he could do business with us," she replied evenly.

Her phone buzzed. "Dar, is Mr. José on numero uno for you."

Dar sighed. "Thanks, Maria." She hit the button. "Yeah?"

"What is this I hear, you cut loose Interlock?" José's voice came through, thick with outrage. "What's this shit, Dar?"

"That's right, I did," Dar replied flatly. "He said he couldn't work with us, so I cut him loose. Got a problem?"

"Hell yes, I have a problem with that!" José shot back. "What do you think you're doing? We had a business plan in Idaho. I am having seven major contracts going in there."

"Not with his cooperation. Try something else," Dar commanded. "Go around him."

"Mierda, that's a load of…what was his problem?" José demanded.

Dar hesitated, then her jaw clenched. "I was."

Dead silence. "You?" José spluttered. "Jesú, it figures. Did you tell him off or…no, I bet he found out you're sleeping with that little slut of yours, and I tell you—"

Duks leaped around the desk and grabbed Dar's hand, slamming his own down on the mute button. "Dar!" he hissed, seeing the pale blue eyes go gray with fury. "Hold it."

"Let me go, Louis." Dar felt the tremors start. "I'm gonna fire his ass."

"Come on, listen to me." The Finance VP stood his ground, speaking softly. "He's an ignorant jerk, but life's full of them, and so's the company. You can't fire them all, my friend."

Dar sucked in a breath, and released it, trying to keep a lid on the anger. "I can fire this one, and maybe the others will get the message," she finally said, in a low voice. "I am not going to put up with it, Louis."

"Okay, okay, but, please, please, my friend, give him one warning. Just one. Keep our asses out of the courts, all right?" Duks asked reasonably. "You know he'll do it again, Dar—please."

The dark-haired woman let her hands fall to the desk, and she leaned on them. For a long minute she stared at the wood surface, then hit the mute button. "José?"

"Sí? I knew this was going to get us into trouble, and I tell you—"

"Shut up."

Silence.

"I want you to listen to me, all right?" Dar enunciated her words carefully.

"Sí?"

"If you ever make a statement like that about anyone who works here ever again, I'm not only going to personally fire you, I am going to come down to your office, pick you up, haul you outside, and beat the living daylights out of you in front of the entire company," Dar stated softly. "Do you understand me?"

Long silence.

"I asked, do you understand me?" Dar requested dangerously.

"Sí," José came back, very subdued.

Dar exhaled. "Good. Now, he had two issues: me being gay, and you being Cuban. I didn't figure either of us was going to change any time soon, so I told him to take a hike."

Long pause. "That puta had a problem with me?" José's voice rose. "My father came over to this country with nothing but a cigar wrapper and six banana leaves, and ended up owning half the real estate in Hialeah, so he can kiss my Cuban ass."

"Yeah, well, so find another way up there," Dar reiterated, then disconnected the call. She stared at the fighting fish as her blood pressure slowly dropped, aware of Duk's close presence. "I think he owes you a thank you."

"Mm," Duks murmured.

Dar glanced up. "I think I do too."

The accountant shifted a little. "My friend, it's hard, I know. I understand."

"Somehow I doubt the majority of the company considers you and Mari an abomination in the eyes of God, Lou," Dar replied, as she sat down, and rested her hands on the desk. "You try not to care, but it gets a bit much sometimes."

Draefus turned and sat on the edge of the desk, studying her. "You know, Dar, I'm sure there are people who feel that way, but I don't think it's the majority."

"No." Dar had to laugh shortly. "The rest of them just hate me because I'm a bitch." She gave Duks a wry look. "They don't really care who I sleep with."

Duks sighed, and patted her on the shoulder. "Some of us are just pathetically glad you're here, and as good as you are, my friend, and I think there are more of us than you would ever imagine." He paused. "Come, let's take a walk downstairs, get some coffee, hmm?"

Dar studied her hands. "Go on down. I'll meet you there in a minute."

Reluctantly, the accountant left, closing the door softly behind him. Dar rubbed her face and leaned back as her stomach slowly untied itself from its knots. "What a completely sucky day," she informed the ceiling. "A few more like this and I'm going to chuck it all and become a diving boat captain."

A moment later, a soft knock came on the door, and she tilted her head towards it. "Yeah?"

The door opened, and Maria came in carrying a tall mug, a faint curl of steam visible over its edge. "Jefa, I know this is so bad for you, but today is not good." She put down the mug, and Dar caught a scent of hot chocolate.

It made her smile. "Thanks, Maria." She blew out a breath. "Yeah, today's been a bitch all right." She watched the secretary settle in the visitor's chair. "I'm sure the stories are flying."

"Sí." The woman nodded. "They have been, is true." She straightened a little. "You know, Dar, when I came here from my country, in my country I was in the office, the numero uno, you know? And when

I came over to this country, all the people looked at me, and it was…" She made a tiny, discreet spitting noise. "Immigrante."

Dar watched her curiously. "Hmm."

"It did not matter that I was good in church, or that I was running this big law office, or that I raise my children…. No, it was just, ptooey. Immigrante."

Dar steepled her fingers. "That must have been hard for you. We take our citizenship for granted, a lot of the time."

"Sí," the secretary agreed. "You do. I had to be studying many hours before I passed this test, you know? And you do not have to take it, but anyway, what I learned from this, Dar, is that what is important is what is on the inside of people, not on the outside."

Dar gazed fondly at her secretary. "A lot of people never quite get that, Maria."

"Sí, you are right, they do not," Maria agreed. "Even in my church, which is writing that all people must love each other, still, they think that God makes this kind, or that kind better than the other." She folded her hands. "Dar, you are a good person."

The taller woman smiled. "Thanks. I think you're a very good person yourself."

"Gracias." Maria smiled. "Kerrisita is a very good person."

"Yes, she is," Dar agreed, softly.

"When two good people love each other, Dar, God smiles on them, and he does not care what they are looking like," Maria said, gently. "That is what I believe, that you have been very blessed."

It was like a warm blanket settling over her, coming from the most unexpected source imaginable. "Thank you, Maria," Dar replied softly. "That means a lot to me."

Maria looked pleased. "You are welcome, Dar." She hesitated. "One more thing: my youngest daughter, Conchita, is having her quinces next month. I would very much be honored if you and Kerrisita would come and celebrate this with my family."

It was a shock. Dar knew enough about traditional Cuban culture to be honestly surprised at the request, but she also knew enough not to refuse. "We'd be honored," she replied, simply. "Thank you."

"Gracias," Maria said in a dignified tone as she stood and brushed off her skirt. "How is Kerrisita?"

"She's doing all right," Dar answered, taking a long sip of her hot chocolate.

The secretary glanced at the window. "It is five o' clock. I am to be leaving; do you not think those herbs would do better if Kerrisita gets them soon?"

Dar chuckled softly. "Are you telling me to get out of here, Maria?"

"Sí." The secretary smiled. "I think I am doing that. It is very bold of me, no?"

Dar stood up and turned her monitor off. "Sounds like a good idea to me." She grabbed her keys and shouldered her laptop. "It's been a long day."

"And there will always be tomorrow," Maria added, "for new problems."

Dar followed Maria out the door and shook her head. "Isn't that the truth."

🐄　🐄　🐄

Kerry watched the late afternoon light pour in the front windows and spill across the tile floor, painting golden stripes across the table. She was curled up on the couch with Chino tucked in next to her and a cup of hot tea resting on the end table near her head.

She felt pretty good. The drugs had mostly taken care of the pain, though she was feeling a little lightheaded from having to take so much, and she'd been quite productive, so she wasn't feeling any guilt about simply lounging around watching cartoons all afternoon. It was nice just to have a day off, she reflected, and spend the time mindlessly relaxing, not having to worry about lines going down, or people yelling, or things like that.

She was a little worried though, since she hadn't heard from Dar since the morning, and a recent call to the office had gone to voice mail. She felt a little uneasy about her friend in a vague unsettled way, but resisted the urge to use her pager or the cell phone, because if there was something going on, surely Dar would have called.

Right?

Kerry sighed, and put her head down on the soft couch arm, breathing in the scent of the leather as she tugged a soft quilt around her body. Her eyes closed, and she let the warm comfort lull her into sleep.

It was a strange dream, full of children's laughter and the smell of hickory smoke. She was snoozing in what felt like a hammock, wrapped in a soft blanket that bore a hint of woods and leather.

Footsteps came close, and she felt a nearby presence, a warmth that brought a smile to her face, even as gentle fingers brushed her hair back, and she felt a kiss touch her lips. Her eyes fluttered open, to see familiar blue ones looking back at her, framed by a face a little tanner, and a little older than she'd expected.

She reached up and hooked an arm around a powerful neck and drew that face down, kissing her again, and reveling in the sweetness, and the passion, and the sense of belonging to each other that had no match in anything else she'd ever known.

And as she did, the children's laughter faded, and the hickory scent shifted to the tang of wood polish, and she opened her eyes to see those same blue ones looking down curiously at her as a faint smile played about Dar's lips.

"Oh." A little fuzzy, she reached up and brushed her fingers across Dar's cheek, where a tiny scar had shown in her dream, and now was gone. "You're home." Chino was wriggling up against her and nibbling her fingers.

The lips moved into a gentle smile. "Yes, I am." Dar seated herself on the edge of the couch. "How are you feeling?" She scratched the puppy behind the ears.

Kerry glanced at the window, which was darkening into twilight. "Um, better, thanks. I was watching tv, and I guess I dozed off. How long have you been here?" She peered up at her lover. "You look beat."

Dar sighed. "I am. I had a tough day," she admitted softly. "I've got a headache you wouldn't believe, and I gotta tell you, it's just nice to see a friendly face."

Kerry tugged her down and pulled her into a hug, feeling the long breath Dar released as she did so. She rubbed her lover's back, feeling the warm skin beneath the silk shirt. "I missed you. What happened?"

Dar allowed herself a few more seconds of bliss before she reluctantly straightened and tucked the quilt back around Kerry. She'd been debating with herself since she'd left the office as to whether or not to tell Kerry, then she figured that the blond woman was probably going to hear sooner or later, so it would be best to come from her. "Nasty stuff. I had to terminate a contract today because the company we contracted with felt they couldn't do business with us." She pushed Kerry's very disheveled hair out of her eyes, and reflected on how cute she was when she just woke up. "They didn't like our diversity."

Kerry cocked her head to one side. "Diversity? I don't…what do you mean?"

No way to soften it. "They heard about you and me and they spent some time in the lunchroom and heard the different languages…they didn't like that."

Kerry stared at her. One blond brow rose up to her hairline. "What jerks. Tell them to go contract with the KKK."

Dar felt a smile coming on. She should have known better than to worry about Kerry's reaction. "It was a pretty ugly scene, and then I had to explain to everyone, and that got pretty ugly too. Duks kept me from firing José outright."

"Wow," Kerry murmured. "What did he do?"

Dar bit her lip. "He said something I didn't like about you."

"Oh." Kerry considered that. "I'm glad you didn't fire him for that." She stroked Dar's face. "Sticks and stones, and all that stuff." She felt bad, but not as bad as if Dar'd fired him. "I'm sure you handed it in a very professional manner."

Blue eyes glinted in the soft twilight at her. "Um, actually, I told him if he ever said anything like that again, I'd take him outside and beat him silly in front of everyone."

Kerry clapped a hand over her mouth. "Oh." She muffled a laugh. "Jesus, Dar! To a Cuban man, that was worse than firing him."

"Mm," Dar agreed softly. "On the bright side, we got invited to Maria's daughter's quinces."

"We did?" Kerry was surprised. "We, as in you and I, did?"

Dar nodded. "We, definitely we, got invited," she confirmed. "Maria said some really nice things to me after everything happened…she's really a sweetheart." She tugged on Kerry's t-shirt. "We'll have to go shopping for some really snazzy gowns."

"Uerrg. I haven't worn a gown since my prom, Dar." Kerry made a face. "And you don't want to know what I looked like for that."

"Sure I would," Dar objected, with a grin. "You haven't shown me all your embarrassing pictures yet. Tell you what: how about we get dinner sent over, and we can trade. I was a really dorky kid."

"Eek." Kerry rested a cheek on her shoulder, and bit her lip. "Okay, but you have to promise not to laugh—I tried to perm my hair for the occasion."

"I promise." Dar crossed a finger over her heart. "But you can't ever admit to seeing the ones from my grade school play."

Mischief filled the green eyes. "Ooo…you got a deal," Kerry agreed, curling her fingers around Dar's. "Go get into your jammies… I'll call the beach club."

Dar smiled and walked towards the bedroom, then glanced over her shoulder. "Could you have them send…."

"A chocolate milkshake?" Kerry supplied, dialing the phone. "Sure."

Dar's eyes twinkled as she disappeared into the bedroom. She could hear Kerry's low voice, and she looked down to see Chino tugging on her shoe, and it made her smile.

Home had such a different meaning now. Dar tossed her jacket over the chair near the mirror, then quickly changed out of her suit, feeling a sense of relief as the soft cotton of her favorite sleep shirt draped over her shoulders. She sat down for a minute on the edge of the waterbed, and picked Chino up to play with her. "Hey there girl. Whatcha up to?"

The puppy nibbled at her chin, then licked her face. Her brown eyes gazed adoringly up at Dar as her paws scrabbled for a good hold on her neck. Dar hugged the puppy to her, feeling a silly grin take over her face. Then tucked Chino under her arm as she made her way back out into the dimmed living room. Kerry was standing by the coffee table lighting two sturdy, scented candles. Her blond lashes caught the candlelight, which threw interesting shadows up her body as she turned towards Dar and smiled. "Dinner's on its way."

Dar gazed at her, imagining what it would have been like to come home from a day like today and not have Kerry or Chino there. A sigh trickled out of her, and she put the puppy down, then went over and enfolded Kerry in a hug that came right from her heart.

"Urk." Kerry was surprised, but obligingly slid her arms around her lover and hugged her back, loving the feel of the strong body pressed hard against her own. "Mm. What was that for?"

"I'm just glad you're a part of my life," Dar answered with a dazzling smile.

"Really?" Kerry murmured.

"Of course." Dar released her, and leaned back a little.

"Funny you should say that." Kerry sat down on the love seat, and pulled her down as well. "I've got something to ask you, and before I do, I want you to know it's okay for you to say no."

"It is?" Dar responded faintly, unsure of what to expect.

"Yes." Kerry took both her hands and held them. "I got a call today." She took a breath. "It was from Pastor Robert… I told you about him, remember?"

"Yes," Dar answered cautiously.

"He's in town."

"Oh, that's nice. You want to have him here for dinner?" Dar offered, hesitantly.

"No—well, I mean, sure, but that's not the question." Kerry squared her shoulders. "He offered to, um…" She stopped, then took a deep breath. "He said he'd perform a ceremony for us, if I wanted…I mean, if we wanted him to."

Dar blinked at her.

"Listen, I know you're not into that, Dar. I know it's not been something you had growing up, and I know it doesn't really mean…oh." Kerry shut up as Dar cupped her cheeks and kissed her passionately. They broke apart.

"I'd love that," Dar stated sincerely. "You're right, I don't know much about it, and I've never been into stuff like that, but I know it's important to you, and that makes it important to me."

Kerry smiled gently at her. "Wow." It felt wonderful. "Great. You can figure out a place to do it, because I don't know if I want to have it inside a church, even the one on South Beach."

Dar grinned. "I know a place." She cradled Kerry's face in her hands, stroking her cheeks with gentle thumbs. "It's a little short on amenities, but it's got a killer sunrise." Kerry's request had delighted her in ways she'd hardly expected, but she couldn't pretend she hadn't been considering the same sort of thing lately. In fact, a dawn run out to that little spot had been on her list of Valentine's Day things anyway. "Thank you for asking me."

Kerry found herself smiling, just because Dar was. "Sorry you had such a lousy day."

Dark brows knit. "Huh?" Dar asked, honestly puzzled. "What day? Oh, right." She laughed softly at herself. She studied Kerry's face. "Maria was right."

Kerry leaned into the touch, simply feeling the love. "Mm?"

"I have been blessed," Dar stated softly. "I've found my soulmate."

Breathe, Kerry. Her chest moved and sucked in air, making a soft, almost sob. She was crying, and she had no idea why, except that just that word made her feel so…

Complete.

Kerry smiled. "Yes, you have." She reached up and curled her fingers around Dar's hand, then turned it a little and kissed the palm. *After all this time.* The thought echoed gently.

The doorbell rang.

"I'll get that," Dar said, softly.

"I'll get the pictures," Kerry sniffled.

"We've got a lot of catching up to enjoy," the dark-haired woman said, with a smile.

Her soulmate smiled back. "Yes, we do."

Dar slowly let her eyes open, aware of the early morning hour even before the alarm sounded. She shifted her eyes toward Kerry, who was nestled against her on the waterbed. There was something so gentle and so contented in her expression that it tugged at Dar's heartstrings. Dar protectively curled closer around her. Kerry was sleeping peacefully with her hand spread across Dar's chest, her head resting on her shoulder, and her knees between the taller woman's. Dar smiled tremulously.

Her soulmate. Dar stroked the soft pale hair. The word had delighted Kerry, and it really did fit how she felt towards the blond woman, as though they really were part of each other.

Maybe they were. Dar pulled Kerry a little closer. They certainly fit together, like a well-made puzzle, despite their different heights. Dar could feel Kerry's warm breath against her collarbone, and…. Dar smiled. They were breathing in the same rhythm.

It was a nice feeling.

Loving Kerry was a nice feeling. Dar smiled contentedly, and relaxed, thinking about the weekend. More specifically, early Saturday morning, when they'd go out and greet the sun, and tell each other…

Pale blue eyes popped open in mild alarm. Tell each other what? Could they use the standard vows?

Uh, no.

Dar's mind started working. What in the hell could they…okay, okay. How about something simple like "I'll love you forever."

She winced. Not that it wasn't true, but…

Hmm…

You are the light of my life? Augh. Dar, you sound like a bad seventies hit parade. You make my life worth living?

Well, that was true too. *You came into my world, and turned it upside down? Not so flattering, but…*

"Dar?" Kerry's sleepy voice interrupted her studied musing. She glanced down, where the blond woman was still nestled against her.

"Hmm?"

"What are you muttering?"

Dar sighed. "Sorry. I didn't realize I was."

"Mm. So what was it?" Kerry persisted, curiously.

"Umm…nothing, really." Dar cleared her throat gently, and snuggled back down. "G'back to sleep." She firmly closed her eyes.

"Okay," Kerry murmured obediently.

Peaceful silence fell.

"Am I really the light of your life?"

Dar made a noise halfway between a groan and a whine.

"I'm not?"

"Of course you are," the taller woman spluttered hastily. "You weren't supposed to hear that."

"Oh." Kerry's voice seemed disappointed. "Okay, sorry."

Dar gazed down at her unhappily. "Kerry, you're all those things and so much more I can't even begin to tell you. I was just trying to figure out what I was going to say to you on Saturday morning."

"Oh." The inflection was totally different. "You don't have to say anything," Kerry told her softly. "Just your being there's enough for me."

"Oh." Dar's turn to murmur.

"I thought maybe I could just sort of, um…I mean, I have this poem…that I wrote…I thought maybe I could have Pastor Robert use that."

Dar exhaled in relief. "That'd be perfect." She kissed Kerry's head gently. "Thank you."

Silence fell.

"I turned everything upside down, huh?"

Dar rolled over onto her back, pulling Kerry up on top of her. "Yep."

"Awk! Dar, you're gonna be squished," Kerry laughed.

Dar rubbed her back, working the strong muscles with her fingers. "Nope. I like this feeling."

"You like not being able to breathe? Dar, you're demented." But

Kerry's body slowly relaxed completely against her, melding with her own in boneless completeness.

"Mm." Dar savored the feeling.

"Goofball." Kerry nuzzled her neck, nibbling the underside of her jaw. "I love you." She felt the muscles of Dar's face move as she smiled. "It's almost time to get up."

"Uh huh," Dar agreed lazily. "How are you feeling?"

Kerry considered the question. "Like I don't want to get my lazy butt up and go running but I don't have a good excuse not to. So, c'mon, tiger, let's hit the Frosted Flakes and get moving."

Dar laughed softly, and pinched her on the specified body part. "I'll put the coffee up, you let the puppy out?"

It was just the start of another day.

Chapter 16

Kerry yawned. "What a day." She peered out at the sunset they were sailing through on the ferry home from work. "I don't want to see another TCP/IP diagram this week, Dar. I swear I have ping test patterns bouncing off the insides of my eyeballs."

"That's an attractive thought." Dar leaned her elbow on the car window and stretched her legs out. "Did you get a hold of the pastor?"

"Yep." Kerry told her. "He's all set. When I told him he'd get to go out on a boat and see the sun rise, he almost burst a vocal cord cheering." She adjusted her sunglasses and watched the road. "Now, um, I thought I'd ask Colleen to be there, if that's okay."

"Sure." Dar closed her eyes behind her own sunglasses.

Kerry glanced at her. "If I had a few more days, I'd try to get Angie down here, or Mike. Is there...Dar, do you think your father would like to be there?" She watched the fading sunlight outline her lover's profile, and saw the movement as Dar swallowed. "That was a silly question. I know he'd like to be there."

Dar was silent a moment. "I don't think he'd…he won't come with other people there. But it's a nice thought."

"You could ask him," Kerry suggested softly.

Dar turned her head and looked out the window. "Maybe…maybe he won't want to be there, Kerry. It's hard for him, being alone so much."

"What's hard, to see his daughter happy?" Kerry steered the Mustang onto the ferry and parked. "Dar, he doesn't begrudge you anything. Even I realize that."

"No, I know, but…" Dar fiddled with her glasses, pulling them off and rubbing her eyes. "Damn, I looked at that screen too long today," she sighed. "What was I saying? Oh…no, I don't think he begrudges me anything. I just don't want to make him hurt more than he is."

Kerry studied her. "You know, I saw you squinting in that damn meeting today. When was the last time you had your eyes checked?"

Dar froze, then settled her sunglasses back on her nose and slouched in the seat. "There' s nothing wrong with my eyesight." She folded her arms across her chest.

Oo. Kerry settled back in her own seat. *Hit a nerve.* "Okay, just a thought," she replied mildly. "Maybe it was just the glare in there." She gazed out at the water quietly, very aware of the pale blue eyes watching her from behind the tinted lenses of the wraparound sunglasses Dar preferred. "Might be nice to ask Maria, since she asked us to her daughter's ceremony—and helped get us together."

"Yeah, that's not a bad idea. Maybe I could see if Duks and Mari want to come over for it, too," Dar murmured. "And I'll, um, I'll ask Dad. Maybe he'll come over afterwards for a few minutes."

Kerry reached over and took her hand, squeezing it a little. Then she waited, letting the soft hiss of the surf and the lonely cry of a seagull settle between them. She could see the tiny twitches as Dar's jaw muscles moved, and that was a sure indication the taller woman was working something out in her head.

Or deciding to relate something.

Finally, Dar's head turned a little towards her. "They told me I needed glasses in sixth grade."

"Ah. Really?" Kerry mentally ticked herself a point. "So what happened?"

A faint shrug. "I figured if my father didn't need them, I didn't, so I figured out a way to, um…"

"Trick them?" Kerry inquired mildly. "That'd take some doing."

Dar sighed. "Not really. I have almost perfect recall. Memorizing a stupid eye chart wasn't hard."

Kerry turned and looked at her in amazement. "You are joking, right?"

Dar solemnly started reciting the chart.

"Son of a…" the blond woman blurted. "Dar, but you…I mean, you're an adult now. Surely you could…"

Another shrug. "Wasn't that bad to begin with, and I sort of grew out of it, mostly." Dar regarded the waves. "It gets a little annoying when I get tired, though." She gave Kerry a smug look. "I didn't get much sleep last night."

Kerry shook her head. "What I don't learn about you…. Now that I think about it, you were having trouble the night we came back here after I got stranded, weren't you?"

Dar paused, thinking, and smiled faintly. "You know, I honestly don't remember…that wasn't one of the things I retained about that night."

"Ah." The blond woman nodded. "You hit those guys, didn't you?"

Blue eyes regarded her quietly. "Yes." Dar flexed a hand. "I think I fractured at least one jaw."

"Mm." Kerry put the car in gear as the ferry docked, and steered off the platform. The security guard flagged them down, and she pulled off to the side, rolling down her window. "Hi."

"Hey, Miz Stuart, Miz Roberts; you just had a delivery," the man told them, checking a clipboard. "Federal Express box. We had it escorted to your place." He glanced at Dar. "It was for you, ma'am, from New York."

"Ah." Dar nodded. "Yes, I was expecting that. Thanks, Jorge." She smiled as he waved them on.

Kerry rolled her window up. "What's up?"

Dar leaned back in her seat. "My aunt May, the one I got this place from; they found a deposit box with some of her stuff. I'm her only inheritor, so they sent it down. Should be interesting; she traveled all over, so who knows what we'll find in there."

"Oh, sounds fun." Kerry smiled in surprise. "Maybe there'll be ancient scarabs, or something."

Dar chuckled. "Assorted, dried snakeskins, knowing Aunt May." She stifled a yawn. "We'd better keep Chino away from them."

Kerry grinned and drove on.

🐾 🐾 🐾

"Oh, I get it." Kerry finished slicing up the fresh chicken breast. "I'm cooking, so now I'm your favorite, right?" She gave the patiently waiting Chino a droll look. "Don't you look at me like that. Go find your friend the cookie monster."

"Yawp." Chino yawned, then rolled her small tongue out and panted.

The blond woman laughed and turned her attention back to her task. She checked the steamer full of brown rice and started a fire under the wok, pouring in a little peanut oil and waiting for it to heat. "Shh…. You keep quiet now, Chino… don't tell Dar I put all these nice vegetables in here, okay? After I finish making the sauce, she'll never know."

Chino sniffed her ankle, then curled up on Kerry's foot and closed her eyes.

"Oh, great. What am I, a puppy bed?" Kerry sighed. "You're just hoping I drop something."

One brown eye opened and peeked at her.

Kerry smiled, as she tossed thinly sliced red, green and yellow bell peppers into the oil and listened to the sizzling. She stirred them around, then added bamboo shoots, peanuts, and Szechwan peppers. "Ooo, that smells good, huh?" She got the vegetables nice and crisp, then she slid the two pounds of chicken breast into the vegetables and quickly stir-fried it.

"Almost ready," she murmured, adding the sauce, which coated the contents of the wok a nice honey brown. She added handful of sesame seeds, then she turned the fire off and scooped mounds of fragrant brown rice into each of two bowls, and topped it with the stir-fry. "Hey, Dar?"

"Mmm?"

The nearby voice nearly scared the bejesus out of her. "Yeeow!" She almost dropped the bowls. "Dar… don't do that!"

Dar protested, taking them both from her.

"Well, yeah, but I didn't realize you were standing in my back pocket," Kerry laughed, as she grabbed two glasses and a bottle of plum wine. She followed Dar into the living room, and joined her as she settled onto the loveseat, putting the bowls down on the end table.

"So." Kerry curled up with her legs tucked under her and accepted the bowl Dar handed over. "That's some chest." She indicated the trunk that had been delivered. It was a curious item, bound in leather that was carved with intricate, interlocking squares. "It's gorgeous."

"Mm." Dar agreed around a mouthful of rice and chicken. She'd changed into a pair of cutoff sweatpants and a t-shirt, and was wearing a thick pair of very white socks which were intriguing Chino immensely. "Good stuff, Ker." She indicated the bowl.

"Thank you." Kerry's nose wrinkled up as she smiled happily. "It's a new recipe."

Dar's eyes twinkled. "I can feel the healthy vibes coming off of it." She used her chopsticks to retrieve a sneakily hidden vegetable and waved it at her lover. "But you could put this sauce on shoelaces and I'd eat them."

Kerry laughed. "I was counting on that." She took a mouthful and chewed it. "Do you really mind the veggies?"

Dar made her wait for an answer for a moment, then she smiled. "Nah." She took a cheerful bite. "Besides, what right do I have to complain? You're cooking."

Kerry nibbled a bamboo shoot. "It makes me feel better about having chocolate chip ice cream for dessert." She paused, almost laughing at the way Dar's ears perked up. "Double chocolate chip, in fact." She scooped up a bit of rice. "Which reminds me, we're going to have to take separate cars tomorrow. I have my annual checkup scheduled; I almost forgot about it."

"Mm." Dar took a few mouthfuls and chewed them. "Kerry, can I ask you a personal question?"

The blond woman stopped eating, and stared. "Uh, sure."

One dark brow lifted. "Why does chocolate chip ice cream remind you of your doctor?"

"Oh." Kerry laughed, blushing a little. "Yeah, I guess that came out a little weird, huh? It's because she gave me such a hard time last year; apparently I was too skinny for her tastes. She started giving me lectures, and pamphlets on eating disorders." She gave Dar a wry look. "I was imagining her reaction this year."

"Ah, I see." The taller woman nodded in understanding. "Do you think she was right?"

Kerry slowly chewed a mouthful. "I think I'm a lot happier now than I was then, but there's a lot that goes into that." Her eyes searched Dar's face. "I think the biggest influence in getting me to change my mind was the opinion of someone I really respected."

"Mm." Dar didn't quite know how to respond to that, so she merely murmured an agreement, scooping the last of her rice up. "Well, let's see what we have here, huh?" She put the bowl down and eased herself down onto the floor, where Chino immediately tried to crawl into her lap. "Hey!"

Kerry laughed, as she put her own bowl aside and joined her lover on the floor, taking the puppy out of her way. "Ooo, look at that hasp."

Dar took the key that had come with the box and fitted it to the old fashioned lock, then turned it. The metal protested, but released, and she removed the rusted object and set it on the floor. "So far, so good," she murmured, then she carefully unlatched the two catches and released them, tugging the top open and tipping it back.

The scent that came out was the oddest mixture of dust, age, and mystery, and Kerry squirmed closer so she could peek inside. "Ohhh….."

Kerry reached in and pulled out a small wooden box, a heavy, almost petrified wood with a brass band fastening it shut. Kerry carefully undid the clever latch and worked the box open, the wooden edges having warped tightly shut. "Oof. This is kinda…whoops—" The box fell out of her hands as it popped open, and onto the tile floor, spilling its contents. "Oh, damn, did it break? God, Dar, I…"

"Shh…no." Dar reached down and touched the grayish black stones gingerly. Each was attached to the remains of a silver chain, and she picked one up and examined it. "What in the hell is that?" She picked up the other stone and looked at it, then she rotated it and gingerly put both stones together. "Hey, they match."

Kerry leaned close. "They fit together." Her throat felt funny when she said it. "How unusual."

Dar's finger pushed the two stones around in her palm, their edges fitting snugly together. "They sure do," she mused thoughtfully. "Too bad they're so beat up. It might be kinda fun to… um…"

Kerry gently picked the stones up and separated them. "Let me see if I can clean them up a little. I've got some jewelry cleaner upstairs." She glanced up at Dar's face, which was painted in tones of interest and curiosity. "Would you wear half if I can?"

A strange, almost dreamy smile crossed Dar's face. "Yeah...would you?"

A laugh bubbled up from deep inside her, and Kerry released it into the air. "Sure."

In her palm, the stones nestled together in obscure gray contentment.

Kerry took the small bowl out onto the patio with her, seating herself in the early morning sun and propping her bare feet up against the railing. Dar had left a little while ago, and she'd found herself with some time before her nine a.m. appointment.

So she'd decided to clean the rocks they'd found before she got dressed and took the short drive over to her doctor's office. Kerry dipped the rocks carefully in the very mild cleanser and swished them around. "Okay, let's see what we've got here." She gently fished the first stone out and laid it on a soft cloth, then rubbed it carefully. A layer of the dark surface came off onto the rag, and she examined it, then dipped it again. Three or four more dips, and a careful cleaning with the rag, and she was sitting in some amazement, as the sun poured down and sent fractures of colored light through the pure, clear crystal in the palm of her hand. "Wow," she whistled under her breath. "Check that out."

An idea occurred to her, and she carefully dried off the two pieces of crystal, untangling the ruined chains from them. "I think I remember a jeweler close by the office...yeah."

She grinned as she stood up and headed for her bedroom to change.

Dar was seated at her desk, her head propped up on one hand and her mouse in the other. She was clicking through a series of very boring spreadsheets, checking their contents. A soft knock interrupted her, and she leaned back, welcoming it. "C'mon in."

Maria pushed the door open and entered, closing it behind her. She was carrying several folders, which she put neatly on Dar's desk. "Is the three new companies we bring in, Dar," the secretary said. "And Kerrisita just poked her head in to say she is here now."

"Oh?" Dar visibly perked up. "That didn't take long; guess everything's okay then." You never knew with doctors, after all.

"Great...I had a lunch meeting sprung on me that I wanted her to attend."

As if on cue, a popup message appeared on her window.

"Hey...my doctor wants to meet you."

Dar blinked, and glanced at Maria, then leaned forward and typed back.

"Oh really? Everything go okay then?"

"Remember what Maria thought of me? With the trail mix? That's what my doctor thinks of you."

Dar smiled. *"C'mon over."* She turned and put her hands on the desk. "So we have three new acquisitions, eh?"

"Sí."

Dar drummed her fingers on the desk. "Um... so, what did you have planned for the weekend, Maria?"

The secretary gave her a curious look. "Ay, well, nothing really, just some work in the garden, and my husband is going to paint the bathroom," she answered, a little puzzled.

"Ah. That sounds nice. Um..." Dar glanced up as the inner door opened and Kerry ambled in, her green eyes twinkling as they found her lover's face. "We were going to have a little get together on Saturday morning; I'd, um..." The tall woman looked over at Kerry. "We'd like you to be there." Kerry put a paper bag down on the desk and smiled at Maria.

Maria folded her hands, and looked from one to the other. "It is a party?"

Dar looked at Kerry in silent appeal. The blond woman rolled her eyes.

"Sort of." Kerry perched on one corner of the desk. "My former pastor from Michigan is in Miami for a visit, and he offered to perform a commitment ceremony for us."

She does that so smoothly, Dar marveled.

"Como?" Maria took a step forward towards them. "Do you mean to be saying you are getting married?"

Kerry felt the strangeness of the word. "Um, yes, I think you could say that." She turned and looked at Dar in question. The woman was chewing the end of her pen so diligently you'd have thought she had a plastic deficiency. "Right?"

Blue eyes shifted to her face, and then to Maria. "Uh, yes." Dar swallowed, having never really expected to be saying that.

Maria put her hands on her hips, and gave Dar a very severe look. "Jefa, that is not nice."

Dar was startled. "Wh…" Could she have read Maria all wrong?

"What isn't nice?" Kerry was also regarding the secretary in some astonishment.

"You cannot just be doing this without warning, to not give me a chance to get a nice present, that is not fair, Dar. I must get a dress, and…"

"Whoa, whoa! No, no, it's very casual, Maria." Dar stood up hastily. "You don't need to get us anything. We just want you to be there."

"Right." Kerry nodded. "Really. It's very…we just decided to do this the other day, Maria."

"Casual?" the shorter woman repeated. "How you mean, casual, Dar?"

"Well, we're going to take my boat out there." Dar scratched her jaw. "And it's on a little island, before dawn."

Maria stared at her for a long moment. "Dios Mío." She shook her head. "Dar, you are too much."

Dar exhaled softly. "It's all right if you don't want to, Maria. I know it's very short notice, and it's not…"

"Pardon? I do not think so, Dar. I would not miss this for all the, how you say, coffee in India," Maria stated firmly. "I will get my pair of shorts out, just for you." She beamed at them, then turned and bustled out, shutting the door behind her.

"Well." Kerry remarked, turning and giving her lover a smile. Then she walked around and leaned on the desk next to Dar, her blond hair brushing the edges of the wood surface. "Hi."

Dar glanced at the door, then nuzzled her. "Everything okay?"

"Mm hmm. My doctor tells me I'm in great health, much better than before, and you seem to be the cause of it. So you're going to be stuck with me for a long, long time."

A calm silence fell as they stared into each other's eyes, bathed in the warm sunlight pouring into the room, and spilling over them like a golden blanket as the prospects for their future began to sink in.

Abruptly the phone buzzed and broke the spell. "Dar, I have Singapore on uno." Maria's voice entered the room.

Dar took Kerry's hand and kissed it. "All right, I've got it, Maria."

Kerry stroked her cheek, then straightened, and nodded. "See you for lunch?" She motioned towards the bag. "Enjoy breakfast."

"Thanks." Dar smiled as she reached for the phone button. "Yeah?"

"Dar, we've got SITA problems again," said the harried voice. "The overseas net is down in the Far East… can you help?"

Kerry moved to the door and waved before she disappeared.

It was cool out on the patio. Dar leaned against the stone wall, her elbows resting on its top as she gazed out over the water. The salty wind blew her hair back, and she caught a whiff of wood smoke from the barbeque down at the beach club.

If she turned her head, she knew, she'd see Kerry sprawled in the loveseat, writing something she refused to let Dar see. "Tomorrow's soon enough," she'd told her lover, huddling over it.

Tomorrow. Dar looked down and regarded her hands quietly, absently fingering the golden band around her finger. She wasn't nervous, exactly; after all, it was just a few words spoken by someone she didn't even know. She would have preferred that it were just the three of them, but she couldn't grudge Kerry's wish to have people there.

Grumpy old antisocial beach bum, she chastised herself, semi-humorously. *C'mon, it's not that big a step, and it's only Duks, Mari, Maria, and Colleen. Get over it.*

Her page to her father had gone unanswered, and though part of her was concerned at that, another part was secretly relieved, and both parts warred with the big slice battling off disappointment.

Well, they'd take pictures; he'd like that. Dar sighed. The Jacuzzi caught her eye, and she decided a nice warm soak was a good idea. A thought occurred to her: *Bet Kerry would like that too.* Followed quickly by another: *We have fresh raspberries and whipped cream.*

Brightening, Dar went back inside.

Kerry put the last touches on her poem, then untangled herself from a snoozing Chino and trotted upstairs to put the parchment carefully away. She examined the white, casual outfit she'd picked out for the morning, cutoff denim shorts, and the soft white shirt that tied across her ribcage, exposing her belly.

Casual, yeah. Kerry faced her reflection in the mirror and smiled. Dar had picked a worn, stonewashed pair of short overalls, with a white shirt underneath it. It was impossibly cute on her, especially with her tan and the fact that she intended to remain barefoot.

Kerry laughed gently and opened her top drawer, pulling out the wooden box. She opened it to expose the soft, plush velvet she'd lined it with to protect the two crystals nestled inside, the soft lamplight glistening against them and the brand new golden chains draped about them. The jewelers had polished the stones, causing them to reflect the light in brilliant prisms, and she smiled as she imagined giving Dar hers the next morning.

Soft footfalls alerted her, and she tucked the box away, just in time to turn and greet her wind-blown lover as she peeked inside the room. "Hey."

Dar entered, riffling her hair with a negligent hand. "I was wondering if you'd like to share a bowl of raspberries and a hot tub with me."

Kerry grinned hugely. "Would I? What kind of a silly question is that? You betcha." She grabbed her bathing suit from the rack and gave Dar a gentle shove. "Meet you out there?" Dar's eyes twinkled as she nodde, and ambled out, Chino stumbling at her heels.

Kerry tugged on her suit and grabbed a towel and trotted downstairs in time to meet Dar coming out of the kitchen with two plastic containers and a smudge of whipped cream on her face. Kerry stood on tiptoes and licked it off, getting a startled squawk from her taller companion. "Who needs berries?"

They went outside and eased into the bubbling Jacuzzi as Dar put the containers on the edge of the pool. "Mm." She stretched out long legs and leaned back, wondering where her father was.

Kerry rested her head against Dar's arm, feeling her tension. She glanced up. "You nervous about tomorrow?"

"No." Dar brushed the thought off. "Oh, well, a little nervous about getting all those people on the boat and out of Government Cut without ramming into Sovereign of the Seas, but other than that, no." She nuzzled Kerry's hair. "They're going to stock the galley with breakfast for everyone."

"Yum." Kerry moved closer, sliding her arms around Dar's body. "Did you decide on what you wanted to say?"

A smile lit Dar's face. "Yes."

"Ooo…gonna tell me?" Kerry coaxed, easing an adventurous finger under Dar's bathing suit strap.

"Nope," the dark-haired woman responded. "You'll find out tomorrow." She bent her head and nipped a line across the back of Kerry's neck, feeling the soft rise of goosebumps on her skin. Playfully, she reached behind her and dipped a finger in the whipped cream, then put a blob on Kerry's damp nose.

The green eyes crossed slightly as Kerry tried to focus. "Yah."

Dar leaned over and obligingly removed the blob, then moved down and kissed her, exchanging a bit of the sweet stuff while Kerry giggled. "Like that?"

Kerry went back for another taste, easing over and straddling her lover as she floated in the water. After a moment she paused. "That answer your question?"

A dark brow arched. "Want some berries?"

"Later." Kerry leaned forward and brought their bodies into contact, creating a gentle friction in the water. Dar's hands slid across her back and increased the pressure, as their legs intertwined and she felt a touch wander down her hip and tickle her thigh.

She slid a strap down on Dar's suit, and heard a chuckle as her fingertips brushed against newly uncovered flesh. "Hope no one's got the binoculars out."

Dar got both Kerry's straps off at once, and slid the sheer fabric down, exposing her body to the water's currents, a sensual moment. "They'll just think it's a full moon." She tweaked Kerry's behind with a twinkle in her eyes, then arched her back as the blond woman worked her own suit off.

"Bite me." Kerry ducked her head under the water and took a nibble, feeling Dar's whole body jerk in reaction. The combination of subtle touches and the water's stimulation was incredible, and she wanted more of it. Hands slid around her ribcage and pulled her up, and she found Dar's lips waiting. The dark-haired woman rocked back and started a slow, teasing expedition that Kerry enthusiastically joined.

The stars chuckled overhead.

"You ready?" Kerry leaned on the kitchen counter, watching Dar suck a comforting glass of milk. The tall, dark-haired woman was dressed in her overalls and had her hair pulled loosely back into a knot, outlining her angular profile. The dim light in the room caught her pale eyes, and Kerry could smell the clean scent of the soap Dar used and a soft hint of sun dried cotton.

"Yep. I called the ferry dock and left the names," Dar replied, licking a few droplets of milk off her lips. "I told them to escort everyone down to the marina. I figured that was easier than meeting here, then trooping over. Besides, there's parking there." Dar put the glass into the sink and exhaled. "Let's go. I want to get the boat ready."

Kerry picked up a small rope bag and slung it over her shoulder as she followed Dar out the door.

Almost. "Hey!"

"Yeep!" Chino's head almost got caught in the door, and the puppy complained vigorously.

"C'mon, honey, you stay here, okay? I don't think you'd like boats," Kerry told the animal.

"No." Dar put a hand on her shoulder. "Let her come. She's family."

Kerry gave her a surprised look, but opened the door and let the puppy out, watching as she scampered over to Dar's feet and started chewing them. "Okay, but remember you asked me to do this."

Dar scooped up the dog and tucked her under an arm as she got into the golf cart. She set the puppy down on the seat between them and released the brake, starting off in the pre-dawn darkness.

It was really quiet, Kerry mused, as they rolled along the road, the sound of their tires on the tarmac seeming very loud. To one side, she could hear the gentle hiss of the surf, and to the other, the rustle of sleeping birds that roosted in the ring of trees around the small, nine-hole golf course in the center of the island. Dar steered around the curve that circled the beach club and headed down the small path that led directly to the marina. The soft sound of clanking rigging got louder, and as they turned the last curve, Kerry could see the security lights of the harbor lighting the rows of boats. "Beautiful morning."

"Mm hmm," Dar agreed, steering down the dock until she was opposite their slip. The boat rocked gently in the water, and Dar hopped aboard with easy grace. "The club people'll be here shortly." She eyed the front deck, tucking a life preserver away into its bin. "You want to kick the batteries up, make sure we've got plenty of juice?"

"Sure." Kerry ducked down into the cabin and stowed her bag, then checked the boat's electrical system, which was hooked to a portal on the dock. "Looks fine," she yelled up, idly opening the small refrigerator. "Hey." She peered inside, spotting a small tray with two splits of Dom Perignon and a dish of creamy truffles. A card rested there, and she plucked it up, peering at it. "Awww. Hey, Dar!"

"Mm?" A voice sounded right in her ear, almost making her hit the overhead.

"Jesus, would you not do that?" the blond woman yelped. "You're going to give me a heart attack one of these days, Dar."

"You called me," Dar complained. "It's not my fault I was right here." She poked her head into the small galley. "What's that?"

Kerry handed her the card, and retrieved the tray.

Dar studied the writing and felt a smile edge across her face. *This'll take the edge off your nerves. It better, considering it cost more than a damn F-18.* "It's from dad. Wow."

"Open wide." Kerry offered her a truffle, which she obediently accepted. "He's such a sweetie."

"Mmmhf." Dar nodded, chewing.

"Now I know where his daughter gets it from," the blond woman teased gently, catching Dar in mid-chew as a faint blush colored her skin. "Heh."

Dar sighed. "My reputation's in tatters." She swallowed. "Mmm… that's good." Her eyes brightened, and she sniffed after the tray. "More?"

Kerry poured the champagne, and handed her lover a glass, then produced another truffle, which disappeared immediately. "Hey, chew it, okay?" She took a sip of the alcohol and nibbled a sweet, enjoying the contrasting tastes. She looked down as a scrabbling of claws indicated Chino's approach, watching as the puppy stumbled down the stairs and barked at her. "Hello, honey."

"Yawp!" Chino sniffed around Dar's legs, then sat down on her foot. "Urrr."

Dar chuckled. "Thanks, Chino, I needed a footwarmer." She took a swallow of her drink and let it trickle down her throat, then she nudged Kerry. "You hoarding those?"

Kerry put a truffle in her mouth, then bit down lightly, and raised her eyebrows. "Srof?"

The taller woman tilted her head down, and took the proffered half, brushing her lips against Kerry's teasingly. "This is starting out to be a great day already."

Kerry grinned happily, then turned as she heard voices outside. "Well, I think we're about to get things going…awp."

Dar put her glass down, and laced her fingers through Kerry's hair, drawing her closer and into a heartfelt, passionate kiss. They separated after a long stretch of heartbeats and looked at each other. Dar put a warm hand on Kerry's cheek. "I love you," she said simply.

"I love you too," Kerry answered, her voice a little hoarse. "Thank you, for doing this, Dar. It means a lot to me."

Dar smiled tremulously and rubbed her thumb against Kerry's soft cheek. "I know. Me too." Her eyes shifted to the door. "Guess we'd better get going; I think I hear Duks."

Kerry hugged her for a moment, then released her, and followed her up the steps to the deck.

Sure enough, familiar figures were lining the dock, weirdly shadowed in the ochre security lights. "Morning." Dar lifted a hand, stifling a grin as Duks put his hands on his hips and glared at her.

"You know, Dar, it's a very good thing I am a forgiving sort." He shook his head. "You could not have had a sunset affair, eh?"

"Wrong ocean for that." Dar put a bridge down and tugged the lines taut as their guests came aboard. "Go on up into the front. We need to take some supplies on board." She gave a nod to the waiting staff carrying insulated coolers. "Thanks for coming. Hello, Maria."

"Buenos Dias, Dar, Kerrisita." Maria gave her vermilion headscarf a tug and handed Kerry a small box. "I know you are telling me not to get any gifts, but you take this anyhow."

"Thanks, Maria." Kerry took the box, then gave the secretary a hug. "Thanks for coming… we really appreciate it."

"Thank you for asking me." Maria smiled benevolently. "My family, they think I am having a, how you say, a fling, to be sneaking away so early."

Kerry walked with her to the bow to join Duks and Mariana, who were seated on the cushion whispering to each other. "They don't really, do they?" the blond woman asked, a little embarrassed. "I mean, we didn't think about how annoying it would be for everyone else to drag their butts out here before dawn; it's about the time we usually get up."

"Oh, it figures," Mari laughed. "You know, I should have realized if my overachieving, typical Type A friend Dar found a match, it'd have to be someone who was as much in to self-torture as she was."

"What do you do so early in the morning?" Maria asked curiously as she seated herself on a cushion.

Kerry glanced over as Duks and Mari started sniggering. "Actually, we go out running." She stuck her tongue out a little at them.

They both groaned. Maria hid a laugh behind a small hand.

🐾   🐾   🐾

Dar watched the two waiters stow the food and waited for them to leave before she investigated the contents, snagging a corn muffin and some butter and gaining an instantly attentive Labrador puppy glued to her foot. She split the muffin, then cracked open the insulated dish and scooped out a bit of the scrambled eggs it contained, and put some on each half. Then she settled down for a moment's peace, glad to let Kerry do the social honors for the time being.

The rocking of the boat soothed her as she chewed, allowing her nerves to settle. It wasn't the ceremony that was bothering her, she realized; it was that she was about to expose a very personal side of herself to someone other than Kerry.

Ugh. Dar sighed. *Well, get a grip, rugrat; after this whole thing, they suspected you had a marshmallow center anyway.* She shared her muffin with Chino, then took a breath and went back up on deck, carrying a thermal carafe of coffee and a stack of purple styrofoam cups. Purple styrofoam. Where in the hell did these people get stuff like that? She'd asked for plain foam, and gotten a face from Clemente as though she'd asked for paper frigging plates. He'd wanted to provide a china service for the coffee. So this was his compromise, she supposed, shaking her head.

"Hey, Dar."

A voice called from the docks. She turned to see Colleen, dressed in neatly pressed tan walking shorts and a crisp white polo with a tall, heavyset man in a sweatshirt and cutoffs who she guessed was the pastor. "Morning." She waited for them to cross the gangplank and gave them a reserved smile. "If you want to bring this up front, Colleen, I'll get the engines started." She glanced at the pastor. "Welcome aboard."

The man stuck a hand out, which Dar was now free to grasp since Colleen had helpfully snatched the coffee and cups from her. "Hello. You must be Dar."

Dar inclined her head, favorably impressed with his friendly face and firm handshake. "That's right…is it Pastor Robert?"

He laughed. "Sure. It's better than Pappy Bob, which is what my nephews call me." He cleared his throat a little. "It's a pleasure to meet you. From the way Kerry talks about you, I had a feeling she'd found someone special." He smiled a little at Dar's discomfited look. "I've known Kerry since she was a little girl."

A hint of warmth crept into Dar's eyes. "I bet you know some stories, then," she said, gracefully easing the subject away from herself. "Was she a scamp?"

"Oh ho, yes, a boat, er, load." He started laughing. "And yes, she certainly was—especially when she was in my Sunday school classes."

"Ooo, we should talk." Dar bestowed a grin on him, her eyes twinkling with mischief. "G'wan up front. I'm going to take us out." She paused. "Thanks for making it out here. I can't tell you how much this means to Kerry." She hesitated. "And to me."

He beamed. "It's my pleasure, and I'm an early riser anyway. The thought of doing this as the sun came up out on the beautiful Atlantic under God's own canopy...it's perfect."

Dar decided instantly. *I like him.* "Great." She walked over and untied the lines, setting the ship free of the dock. Then she walked to the bridge and started the two diesel engines, trimming them expertly and backing the vessel out of its slip. She heard a laugh from the bow, and glanced over to see Kerry hugging her former pastor, a look of delight on her face.

Dar smiled to herself as she guided the boat slowly out of the marina and headed it towards the Cut. The freshening breeze blew her hair back, and she took a breath of the salty air, remembering all the times she'd faced the dawn just like this.

Except, of course, the boat had been a whole lot smaller.

And she'd been the only one on it.

A solid warmth settled onto her foot, and she glanced down to see Chino curled up there.

Definitely different.

Duks wound his way over to her and leaned against the railing. "So, my friend, how are things?"

Dar glanced at him, then looked back at her gauges. "Weather's great, water's calm, couldn't ask for better. Why?"

Duks scratched his jaw, and regarded the faintly gray horizon. "Is it hard for you, Dar?" he asked gently, regarding her. "Letting all of us into private part of your life like this?"

Dar adjusted the throttles, using that as an excuse to delay her answer. Finally she sighed. "Does it matter?"

The accountant snorted softly. "That's answer enough," he advised her. "If it's any consolation, I think it's been good for you."

Pale blue eyes flicked to his face, then went to the water, scanning it. "It's taken some getting used to," she admitted quietly. "I've had to change the way I think about a lot of things."

He nodded. "I gathered." A gentle peal of laughter rose from the bow, and he looked over to see Kerry hopping up and down a little, shaking a finger at Mariana. He looked back and caught Dar watching the blond woman, an unconscious smile tugging at her lips. He chuckled softly and shook his head.

"All right, so where are we going?" Colleen asked, spreading her arms out against the railing and regarding Kerry. "The Bahamas?"

"No, at least I hope not." Kerry smiled, as she regarded the horizon. "Dar wouldn't say. Or, to be more specific, she gave me a GPS coordinate, which meant to me somewhere in the Florida Straits." She leaned on the railing. "She did say it wasn't that far out, just far enough to lose the city."

They were out of the cut now and heading across the water, the powerful roar of the boat's engines at full throttle as Dar pushed them through the soft graying light. The ocean was calm, just a faint ruffle moving the dark surface and the occasional splash as a fish poked its nose up into the dawn as the horizon went from black to lavender, spreading out a band of faint color across the rim of the world.

After about twenty minutes, the roar lessened and Kerry moved to the railing, leaning over and spotting a small bit of land in the growing light. "I guess we're here," she announced with a grin. "It's an island."

They all clustered around her and peered out, gazing at the cluster of trees outlined in the dusky light. A tiny ridge of coral, it seemed, with just enough dirt to allow a cluster of sea grapes and mangroves, its sandy edge sloping up out of the water.

Dar moved the boat in close and wound a rope around an overhanging branch, securing them, then cut the engines, the sudden silence almost startling as the lap of the waves and the soft hiss of the water brushing the shore became very evident.

Everyone peered at the grayish, licking waters between the boat and the island, then at Dar. Kerry walked over and put an arm on her shoulder. "Um, Dar?"

"Yes?" Innocent, innocent blue eyes.

Kerry chewed her lip. "Did you think this all out?"

"Yes." Dark lashes batted at her. "Why?"

Kerry leaned close to her. "I don't know if everyone here can swim, sweetheart," she whispered. "Unless you wanted to have the ceremony on the boat."

"Nah." Dar patted her on the shoulder. "Be right back." Putting her hands on the railing, she vaulted over, landing in the water with a clean splash. The waves came up to her mid-thigh, and she waded towards the island with a purposeful stride.

"What is she doing?" Colleen came up next to Kerry at the railing and peered over. The rest of the group joined her; even Chino poked her head through and sniffed.

"I have no earthly idea," Kerry murmured. "It must be a sand bar. Look how shallow it is here."

Eyes turned to her. "Hope we don't get stuck," Mari remarked with a grin. "Can you imagine the story that would make?"

Kerry peered out into the slowly growing light, chuckling. "No, she anchored us in a deep enough draft; it slopes up there. I can see the water getting lighter." She leaned over. "Hey Dar, what are you doing?" They could hear splashing noises coming towards them.

The water parted, and then Dar reappeared from around a bend, her overalls damp almost to her groin and a rope over one shoulder. She moved steadily towards the boat and as she came closer, they saw something trailing behind her. The wind tugged at her knotted hair, sending tendrils of it whisking around her face, and a flash of white appeared as she smiled up at them. "Here you go." She handed up the rope. "Pull."

Duks took hold and tugged, and they watched as a barnacle-be-decked wooden platform came towards them. It was old, but it seemed to be in one piece, consisting of sun-bleached wood on rubber pon-toons.

"Dios Mío, it's a sidewalk," Maria said, surprised. "How clever you are, jefa."

Dar leaned against the boat and pulled the wooden bridge into place, tying it securely to the railing. "Well, actually I made this in my much less clever days." She gave them all a wry look. "High school, to be exact." She used the railing to pull herself up, standing on the bridge and removing a piece of impudent seaweed that had attached itself to her thigh. "Water's nice."

Kerry had retrieved the diving ladder from its hooks and set it into place, then climbed down onto the bridge. It bobbed under her weight, but held firm, and she bounced up and down on it a few times. "Well, for a high school shop project, it sure feels sturdy." She gave her lover a warm smile. "Okay, let's go, folks."

With some hesitation and muted screams, they did, and landed safely onto the bridge with little incident, moving along it towards the small beach they could see ahead. Dar waited to bring up the rear and collect Chino, then she followed along, not surprised to find Kerry waiting for her. "Hey."

"Hey." Kerry looked around. "So this is an old haunt of yours, huh?" She smiled. "It's nice out here."

Dar took a deep breath of the familiar air. "You could say that. Most kids have treehouses; this was mine." She stepped off the pontoon bridge onto the soft, sandy beach. "It's too small for anyone to bother with it, and it's about the best place I've ever known to just sit and watch the sun rise." She paused, as they walked towards the small group standing on the beach in the growing light. "Or just to daydream."

Kerry looked up at her. "Bet you had some great parties out here." She nudged her lover in the ribs.

Dar regarded the intertwined mangroves reflectively. "You're the first people I've ever brought out with me," she remarked quietly.

Kerry sucked in a surprised breath. "Oh." Then she put an arm around Dar and leaned against her as they walked along in silence.

They joined the small group on the beach, where the waves were rolling gently up and hissing back with almost hypnotic regularity. Seagulls coasted overhead, circling lazily, waiting for the sunrise now painting the eastern horizon in bands of coral and deep russet. Only a thin tracing of clouds obscured the view, and the breeze grew stronger as if in anticipation.

Dar put Chino down and watched her dash excitedly over the water, almost immediately encountering a startled crab.

"Yawp!" Chino barked, watching the crab skitter backwards. "Yawp!"

The group laughed. "Chino. Don't got there," Colleen warned, shooing the crab down its hole. "You're gonna get your little nose bitten."

Dar cleared her throat. "Thanks for coming out here, folks."

"Thanks for inviting us," Mari answered promptly. "I can't think of a better way to spend a Saturday morning."

The taller woman stuck her hands in her pockets and regarded the horizon. "I know sunrise isn't everyone's favorite time of day, but it seemed appropriate to me because I always regarded dawn as being a time of…" She paused. "A time to start things."

Duks chuckled softly. "I always suspected the reason you were constantly one step ahead of us was because you just woke up earlier, my friend. It is nice to have that confirmed."

Even Dar laughed. "Thanks," she drawled in response, then fell awkwardly silent.

"Well, you can't take the blame for this," Kerry spoke up, as she moved to Dar's side, and they faced the oncoming dawn. "Pastor Robert here was visiting in Miami. He's been my pastor since I was…well, let's say a long time." She paused, sucking in a slightly nervous breath amid another round of gentle laughter.

"And he offered to preside at a commitment ceremony, and I kinda talked Dar into it, so it's my fault we're all out here," she continued bravely. "So I guess it's time to get started." She actually heard Dar swallow audibly at this, and she gave her lover a mildly concerned look.

Pastor Robert stepped in front of them, his plain, black sweatshirt highlighting the polished silver cross on his chest. He drew out a small bible and held it, regarding them with kindly eyes.

Kerry smiled back at him, her hand instinctively finding Dar's, and feeling the faint tremor run through it. She glanced at the taller woman, and saw the brief tightening of her lips, and the sudden movement as her jaw muscles clenched under the skin. A gentle squeeze of her hand brought a smile to the tense lips, however.

The pastor folded his hands. "My children," he began softly, then glanced at Dar. "It's okay to call you that, isn't it?"

Dar nodded. "Sure." She let out a breath, unsure of what to expect from him. Kerry had merely said he had words prepared, but…

"Good." He exhaled, then started speaking, his voice taking on a rounder, more mellow tone. "My children, we stand here in the eyes of God, beneath his sky, and amongst the waters of life he put upon the earth. And as those things are by his mercy, and out of our control, so too is the coming together in love of the two people who stand before me, so this ceremony is not a thing of permission, or of sanction, or of regulation, but rather a simple affirmation of a truth that is one of the greatest gifts our Lord has bestowed on us."

The sky brightened, and the sea eased from gray to a thousand shades of green.

Dar drew in a breath, and released it. Waiting.

"So I will state here, in the name of God, whose servant I am, that no person shall sunder what the Lord has chosen to join together. May his gentle hand guide you and watch over you for all the days of your lives." The pastor turned to Kerry, his eyes twinkling a little. "Kerrison, I have known you since you were a small child running rampant in my classrooms."

Kerry bit back a nervous chuckle, but nodded. "Yes, you have."

"I have never known you to give your word and not mean it, or enter into a thing if you didn't intend to carry it through, so if you say to me you wish to spend your life with this person, she'd better watch out," Pastor Robert intoned. "Because for you, I know in my heart, that forever means just that."

Kerry felt tears sting her eyes, and she just nodded in affirmation.

Now the pastor's eyes shifted to Dar. "I have just met you." His voice was quiet, and thoughtful. "But the person I see before me is someone I believe would be steadfast, and loyal, and a friend you could depend on above all others."

Startled, the pale blue eyes flicked to his face.

"And I feel that your word, once given, is never taken back," the pastor went on.

Dar hesitated, then nodded quietly.

Robert nodded as well. "Then sit at the side of the Lord, for his hands cup your souls gently together." He held out the book and took their joined hands, resting them under his own. "Go with God, and know that where love exists, he is present, now, and forever." A pristine rose light spread over them as the sun hit the horizon, sending a palette of reds, and golds, and tropical tints across the sky.

The pastor squeezed their hands, then let his drop, watching as they turned towards each other, the sound of the surf suddenly loud as he stopped speaking.

Kerry felt very nervous, conscious of the people watching and the expectant air. Then she lifted her eyes to meet Dar's and found herself swallowed into them, sparkling there in the rosy light, warm and familiar, and her nerves settled. "Me first, I guess." Screwing up her courage, she took a breath, hoping she'd remember all the words in all the right places. "I'm not really sure where this came from; I was sitting outside looking out over the water, and thinking of you, and when I looked down, there it was, in my handwriting." She paused, reflectively.

"It was like my heart wrote it for me...but anyway..." Kerry cleared her throat and began to recite.

"When I look at you
I see sunlight and shadows
Deep, still waters, and wild rapids
A fiery heart and a cool, clear mind.
When I look at you,
I see all that I am, and all that I could hope to be.
My past, and my future,
My one safe harbor in a terrible world.
When I look at you,
I see my best friend and playmate,
My protector and defender,
The love of my life and the holder of my soul
Losing you, I would also lose myself
And be left in a darkness so deep,
No light could ever find me."

"So where you go, I go," she finished in an almost whisper.

The sun's rays now poured over them, throwing part of Dar's face into shadow, and her chest heaved suddenly as she resumed breathing. "That was beautiful," she whispered, unnerved at the familiarity of the words, and the deep, resonant chime they sounded inside her.

Kerry dropped her eyes, then lifted them again. "Thanks."

A tiny, awkward silence fell. Then Dar closed her eyes, and sucked in a deep breath, visibly straightening. "Well, I'm really not one for speeches."

A soft chuckle rose.

"And I've never really known how to use words to express what I was feeling, so I guess I'll just have to improvise." Her shoulders dropped a tiny bit, then she opened her mouth and started singing.

Kerry stared at her, completely mesmerized, to the point where she almost missed the words.

But not quite.

"I feel like I was born today
Like all my life before's only been a dream,
Only touching the surface, never going further
Never being a part of the world.
I feel like I was born today
Knowing I have to walk a wider path from now on.

Wide enough for two of us, walking side by side
Facing the future together.
The sea is wide,
Our love is wider,
Covering the earth from end to end.
Walk beside me,
Through wind and weather,
For all the years on earth we'll spend.
I feel like I was born today
We leave behind a past of sorrow.
Going forward through the sunlight,
Hand in hand, and souls united."

Dar let her voice trail off, and she fell silent, uncomfortably aware of the stares focused on her. What had she been thinking of? She sighed. At least it was over. She lifted her eyes to Kerry's face almost furtively, then stilled, seeing the tears running down her lover's cheeks.

In pure reflex, she lifted a hand and brushed them away. "Wasn't that bad, was it?" she joked faintly. "I didn't get a chance to practice it. Much."

"Wh…" Kerry's voice broke, and she cleared her throat and tried again. "It was gorgeous…awesome…where did you find it?" she asked. "The song? And my god, Dar…you should sing more often. You have a beautiful voice."

A murmur agreed with her, causing Dar to glance around self-consciously. "Thanks." She was painfully aware of the deep blush coloring her skin, and hoped that her base tan concealed most of it.

Kerry moved closer and enfolded her in a hug, burying her face into Dar's chest and squeezing her tightly. She returned the hug, looking over Kerry's shoulder to see quietly respectful glances back at her. *Well. That went better than expected.* "So…I um…" Dar realized she was rooted in place by her blond lover. "Hope everyone's hungry; they packed enough food to feed half the office."

That broke the reverent tension, and everyone relaxed. Dar smiled as she felt Kerry's hands clench in her shirt.

Yeah. Definitely different.

Kerry sniffed, and backed off a little, lifting her head to peer up at Dar. "Hang on. I've got one more thing."

Everyone turned to watch her as she pulled the wooden box from her bag, then handed the bag back to Colleen. She opened the case and the sun poured in, sparking brilliance from the crystals.

Dar blinked. "Wow."

Kerry held her hands out. "Hold the box for me?"

Dar did, cradling it in her palms as Kerry pulled the joined crystals out.

"I'm…um, I'm not sure where these came from, originally," the blond woman stated softly. "They probably have a history we'll never know, but I really liked the way they're both very unique." She parted the two pieces, holding them up to the light. "But they fit together so perfectly." She mated them with a tiny, satisfying click. "I hope we can do the same."

Dar smiled at her. "I love it… they're beautiful. I can't believe they turned out so nice."

Kerry beamed, then looped one chain over her hand and opened the other, leaning forward, and lifting her arms up.

"Wrong one," Dar stated softly, then she blinked, a little startled.

Kerry looked at her for a long moment, then she nodded and changed hands, fastening the other necklace around Dar's smoothly tanned neck. She kissed her gently, then stood back, as Dar took the other chain and fastened it around her, and the crystal nestled itself into the hollow of her throat with a sense of quiet belonging.

Blue eyes met green, in a glance as old as time.

They kissed again, and the sun bathed them, sparkling the waters that surrounded the island as though dancing off crystal walls.

They were seated in the shade, sprawled in the soft sand as they lingered over breakfast, the warm sun and the steady breeze making it too comfortable to want to move. Dar was stretched out, her feet half buried in the sand, leaning on a piece of driftwood with Kerry curled up on her side pressed against her. She glanced up as Chino started barking somewhere of in the brush to their left. "Chino!"

The puppy just barked harder, then the brush rustled sharply.

"I'll get her." Dar sighed, then hoisted herself to her feet and brushed a layer of sand off her legs. She plowed off through the soft surface, heading towards the sound of the excited puppy. "Chino!"

She pushed through some brush, then froze as she heard a low voice. A moment later, a grin spread over her face and she hurried forward.

"Would you shut up, ya little bag of mouse squeaks?" the voice was saying, in a loud whisper.

Dar parted the last bushes and peered through. "Hey."

Cantankerous blue eyes glared back at her. "Damn dog."

Andrew Roberts was hunkered down in the brush, a light three-quarter wetsuit covering part of his body and a neatly stacked pile of diving equipment just off to one side. In the sharply patterned sunlight, the horrible scars on his face were very evident, but even that couldn't hide the smile as he gazed up at his daughter. "Hey there, rugrat."

Dar ambled over and dropped to her knees next to him. "Thanks for the treats. I'm glad you could make it out here, but how…?"

"I could just go all military on you and say that is classified information," the older man rasped. "But the truth is your little kumquat got hold of me and batted those pretty green eyes."

Dar smiled and glanced down. "She's really something else, huh?"

"Ya got that right." Andrew studied his hands, which were petting a contented Chino. "That was a real nice ceremony," he told her. "Who's Grizzly Adams?"

A soft chuckle. "Kerry's pastor from Michigan. He's on vacation."

A little silence fell. "Ya know… I always wondered what I'd do if I had to walk you down some long damn aisle," Andrew mused. "I didn't think anyone living could convince me whoever was standing up on the other end was good enough for my kid."

Dar sat down in the sand next to him and circled her knees with both arms. "I can remember thinking that I wouldn't get married unless I could find someone just like you," she revealed, feeling a hand settle on to her shoulder. "Then I realized you're one of kind."

"Paladar, if you make me start crying, I'm gonna whup you," her father growled. "Bad enough I had to listen to all that pretty poetry and you singing and all that. I like to have drowned back here. I almost had to get my damn desal kit out."

Dar had to let out a soft laugh. "Sorry." She studied the ground, a soft gray sand mixed with broken seashells. "Thank you for coming. It means a lot to me."

Andrew reached over and awkwardly stroked her hair. "Makes me feel good to see you feel good, rugrat," he murmured. "I think you found a real good one there."

Dar turned her head and gazed up at him. "Thanks. I do, too." She paused. "You want some breakfast?"

"You telling me you had that yacht catered?" He laughed.

A sheepish chuckle. "Something like that. C'mon; come sit by us, and join the party."

A quietly sad look colored his eyes. "Naw… you know I'm not one for company, rugrat."

Dar nodded. "Me either. But I found out that sometimes what matters is what's important to other people, and I'd really love to introduce my friends to my father." She kept her gaze even. "Please, daddy?"

Andrew looked at her for a long, tense moment. A terrible, aching fear was the chief emotion Dar could see in his eyes, which fluttered closed, then opened again as he let out a breath. "You don't know what you're asking me, Paladar."

Dar smiled wistfully. "Yes, I do."

Then she waited, listening to the soft sound of the waves rustling all around them, and the contented breathing of the puppy curled at their feet.

"All right." Her father finally said. "If you could get up and sing in front of all them people, I guess I kin do this," he grumbled. "C'mon already… I'm hungry."

Dar pushed herself to her feet and took his hand as she led the way back towards the beach.

🦋   🦋   🦋

"Where did she go off to?" Kerry worried, getting to her knees. "This is a really small island, and that's a really big puppy; she can't have gotten that lost that fast." She peered into the brush and her breath caught. "Oh."

"She got someone with her?" Duks lifted himself up on one elbow. "Where did he come from?"

Kerry watched the approaching duo with a sense of wonder. "I can't believe it." She got up and trotted over, giving Andrew a big smile and throwing her arms around him. "Dad…this is great."

Dar's father stopped dead and managed to give the impression he'd been attacked by a large, friendly, talking alligator. "She do that to everyone?" he asked Dar, who was biting her lip to keep from laughing.

"Nope," Dar told him. "Only people she likes."

Andrew sighed, then hugged the blond woman back. "Hi there, kumquat." He joined them as they walked back to the rest of the group, facing curious eyes that glanced at the tall man, then flicked to Dar in question.

"Folks, say hi to my father," Dar announced quietly. "His name's Andrew. Dad, this is Duks, Mariana, and Maria, who work with us, and Pastor Robert, from Michigan."

Everyone was a touch awkward, but Andrew rose to the occasion and settled down, his wetsuit creaking slightly. "Nice ta meet you all," he stated bluntly, then glanced at his daughter. "Were you saying something about eggs?"

"Dios Mío!" Maria said suddenly. "You are the one who is sending those beautiful flowers! I am recognizing your voice."

"Oh, the coral roses?" Mariana smiled. "I was wondering…"

Andrew glared at them. "Well, ya plastered her picture all over the city, I had to do somethin'."

All of them smiled and glanced at Dar knowingly.

Dar nodded a little, then went to grab her father a plate. She felt a hand touch her shoulder, and turned to see gentle sea green eyes looking warmly back at her. "He came."

"Mm hmm," Kerry agreed. "You got him to come out with us…Dar, that's amazing."

Dar added grits to the plate and drizzled gravy over them. "It's a day of new beginnings." She looked out over the water, then back at the blond woman. "Wonder what'll happen next?"

Kerry took the plate from her, and slid an arm around her waist as they walked back over. "I can't wait to find out."

The End...

Tristaine, by Cate Culpepper, focuses on the fierce love that develops among strong women facing a common evil. Jesstin is an Amazon from the village of Tristaine who has been imprisoned in the Clinic, a scientific research facility.

Brenna, the young medic assigned to monitor Jess's health, becomes increasingly disturbed by the savage punishments her patient endures at the hands of the ambitious scientist Caster, and a bond grows between the two women. The struggle Brenna and Jess face in escaping the Clinic and Caster's determined pursuit deepens the connection between them. When they unite with three of Jess's Amazon sisters, the simple beauty of Tristaine's women-centered culture weaves through the plot, which moves toward a violent confrontation with Caster's posse.

And now for a special preview from the soon to be released JHP book by Cate Culpepper, *Tristaine*.

Tristaine

Cate Culpepper

——— *** ———

An Excerpt

Jess expected to be executed when they took her from the communal cell. The two young Amazons imprisoned with her had the same thought, and the guards had to use pepper spray to get her out of there.

A beating was better than execution. Jess reminded herself of this, as she had every time she'd been beaten since her arrest. She had never understood the purpose of the beatings—her captors didn't seem interested in interrogating her. Tonight's session was as mystifying in purpose as the others had been, but it was thorough.

The harsh glare of the cell's overhead lights began to blur as the blows rained down on her body, and she felt her senses start to fade at last. *As long as they leave Kyla and Camryn alone*, Jess thought. *As long as they're okay, we can give Shann time.*

She was unconscious when she was transferred to the Clinic.

—— *** ——

Biting cold woke her.

Jess surfaced through the familiar, unpleasant haze bestowed by blows to the head. She found herself strapped into a jointed chair, a kind of reclining restraint that left her head elevated, equipped with arm and ankle cuffs. Her long body lay full-length on its padded surface, and the cuffs were tight, but not biting. Jess figured if she hadn't been freezing, and aching with fresh bruises, she'd be comfortable enough.

Another intense light flooded her, courtesy of a floodlamp suspended over the recliner. It took Jess several tries to squint her eyes fully open. She still wore Prison blacks, a standard-issue sleeveless shirt and slacks, and she was barefoot. Her wrists were cuffed to the chair at her sides. Her ankles were similarly bound at the base of the recliner.

She leaned as far as the straps would allow and spat a small mouthful of blood to the concrete floor. Wincing at the pain in her side, her blue gaze ticked methodically around the small, antiseptic room. A detention cell, judging by the heavy steel door—empty except for the reclining restraint and shelves of medical supplies, and cold as a Fed's heart.

The frigid air smelled astringently sterile. Jess longed again for the light pine spice of Tristaine's mountain breezes; and wondered if this eye-watering chemical stench would burn it from her memory forever.

The dark woman shivered, and craned her neck—she couldn't see the cooling unit in the wall behind her, but judging from the chill blasting through the cell, it was cranked high.

She lay still and concentrated on her breathing. The crease between her arched eyebrows faded as she relaxed. Jess knew she wasn't badly hurt. She was cold and hungry, but she'd been hungry for months. She still had a pulse. She could wait this part out.

She was too cold to sleep, but she could pass the time thinking of home, a rare luxury. To Jess's unrelenting, lifelong dismay, she had no control over her tear ducts. She hated it, but she cried easily. Her mentor, Dyan, taught her warriors never to shed tears before an enemy. Jess didn't risk remembering Tristaine these days unless she was alone.

The tall Amazon's bare shoulders eased against the leather surface of the restrainer as her mind filled with images. Nothing drawn out, just quick, fragmented memories of her adanin, and her home.

All the clichés of poetry applied to Tristaine—sunlit meadows, racing streams, brooding, craggy peaks looming above lush old-growth forest. Shann and Dyan, sitting quietly in meetings of Tristaine's high council, listening more than speaking, their hands joined loosely on the oak table. Dyan's scarred knuckles, her blunt fingers stroking Shann's wrist.

Camryn's sweet younger sister, Lauren, following Dyan around everywhere she went, like a worshipful puppy. She blushed crimson whenever Dyan spoke to her, and raised her hand to hide her crooked front teeth when she smiled.

Jess's eyes filled long before she remembered Dyan, and young Lauren, trapped on a dark mountain trail, dancing under a deadly spray of bullets.

She heard the pneumatic pump over the door whoosh as a young blonde elbowed it open. She was carrying a clipboard, and she wore a white coat. Jess blinked quickly to clear her eyes.

"What the—?"

There was surprise in the girl's voice. The white coat was too big for her, and she wrapped it more tightly around her shoulders as she went to check the cooling unit behind the jointed chair. Jess noted that she moved like an athlete in spite of her diminutive size.

The young woman studied the tall prisoner's restraints silently for a moment. Her green eyes narrowed when she saw the blood on Jess's face. Then she sighed, and blinked at the steam her breath made in the cold air.

"My name is Brenna. I'm staff." She sounded angry as she consulted the form on her clipboard. "Who left you in here like this?"

"Pleased to meet you, Brenna." Jess flexed her sore jaw. "I'm Jesstin."

The medic blew tousled bangs off her forehead and slapped the clipboard against her thigh. "Well, this tells me exactly jack. You came in when, last night?"

Without waiting for a reply, Brenna snatched the penlight out of the breast pocket of her white coat, thumbed it on, and moved the beam across Jess's glassy eyes.

"Were you examined on arrival, Jesstin?"

"No. I'm all right." It would have sounded more butch if her teeth hadn't been chattering.

Brenna measured her pulse at the throat, and frowned at her blood-shot eyes. "How long since you've had any solid sleep?"

"Couple of days."

The smaller woman muttered something derogatory about the idiocy of Prison healthcare as she palpated the base of Jess's jaw, her eyes unfocused over her shoulder.

Brenna tried to concentrate. She'd been told she might find some of the subjects admitted to Military Research in rocky shape. Apparently beatings were common practice before a prisoner was transferred from the Prison to the Clinic. She had no idea how this stupidity was justified, and questions from new medics were not encouraged. But judging from this woman's bruises, emerging and faded, she had been beaten more than once in the recent past. Brenna wondered uneasily what this prisoner, with her mild brogue, had done to merit such treatment.

Jess wondered uneasily when the Feds had started handing out hypodermics to schoolgirls. However, she had to admit that this Brenna's touch was light and efficient. She'd seen that same look of focused concentration in Shann's eyes when she tended one of Tristaine's wounded. At least the girl had good instincts—and probably decent training. City-dwellers were tested for aptitude in childhood, then educated rigorously in a single discipline. Hopefully this girl hadn't held dreams of teaching or practicing law—medicine had been her only career option.

She tightened as Brenna's fingers probed a tender area low on her right side. The medic's green eyes shot her a look of concern before she continued. This blonde pixie didn't strike Jess as callous enough for Government work.

"Were you given anything for pain at the Prison?" Brenna asked.

"They don't keep analgesics at the Prison. Your hands are cold, Brenna."

"Jesstin?" Brenna cleared her throat, and straightened. "You're supposed to answer my questions as simply and briefly as possible. If you're insolent, or too familiar, or uncooperative, there'll be consequences. You know that, right?"

"Right."

"Great, we understand each other." Brenna pulled a thick blanket from the stand beneath the restraining chair. She caught Jess's eye, and the corner of her mouth lifted. "I may be short, but in your condition I could deck you with one gut-punch. Don't forget it, please."

She flipped the blanket out and settled it over Jess, then tucked it around her sides with an odd gentleness. "Okay. I'll find someone in Maintenance to turn down the damn cooler. We'll make you comfortable enough to rest. Sound all right?"

"Yes'm."

Brenna glanced at her, wary of sarcasm, but the tall woman's sky-blue eyes were guileless. She smiled, briefly, and left the cell.

—— *** ——

Brenna opened her locker and pulled out a small silver flask. She tipped it twice, angry with herself for letting emotion goad her. Beating a woman senseless seemed pointlessly brutal, but an entry-level medic had no control over transfer protocols. Caster had warned her that too much empathy could be dangerous here. Military Research was a prime assignment, and she had no intention of making waves.

When she pushed the heavy door open again, she was relieved to note some improvement. While still cool, the cell's temperature was bearable. The dark woman lay quietly under the blanket. She opened those disconcertingly blue eyes when Brenna approached her.

"What do you say we start again." She folded her hands behind her. "I'm Brenna, I'm staff. I'm going to take care of your health needs during your clinical trials, and be your medical advocate while you're in the Military Research Unit. Remember that I have the authority to discipline or disable you at any time, if necessary. Is all of that clear?"

Jess felt her gut clench. "Military research…."

Bad enough that she had awakened in the Clinic—stories of the place abounded in the Prison's communal cells—but she had still harbored hope for a civilian unit. Jess would have preferred organ harvesting, or the morgue, to this. Military research meant the Government intended to use her against Tristaine.

"Caster is the scientist in charge of your project. She'll explain all of that to you later." Now Brenna's voice took on a practiced, soothing cadence. "You just need to concentrate on following directions, Jesstin, and obeying rules, and you'll be fine. All that clear?"

"Clear," Jess said. She smelled whiskey. Wonderful. Clinical trials, Military research, and a Government pixie with a fondness for spirits and access to long needles. The luck of Tristaine's women hadn't turned yet.

"Also." Brenna rummaged in the pocket of her lab coat, her brows lowering with unconscious distaste. "I should have read this to you earlier." She pulled out an index card, and cleared her throat again.

"'Jesstin, your transfer to this medical facility was arranged under conditions of highest security. Be aware that armed peace officers—'" Brenna glanced up. "They mean orderlies with guns. 'That armed peace officers, stationed throughout the Clinic at all times, will ensure your compliance with unit rules.'"

She sighed, and put the card back in her pocket. "It goes on like that for a while. Basically, you can rebel or try to escape, if you wish, but someone will shoot you if you do."

Jess nodded. This girl must not know that the Feds had assured her compliance beyond the firepower of Clinic staff.

"I need to patch you up." Brenna surveyed Jess critically. "Save us both time, tell me where you're hurt."

"My head stings." Jess thought about it. "My side hurts. Other than that, cuts and bruises."

Brenna unbuttoned the tall woman's shirt, feeling the blue gaze on her face as she spread the black cloth apart. Standing on her tiptoes and leaning over, she spotted a thunderhead bruise low on Jess's right side. "That's got to hurt like hell, Jesstin. You might have a couple of fractured ribs."

"Don't think so."

"Well, I need to be sure." Brenna folded her arms and regarded Jess soberly. "I'll have to palpate that bruised area to see if you need x-rays. That's going to be painful. And I need to stitch the cut on your head." She sighed. "You were right about analgesics, Jesstin. I checked your orders, and I can't give you any.."

"Brenna?" Jess squinted up at her. "Just curious. How in blazes did you get here?"

"What do you mean?"

"You don't seem to enjoy inflicting pain." The cobalt eyes were weary, but curious. "I'm trying, but I can't see you as the bloodthirsty type."

"I'm a certified medical technician, Jesstin. I may be new to this particular unit, but I've been ankle-deep in blood before, believe me. Don't worry, I'm not some green nurse's aid—"

"You're a kid." Jess closed her eyes. This girl was only a few years older than Kyla and Cam. "You seem a capable medic, lass, but how you got assigned to a gruesome outfit like Military Research—"

Brenna laid the flat of her hand over the bruise on the prisoner's ribs and pressed, gently but deliberately. Jess gasped and stiffened, hard, in the restraints.

"Okay." Brenna straightened, and let out a long breath. "Now you know I'm not just a capable medic, I'm also capable of correcting you, if I have to." She studied Jess's pale features and folded her arms. "Look . . . we have to apply a pain stimulus like that with a new patient, sometime during the first examination. That makes it clear to you that I'll do what I—"

"Clear," Jess gasped.

Brenna nodded and pushed up the sleeves of her coat, as if to reset her professional mode. She started to speak, and then waited, uneasily, until the dark woman was able to relax again in the restrainer.

"The other Clinic unit I was assigned to didn't do military research, Jesstin. But we did several civilian projects, and I've worked with lots of prisoners in clinical trials. Some of my patients did well, and they were released. Some of them messed up, and they went back to Prison." Brenna shrugged. "It didn't matter to me, my pay was the same. So don't push me, okay?"

Neither of them spoke while Brenna stitched the cut above Jess's brow. The medic's deft fingers were cold on the rugged face. She'd never stitched anyone without at least a numbing spray before, and she found her patient's utter stillness beneath the fiery needle unnerving. To Brenna's credit, however, her stitches were characteristically neat and even. She held herself to high standards when it came to patient care.

The blonde woman moved to the other side of the recliner and used her palms and the flats of her fingers to detect any sign of fracture in the prisoner's ribs. She applied salve and bandages as needed. Then she wrote clinical notes on the clipboard for some time while the dark Amazon dozed beneath the blanket.

Brenna brushed one hand through her bangs and noticed she'd gotten a smudge of blood on the corner of the blue intake form. She slapped down her pen in annoyance and went to the sink. She didn't realize her hands were trembling until she held them beneath the water, and she thought of the flask in her locker again, longingly.

She took a white cloth and folded it. The tall woman was still shivering, probably from exhaustion as well as the lack of an analgesic. Brenna patted Jess's forehead with the cloth, damp with sweat in spite of the cool room, and summarized her clinical impressions.

Jesstin of Tristaine was a caucasian female in her late twenties. She was slightly malnourished, but she looked as if she'd been healthy and active before her incarceration. To say the least, Brenna thought—she looked as strong as a horse. Her shoulders were broad, and her powerful arms and legs required constant restraint, according to her orders. She might have been sentenced to fieldwork at the Prison, judging by the healing scratches on her long-fingered hands.

Brenna unsnapped Jess's shirt again and patted the cloth over her throat before moving it over her stomach and sides. She found that she avoided touching the firm, pale breasts.

"I'll tell you a secret of the medic's trade, Jesstin." Brenna ran the soft cloth down each muscled arm. "If you know how, and when, to administer pain—and your patient knows you're willing to…you don't have to do it very often. Makes life more pleasant for both of us."

"Did you learn that bit of wisdom from this Caster, Brenna?" Jesstin's brogue softened the words. "That's the credo of a bully, not a healer."

Brenna drew a breath, but she saw another small tightening around Jess's eyes as pain flickered through her, and decided to let the comment pass.

A few minutes later Brenna folded the cloth, and the corners of her green eyes crinkled as she smiled. "I think you're patched for the night, Jesstin. Can you sleep for a while?"

"Sure." Jess shifted stiffly, and another shadow of pain crossed her face.

Brenna studied her pensively, then flicked off the floodlight above them, plunging the cell into blue-hued darkness. Her searching fingers touched her patient's shoulder, then slid gently beneath her dark hair. She cupped the strong neck, noting the velvet-sheathed tension thrumming in her palm. She began working the tight muscles with strong fingers, closing her eyes in order to concentrate.

"You're like me," Brenna murmured. "We carry all our tension in our shoulders and neck. My little sister can put me to sleep in ten minutes doing this. Try to relax, Jess."

She probed the steely muscles silently for a while.

Jess let herself drift with the memory of Shann's cool, healing touch, and she let the darkness hide the welling in her eyes.

"Listen." Brenna kept her voice low and soothing. "If less stress will help you heal, your chart says you've got nothing but physical therapy for the next week. Caster wants to build your strength for the clinical trials. That means bed rest, decent meals, light exercise when you're ready for it...."

Brenna heard a light, buzzing snore in the darkness. She smiled, and edged her hand carefully from beneath Jess's thick hair. She smoothed a stray lock off the sleeping woman's brow, sifting its softness through her fingers. "I'm so good," she murmured.

To read the rest.... please visit our website at http://www.justicehouse.com and order this exciting book.

A Year in Paris, by Malaurie Barber,

When student Chloe Jones becomes an au pair, all she's looking for is an interesting year abroad in Paris, but she gets more than she bargained for in the mysterious Glairon family. While caring for sweet little Clement, Chloe begins to care a great deal for his beautiful but haunted half sister, Laurence, too. But not even the most romantic city in the world can help these two when the family's secrets threaten to destroy them all.

And now for a special preview from the soon to be released JHP book by Malaurie Barber, *A Year In Paris*.

A Year In Paris

Malaurie Barber

_____ *** _____

An Excerpt

The ride to Paris was faster than the night before. Laurence had explained to Chloe that they were going to see a friend she had not seen in a long time. The meeting had been set for 4 p.m. in front of the fountains at Les Halles market. At 4:15 Laurence parked her bike on a side street and took off her helmet.

"Okay, here we are. We're not too late. Hopefully Tony is still there."

The street was crowded. Artists were painting portraits, jugglers were putting on a show, and guitarists were playing, hoping for some pocket change. The ensemble created a very busy atmosphere full of music and laughter.

Laurence and Chloe walked into a brasserie called "A la Crepe." Laurence scanned the room for Tony and spotted him in the far corner reading a newspaper. She called across the room. "Hey, Tony!"

Tony waved and got up to meet them.

"Te voilà. Toujours ponctuelle à ce que je vois," said Tony, grabbing Laurence and planting two kisses on her cheeks.

Laurence laughed and moved aside to introduce Chloe.

"C'est mon amie Chloe. Elle ne parle pas très bien le Francais." She then turned to Chloe and introduced Tony to her. "Chloe, this is Tony, a longtime friend."

"Bonjour," said Chloe, shaking Tony's hand.

"My English isn't as good as Ms. Perfect over there, but I will try," said Tony with a heavy accent as he sat and gestured to Chloe to sit next to him. Chloe smiled and took the offered seat.

The conversation started in English, but as it got more animated French took over. Chloe tried to follow the conversation but soon gave up. Her mind drifted back over the past few days and how much time she and Laurence had spent together. *She is quite something. I'm really going to miss her. Boy, I wish she could stay. I wonder if Tony is one of her ex-boyfriends.* This last thought somehow bothered Chloe. *I can't imagine her with him...or with anyone, for that matter. Come on, Chloe! What is wrong with you, girl? She probably has boyfriends left and right. Look at her, she's stunning.* Chloe looked at Laurence from the corner of her eye. She was engaged in a spirited conversation with Tony. The heat of the restaurant had given Laurence a nice pinkish shade on her cheeks, highlighting her clear blue eyes. Her red tee shirt showed muscular arms tapering to very elegant hands. Chloe sighed and took a bite of the chocolate crêpe she had ordered.

"Are you okay? I'm sorry, it must be really boring for you," said Laurence, looking at Chloe with concern.

"No, I'm fine. I was just thinking."

Tony watched the exchange between the two women and smiled to himself.

"Girls, I have to get going anyway. I tell you what. I'm going dancing with some friends tonight. Would you like to come along?"

"Wow, Tony, that would be great," answered Chloe with enthusiasm. "Well...that is, if Laurence wants to," she added. Laurence had thought of calling it a night early because she still had to finish packing and wanted to have an early start in the morning. She glanced at Chloe, who was looking at her expectantly.

"Yes, but we can't stay late."

"Awesome," exclaimed Chloe, giving Laurence a quick squeeze on the hand across the table. Tony's smile grew even larger.

"Great. We'll meet at 11 p.m. at La Joconde, Porte de La Chapelle," said Tony, smiling.

"Tony…" growled Laurence.

"What?" asked Tony, innocently.

"You know what. Don't even think about it!" Laurence was looking menacingly at Tony.

"What's wrong? What's going on?" asked Chloe. If Laurence heard she didn't flinch, but instead kept her gaze on Tony.

"Laurence?" asked Chloe again, not understanding the situation.

"Be there at 11, and I promise you, no set up," smiled Tony.

"You better be true to your word, my friend," answered Laurence.

"I will. Bye, Chloe…see you guys tonight." With those words Tony left the restaurant.

Laurence was fiddling with her napkin, not looking at Chloe.

"Hey, Earth to Laurence…what just happened here?"

"Nothing to worry about. Want to walk around before we go home to change?"

"Don't change the subject on me. Come on, what happened?"

"You don't take no for an answer, do you?" said Laurence, smiling.

"You know I don't. So, are you going to tell me?"

"You asked for it…Tony always tries to set me up when we go to clubs."

"Okay, but I don't see where the problem is. You're a big girl, you can say no."

"Chloe, do you know what kind of club we just got invited to?"

"Nope. I figure your clubs can't be that different from ours."

Laurence laughed out loud. "Chloe, you're so innocent. We just got invited to a gay club." Laurence took the last bite of her strawberry crêpe and waited for Chloe's reaction.

"What?"

"La Joconde is one of the biggest gay clubs in town." She finished her drink and took her wallet out of her jacket.

"Is Tony gay?" asked Chloe, hesitantly.

Laurence dropped 40 francs on the table. "What do you think? Come on, don't tell me you didn't see it."

"Uh…no, I didn't. I don't think I've ever met anyone gay." Chloe, suddenly feeling shy, reached for her wallet and busied herself counting her cash.

"No need to, I took care of it," Laurence said, pointing to the money on the table. "Maybe we shouldn't go tonight…"

"No, I want to go," exclaimed Chloe.

Laurence sighed. "Okay, but you might be in for a shock."

Chloe nodded. "Laurence, you said that Tony always tries to set you up when you go out with him… if it's a gay club…" Chloe's voice trailed off.

Laurence looked intently at Chloe and waited for her to finish her sentence.

"…he sets you up with other women?" asked Chloe shyly, finishing her sentence.

"He tries."

"Oh," answered Chloe. Not looking at Laurence she asked, "is he ever successful?"

Laurence smiled at Chloe's shyness. "Chloe, look at me." Chloe slowly brought her eyes to level with Laurence. "The answer is no. He has never found a match for me."

"Oh…can I ask you a question?" Laurence nodded. " Are you…"

"…gay?" asked Laurence finishing Chloe's question.

"Yeah."

"If being attracted to women makes you gay, then yes I am. But, if having ever had a relationship with a woman is what makes you gay, then no, I'm not."

"I don't get it," said Chloe.

"Tony thinks I should get involved with another woman because every guy I've been involved with so far has been a jerk. I don't really care at this point if the next person I'm with is a man or woman, I just want them to love me for who I am."

"Oh…that makes more sense."

"I'm surprised you haven't left screaming yet," said Laurence sarcastically.

"Why? You're my friend. It doesn't bother me…and thanks."

"For what?"

"For telling me—and for the crepes."

"You're welcome," said Laurence with a smile.

They left the restaurant and walked around Les Halles for a little while. It was close to dusk, and the heat of the day evaporated from the pavement, giving place to the cooler air of the evening. The streets were less crowded than earlier in the day. A couple sat next to a fountain murmuring soft words to each other, the artists were packing up their palettes and pencils, and the musicians were putting away their instruments.

"Wow, it's true what people say," whispered Chloe to herself.

Laurence's acute hearing picked up on Chloe's remark. "What do you mean?"

"I read somewhere in a magazine that everything stopped in Paris around 7 p.m."

Chloe looked around her and took it all in: the orange and red of the sunset reflecting on the pavement, the smell of fresh bread being baked, the sound of the city getting ready for the evening, and the way Laurence's hair shone with the last sun ray of the day. Chloe shyly smiled at Laurence. "I wish you didn't have to go tomorrow."

"I wish I didn't have to go," softly answered Laurence.

"Lo, would you do me a favor?" asked Chloe, stopping and facing Laurence.

"Anything, just ask."

"I know you probably are going to be really busy once you get back to school, but would you…." Chloe stopped, suddenly feeling timid.

"Would I what?"

"Call me once in a while? I mean…I don't really know anyone around here. Well, I did meet this guy on the plane, but I mean, I like you, and…"

"Yes," answered Laurence, speaking over Chloe's mumble.

Chloe, oblivious to Laurence's answer, kept on going. "…we spent so much time together. I understand if you don't think you'll have time. It's okay, really…"

"Chloe, didn't you hear?" asked Laurence, grabbing Chloe by her shoulder.

"Hear what?"

"Yes, of course I'll keep in touch. Of course I'll call you."

"Really?" Laurence nodded, not releasing her hold on Chloe's shoulder.

"I'll do my best…I…really like you, Chloe. I wonder how you put up with me, but I'm glad you do," said Laurence sincerely.

Chloe looked at Laurence, feeling relief wash over her. *I don't know why I care so much, but I'm glad she didn't turn me down.* "Thanks."

Laurence let go of Chloe's shoulder and teasingly poked her in the ribs. "You're welcome. We're friends, you said so yourself." Laurence looked at her watch. "Listen, we probably should get going. By the time we get home and get ready it'll be time to drive back."

"Okay, let's go. I like this part of Paris. It's so exotic."

"I've never heard anyone call it that, but if you say so." Laurence led Chloe back to the bike.

——— *** ———

They got off at Porte de La Chapelle. Chloe had been surprised and outraged by the number of homeless begging for money inside the train. They would climb on at a stop, give a little speech and go down the aisle with their hands extended, expecting money from people. Chloe's heart had been broken when she saw a young mother entering the train with her newborn to beg for food and money. She had reached for her wallet, but Laurence had stopped her.

"Don't. If you start giving you'll never stop."

They were now walking out of the metro station. The polluted air of Paris seemed almost fresh compared to the smell of sweat and un-washed bodies found in the metro.

"Yuk," said Chloe once they were outside. "God, your metro is gross and dirty. Do all those homeless people sleep in there?"

"For the most part, yeah. It's dirty, but it gets you where you have to go. Not all stations are this bad."

"Glad to know that."

"The club is a few blocks away. Chloe, it's not the best area, so stay close to me and keep one hand on your wallet." Laurence crossed the street, followed by Chloe.

The walls were covered with graffiti and a trashcan had been tipped over, its contents spilled across the pavement. The remains of a burned car stood next to the sidewalk.

"I'm glad I'm not here alone," said Chloe, getting closer to Laurence.

"It's creepy, but I've walked those streets alone, and nothing has ever happened. Don't worry."

"Okay, I'll take your word for it," Chloe answered, speeding her walk.

They took one last turn and found themselves in front of La Joconde. A large crowd was waiting in line, and two bouncers were letting people in after searching them.

"What are they doing?" Chloe asked, taking her place in the line.

"Checking for drugs and weapons."

"Boy, and I thought Paris was the city of love, city of peace."

Laurence laughed. "Come on Chloe, aren't there any bad areas in Washington?"

"Oh yeah."

"Same here. We just happen to be in one of them."

"Why put a club in a place where people are scared of walking alone?" asked Chloe sarcastically.

"Because French people are very narrow minded and would never put a gay club in a fancy neighborhood, that's why."

"Oh…" Chloe had not thought about that. She had always been told that the French were very promiscuous and open to any kind of sexuality.

"I know what Americans think of the French, that we sleep with everyone and cheat on our partners. Isn't that true?" asked Laurence.

"Well… It's what I heard."

"Chloe, you can't believe everything everyone tells you. I know that my family is not the best example because of Beatrice, but trust me, people don't make a habit of cheating on their spouses. Also, the French are very old fashioned, so the gay movement is not very popular." Laurence pushed Chloe forward. "Go on, it's our turn."

Once the bouncer opened the door, the music burst out, enveloping Laurence and Chloe in its rhythm. They entered a large room with people dancing in the middle, bars surrounding the room on each side.

"Tony is upstairs. Come on," said Laurence, shouting to be heard above the music. Wooden stairs were placed at the extreme right of the room. The upstairs consisted of balconies overlooking the dance floor below. Different opened rooms were accessible. Laurence pushed Chloe toward the furthest room on the right. Tony was sitting with three friends on a couch at the end of the room. The room was small but nicely decorated. Black and white photographs of men and women hung on the walls, and a leather couch and black coffee table complemented the atmosphere. Tony spotted Laurence and Chloe.

"Hey, girls! Over here," he yelled.

They made their way to Tony. Laurence kissed him lightly on the cheek and shook hands with his friends.

"Guys, this is my friend Laurence and her family's adorable new au pair coming straight from the States. Honey, what's your name again?" Tony asked, putting his arm around Chloe's shoulders.

"Chloe."

"Chloe, Laurence, those are my friends Sylvain and Marc, and this is my special friend Clovis." Tony plopped himself back on the couch and took Clovis's hand. Laurence smiled and grabbed two chairs from a near by table. She offered one to Chloe, who sat down smiling at her to thank her.

The room was far enough from the dance floor that conversation was possible, although the music was still loud.

"Do you girls want to drink something?" asked Tony.

"Yeah, but I'll get it," answered Laurence. "Chloe, would you like something?" asked Laurence, getting up.

" A coke, please."

"J'croyais que les Americains étez élever à la bière," said Sylvain sarcastically while sipping his drink. Chloe looked at him. She understood what he had said, and knew he was probably joking, but she could not find the words in French to answer.

"Hey, play nice," said Laurence. "Chloe doesn't speak much French, so the rule is that if you want to make fun, you have to do it in English, so you guys are on equal ground. Get it?" Laurence's face bore a smile, but her eyes were intensely fixed on Sylvain, leaving no doubt that her request had better be agreed to.

"I was just joking," answered Sylvain.

Laurence ignored him and turned to Chloe. "I'll be right back."

"'kay."

"I'll keep an eye on her," joked Tony, smiling at Laurence. Laurence left the room, but not before glancing one final time at Chloe. "Boy, she sure is protective," commented Tony.

Tony lit a cigarette and offered one to Chloe.

"No thanks. I don't smoke," she answered.

Tony nodded. "So, Chloe, how do you like your stay so far?"

"I like it. Laurence took me to the castle of Versailles yesterday. It was great." Chloe smiled at the memory.

"You're here for one year?"

"Yeah."

"Beatrice hasn't driven you crazy yet?" asked Tony with a smile.

"You know about her?" Chloe was somehow surprised.

"Yeah, Laurence and I go back a long way." Tony took a puff from his cigarette and seemed to be contemplating his next question. "You guys seem to get along very well."

"I think so. We didn't start out that way, but we have come a long way." Chloe looked at Tony, wondering where this round of questions was taking her.

"She's been through lots of crap, so treat her well." Before Chloe had time to ask what he meant by that, Laurence had made her way back to the table with their drinks.

"Here you go." She handed Chloe her drink and sat down. "Tony, I hope you haven't been bothering Chloe," she said, only half joking.

"No, I've been a perfect gentleman." Tony suddenly stood up and grabbed Clovis's hand. "I love this song. Come on, let's go dance." Clovis got up and laced his fingers with Tony's. "Are you girls coming?" asked Tony.

"Let's go, Lo," said Chloe getting up.

"No, go right ahead. I'm just going to sit here for a while."

"You're such a party pooper," said Tony, putting his free arm around Chloe's shoulders. "Come on babe, let's go boogie. Are you guys coming?" he asked Sylvain and Marc. Without further delay, he led Clovis and Chloe out with Sylvain and Marc following close behind. Chloe glanced back briefly at Laurence before being dragged out. Laurence sat back in her chair, and let her gaze wander over Chloe's form until she was out of sight. She slowly brought her glass to her lips and let the cold liquid go down her throat, the bitterness of the alcohol making her wince.

Meanwhile, the others had made their way downstairs. They forged a path through the crowd of dancers and started moving to the music. Chloe let her gaze wander around the room and fixed on two women locked in a kiss, dancing to their own rhythm, oblivious to the crowd. She had expected to bolt or even feel disgusted, but instead she was riveted and could not tear her eyes away. Tony followed Chloe's gaze and smiled to himself.

Chloe finally turned her focus back to her friends, and she smiled faintly at Tony. The crowd of dancers had gotten larger and space was more and more limited. Tony and Clovis were dancing closer and closer, their bodies almost rubbing against each other. Couples were forming and the throbbing lights were pulsing to the increasing rhythm of the music. Chloe started feeling oppressed, her movements were restricted and breathing was becoming difficult because of the hot smoky air. She suddenly stopped dancing and brought her hand to her forehead, wiping the sweat off.

"Chloe, are you okay?" asked Tony, touching Chloe on the shoulder.

"I feel a little dizzy. I…I think I'm going to go sit down for a while. I'll be back." She abruptly pushed past Tony and headed for the stairs, elbowing people out of her way. Once she arrived in the room, she stopped dead in her tracks at what she saw. Laurence was sitting on the couch sipping her drink talking to some unknown woman. Chloe knew she should make her presence known, but something told her to stay back. Laurence threw her head back and her laugh reverberated through the room. The stranger scooted closer to Laurence and caressed her knee with one hand while she turned Laurence's face towards her with the other. Chloe's heart sped up at the sight and the dizziness she felt earlier came rushing back. She passed her hand through her hair and propped herself against the wall to keep her balance. She bravely looked in Laurence's direction, expecting to find the two women in an intimate position, but instead she found herself staring into Laurence's eyes. Chloe broke the gaze, turned around and ran down the stairs. She elbowed her way through the dance floor, passing Tony and Clovis, but ignored them.

"What the… Go get Laurence, I'm going to go make sure she is all right," Tony said to Clovis. Clovis nodded and hurried upstairs. Tony went outside in search of Chloe, who was sitting on the sidewalk, her back against the wall, eyes closed.

"Hey, you're okay?"

She recognized his voice and kept her eyes closed. "Yeah, I just needed some fresh air."

"What happened back there?"

"Don't know." She didn't want to answer and just wanted to be left alone. Yes, the throbbing lights and the smoke had been part of her sudden nausea, but what had pushed her to run was the sight of Laurence almost being kissed by a woman. *I don't get it. Why should I care what she does? I'm not attracted to women… I'm not supposed to be attracted to women. What is wrong with me?* "Clovis went to get Laurence. Can I get you a glass of water?" asked Tony.

Tony, I just wish you could go away right now so I can sort out my emotions…as if bringing Laurence here is going to help.

"No thanks, Tony. I'll be fine in just a minute." The door opened suddenly, and Laurence came rushing out, followed by Clovis. She knelt next to Chloe.

"Chloe, what's wrong?" She had been frantic with worry since Clovis had told her to come quick because Chloe wasn't feeling well. Laurence touched Chloe's forehead, her cheeks, and finally grabbed her hands. Chloe had opened her eyes at Laurence's first touch and was now looking at their joined hands. She felt warmth going through her and a sense of security.

"I just felt a little dizzy inside. Nothing to worry about. Probably the smoke, I'm not used to it."

Laurence brushed the back of her hand against Chloe's cheek and kept one hand intertwined with Chloe's. "You feel warm to me. I think I should take you home."

"No. I don't want to spoil your last night in town. If you call me a cab and give him the address I can go back by myself. Please don't cut it short because of me."

"No way I'm letting you go back alone." Laurence stood up suddenly and extended her hand to Chloe. "Can you get up?"

"Yeah, I think so." She grabbed Laurence's hand and let herself be yanked to her feet. As soon as Laurence let go of her hand, she started to crumble. Laurence caught her and held her up. "We're going home."

"Okay," said Chloe, defeated.

Laurence turned to Tony and Clovis who were still standing outside. "Guys, we are going to call it a night. Thanks for everything."

"Okay, call me when you get back to school." Tony lightly kissed Laurence on the lips. "Bye Chloe, I hope you feel better." He gave her a quick squeeze on the arm, grabbed Clovis's hand and left.

"I have to hail a cab. Do you want to sit back down?"

"No, I'm okay. Go ahead." Laurence slowly let go of Chloe. She stepped off the sidewalk and starting waving at cabs passing by. After a few minutes, one stopped. She went back to Chloe and helped her get in the cab. Once Chloe was secured, she got in the other side. "Versailles, rue de Provence."

"Oui madame," answered the can driver. "Voulez vous prendre l'autoroute ou le periferique?"

"J'm'en fiche, le plus rapide."

"D'accord."

Laurence turned to Chloe who was propped up against the door, her eyes closed.

"How are you feeling?" asked Laurence.

"I'm okay. Really, we could have stayed longer."

"Come on Chloe, cut the crap. Five minutes ago you could barely stand up." Laurence's reply was made with more animosity than she intended to.

"Please, Laurence, don't be mad…I'm sorry," Chloe said softly. For a brief moment she thought she had been reacquainted with the Laurence she first met, abrupt, rude and constantly annoyed with her.

Laurence's annoyance vanished as soon as Chloe's words were spoken. Chloe looked so miserable, her hair hung in her face, and she was staring at her hands lying on her lap.

"I didn't mean to sound bitchy. I'm sorry. You're not feeling well, and I'm being

obnoxious," said Laurence, scooting closer to Chloe.

Chloe looked hesitantly at Laurence who was now only a few inches away. "Sorry I ruined your evening, and I didn't mean to spy on you earlier"

"Don't worry about it. I was trying to find a way to get rid of this person, so perfect timing."

"I still feel bad."

"Please don't… I was worried about you," whispered Laurence.

"Really?"

"Yeah." She pulled Chloe towards her, so she could lay her head on her shoulder. "Use me as a pillow, I'll wake you up when we get home." Chloe let Laurence wrap her arm around her shoulder, and softly put her head down. She tried to fight sleep, but her eyelids felt heavy.

"Don't try to stay awake. I promise I won't leave you in the cab," kidded Laurence, her breath softly brushing against Chloe's hair. So, as the car went down the highway and Paris was left behind, Chloe closed her eyes and surrendered to sleep.

———— *** ————

Laurence sat in the cab with Chloe asleep in her arms, and watched the street lights go by, adjusting her hold on Chloe. *I don't know what's wrong with me. I was so worried for her. Why? Less than a week ago we were strangers. Going away is going to do me some good. I'll go back to school and forget about this week. Forget…yeah, that's probably the safest…*

The cab pulled up to the gate. Laurence softly shook Chloe awake. "Hey, sleepyhead, we're home. Come on, wake up."

Chloe opened her eyes, and sat up. "Are we there already?"

Laurence chuckled. "Yeah, you slept all the way. How are you feeling?" she asked while handing the cab driver money and opening the door. She stepped out and turned to help Chloe.

"I'm okay."

Laurence slammed the cab door. "Good. A good night's sleep, and you'll be as good as new."

"Guess so." Chloe yawned and followed Laurence who had just opened the gate. They stepped inside the courtyard. The high brick walls made it a nest away from the city noise. A light was still burning on the second floor of the house next door.

"Guess our neighbors are burning the midnight oil," remarked Chloe.

"Yeah, guess so." Laurence opened the front door and walked into the dark house. She felt around for the light switch. "Damn, where is it? I can never find this damn…here we go," she exclaimed turning the light on.

Chloe walked past Laurence into the kitchen and poured herself a glass of water. "Want some water?"

"No, I'm going to call it a night."

Chloe walked into the family room and sat down on the couch, sipping her water. The dizziness of earlier had disappeared. *Must have really been the smoke,* she thought, putting her glass down on the coffee table and unlacing her shoes. "Lo, when are you leaving tomorrow?"

"Since I can't see Clément, first thing in the morning."

"Will I see you?" asked Chloe, her heart suddenly beating faster with anxiety.

"Don't think so." Laurence started going up the stairs. "It was great hanging out with you. Bye." With those words she left.

Chloe sat dumbfounded for a few minutes. *What? That's it? Great hanging out with you, bye? What the hell?* Tears started slowly falling down Chloe's cheeks. *She can't just walk away like that after everything we shared.*

"Damn her. I'm not going to let her get away so easily." Chloe got up angrily and ran up the stairs, decided to at least get a proper goodbye out of Laurence. *Who the hell does she think she is?*

Laurence's door was closed, but Chloe didn't even bother knocking. She barged into the room in a fury. "Laurence, what the hell was all of that about? Great hanging out with you, bye. I thought we had a little more going on than just the usual great to meet you," yelled Chloe, walking toward Laurence who was standing at the window with a surprised look on her face. "What was all this fuss about being worried about me earlier if you feel like you can just turn your back on me and leave?" Chloe stopped to catch her breath, tears rolling down her cheeks, her eyes a deep dark green, face red with anger.

Laurence had not moved. She was standing near the window, not knowing what to do, not knowing if she should let herself do what she really wanted to do. Her fists were clenched and she was staring intensely into Chloe's eyes, her heart melting at the view of the tears she had caused. Suddenly she made a decision and stepped forward. She reached for Chloe's face and gently wiped her tears away, not once looking away. They spent what seemed an eternity staring into each other's eyes. Chloe's tears had stopped, and she could only feel the warmth of Laurence's hands on her face. Slowly, Laurence took a step forward and drew Chloe into her arms, wrapping them tightly around her. Chloe let go of the tension she had been holding and started crying again. Not a word had been exchanged. Laurence tightened her grip on Chloe and lightly kissed the top of her head.

"I'm sorry. I don't know how to let you go. It scares me, Chloe. I thought that by just walking away, it would be easier. I was selfish, I only thought about myself. I never thought you cared. I'm sorry, please don't cry. I really was worried earlier, and it scares me to think I could care so much."

Chloe's tears had dried, giving way to soft sniffles. She lifted her head up and looked at Laurence with red puffy eyes. "I'm sorry I burst into your room like that, but the thought that you could leave without really saying goodbye horrified me. It hurt after what we shared this week that you could walk away so easily."

Laurence sighed and squeezed Chloe one last time before releasing her. She walked to her bed and sat down, patting the area next to her for Chloe to sit down. Once Chloe was settled next to her she spoke again. "I don't know what's happening to me Chloe. When I'm not with you, I think about you. When I'm with you, I can't stop looking at you. I…" She stopped at lost with words.

Chloe reached for Laurence's hand. "Please…go on."

Laurence looked at Chloe and nodded. She took a deep breath and tightened her grip on Chloe's hand. "Do you remember what we spoke about this afternoon? About what Tony believes about me?" Chloe nodded. "I think he might be right." Chloe suddenly withdrew her hand. "I'm sorry Chloe. That's mostly the reason I thought it would be better to just leave tonight without properly saying goodbye." Laurence stared at the door, not daring to look at Chloe.

Chloe had been surprised by Laurence's statement, but still wasn't sure about one thing. "Laurence, do you think you like me…I mean do you think you…"

"Yes, I think so…Oh, I don't know, I'm confused. It's all new to me," interrupted Laurence, roughly passing her hand through her hair.

"What about earlier at the club? That woman…"

"I told you I didn't know how to get rid of her. I've been battling with the feeling I have for you for a while, and maybe I wanted to see if it was just you or…I don't know what I'm talking about." Laurence passed her hand through her hair nervously.

"What do you want from me?" asked Chloe hesitantly.

"Nothing," exclaimed Laurence abruptly. "Chloe, I'll deal with it. I know that until today you had never even been in touch with a homosexual…I'm…. I'm not asking you for anything except your friend-ship. I'll go away for a few months and deal with that on my own. You'll see, it'll be all gone by the time I come back," said Laurence, rushing through.

"What if I don't want you to?" whispered Chloe, fiddling with the blanket.

"What?"

"What if I don't want you to?" repeated Chloe loudly.

"What do you mean?"

"What if I didn't want you to stop thinking about me this way?" asked Chloe timidly.

"Chloe, you don't know what you're asking."

"You assumed I want to run away from this. Why? Because I had never been exposed to homosexuality before today? Why do you as-sume you're the only one having those feelings?"

"Chloe…"

"No, let me finish. The smoke wasn't the only reason why I was sick earlier. Confusion was a big part of it. While I was dancing I saw two women kissing and wondered what it felt like. I couldn't help think-ing about you. My brain was telling me no, but my heart was saying yes, then I went back upstairs and I saw you with that woman, and it hurt. I'm as confused as you are Laurence, but I know one thing."

"What's that?" asked Laurence, stunned, swallowing with difficulty.

"There is something strong between us, and I'm not willing to just brush it away and pretend it's not here."

A long silence established itself. The only noises in the room were those of far away cars and a barking dog. Laurence broke the silence. "What do you suggest we do?"

"I don't know," answered Chloe, suddenly feeling drained. "I don't know how much I'm ready for or what I can give you."

"Let's take it slow. No strings attached. I don't know what I'm ready for either."

Chloe nodded. "I guess I should get going." She got up and slowly walked to the door.

"Chloe, wait…please stay…" Laurence got up and extended her hand to Chloe.

"Lo, we just said let's take it slow."

"I just want to hold you through the night. I'm leaving tomorrow, and I want to know I was with you until the last minute." Her hand was still extended. Her blue eyes were almost begging. Chloe paused a few moments, unsure. She looked at Laurence's hand, and she reached for it. Laurence smiled and walked toward the bed. She removed the top cover, took her shoes off, and lay on the bed. Chloe climbed in next to her, not daring to touch. Laurence scooted closer and shyly snared Chloe's hands. "Is that okay?" she asked uncertainly.

"I have a better idea," answered Chloe, moving up on her side and laying her head on Laurence's shoulder. "Is that okay?"

"Yes. More than okay," answered Laurence. She reached for the switch, turned the light off, and pulled the blanket over both of them. "Good night Chloe."

"Good night, Lo." Chloe snuggled closer and closed her eyes. She quickly drifted off to sleep, feeling safe and secure.

Laurence lightly kissed the top of Chloe's head. Her last thought before falling asleep was, *What do we do now?*

To read the rest.... please visit our website at
http://www.justicehouse.com and order this exciting book.

Justice House Publishing

Accidental Love
BL Miller

Rose Grayson, a destitute, friendless young woman, and Veronica "Ronnie" Cartwright, head of a vast family empire, are thrown together when Ronnie rescues Rose from certain ruin and nurses her back to health after a crippling, near fatal car accident. What happens when love is based on deception? Can it survive discovering the truth?

The Deal
Maggie Ryan

In an inside look at television news, two dynamic women fall for each other behind the cameras, but there's a catch: one's the boss. Can Laura Kasdan and Christine Hanson fulfill both their contracts and their hearts? Details at eleven.

Of Drag Kings and the Wheel of Fate
Susan Smith

A sultry, mystical novel of love and destiny, of leather jackets and cigarettes,
Of Drag Kings and the Wheel of Fate will draw you into its passion, power, and magic, leaving you spellbound.

Rosalind, a college professor, moves to Buffalo for her first job where she meets Taryn, a young butch tattoo artist, and they set the harsh upstate winter ablaze with their intense attraction, but find out it is so much more than that—all the world's their stage, and they must act on the demands of fate, or lose everything.

Smitty's eloquent prose lures you with its beauty and captivates you with its unashamed honesty; its intensity will overwhelm you and make you beg for more as the words burn into you. Rosalind and Taryn will reside in your heart and soul long after you've read this book for the 20th time. You will find the meaning of life, you will be entranced in the sublime, and you will be grateful for the moment.

Several Devils
K. Simpson

What do you do when you live in the most boring city in America, you hate your job, and you're celibate? Invoke a demon to shake things up, of course. Join Devlin Kerry on her devilishly funny deconstructive tour of guilt, fear, caffeine, and suburbia.

Above All, Honor
Radclyffe

Single-minded Secret Service Agent Cameron Roberts has one mission-
to guard the daughter of the President of the United States at all cost.
Her duty is her life, and is the only thing that keeps her from self-
destructing under the unbearable weight of her own deep personal
tragedy. She hasn't counted on the fact that Blair Powell, the beautiful,
willful First Daughter, will do anything in her power to escape the
watchful eyes of her protectors, including seducing the agent in charge.
Both women struggle with long-hidden secrets and dark passions as
they are forced to confront their growing attraction amidst the escalating
danger drawing ever closer to Blair.

From the dark shadows of rough trade bars in Greenwich Village to the
elite galleries of Soho, Cameron must balance duty with desire and,
ultimately, she must chose between love and honor.

Hurricane Watch
Melissa Good

In this sequel to Tropical Storm, Dar and Kerry are redefining themselves and their priorities to build a life and a family together. But with
scheming colleagues and old flames trying to drive them apart and bring
them down, the two women must overcome fear, prejudice, and their
own pasts to protect the company and each other. Does their relationship have enough trust to survive   the storm?

Josie & Rebecca:
The Western Chronicles
BL Miller & Vada Foster

At the center of this story are two women, one a deadly gunslinger bitter
from the injustices of her past, the other a gentle dreamer trying to
escape the horrors of the present.

Their destinies come together one fateful afternoon when the feared
outlaw makes the choice to rescue a young woman in trouble. For her
part, Josie Hunter considers the brief encounter at an end once the girl
is safe, but Rebecca Cameron has other ideas....

Lucifer Rising
Sharon Bowers

Lucifer Rising is a novel about love and fear. It is the story of fallen DEA
angel Jude Lucien and the Miami Herald reporter determined to unearth
Jude's secrets. When an apparently happenstance meeting introduces
Jude to reporter Liz Gardener, the dark ex-agent is both intrigued and
aroused by the young woman.

A sniper shot intended for Jude strikes Liz, and the two women are
thrown together in a race to discover who is intent on killing her. As their

lives become more and more intertwined, Jude finds herself unexpectedly falling for the reporter, and Liz discovers that the agent-turned-drug-dealer is both more and less than she seems. In eloquent and spare language, author Sharon Bowers paints a dazzling portrait of a woman driven to the darkest extremes of the human condition-and the journey she makes to cross to the other side.

Redemption
Susanne Beck

Redemption is the story of a young woman who finds out that the best things in life are often found in the last place you'd look for them. Angel is a small-town girl
who finds herself trapped within her worst nightmare-a state penitentiary. She finds inner strength, maturity, friendship, and love, while at the same time giving
to others something she thought she'd lost within herself: hope. It is the story of how Angel rediscovers hope blazing within the piercing blue eyes of another inmate, Ice.

Ok, so where's the book? Right now its at the printer people's plant. Should be shipping to us for distribution soon. The suspense is suspenseful.

Tristaine
Cate Culpepper

Tristaine focuses on the fierce love that develops among strong women facing a common evil. Jesstin is an Amazon from the village of Tristaine who has been imprisoned in the Clinic, a scientific research facility. Brenna, the young medic assigned to monitor Jess's health, becomes increasingly disturbed by the savage punishments her patient endures at the hands of the ambitious scientist Caster, and a bond grows between the two women. The struggle Brenna and Jess face in escaping the Clinic and Caster's determined pursuit deepens the connection between them. When they unite with three of Jess's Amazon sisters, the simple beauty of Tristaine's women-centered culture weaves through the plot, which moves toward a violent confrontation with Caster's posse.

Tropical Storm
Melissa Good

A corporate takeover pits mercenary IT executive Dar Roberts against soft-hearted manager Kerry Stuart. When Kerry comes up with a plan to save her employees' jobs and help Dar's company turn a profit, Dar discovers a new way to do business—and her heart. But when Kerry's father, a powerful Senator, gets wind, all hell breaks loose on the coast of Florida.

A Year in Paris

Malaurie Barber

When student Chloe Jones becomes an au pair, all she's looking for is an interesting year abroad in Paris, but she gets more than she bargained for in the mysterious Glairon family. While caring for sweet little Clement, Chloe begins to care a great deal for his beautiful but haunted half sister, Laurence, too. But not even the most romantic city in the world can help these two when the family's secrets threaten to destroy them all.

Join the legacy of
Justice House Publishing

☐ **Accidental Love** BL Miller
0-9677687-1-3 $16.99

☐ **The Deal** Maggie Ryan
0-9677687 $17.99

☐ **Drag Kings** S. Smith
change isbn here $17.99

☐ **Hurricane Watch** Melissa
Good
0-9677687 $17.99

☐ **Josie & Rebecca:
The Western Chr.**
BL Miller & Vada Foster
0-9677687-3-X $16.99

☐ **Lucifer Rising** Sharon Bowers
0-9677687-2-1 $16.99

☐ **Redemption** Susanne Beck
0-9677687-5-6 $17.99

☐ **Tropical Storm** Melissa Good
0-9677687-0-5 $16.99

If not available through your local bookstore send this coupon
and a check or money order for the cover price(s) + $5.95 s/h to
Justice House Publishing (JHP), 3902 South 56th St, Tacoma,
WA 98409. Delivery can take up to 8 weeks.

Name:_____

Address:_____

_____

I have enclosed a check or money order in the amount of

$_____

Or order on line at our web site at
www.justicehouse.com